Sword and Mirror

Kate Grove

Sword and Mirror

Written and published by Kate Grove
Copyright © 2019 Kate Grove
Kate Grove asserts the moral right to be identified as the author of this work, under the Act LXXVI of 1999 on Copyright. A catalogue record for this book is available from National Széchényi Library.

ISBN (paperback): 978-615-00-6226-6
ISBN (e-book): 978-615-00-6227-3

http://kategrove.net

First edition.

Cover design © Lauren Bearzatto of Sly Fox Cover Designs
Editorial work by Red Loop Editing

This novel is a work of fiction. People, names, places and events portrayed in it are purely products of the author's imagination. Any resemblance to actual people, living or dead, places, or events is entirely coincidental.

Thank you for purchasing this book. Enjoy!

To my first readers on Tapas and Patreon

$\mathcal{T}$he car accident had changed everything.

Ciara accompanied her student on the piano as Marla practiced scales to warm up her vocal cords. Pressing keys with a pause in between was Ciara's limit. Keeping the grand piano dusted off was her duty. Gone was the talented master pianist.

Ciara turned to her student when they finished warming up. "What would you like to learn next?" Marla was standing in the middle of the living room, and her eyes sparkled in excitement.

"The Queen of the Night aria."

Ciara froze for a moment at hearing that before reaching for her phone on top of the piano.

"You're not going to sing it to me?"

"I'm sorry, I can't." She flashed her an apologetic smile.

"Because of the high note?"

"You could say that." Ciara found a record of the aria. "Let's hear it first."

Marla nodded, pricking her ears, listening to the voice of the opera singer on the record. Ciara could see the wonder on her face and silently pondered if she wore the same expression at that moment. Mozart's music always enchanted her.

"Wow…"

"Indeed," Ciara chuckled. "Marla, you have a beautiful soprano voice, but let's not strain your vocal cords right at the beginning. Let's start with a lower note."

Marla seemed to think it over. Eventually, she nodded, happy with the decision.

Ciara pressed a key on the piano. "This will be your starting note. Let me replay the first ten seconds…"

The class went on in a similar style. Marla was satisfied when they finished, having gotten to sing the famous part of the aria, albeit a few notes lower than how it was originally written. Ciara knew few people could sing such a high note, herself included.

"See you next week! And don't forget to warm up your vocal cords *before* you sing! We don't want a repeat of last month!" Ciara said as she walked Marla to the door.

"Yes, ma'am!" Marla saluted dutifully as she exited. She disappeared down the corridor the next moment.

Ciara grabbed the letters lying on the threshold, her chestnut-colored hair falling over her shoulder. She brushed it away as she straightened up and quietly closed the door.

"Is she gone?" She jumped at the voice coming from behind her.

"Karen?! I thought you were at the uni."

"My morning lecture was canceled." Her cousin poked her blond head through the doorway from her room. She looked around and ventured out to the living room. "Thank Goddess, she's gone. I thought I'd have to pee on the carpet!" she exclaimed before disappearing into the bathroom. The only way to the restroom from Karen's room was through the living room where Ciara usually held her lessons.

Ciara snorted at Karen's outburst and walked to the fridge, thinking about their current situation. Her cousin had just started studying at the local university and was probably going to stay for the next couple of years, not counting the breaks. Ciara had to come up with a solution so Karen wouldn't need to go out every time there was a lesson. She wanted her little cousin to consider this place a home away from home.

Her gaze landed on the small pile of letters. One of them was a medical bill. Ciara had seen the logo on the left top corner enough times in the last five years not to miss it. She scowled and threw the letter to the far corner of the counter, unopened, then she turned to pour herself some orange juice.

Just then, Karen exited the bathroom and came over to Ciara. She was wearing a T-shirt with an anime character on the front, and she was just tying up her long hair.

"Juice?" Ciara asked.

"Thanks."

She grabbed another glass and filled it to the brim. "Cheers!"

"Kanpai!"

They grinned and downed the refreshing orange juice. A moment of silence passed between them before Ciara spoke.

"So, when is your next class?"

"I've a seminar at noon. I still need to look through my kanji list, though. You?" Karen adjusted her glasses.

Ciara glanced at the clock on the wall. The clockface looked like a piano sheet, and the fingers reminded her of clefs.

"I need to leave soon."

Karen grabbed a block of cheese from the fridge and looked at her older cousin.

"You're doing a house call? That's rare."

"Yep."

Karen fished a knife out from one of the drawers and started cutting the cheese into tiny cubes.

"You're not happy about it," she observed while dicing.

Ciara made a face and went around the apartment to gather her things.

"Truth is, he was a bit rude on the phone."

"Then why accept him as a student?" Karen asked. "Just don't."

"It's not that simple…"

"You know I hate it when you treat me like a kid."

"I didn't mean to," Ciara replied but didn't elaborate. Karen sighed, deciding to change the subject.

"Have I told you yet you're my favorite cousin?"

Ciara stopped in her preparations and looked at Karen with suspicion in her eyes.

"Not today. Why, what do you want?"

"Oh, don't be such a cynic!"

"Karen." Ciara's tone changed in warning.

"I was hoping you would come back with me for Thanksgiving."

"Thanks, but no thanks."

"But—"

"No means no, Karen." Ciara was adamant as she grabbed her purple sunglasses.

Her little cousin sighed sadly. She mumbled, barely audible, "Promise me you'll at least think about it."

Ciara doubted her aunt would want to see the face of the person responsible for the death of her beloved sister. If only she hadn't taken such a long time that day to get ready and make her mother drive faster, the accident wouldn't have happened. Ciara's thoughts were going in a dark direction.

Karen opened her mouth to nag her more.

"Don't try to convince me." Ciara's voice had a weird tint to it. Karen shut her mouth immediately.

"See you later?" Ciara quickly changed the subject, feeling awkward.

"Yeah, take care." Karen walked to her room with a small plate of cheese cubes.

"You too!"

Karen waved at Ciara, disappearing behind her door. Ciara exited the apartment and sighed, trying to calm her turbulent thoughts. Her hands trembled as she put on her sunglasses, reminding her of the medical bills which had arrived with the post. She needed to focus to handle the unpleasant man who would be her new student. He had silenced all her protests when he told her a price. She couldn't say no to such an offer.

2

*C*iara had jogged to catch the bus to the other end of town. If she missed it, she would be twenty minutes late. Now that she sat on the bus, panting a little, she could be sure she'd be early by half an hour.

She hated public transportation, but she had no other choice. She wasn't going to drive again. Hell, she wasn't going to sit in a car again, even as a passenger, if she could help it.

The seats were uncomfortable, and she idly wondered how to best position herself for the long bus ride. It took her a while to settle down, and just as she did, they arrived at the next stop. A group of kids got on with a couple of adults. The children chatted away noisily as they sat down, herded together by the teachers. The bright yellow, high visibility jackets the kids wore and their loud voices made Ciara feel dizzy. She closed her eyes and sighed. She didn't have anything in particular against children, but all the noise was giving her a headache today. She wished they'd quiet down, but the teachers either didn't care or didn't notice how disruptive the group was.

"Let it go!" A boy argued with another as they both refused to relinquish a toy to the other. Their shouting quickly grew louder.

"Quiet…" Ciara murmured as she dug around her pockets to find her earphones. "I need some *quiet*."

Suddenly, it was as if someone put a mute button on the world. She looked up and saw that everyone on the bus stopped talking. Ciara blinked in surprise to take in the vacant stares of everyone as they kept silent. An eerie pressure weighed down on the passengers.

A gasp escaped Ciara as she realized she had accidentally caused this strange phenomenon. But it was too late for her to do anything about it; she didn't remember how to undo it. *I swore never to use this power again, yet here I am, restricting people's free will.*

Until the effect wore off naturally, these people would remain quiet, just as she had wished. Since there was nothing she could do, she plugged in her earphones and started her playlist. As she listened to *The Swan Lake* theme song, undisturbed, she hoped today wouldn't keep another strange thing in store for her. She had had enough surprises for one day.

———

This part of town was full of mansions, and Ciara wandered around until she spotted the home of her new student. The building was made of orange-hued bricks and had an early nineteenth-century feel to it. Ivy ran up one side, and wrought-iron fences embraced the estate. It looked a little bit run-down, and Ciara silently wondered why the owner wouldn't maintain their mansion if they could afford to pay her such a high hourly rate.

She shrugged and checked the time again. She still had

twenty or so minutes until the lesson began. Looking around, she spotted a park nearby and decided it would be a pleasant place to wait. Finding a bench, she sat down to check new emails.

Great. She received an e-mail from her medical insurance company. The next installment of paying for her latest operation was due in a few days.

As soon as I get home, Ciara thought, *I need to check what's in the envelope.* She sighed, checking her credit balance.

She winced at the information on the screen. Rude or not, she really needed this new client's money to pay off her debt. Until then, she couldn't even entertain the idea of the new method she'd read about that could help heal her hands. Thin, white lines could still be seen on her once-smooth palms and on the back of her hands.

Her fingers trembled.

Next, she checked her debit card balance and was pleasantly surprised when she realized her aunt had once again transferred Karen's rent. Ciara didn't know whether to be annoyed or grateful. She had clearly told Kelly there was no need for Karen to pay rent, but her aunt ignored her request and sent the money anyway.

Ciara quickly transferred the full amount to a savings account. She had set it up after the first two instances of Aunt Kelly transferring the money and refusing to take it back. Ciara was adamant about not accepting rent from family, so this was the only solution she could came up with. She was sure Karen would find it useful later whenever she eventually told her.

Her phone rang, and Ciara's eyes widened. She was one minute late, and her new student was already calling her! She quickly grabbed her bag and answered the call as she started speed-walking in the direction of the mansion.

"Hello?"

"Where are you?"

"I'm just outside. Give me a couple of minutes."

"We agreed on eleven. It's past eleven."

"I know, I'm sorry." Ciara ground her teeth, swallowing her retort. "See you in a moment."

She ended the call, already frustrated with him. It was only one frickin' minute! She huffed and marched to the orange-hued mansion. She was about to ring the bell, but the gate opened automatically as she approached.

"Hn." She was *not* going to be impressed by that.

Ciara walked along the short path to the door and took the few stairs until she arrived at the entrance. Once again, when she was just about to knock, the door opened a crack.

"Hello?" she called as she opened the door. Silence answered. "Hello, can I come in?"

No reply. She shrugged, deciding to enter. After all, he sounded impatient on the phone. As she made her way inside, she was surprised not to hear any signs of life.

"Anyone—" Ciara's sentence ended in a shriek as the door loudly shut behind her. She jumped and whirled around, her heart hammering in her chest. Only now did she realize how stale the air smelled. Her suspicion increased when she looked around and saw white sheets covering every piece of furniture.

She pushed the sunglasses to the top of her head as she stopped in the middle of the foyer and redialed the last caller. A moment later, she heard the ringtone coming from upstairs. A long, winding staircase led up to the second floor. She waited a little before making her way upstairs. Nobody answered the phone, but it kept on ringing. Maybe something happened to her new student?

What if he collapsed? What if he had a heart attack? She took two stairs at a time and sprinted toward the sound of the ringtone. Every second counted in a situation like this.

Finally, she arrived in the room with the cell phone. She ended the call and looked around. There was a big mirror with an ornate frame; it looked oriental. The silver surface was blackened in some spots, betraying its age. Her gaze stopped at the grand piano occupying most of the room. Mesmerized, Ciara made her way to it, stroking the keys lightly as if in a trance.

Wait, where is he? Ciara thought, glancing up, but she couldn't see anybody. She was alone.

"Hello?" she called out again. She couldn't hear any movement in the mansion. What if he really did collapse? She headed for the door when she caught sight of a cell phone lying in front of the mirror. She decided to get it, just in case.

"Where's your owner?" Accusation was clear in her voice as she squatted down to reach for the phone.

"No need to worry about me."

Ciara spun back and saw a black figure. His face was visible only for a moment before she was pushed forward. Her sunglasses flew off, and she screamed as she realized she was going to hit the mirror.

---

3

*H*er muscles tensed as she readied herself for the impact, and she covered her head with her arms. She could only hope the shards wouldn't hit something vital. For a terrifying moment, she was thrown back in time as memories from the car accident resurfaced from the depth of her mind.

She couldn't distinguish her mother's wild, red hair from the blood on her face and arms. Her mother was leaning back in the driver's seat, her brown eyes glassy as she stared at nothing. A large glass shard was sticking out of her neck, and rivulets of dark crimson blood poured out from the edges.

Mom... Ciara's voice was struck in her throat. She tried again, but no sound came out.

Ciara was dragged back to the present by distant sobbing. After a moment, she realized she was uninjured, and curled into a tight ball. She was the one sobbing.

She immediately stopped and tried to calm her erratic breathing. Slowly, she unwound herself from the fetal position, and as she realized she wasn't in pain or danger, the adrenaline dissipated in her body and her muscles relaxed. Too bad she was still trembling like a leaf in the wind.

She heard voices around her but couldn't recognize the language. She blinked up at an unfamiliar dark wooden ceiling and noticed a yellow paper lantern hung directly above her. Candlelight lit the tears streaming down her face, and she wiped them away as she sat up, disoriented.

What happened? Why was she crying? She closed her eyes for a moment and suddenly found herself back at the site of the car crash. Her eyes flew open, and she took a deep breath. She had to center herself.

Someone was talking to her, and she looked at the man squatting down next to her. He repeated the question.

"I don't understand you," she croaked. "What happened?"

Ciara looked around and saw a familiar mirror right behind her. It was the very same she had found at the mansion of her new student. The frame looked exactly the same, however, the mirror's surface had no black spots marring it and looked brand new. Was it really the same mirror? She racked her brain but didn't remember hearing shattering. Then again, she did remember sitting in a car, so maybe her mind was playing tricks on her.

The man next to her gestured to someone, and a young boy emerged from the shadows where the lantern's light couldn't reach. He gave the man a large book, which looked like one of those tomes that would appear in one of Karen's favorite history doramas.

Ciara felt a spark of curiosity. Where was she? The man told something to the boy who then scurried off. The two of them stayed in silence until he got back with a lit candle and held it up for the man to read. That's when Ciara noticed the man had a topknot. She was taken aback and looked at him again. His clothes looked like traditional

Japanese clothes. Candlelight exposed two sword handles at his hip.

He looked like a samurai.

Ciara snapped her gaze up when he yelled at her.

"What?" she grumbled, not liking his tone.

He grinned at her, and she realized with horror that she couldn't see any teeth in his mouth. He moved closer while Ciara leaned away, but he followed and grabbed the back of her neck.

Oh no, oh no, oh no! Her thoughts ran in a loop and she desperately tried to get away from the man.

Ciara tried to turn her face away but couldn't. The man murmured something, but she couldn't understand what he said. Then he pulled her close and kissed her. Ciara closed her lips tight and pushed on his chest with all the strength she could muster.

He was like a boulder and didn't move an inch. His tongue ran over Ciara's lower lip and in a final, desperate attempt to get him off her, she hit him over the head with her fist.

The creepy samurai pulled away with a frown, and Ciara gagged, turning away from him. She wiped her mouth furiously and cussed all the while.

"Are you done?"

"Are *you*?!" she shot back. "Don't you ever..." her eyes widened as she realized she could understand him. "...do that again."

"Or what?"

"How come I can understand you?"

"Now that we've sorted that out, follow me."

Ciara stood up but didn't move from her spot.

"What? Why? What do you want? Who are you?"

The samurai whirled around and stepped in front of her. Ciara took a step back, and the empty grin appeared on his face again. She realized she couldn't see his teeth earlier because they were all black. *What in the world?*

"You are here to assist me."

"Oh, hell no!"

He grabbed her arm. Ciara prayed he wouldn't sense her trembling. She made a fist and tensed her muscles.

"Silence!" he yelled at her. His putrid breath hit her, and she turned away, horrified. She was going to wash her mouth with soap as soon as she found a bathroom. The samurai used his free hand to grip her jaw and turn her head. She glared at him.

"You'll do as I say, or I'll cut you down where you stand. Is that clear?"

"What the hell?"

He backhanded her with such force that if he wasn't holding onto her arm, she probably would've ended up on the floor. Ciara saw stars dancing in front of her eyes and tasted blood in her mouth. She didn't even have time to recover from the shock. He was already dragging her away.

Ciara's head spun as he pulled her through dark corridors. She tried to understand what had happened. She was at the student's house when suddenly, she was pushed forward and fell into the mirror. Did she actually fall *through* the mirror? Was it a secret door to a secret room? And now they're going through secret corridors? The mansion was big enough to have something like that.

But who was this man who made her skin crawl with disgust? Who didn't know how to treat others with respect? Ciara's eye twitched in anger.

Maybe she ended up in an escape room? She had heard of those attractions but have never tried one herself. She wasn't good with closed spaces. Already she could hear the blood pumping in her ears and her breathing becoming ragged. She had to get outside, otherwise—

She took a deep breath when her brain registered the fresh air around her. *Finally!*

"Don't lag behind."

"Yes, my lord."

Ciara jumped at the voice of the boy behind her. She completely forgot he was there with them; she didn't even hear his footsteps. The samurai yanked her arm, and she gave a sound of protest, which he conveniently ignored.

They were outside, but Ciara could hardly see anything in the darkness of the night. *Wait, wasn't it before noon just now?* Maybe she lost consciousness and was out for hours? Was that possible?

No streetlamps lined their path; however, a torch flame lit the way at regular intervals. There was no pavement, no traffic lights, no cables hanging over the buildings. As Ciara looked up, she was amazed for a second, realizing she'd never seen the stars so clearly.

This all felt wrong. There was no sign of electricity or paved roads. Not even a car was in sight. Ciara tensed as her subconscious came up with a crazy idea. Either she was somehow transported to a tiny village without the conveniences of modern time or…

She immediately rejected the other idea and tried to come up with a more possible solution. Maybe these people chose to live like old times? No modern technology, just a simple life based on Japanese history? That seemed like a possible, if somewhat forced explanation. Right? But why was she kidnapped?

A scary thought entered her mind. What if that samurai-looking guy was a guru and he intended to initiate her into his cult? What if he kidnapped young women to be…to be…?

She didn't want to finish her thought.

"Let me go!" she shrieked as she tried to get out of his grip. He tightened his hold on her.

"Silence! I do not like to repeat myself, wench."

"What the—"

He backhanded her again, this time on the other side of her face. His eyes flashed angrily as he stopped to put her in place. Ciara's cheek was numb as she glared at him.

Blackteeth turned away and kept dragging her toward a tall building. Dawn was breaking, as was evident by the orange-purple colors appearing behind them on the Eastern sky. It slightly illuminated the big building before them. As she glanced up, she realized they were headed toward a Japanese-style castle through the courtyard. Her jaw slackened at the sight.

He must be a very wealthy guru. Where the hell was this hidden? It's bigger than the mansion! Ciara paled as her last hold on finding a sane solution to her situation slipped through her fingers. This was a nightmare.

"Bōya, check if our other…*guest* has arrived yet."

"Yes, Kawayuki-sama." The boy following them scurried off in a random direction.

Ciara noticed guards standing at every intersection. Moreover, she had seen some patrolling the courtyard. The security was not taken lightly in this place. She felt despair creep up her back as she realized her odds of escaping were diminishing by the second. Her hands trembled in response to her dark thoughts.

4

*I*t started as any other day for Katsuo Kitayama, lord of Shirotatsu castle. He woke up at dawn and quickly made his way to the pagoda, which was off-limits other than members of his family. It was built on the castle grounds, visible from a fair distance. Here, he could be alone with his thoughts and could train without interruptions.

He took his time going through the motions, cherishing a moment of respite in these turbulent times. He never knew when he had to head to battle next. Katsuo finished his kata and took a moment to meditate. The sun was peeking between two stories of the pagoda when he was done.

On the way back to his quarters, he made a detour to check on his soldiers' training and was satisfied to see that everyone who was not on duty was there, even his samurai officers.

"Brother!" Takeru shouted as soon as he spotted him and hurried over, his dark ponytail swinging side to side.

He looked to be, nearing the end of his teenage years, and eagerness reflected in his brown eyes. Katsuo nodded to him in greeting.

"What brings you here? We'll have sparring sessions as soon as they're finished with this kata. Do you want to join us?" Takeru asked, hopeful. It was a rare occasion whenever Katsuo joined them.

"Maybe next time," Katsuo replied.

"I see."

"How are the new recruits doing, Takeru?"

"Well…" His little brother glanced to the left side of the group where the beginners practiced. "Good for their second week."

"Make sure they're ready for the battlefield soon."

"Yes, brother." Takeru seemed as if he wanted to add something else, and Katsuo waited patiently for the young man to gather his thoughts. "Do we need to be ready soon? Is there a battle coming?"

"Takeru"—Katsuo put a hand on his little brother's shoulder—"we always need to be ready." He glanced over to the soldiers once more before striding off and waving.

"Keep up the good work, Takeru!"

"Yes, brother!"

After saying goodbye, Katsuo walked to his office to have a quick breakfast and start on the paperwork. That was the least favorite of his duties as a warlord, but it was as important to keep order in his territory as it was to hear out the grievances of his citizens. Happy underlings made for a flourishing economy, which made for a strong warlord.

Most days, he skipped lunch for the sake of an abundant evening meal, spending his time in ongoing strategy meetings unless something urgent came up or he was off to war. His days usually followed the same pattern. He was looking forward to the evening where he could finally spend some time with his daughter. His vassals respected his family-time and would never dare to intrude at this time of day.

"Join us, Taiki," Katsuo invited as he settled down for dinner. Taiki was in his mid-twenties and was his head of security. He was dressed in black and was just about to vanish into the dark night. He was the only ninja to serve Katsuo.

"With all due respect, my lord, I thank you for your invitation, but I must refuse."

"Are you not hungry?" Ayaka, Katsuo's daughter asked. Taiki seemed to consider his reply.

"Not really, Ayaka-dono."

"Then at least take this onigiri so you won't get hungry later." Ayaka got up and gave him a rice ball. "It's filled with tuna. I know you like it."

Taiki looked at his lord for help, but Katsuo pointedly looked away. He calmly took a sip of his sake, as if he didn't notice Taiki's predicament. The ninja glanced at Takeru, who was just arriving, for help.

"Oh, hey Taiki. Are you going to join us finally?"

"No," he bit out as he accepted the rice ball from the little girl. He smiled at her. "Thank you, Ayaka-dono."

"You're welcome, Taiki. Bye!" And she went back to the low dinner table to sit down.

"I'm going," Taiki said, pulling up his mask to cover the lower half of his face. He didn't expect a reply, so he was surprised when he heard his lord say, "I'm counting on you."

Taiki nodded almost imperceptibly and slid the door shut behind him as he exited the room. They didn't hear his retreating footsteps.

The family ate in relative silence, with the occasional

comment from Ayaka. When they finished eating, the little girl immediately lunged into recounting her day. Katsuo and Takeru were content to listen to her chatting away. When she asked them about their day, Katsuo replied with a few words. Takeru, however, told her about something interesting that happened during training.

"Will you play something, Daddy?" Ayaka asked when story time was over. She was blinking rapidly, a sure sign she was tired.

"Aren't you sleepy?"

"No!" She opened her eyes wide and leaned forward. "See? I'm very awake."

Katsuo chuckled. "Well, if you insist… maybe one song before you go to bed."

"Three!"

"Two."

Ayaka seemed to think his offer over. Eventually, she nodded. "Two songs."

Katsuo stood up and walked over to the cupboard to get the biwa. Meanwhile, Ayaka crawled into Takeru's lap and made herself comfortable. Takeru felt her arms were cold and hugged her to keep her warm. It was late fall, and a chill could already be felt after sunset. Katsuo started to play a happy melody.

The last note of the first song still hung in the air when Katsuo's ears pricked. He could hear pounding footsteps coming their way and placed the instrument down, looking at the door.

"What is it, Daddy? You promised two songs."

"Someone's coming," Takeru replied instead.

Ayaka looked up to him, puzzled. She didn't hear anything, but she had long since learned that her family had better ears than anyone she knew.

They heard a thud and someone's harsh breathing.

"Katsuo-sama!" Someone called him from the other side of the door.

"What is it?" Katsuo barked, annoyed his time with his family was interrupted. It had better be an emergency, or—

"Orihime-sama has just arrived."

Eerie silence was his response.

"Please repeat that."

The soldier winced at his lord's icy tone. Oh, he was pissed all right.

"Orihime-sama unexpectedly showed up at the castle gates just now."

The poor soldier jumped when the sliding door opened with such a force that it fell off its tracks.

"Damnit, brother, not the furniture again," Takeru mumbled in the room. He lifted Ayaka as he stood and joined Katsuo standing over the trembling soldier in the doorway.

"Where is Taiki?" Katsuo asked.

"Receiving Orihime-sama and her entourage."

"Her…" Katsuo took a deep breath. His eyes flashed golden. *"Entourage?"*

"Fi-fifteen of them, my lord," the soldier bowed so deep, his forehead touched the floor.

Katsuo didn't say anything as he strode away. His steps were heavy with suppressed anger.

Takeru yelled at his retreating back, "Cool down, brother!"

Katsuo stopped mid-stride and glanced back at him. His eyes were still golden.

"You don't want to scare them away."

Katsuo growled. "Maybe I do."

"You know what I mean."

As Katsuo blinked, the golden hue from his eyes faded. He nodded at his little brother and disappeared down the corridor. Takeru glanced at his niece sleeping in his arms then down at the soldier cowering at his feet.

"Get up."

"Yes, sir!"

The soldier was still trembling after seeing his lord in such a mood.

"Why are you afraid?"

The poor guy looked him in the eye before glancing away nervously.

"Look at me," Takeru ordered in a calm manner. The soldier met his eyes. "I know you're new, but remember this. Katsuo is not the kind of person to cut down the bearer of bad news. He'd rather hear it as soon as possible so the situation can be solved quicker. Understood?"

"Yes, sir."

"Good. Now, take her to her room." Takeru gave the sleeping Ayaka to the soldier. "I'll go assist my brother."

"B-but—"

Takeru was already walking away. At the hesitation in the soldier's voice, he glanced over his shoulder. "What is it?"

"What if the tiger is still here?"

"What are you talking about?" Shocked, Takeru turned to fully face him.

The soldier's eyes were looking around frantically. "You know, the tiger that made that growling sound just now."

Takeru's lips twitched. Wait until he told Katsuo he was mistaken for a tiger in his own home! He tried not to laugh out loud.

"No need to worry. The *tiger* is gone."

"How would you—"

"Another thing you need to learn is to trust your lords," was all Takeru said as he rounded a corner and vanished.

The soldier looked down at the sleeping little girl in his arms. He had no idea where her room was.

5

*K*atsuo was still in a bad mood when he arrived at the castle gates. Taiki silently slid next to him.

"My lord."

"Report." Katsuo's terse reply didn't faze the ninja.

"Orihime-dono swears she sent a message ahead, but we have not received such a thing. She insists on staying here until…"

Taiki trailed off, which was rare for him. Katsuo gave him a sideways glance.

"Until?"

"Until the wedding."

Katsuo froze, opened his mouth, then realized he was already in the courtyard near the gate, and if he lost his composure, everyone would hear. As a dependable leader, his men needed to know they could count on him through better or worse. If he lost his temper, then who would they rely on to bring them home safely from the battlefield?

"Your eyes, my lord."

"Stop calling me that!" Katsuo snapped, turning and

continuing his march to the uninvited guests. He could only hope he had calmed enough for his eyes to be back to normal. If not, he'd just have to blame the torches' light.

"Orihime-dono," he greeted.

"My lord, Katsuo-sama!" The woman twirled around, a big smile plastered on her face. She was pretty. Her long, raven black hair was tied up in an elaborate design, and she wore a crimson kimono. The colors contrasted with her smooth, alabaster skin, which seemed to luminesce in the weak light of the torches around them.

She hurried up to him, full of energy. Her big, brown eyes were wide as she gazed up at him and batted her eyelashes. Katsuo was mesmerized before he reminded himself what happened the last time he submitted to such a look.

"To what do I owe the surprise of your presence here?"

"Oh." Orihime put a hand over her mouth as she gasped. "Haven't you received my message, my lord?"

"Apparently not." Katsuo quirked an eyebrow. He wouldn't let her play this game.

"My honorable father has decided it was time to start on the wedding preparations." Orihime stepped closer and reached out to touch Katsuo's arm. He stepped away before she made contact.

"I do not recall sending a response to the proposal."

"Well, yes, but…" Orihime was uneasy, fidgeting with a lock of her hair that escaped her bun. She glanced down shyly. "It's a good proposal. Why would you refuse? So, I thought—"

"You thought wrong." Katsuo was fed up with the charade. He didn't have time for a wedding and certainly not with such a sly woman. He took another step back. "As it is very late, please stay here for tonight. I shall write to your father come morning. And excuse us for the ill-prepared rooms. We weren't expecting you."

Katsuo made a quick escape with as much politeness as he could muster.

"Wait!" Orihime reached out after him. "Won't you reconsider? Our families—"

"Good night, my lady." Katsuo cut off her further protests as he walked out of sight. Takeru bumped into him just as he was rounding a corner. He tensed as he looked at Katsuo's face.

"Brother... your eyes..."

"I'm going to my room. Tell everyone not to bother me."

"Sure. Did she say why she travelled here?"

"She is under the illusion that she is to be wed to me."

"Didn't you reject the proposal?"

Katsuo sighed. Finally, the gold hue receded from his eyes as he forced himself to calm down.

"It seems I had forgotten to send a reply between the recent border skirmishes."

"Ah, that's bad."

"I'm leaving. Just one more thing, Takeru," Katsuo said as he stopped at the veranda.

"Yes?"

"Find some rooms for them."

Takeru grinned, an idea already forming in his head.

"Leave it to me, brother!"

He sounded way too happy about it, but Katsuo didn't have the energy to contemplate that. He suddenly felt drained. When was the last time he had a good night's sleep? He couldn't even remember.

He was awakened near dawn by a nagging feeling that told him he was in danger. Katsuo's hand slid under his pillow, and his fingers wrapped around the handle of the dagger he kept there. Whoever was trying to take advantage of his sleeping hours, they were in for a nasty surprise.

He doubted anything could get close to him under Taiki's supervision of security, but ever since the incident with his ex-wife, he had been prepared to expect the worst.

Katsuo suddenly tensed and threw the dagger in a wide arc. It sank in the wall next to the door. He was alone in the room, but something still didn't sit well with him. He calmed his erratic breathing and stood to retrieve his weapon.

He was halfway to the door when it unexpectedly slid open. Taiki stood on the threshold. If the ninja was surprised to see his lord awake, he didn't show it. Taiki eyed the dagger with suspicion.

"Is everything all right, my lord?"

"Yes," was the terse reply as he pulled the dagger out from the wall. He brushed his long hair to the side. "Why are you here?"

Taiki never sugarcoated anything. He went straight for the kill.

"Ayaka-dono was kidnapped during the night."

Katsuo thought he heard wrong. He inclined his head.

"Care to repeat that?"

"Ayaka-dono was kidnapped."

"Talk to me." Katsuo hastily wrapped a haori[1] around his torso, grabbed his wakizashi[2], and headed to Ayaka's room in a hurry.

"It happened sometime after dinner and before the early morning shift. I've just discovered the body."

"What body?"

"There was a guard outside her door. His throat was slit, and Ayaka is gone."

"I don't remember placing a guard outside her room."

"Neither do I. It's..." Taiki racked his brain for the appropriate word. "Intriguing."

Katsuo knocked on Takeru's door before continuing to Ayaka's. Takeru slept as light as he did, so Katsuo knew he would be soon on his way. By the time he arrived at his daughter's room, Takeru had caught up to him. He was only wearing a hakama³. His unbound hair was messy, but his eyes were sharp.

The three looked at the lifeless body of a young soldier. Takeru squatted down, examining his face.

"This was the guy who told us of Orihime's arrival. I tasked him to bring Ayaka to her room," Takeru informed them. His voice quieted. "This was only his second week here."

And I told him to trust us. Takeru closed his eyes and bowed his head, mourning for the loss of a good man.

"Other than his injuries, there are no signs of scuffle," Taiki added.

"She was probably asleep," Katsuo murmured as he entered his daughter's room. Nothing was out of place, except the missing little girl.

"Who could've done such a thing?" Takeru followed his brother inside the room. "Slit someone's throat then kidnap a child? That's just cruel."

"War is cruel. You should know by now."

"Ayaka has nothing to do with war," Takeru protested. Silently, Katsuo agreed.

"My lord," Taiki said as he crouched down. He held up something in his hand.

"What is it?" Katsuo asked as he walked over. Takeru followed him immediately.

"A piece of paper," Taiki replied and held it out to them. Two characters were written on it. The ninja was taken aback as both men's eyes flashed gold. He was used to such display from his lord but not from Takeru.

"That bastard Kawayuki! I'm going to kill him!"

"Takeru." Katsuo's icy voice stopped him. He turned back.

"You're not going to tell me to sit here while he has his disgusting paws on my niece!"

"Of course not. But we need to come up with a strategy. We can't just rush into this," Katsuo said. His body was so tense, and he resembled a snake coiled to attack any moment. Seeing his brother in such a state made Takeru calmer. At least one of them needed a cool head to come up with something.

"I understand. Shall I gather our strategists?"

"No."

"What? Why?"

"Nobody has seen anything," Katsuo replied. "Nobody has heard anything. Doesn't that make you suspicious?"

"What do you mean?"

"Do you think they had help from inside, my lord?" Taiki asked, his eyes narrowing.

"Anything is possible. Right now, you two are the only ones I trust in this household. I'm counting on you. Get ready and meet me in the council room."

Takeru nodded and hurried back to his room.

"Get someone to confirm her kidnapper," Katsuo ordered the ninja. Taiki bowed and melted into the shadows of early morning.

---

1. overcoat
2. samurai's short sword
3. loose trousers, with folds

6

*C*iara was forced into simple clothing that was of a similar style to the one the young servant boy wore. Her belongings had either been left in the room with the mirror or were taken away when she had to change. Even her sunglasses were missing, and as the sun slowly made its way higher, she had no doubt her unusual eye color would be noticed. She couldn't even cover it with her hair, as it was twisted up and secured with a headcloth on the top of her head.

She looked like a washwoman from a periodic drama.

The boy from earlier came to get her to lead her to a small room, and guards flanked her from both sides as they made their way through the castle corridors. The wooden planks under her bare feet were cold, and Ciara pondered for a moment the possibility that she was sleeping back in her home and her feet had peeked out from under the blankets.

As she stumbled, a guard caught her arm and steadied her. His grip tightened a fraction before he released her. Pain shot up on Ciara's arm momentarily, and she was reminded of the two hard slaps she had received not long after arriving here. She was most definitely awake in this twisted world.

She fidgeted as she was ordered to sit down in a small room. The guards had exited and stood outside the sliding door. Everything to the last bit of detail reminded her of how she would imagine old world Japan. The young boy stared at her, and she decided to try to get some information from him. Maybe he'd be more compliant than Kawayuki.

Ciara smiled at him gently.

"Do you live here?"

He didn't reply.

"My name is Ciara. Yours?"

She thought he wouldn't reply this time either, but he did.

"Kazu."

"Kazu," Ciara repeated, happy to know. "Can you tell me what place this is?"

The boy cocked his head to the side.

"Kawayuki-sama's castle."

"Is it in Japan?"

"Nippon? Yes." Kazu looked as if he wanted to ask something but stayed silent.

"What is it? Tell me," Ciara urged him with a small smile.

"You are strange."

She was taken aback for a moment, not sure what to make of this remark. Eventually, she nodded.

"I suppose I am, for your eyes." A moment passed. "Do you know why I'm here? I only remember falling into a mirror."

What if she had a concussion and is out cold in a stranger's house, with no help on the way? Her eyes widened. No, no. She had definitely felt those injuries. She shook away the disturbing thoughts and focused on Kazu's answer.

"Kawayuki-sama brought you here. He wants something from you. He always wants something from people." Kazu let out a small sigh as he told her.

"Who is he? This Kawayuki?"

"He is he lord of this castle. One of the daimyōs."

Daimyō[1]. It triggered a distant memory, Karen preparing for her Japanese history class, murmuring about daimyōs and tiny countries. Ciara felt fear settle heavily in her stomach. She licked her lips, preparing for the inevitable question.

"What year is this?"

"It's interregnum year-"

"Boy!"

Ciara jumped at Kawayuki's booming voice. Kazu walked to the door opposite from where they had come in, knelt, and slid it open. A huge meeting room revealed itself. There was a dais on the closer end of the room, where Kawayuki sprawled, overlooking the entire place.

He reminded Ciara of a rooster standing on top of the—

"Now!" He looked Ciara straight in the eye.

Without meaning to, she stood up and walked toward him as if in a trance. Slowly, she made her way to his side even though that was the last thing she wanted. It was as if an invisible force made her walk over to him and sit down next to his legs.

As soon as she sat down, the strange feeling passed away, and she shook her head to clear her mind. What was that? Was this how people felt whenever she accidentally used the Voice? Disturbed, she looked around.

At least a dozen people lined both sides of the room. All

of them were dressed in rich, silk clothing and had the ridiculous hairdo Kawayuki sported. Maybe they wanted to imitate him? Each of them had some symbol on their overcoats, and their swords rested next to them, just in reach. Goosebumps ran over Ciara's arms at the sight.

"You know the first part of our plan. We have his daughter. And this here is the second part." Kawayuki gestured to Ciara.

She couldn't help raising her eyebrows in question. *This? Really?* If there was an Olympic category for being offensive, Kawayuki would have an easy win. There was still time for the 2020 Tokyo Olympics—

Ciara's hands trembled and she gathered them in her lap. The small talk with Kazu indicated she wasn't in a secret, crazy escape room, but in a different world. Maybe even a different—

"Time," Kawayuki was saying, "is on our side. Kitayama won't have enough time to prepare a counterattack so quickly. We must make use of this wench's skills in the meantime."

"What skills, my lord?" asked one of his vassals.

What is he talking about? Ciara mused, glancing up at Kawayuki. He smiled with his black teeth at her, and she shuddered at the horrible memory it brought up.

"She will infuse our weapons with magic. They'll be ten times stronger than average weapons. They will cause more damage than imaginable and prevent healing injuries."

Ciara's eyes widened in shock. He was crazy! How did he come up with such a mad plan? The things he had talked about were impossible! Maybe not for Karen, but—

Oh, shit.

Karen. It was Karen's inherited power, not hers. But if they knew they had grabbed the wrong person, then she'd probably be killed and Karen would be kidnapped. The only way out seemed to lead them on until she could escape. But how would she trick them into believing she had these skills? As soon as Kawayuki ordered a demonstration of power, she was dead. And Karen would be in danger. She didn't like either option.

"No need to be shy." Kawayuki grinned at her, seeing her face pale. "I know all about your special powers, purple-eyed witch."

Ciara bit her lip and made a fist of her trembling hands. She needed to come up with an escape plan, ASAP. If she couldn't get back to the mirror, then she had to get as far away from Kawayuki as possible.

The new room she had been led to was full of weapons of all sorts, long and short swords, bows and arrows, daggers, spears of every imaginable shape, and Ciara even spotted some throwing stars!

"Get to work," Kawayuki said as he pushed her inside. Ciara stumbled and twirled around.

"All this?"

"But of course. Did you think you were here on a leisure trip? Don't let my kiss fool you, wench."

Ciara involuntarily shuddered, trying to forget all that had to do with that incident. It didn't help that she was reminded of it every time he grinned.

Kawayuki slid the door shut, and darkness surrounded her in the windowless room.

"Damnit. Where's the light?" Ciara was touching the wall near the doorframe, then remembered her suspicion about the timeline. "Right, no switch." She set about to find a candle or something that would help her see but shortly realized that even if she did find a torch, she had no way of igniting a flame.

Her foot slipped on something smooth and round, making her stumble into a pile of... spears? Ciara prayed she didn't injure something vital. Thankfully, she only collected some new bruises. She managed to crawl to her knees and hands when the door slid open. Ciara hissed at the sudden brightness and put a hand over her eyes.

"What in hells are you doing?" She heard Kawayuki's voice. Great, he was back. "Never mind that. You're coming with me. Up!"

He didn't have the patience to wait for her to get up properly but grabbed her arm and dragged her out of the room and through the corridor. Kazu joined them soon with a little girl and a guard. Ciara didn't have time to assess the situation as she was dragged to a window which overlooked the courtyard.

Kawayuki grabbed the back of her head and pushed her face to the window opening. Thankfully, there was no glass. For some curious reason, Ciara didn't expect there to be any.

Soldiers in black ran in the direction of the gates, trying to push back the enemy, who had crimson uniforms.

"See that? You're already too late, you lazy wench." Ciara tried not to gag as Kawayuki's putrid breath hit her face. "Now get to work!"

He hit her head on the window frame, which cracked under the pressure. Ciara hoped her head fared better. She touched her forehead and felt a bump already forming. Thankfully, there was no blood on her hand when she checked it. She grimaced, thinking her face was probably already deformed by the slaps and hits she had to endure since she had gotten here.

"Here, enhance this," Kawayuki pointed to his sword.

"I can't do it like this," Ciara said, and he lunged for her. She took a step back and raised her hands. "I need to hold the item to do that!"

Kawayuki raised his eyebrows.

"Nice try," he admitted. "But I don't believe you."

Damn, there goes that plan. Ciara forced a blank expression on her face.

"I can read you like an open book," Kawayuki said, but Ciara ignored him, hoping against hope he was bluffing just as much as she was.

"Boy!"

Ciara snapped her gaze to Kazu who had grabbed the little girl and drew her to him. A dagger flashed in his hand as he pointed the blade to the girl's neck. Ciara's eyes widened in shock. She couldn't believe what she was seeing.

"Kazu!" Shock made her voice tremble.

"If you don't enhance my katana, *without* any ulterior motives, he *will* kill her," Kawayuki warned her. Ciara's hands shook as she thought over her choices.

She didn't know the little girl, but she didn't want anybody to die because of her ever again. Maybe she could atone for her sin if she were to save this girl. The blade pressed into the girl's tender neck.

"STOP!" Without meaning to, Ciara used the Voice on all of them. As soon as she realized everybody but her had frozen, she freed the little girl and ran away with her.

"After them! Do not let them escape!" Kawayuki roared in anger a heartbeat later when the effect was gone. Ciara picked up the pace, and surprisingly, the girl matched it. They arrived at a turn, and Ciara went for the right corridor.

"Not that way!" The girl yanked her arm toward the left. "This leads outside."

Ciara didn't stop to argue. They were being chased by armed men, and clearly, the girl felt more at home in a castle than she'd ever be. She followed her, and they soon ended up at the long staircase in the middle of the castle.

"Come!" The girl let go of her hand and ran downstairs. Ciara followed with urgency.

"What's your name?"

"Ayaka. Were you kidnapped, too?"

"Yes," Ciara huffed as they reached the ground floor. She took a deep breath.

Ayaka was already at the end of the corridor.

"Hurry!" she screamed at Ciara, who immediately continued running. Thankfully, her lungs were doing all right, but her legs felt weak. Ayaka was so fast compared to how small she was. Ciara briefly wondered how she did it as she sprinted after her. She could already hear pounding footsteps approaching from behind.

---

1. feudal lord

7

*F*inally, they reached outside. Ayaka didn't stop as she ran to the edge of the veranda and continued barefooted across the courtyard. Ciara sighed, following her and wishing she had shoes.

The sounds of metal clinks coming from behind spurred her into action, and she sprinted across the courtyard with all her might. She could smell burning wood in her nose. Ciara glanced to the side and realized a building was on fire.

"The mirror! Get it!" Kawayuki hollered at his soldiers, pointing to the burning building.

Shit, the mirror was there, Ciara realized, and her steps faltered for a second when her foot slipped. She stumbled to the ground just as a blade swept through the air where her torso had been a second ago. Shocked, she turned around on the ground and looked up at her assailant. The second shock hit her when she realized the figure who stood above her was only a teenager about the same age as Karen or possibly younger.

"What—?" Ciara registered the crimson uniform,

immediately realizing he was one of Kawayuki's enemies. *The enemy of my enemy is my ally.*

"W-wait!" She held up her hands as he lifted on of his short swords. "I'm not working with Kawayuki!"

He snorted in amusement.

"Of course not, you're his servant."

"What? No, I'm not!"

He pointed his blade at her head and cut her headscarf. Ciara's long brown hair unfurled and fell on her shoulders.

"Your clothes say otherwise," he pointed out but stopped at the sight of her chestnut-colored hair. He took a second look at her, intrigued. He kept hold both of his short swords in one hand and squatted down before her, curiosity written over his face. "You're a foreigner."

"I suppose?"

He reached for her hair with his free hand. Ciara waited with belated breath to see what he was planning to do. He seemed more interested in her hair than in killing her at the moment, which was a better situation than the one she had been in a second ago.

"Takeru, we're on a battlefield. Don't flirt."

"Brother…" The teen mumbled and got up to tell him something when Ciara noticed a white streak from the corner of her eye. She shrieked and jumped back. A hand caught the thing, and Ciara came eye to eye with a white snake. Her breath caught as the snake's tongue flicked out. It was so close she could swear its tongue touched the tip of her nose.

"Aaaaah!" She crawled back on her hands and quickly stood up. The snake rose and drew back. Ciara blinked and realized a hand had closed around it. She dragged her gaze up on the toned muscles of the man's arm, to the crimson uniform with a silver sash and a white dragon symbol on it, then finally settled on the handsome face of her savior.

They stared at each other for a long moment. The stranger had dark brown eyes, which glinted with alertness and studied Ciara. His black hair was gathered in manbun on top of his head. A slight breeze swept at Ciara's long hair, briefly blinding her and breaking the moment. She didn't dare move a muscle as she stared at the stranger.

"Thanks," she finally said, still not quite over the shock. He nodded and stroked the back of the snake before throwing it away.

"You're not killing it?"

"Why would I? It didn't do anything wrong."

Ciara gaped.

"Isn't it poisonous?"

"Takeru, why did you let her live?" The man asked the teen. Ciara's legs felt weak. She balled her trembling hands into fists as she tried to fight the panic attack that was looming in the back of her mind. How did she ever think him attractive? She should run while she still had her head!

"She says she's not of Kawayuki's household. And I've never seen such pretty hair," replied the guy who had almost cut her down. He twirled the swords in his hands.

Are they for real? If possible, these men seemed more insane than Kawayuki. She slowly backed away.

"Do you think Kawayuki would spare you if you kept your hair nice?"

"No." Much to his surprise, it was the woman who replied. Katsuo took a second glance at her. Takeru was correct in his assessment of her long brown hair. It was indeed beautiful in its unusual color. Her face had gentle features, and elegant eyebrows framed dark purple eyes.

Katsuo could see the bruises already forming on her

cheeks and a small bump on her forehead and noticed her split lips. Kawayuki wasn't gentle while handling her, and Katsuo idly wondered what she could have done to deserve such treatment. Maybe nothing. Kawayuki thrived on hurting people weaker than him.

"Go," Katsuo waved at her.

She blinked, and a puzzled expression came over her face.

"What?"

"I don't want to repeat myself," Katsuo said, bending down to retrieve the katana he had dropped when lunging for the snake. The woman took a step back and stumbled. She ended up falling on her bottom and looked at him as if he had threatened her life.

Katsuo ignored the sudden pang in his heart and turned to his brother. "Let's go find Ayaka," he said, walking away. Takeru quickly followed him.

"Wait!" the woman shouted after them, hastily standing. He ignored her. "Did you say Ayaka? The little girl with who was wearing a pink robe with bunnies on it?"

Katsuo tensed hearing that. *She had met Ayaka,* he thought and glanced back over his shoulder, a question in his eyes. The woman nervously wet her lips.

"She was just ahead of me."

"She has escaped?"

"Yes, we escaped together, then she ran ahead," she explained, looking around. "She must be somewhere nearby."

"Did you see which direction she went?"

Her expression fell as she turned her gaze on him. She was so sad yet beautiful in her own way.

"No, I'm sorry."

He let out a frustrated sigh before turning away and continuing on his way.

"Wait!"

Takeru let out a small chuckle, which earned him a glare from Katsuo.

"Can I help you?"

"*Help* us?" Katsuo asked, flabbergasted as he fully turned back to face her. "You can't even protect yourself from a snake."

If she felt offended, she covered the feeling with her pride as she puffed out her chest – he only just noticed how abundant she was in that area – and straightened her spine. Katsuo flicked his gaze back to her eyes.

"I might not be of much help in a fight, but I can help find a lost little girl!"

"Well, she might prove useful…" Takeru whispered to him.

"I don't have time for this," Katsuo sighed. He nodded at the woman. "Come if you must."

A bright smile appeared on her face at his words, and Katsuo felt his heart skip a beat. He cursed.

"What is it?" Takeru asked, suspicious of his behavior.

"Nothing," he replied. When the woman caught up with them, he decided to split the party up. Takeru would go alone and he with the woman. His brother happily accepted and winked at him before jogging away. *Oh no, he totally got the wrong idea.* Katsuo dreaded the hour when they would arrive back at Shirotatsu castle.

He turned in the opposite direction Takeru had gone, and the woman fell in place beside him. Katsuo furrowed his eyebrows. It was not customary for a woman to walk next to a man. Before he opened his mouth to correct her, he was reminded of her foreign status as she looked up at him expectantly with her purple-hued eyes. He didn't remember seeing anyone with such eye color.

"What is it?" she asked, curious.

Katsuo turned back to the path.

"How did you meet Ayaka?"

A troubled sigh escaped her.

"This bastard, Kawayuki, threatened to hurt her if I didn't do something for him."

The path narrowed to only one person wide. Katsuo took the lead, walking further into the woods.

"What did you tell him?"

"Well, I didn't want her to get hurt, but Kawayuki was asking for the impossible."

"Why?"

"I don't know. I don't see into his depraved mind," she quipped, and his lips twitched in amusement. He cleared his throat.

"I mean, why would you want to help Ayaka? You don't know her."

The movement behind him stopped, and he turned around to see the woman looking at him like he was a big idiot. He raised an eyebrow, but that didn't faze her.

"She's just a little girl," was all she said. Katsuo sensed there was more to the story but didn't pressure her. He turned around to continue his search. This part of the forest was dense.

"Ouch!" Katsuo heard her painful hiss. Sighing, he turned back around. *What now?*

"I-it's okay, I can keep on going," she said. "Maybe a bit slower. Sorry," she said, looking down at her feet. *Had she been walking barefoot all this time?* The forest floor was full of small rocks with jagged edges, twigs and, whatnot.

Katsuo was about to reply when a nearby bush rustled and someone jumped out at them. His blade moved before he could register what color the uniform was. When he realized it was black, he cut down the enemy in one move.

The woman stood there in shock, trembling from head

to toe. She gulped as their eyes met. She broke the stare first as she looked away. Her small hands made a fist, slightly trembling.

Then she ran to the nearest bush to empty the contents of her stomach.

8

*C*iara wiped her mouth and straightened from her hunched position behind a nearby bush. *Well, that must've been very attractive.* She looked for a big leaf to wipe her hands.

Disgusting, she grimaced as she cleaned her hands and mouth with the leaf. *I need fresh water.* She glanced down at her clothes and was relieved to see they didn't get dirty. Her hair was safely tucked in at the back of her neck, and her stomach was still queasy after all the work.

She risked a glance at the man who had cut down another. He was just wiping the blood down from his sword in the fallen man's uniform. Ciara felt her stomach churn, but she pushed the feeling down and stepped around the tree, away from the bloody scene.

How could he just...doesn't he feel any remorse? He's just killed a man, and he's calmly cleaning his sword as if nothing was more natural in the world! Ciara took a deep breath and hobbled away. Her feet hurt, and she felt sick as she made her way through the forest.

A moment later, she heard pounding footsteps as the

man caught up to her. She felt his touch on her arm and jumped at the unexpected gesture.

"Are you all right?"

Ciara looked into his deep brown eyes. The edges of the irises were golden, like honey. *No, I'm not. How could I be all right after all this?* She felt tears threaten but gulped them down like a bitter pill. She nodded hastily, looking away.

"I'll be fine."

He retreated his hand, his expression puzzled. He glanced down and caught her trembling hands in his. Ciara held her breath as she slowly dragged her gaze up. From this close, she could smell his distinctive scent under all the sweat, dirt, and blood, a fresh masculine scent, like forest and soap. She discreetly took a whiff, and calmness immediately enveloped her. Ciara leaned closer to him. She was surprised at her own reaction.

He was about to tell her something when, again, they were interrupted by movement nearby. This time, it was crunching noise coming from Ciara's left. The man released her hand and gripped his katana with both hands as he stepped in front of her. His muscles were so tense, he reminded her of the attacking snake. She shuddered at the memory.

Finally, a figure emerged from behind a cluster of bushes. The man relaxed and sighed in relief.

"Ayaka."

Ciara peeked out from behind him, seeing the little girl stop and stare at them. Then she lunged for the scary man.

"Daddy!"

What?

Ayaka lunged at the man who crouched and gathered her in his arms. She hugged his neck tightly, and he patted her back. After Ciara got over the shock, she sniffled at the reunion. She was happy Ayaka had found her father and now they could go home. If only she could go home, too…

Ciara looked to the distance, not even sure which direction the mirror was in. She was sure if she could get back to it, she'd be able to go home. But a battlefield and countless maimed bodies stood between her and her way home, not to mention Kawayuki's crazy minions. She sighed deeply, suddenly realizing she wouldn't get home without help.

"Are you inju—" the man started to ask when he drew back from his daughter and noticed the angry red line on her tender neck. His eyes flashed golden for a moment, but when Ciara blinked, it was gone. Was it her imagination?

"I'm fine, Daddy," Ayaka said and turned to Ciara. She reached out her hand toward the woman. Ciara grabbed her fingers with a small smile. "The pretty lady helped me."

"My thanks." The man nodded at Ciara. For the first time, Ciara felt he had appreciated her presence.

"No problem."

He let Ayaka down and grabbed a horn from his belt. It was a conch shell with a metal mouthpiece. He took a deep breath and played a short tune. He repeated it twice, and Ciara was caught in the moment, enjoying the music.

"Let's go," he said to Ayaka and reached out for her, but the little girl skipped over to Ciara, who bent down.

"What is it?"

"What's your name?"

"Ciara."

"Shiara?"

"Ciara."

Ayaka nodded with a serious expression on her face.

"You said you were kidnapped. Do you need help getting home?"

Ciara opened her mouth then closed it. Her lips repeated the movement, not sure how to answer.

"W-well, I suppose so." Hesitating, she glanced up at the man standing behind Ayaka. His penetrating gaze made her shudder. Just what was he thinking? Ciara quickly looked back at the little girl. "But don't worry about me. I'll find my way home."

She hated the fact that her voice trembled.

Ayaka turned to her father with a question in her eyes. Katsuo could never say no when she looked at him like that, and he suspected she knew that, too. He suppressed a sigh and tried to look intimidating, crossing his arms and frowning, but his daughter wasn't buying it. As long as the woman thought him frightening and not take up on the offer, though…

It wasn't like him. He was a daimyō, bound to help the people under his protection, and as soon as the woman offered her assistance in finding Ayaka, she became one of those people. Especially after learning she had helped his daughter escape from his enemy's stronghold. He wondered if she had an ulterior motive and expected something in return.

"Daddy!" Ayaka's voice actually sounded admonishing.

"I'm going." Ciara stood up, her legs shaky. "Take care, Ayaka." Then she glanced at him, bowed a little, and turned to go away.

"Wait." The word left his lips before he could register it. For some unexplainable reason, it hurt to see her turn her back and walk away from him. His instincts screamed at him not to let her walk out of his life.

Katsuo blinked in surprise. He'd never experienced

such an emotion before, not even when he met his previous wife. It was as if something was drawing him to her.

Ciara was waiting for him to continue with a sad smile on her face , which deepened the longer he stayed silent. She moved to turn away again.

"You have helped Ayaka," Katsuo said, "and I am grateful for that. Let me help you in return."

Ciara glanced in the direction of Kawayuki's castle for a moment before turning back to him.

"Thank you, but I have yet to figure out how to get home."

"Is it far away?" Ayaka asked, curiously.

"Yes, very far, I'm afraid," she replied.

"Then you can come with us until you figure it out!" Ayaka offered.

"Erm…" Ciara fidgeted, uncomfortable. She glanced at him, nervously. "I'm not sure your Daddy—"

"The name's Katsuo." It bothered him that she wasn't calling him by his name. She fell silent, waiting for him to continue. "Ayaka is right. You may come with us."

"I…" She choked on her words and looked at him with misty eyes. Oh gods, no, not another woman trying to manipulate him with tears! But she gulped those tears down and took a shaky breath. No tears had fallen. She even mustered a smile on her face as she said, "Don't be offended if I take you up on it!"

"Of course not. You may stay as long as you need."

"Thank you, I am very grateful, Katsuo," she said, hastily wiping at her eyes.

"Come, come!" Ayaka grabbed Ciara's hand and dragged her toward him. Katsuo turned to walk back to where they had left their horses. He wondered at the funny feeling in his stomach when she called his name without honorifics. Were all foreigners this informal?

That was so embarrassing. I almost cried in front of him! Ciara thought as Ayaka led her. She snuck a peek at Katsuo, curious. He was a puzzle. One minute, he was cold and threatening her, the next, he saved her, and the way he treated Ayaka told her he had a soft spot for his little daughter. He couldn't be a bad person.

The image of an attacker cut in half flashed before her eyes. There was no way she was going to trust someone who handled killing people with such ease. How did he do it when she could hardly bear the guilt of causing one person's death?

Ciara's gaze wandered over his broad back and wide shoulders and settled on his toned arms. The way he held himself reminded her of watching a dangerous predator, built for war. He glanced back, and their gazes locked for a second. She looked away, embarrassed that she was caught staring. *I'm not going to make a fool out of myself. He's like all other guys, he'll walk away soon enough.*

"Shiara," Ayaka called her, and she turned her attention to the little girl. "What do you do at home?"

"I'm a voice trainer and singing coach."

She crunched her nose up as she concentrated to understand.

"You teach people to sing?"

"Among other things, yes. Why?"

"I like singing."

"That's wonderful!"

"Takeru sings well, but Daddy is—"

"Ayaka," Katsuo cut her off firmly. That one word was

enough for the little girl to stop chattering. Ciara raised her eyebrows, curious how Ayaka intended to end the sentence. Clearly, Katsuo was of another opinion.

"I can teach you if you want," she told Ayaka.

"Really?"

"Sure."

"Thanks, Shiara."

Maybe work on pronunciation first.

9

*T*hey had soon reached the horses in a nearby clearing. Takeru was already there, waiting for them with a small group of soldiers.

"My lord." They all bowed to Katsuo. Ciara glanced at the samurai with surprise in her eyes but otherwise didn't comment.

"Takeru!" Ayaka ran up to the teen, who picked her up easily.

"I'm so happy you're here, Ayaka!"

"Me too!" She buried her face in Takeru's neck.

Katsuo looked around.

"We're still missing a few people."

"They didn't make it back." Takeru reported, wearing a dark expression.

A moment of silence passed the group.

"Let's go home, men!"

Cheers erupted at Katsuo's order. He walked over to Ayaka, but she hugged Takeru's neck tighter.

"You're going to kill me, Ayaka," he wheezed, and she loosened her hold a little bit.

"Do you want to ride home with Takeru?" Katsuo asked.

She nodded.

"I think she's missed her favorite uncle," Takeru chuckled, patting Ayaka's head.

"You're her only uncle," Katsuo murmured and went to get his horse, but a soldier was already there with said horse. Katsuo looked back at Ciara. "You can use one of those horses."

Ciara paled and gaped at him. She whispered something in a squeaky voice.

"What was that?" Everyone's attention was on her, and she felt as if she was on stage again, which made her voice instinctively rise as she announced proudly that she couldn't ride a horse. Her face reddened as soon as she saw the men's flabbergasted expressions.

"You'll ride with me, then," Katsuo said and walked over to her, leading his horse. Takeru exchanged curious glances with the soldiers, who knew even less about the woman who was to ride with their lord.

Katsuo picked her up and Ciara was surprised for a moment at his gentle touch. The last time she thought herself light as a feather was when she was a child, but at this moment, as Katsuo lifted her with care and ease, a funny feeling bloomed in her stomach. She wasn't sure what it was, but it was a pleasant feeling. Katsuo placed her in the saddle and quickly jumped up behind her. Ciara made herself as comfortable as she could. Even though her whole body tensed up when Katsuo settled behind her, it was still better than running around barefoot.

"Move out!" he yelled, and she winced at the loud voice. Ciara held on for dear life when the horse broke into a gallop.

"Relax. You make the horse nervous," Katsuo said as he

leaned closer and circled an arm around her waist, making Ciara tense up more.

"Horses make *me* nervous," she shot back. The horse jumped over a fallen log, and she clutched Katsuo's arm that held her.

"How long is the ride?"

"Two days."

Silence.

"Sorry, I think I've heard wrong. *Two entire days?*" Just how slow was a horse compared to the modern conveniences she was used to? Were these people time billionaires?

Katsuo chuckled behind her, and she could feel the rumbles on her back.

"I'm just jesting. It's only half a day."

"Half a—That's way too long," she mumbled, slumping back. She didn't even realize she had leaned back until Katsuo cleared his throat nervously. She straightened up.

"Don't. You'll fall off at this speed."

Ciara leaned back, acutely aware of the muscles behind her and the arm around her waist. She sat in a cloud of fresh forest and soap, and slowly, she relaxed. She suppressed a yawn, suddenly realizing she had been up and around for a whole day if her estimate was right. The sun had reached its zenith in the sky, and it stood in the same position when she went to that fateful meeting with her new student. Just who was that man in black that pushed her into this world? Did he know what would await her when she arrived? Was it an accident or on purpose?

Katsuo felt Ciara's form go limp in his arms. He glanced at her face, seeing her eyes closed. Her breathing was slow, and everything indicated she was asleep. He shook his head in disbelief. How could she fall asleep in the arms of a stranger? She was lucky he was a man of honor.

He took a deep breath to center himself and caught a whiff of Ciara's scent. Something spicy and vanilla. He couldn't help sniffing her hair to catch the pleasant scent again. When Katsuo realized what he was doing, he straightened and put a little distance between his nose and her head.

She was a curious little woman, helping Ayaka when she couldn't protect herself physically, frightened of him one second, then talking back the next minute. And now she fell asleep, unaware of the world around her. Katsuo wondered what Kawayuki had wanted with her. That person never did anything unnecessary.

He stole another glance at her sleeping face. She had a noble profile and exotic features. Her alluring scent surrounded them, and he shook his head to get rid of this ridiculous attraction he felt toward her. The last time he gave into temptation and even married a woman he had thought to be the love of his life, it turned out she only wanted to marry him for the title and money. And then tried to get rid of him immediately after the wedding.

It didn't end happily, and it still stung whenever he thought back to that fateful night many years ago. His hands instinctively tightened as he remembered why he kept a dagger under his pillow. He wouldn't let himself be caught defenseless again. A whimper in his arms drew his attention, and he realized he was squeezing Ciara's waist. He loosened his hold on her and leaned back a little bit. He hoped to clear his head before they arrived back at Shiro-tatsu castle.

Katsuo was the first to reach the gates, with Takeru and the others close behind. The sudden stop jolted Ciara from her half-asleep state, and she blinked around sleepily. Katsuo got off the horse first then helped Ciara down. She felt a little wobbly on her feet after so many hours of horseback riding. She hissed as she stumbled around on her bare feet. She steadied herself by leaning a hand on the horse's side.

Her head pounded, and she felt a little dizzy. *Is this what jetlag feels like?* she silently wondered, shaking her head to get rid of the fuzziness.

"My lord Katsuo-sama!" a shrill voice penetrated the fog in her brain, and she looked up, barely avoiding wincing at the loudness of it. A beautiful woman hurried toward them with tiny but quick steps. She had an entourage behind her. Ciara's eyes widened seeing that image. At least ten people hurried after her, maids and soldiers alike. They all wore simple clothing, but the woman who had greeted Katsuo had a lavish kimono on. It had orange and golden hues with a maple leaf pattern.

Ciara thought she looked absolutely stunning. Now if only she would stay quiet. Ciara massaged her temples as the other woman arrived. She bowed deeply before Katsuo, who had walked ahead to meet her. He had an annoyed look on his face.

Takeru could easily read his brother's expression. He had completely forgotten about Orihime. The teen let Ayaka down, who immediately ran over to Ciara, asking if she was all right. Satisfied his niece was in good hands, Takeru joined his brother in greeting the guests.

"Orihime-dono." He nodded his head at her. She flicked her gaze toward him but otherwise did not acknowledge his presence. Takeru felt his eye twitch.

"What do you want?" Katsuo was curt with her.

"I heard what happened. My condolences." She bowed

deeply.

"What are you talking about?" Katsuo raised an eyebrow. Had something happened while he was away?

"The little girl—"

"Ayaka is fine," Katsuo cut her off, and Orihime's eyes widened. She looked around, searching for her.

Takeru turned to see Ayaka clinging to an apparently exhausted Ciara.

"Excuse me," Katsuo said with as much politeness as he could muster. "I must attend to my family." That was a clear prod for Orihime, who wanted so much to wed into his family.

"Who is that woman? What a sight, running around barefooted and in rags…" Orihime muttered. "Where did you find her, Milord?" She fluttered her eyelashes at him as she fanned herself with the golden folding fan in her hand.

Katsuo was just about to turn to go to his daughter and the foreigner. He stopped, considering Orihime's words. He looked at Ayaka and Ciara together. The woman who had nothing but offered help to his daughter. She seemed to be doing a little dance on her injured feet as she laughed with Ayaka at something. He could feel his heart hammering in his chest at the sight.

"My lord? Katsuo-sama?" Orihime's voice penetrated the happy image in front of him and he looked at her. Clearly irritated, she continued. "I demand you answer me, Milord! I will not have a strange woman around my betrothed!"

Katsuo thought he heard something pop in his ear, probably a vein as he tried to stop himself from lashing out at Orihime. The audacity of her! She was behaving as if she already owned the place. And if she had it her way, she would be. Katsuo was at the point where he'd explode from the tension.

"As brother said, he is going to attend to our family." Takeru stepped up, putting a hand on each of Katsuo's shoulders. It seemed like a friendly gesture, but both knew it was more like a counter-measure in case Katsuo snapped. Takeru was acutely aware of his brother's subtle transformation that had begun. The golden hue in his eyes, the lengthened fingernails...

If outsiders discovered the family secret, they were in deep trouble. They were more human than anything else, but if all the other daimyōs in the vicinity banded together to attack them because of their true ancestry, their entire household would suffer for it.

Takeru tried to save what he could.

"What are you saying?" Orihime's attention was finally on him.

"Just what I said. That woman over there is to be wed to brother."

Katsuo was strangely silent while Orihime's eyes widened. She looked at Ciara's sorry form again then back to Katsuo.

"Is that true, Milord?"

He didn't reply right away, making Takeru tighten the hold on his brother's shoulders.

Still tense, Katsuo barked out a reply. "Yes. Now let me go," he addressed the latter to Takeru, who immediately released him. Katsuo glared at him but didn't say anything else as he went over to his daughter and Ciara.

Takeru let out the breath he had been holding, and Orihime snapped her fan closed.

"We'll see about that!" she huffed, turning her nose up and marching away with her entourage.

"What have I done?" Takeru sighed to himself, barely audible. Naturally, his brother heard him. There was no other explanation for the second glare.

10

"Sometimes I swear you were dropped on your head when you were little," Katsuo told Takeru after dinner. Ayaka was exhausted, so she went to bed early, but the two brothers stayed at the table and talked.

Takeru poured some sake for Katsuo.

"This won't let you off the hook," he warned as he downed the alcohol.

"I know," Takeru sighed and turned his eyes heavenward. "But what could I do? That seemed like the only solution to get her off your back. And for you not to attack her on the spot."

"It was reckless."

"Half transforming in front of dozen strangers *was* reckless!" Takeru snapped. Katsuo's eyes flashed golden, making Takeru backpedal. "Sorry. But you know it's true."

"We cannot go with this plan."

"Why not?"

"Ciara would never agree," Katsuo replied.

"Oh, because you know her so well?" his little brother asked. "Listen, I can talk to her and—"

"She's a foreigner; she wouldn't understand. Besides, what if she forgets it's all a farce? I most definitely don't want to be tricked to marry again," Katsuo stressed.

Takeru chose his next words carefully.

"It might work *because* she's not Japanese. And not all women are like... *her*," Takeru finished lamely. His brother had forbidden uttering the name of his ex-wife who had tried to kill him on their wedding night.

"Orihime is the same."

"Maybe."

"I know."

"But what do you actually know of Ciara?" Takeru pushed. "We don't really know anything other than she's afraid of snakes and could be killed in an instant on a battlefield. But she does have a good heart. It's proof that she helped Ayaka."

Katsuo seemed to think it over. He sipped his sake quietly. Takeru let him ponder over the options.

After a little while, Katsuo asked, "Are you saying we should give her the benefit of doubt?"

Takeru nodded. "Yes. We'll stay vigilant, but as far as I could see, this foreigner couldn't hurt anyone. We can get Taiki to have someone tailing her if you think we need to."

Katsuo thought back to the woman falling asleep in his arms. Then when she interacted with Ayaka. He felt no ill intention coming from her.

"That won't be necessary. I can keep an eye on her."

Takeru seemed as if he wanted to say something, but very wisely, he changed his mind and stayed quiet. He nodded in agreement then stood up.

"Let me get her."

He hurried out of the room.

"Wait, *now*?" Katsuo yelled after him a little late. He

poured himself another cup of sake. He had a hunch he'd need it.

———————

It was late into the night, and Ciara couldn't sleep. She found a spot on the veranda where she was able to admire the slim crescent of the moon. Her thoughts were in a disarray. As soon as they got to Shirotatsu castle, she felt how exhausted she was. Thankfully, she was quickly led to a guest room where she almost immediately fell asleep.

She vaguely remembered someone trying to wake her up, but she shooed them away and turned her back on them to sleep more. Now that night had fallen and the sliver of the moon was high up in the air, she felt refreshed. Most of the castle had fallen asleep, except for the guards patrolling the castle grounds.

It was a bigger castle than Kawayuki's, and it had a huge courtyard. She could see the top of a pagoda nearby – the other place didn't have one. Musing about her new circumstances, she didn't sense the presence of someone approaching until they stood right behind her and spoke up.

Ciara jumped in fright at the unexpected voice. She turned to the person behind her.

"Takeru... right?"

The teen nodded and stepped next to her.

"And you're called Ciara."

"Yes."

"Come with me," he said. Ciara's eyebrows rose at the order. "Brother wants to see you," he added.

Ciara waited for a moment longer before realizing Takeru wouldn't change his wording. She nodded, resigned.

"Right."

She got to her feet and dusted off her attire. She had found clean clothes in a cupboard in her room and quickly changed after she woke up. There were some bandages prepared, and she used them to wrap her aching feet. They were still painful, but it was way better. Ciara followed Takeru at a slow pace.

It took a few minutes until they reached Katsuo's quarters. He was sitting at the dining table with a bottle of sake and three cups. Takeru gestured for Ciara to enter the room before him. He followed her and slid the door closed.

"Sit," Katsuo said curtly, gesturing to the seat opposite him. Ciara walked over to the pillow and stood there for a moment, thinking which way would be best to sit. Because of the tight style of the clothes she wore, and because the pillow was on the floor, the only possible solution seemed too painful on her injured feet. She looked around for a chair but couldn't find one.

Eventually, she gave up. She didn't want to make her host wait. She grabbed an extra pillow laying around and sat down, mermaid style, hoping it wouldn't strain her feet much. For a moment, neither of them said anything. Katsuo poured sake for everyone. Ciara realized at that moment that she hadn't eaten anything for the last few hours. Drinking on an empty stomach didn't seem like a good idea.

She quickly cleared her throat to cover the sound of her stomach rumbling at the sudden thought. Ciara completely forgot to eat in all the adventures, not that she had any opportunities to do so, and slept through dinner time. Her ears reddened, and she hoped no one had heard her. Katsuo gave a hardly noticeable nod to his little brother, who stood up.

"I'll be back," Takeru said and disappeared through the

sliding door. Ciara looked after him, puzzled. What was so urgent he had to leave in such a hurry at the start of the conversation?

"Is the room to your liking?" Katsuo asked politely. Ciara turned back to him and smiled.

"Yes. Thank you for your hospitality."

Katsuo nodded and put a cup of sake in front of her. Ciara waited patiently for him to bring up the topic of conversation. It didn't take long.

"I've asked you to come here to discuss something affecting your stay here."

Ciara tensed. He sounded way too serious to be talking about helping around the household.

"What is it?" she asked. Her hands trembled, and she discreetly clasped them and laid them in her lap, hiding them in the folds of her clothes.

"I need you to help me out—"

"Sure—" Ciara started nodding as Katsuo continued.

"—with a certain matter. I need you to be my wife."

Ciara stopped mid-nod and felt the blood drain out of her head.

"What?" She choked on her saliva, eliciting a coughing fit from her. She grabbed the cup and drank it in one go. The sake burned her throat for a moment. She cursed.

———

Katsuo's eyes slightly widened at hearing such profane language from a woman. When her coughing subsided, she dragged a trembling hand through her hair.

"You must be joking," Ciara said, her rusty voice laced with disbelief.

"I'm not."

"I'm leaving," she said, trying to get up but failing and

falling back on the sitting pillows. "Damnit!" She punched the pillows in anger then turned her glare at him. She pointed a finger at him. "I'm not having sex with you in exchange for letting me stay here. Forget it!"

She tried to get up again.

"Wait!"

"No!"

"I think you misunderstood," Katsuo said, and she froze.

"What is there to misunderstand?" Ciara yelled.

"It's only a farce. We pretend to be husband and wife."

"You cannot be serious." Ciara looked at him suspiciously, but Katsuo stood her gaze. She narrowed her eyes. "Why?"

"There's this woman—"

"Ah, of course!"

"She is under the illusion that she is to wed me," he continued. "I have no plans whatsoever to marry her."

"Then why not man up and say it?"

Ouch. Katsuo could feel a painful pang in his heart at those words.

"I've repeatedly told her, but she ignores it," he explained. "And Takeru came up with this crazy plan—"

"Why does Takeru want me to sleep with you?!"

The sliding door opened at that precise moment, and they both looked to see Takeru standing there with a platter of food in hand.

"Is this a bad time? Do you want me to come back later?" he asked.

"No, just come here and—" Katsuo started, but his little brother ignored him.

"I'll just leave this here." He put the platter full of food in front of Ciara and hurried out. "You sort this out yourselves!" He shut the door.

"What just—?" Ciara gaped after him. As soon as her nose registered the smell of food, her stomach rumbled. She felt shame flow over her at the whole situation.

"Can I just—"

Ciara held up a hand before Katsuo could finish. He took a breath, reigning his temper in, which was no small feat. She turned to him, her hand trembling, but otherwise, she looked collected.

"Let me just make this one thing clear. I will *not* sleep with you."

"Why not?"

Damn, that wasn't what he wanted to say. She gaped at him, completely at a loss for words. Katsuo used this chance to finally explain the situation.

"I mean, of course, we don't sleep together! We just need to pretend to be married. Then we'll go on our separate ways."

She huffed.

"No."

11

*C*iara was most definitely not the kind of woman who was into flings, and this samurai lord was most definitely too dangerous. So, why did she feel a slight pain in her chest when he said they wouldn't sleep together? That's what she told him she wanted, so why?

"I only ask for one month of your time."

"One month? That's plenty of time!" she protested. She tried to get up again.

"Why won't we make a wager on it?" Katsuo suggested.

"What kind of wager?" Ciara momentarily settled down on her pillows.

"I have this basket…" He stood up easily and went to the nearest cupboard. Ciara eyed his fluid motions in envy. If only her feet weren't injured and she'd worn less restrictive clothes, she'd been out of this place ages ago. When he turned his back, she quickly grabbed a rice ball from the platter and stuffed it into her mouth. Katsuo retrieved the basket from the top of the cupboard, and Ciara realized the rice ball was too dense for her to quickly chew it. She swallowed it as it was, making her choke.

Katsuo was by her side in a second and patted her back, trying to help. Ciara finally got some air into her lungs, and she coughed, hitting her chest a few times. The rice ball finally seemed to be on its way.

"Drink," she croaked, rising her cup. Katsuo poured her more rice wine. She didn't care it was alcohol. She hoped it would burn the rice ball all the way to hell. Ciara downed the cup in one go.

Now she was hiccupping. She closed her eyes, embarrassed. Was there anything else she could do that evening to be more ashamed?

"Here, drink some more."

"I think that's the problem. Don't you have water or something here?"

"Wait a moment," he said, disappearing into an adjacent room. He hurried back with a pitcher and poured water into her cup. She drank it then asked for two more refills.

"Thanks," she sighed when she was done. Trying to think of something other than embarrassing herself further, she quickly came up with a diversion. "You were saying something about a wager?"

"Are you sure you're fine?" Katsuo asked with a strange expression on his face. Was that... concern? Surely not.

"I'm fine, no worries," Ciara said with a smile. "So... what wager? I'm still not sleeping with you."

"You've made that perfectly clear, thank you," Katsuo cleared his throat and went back to his side of the table. He pulled the basket between them. It was full of ping pong balls. At least, that's what they looked like to Ciara.

"What are these?" She picked one up, looking at it curiously.

"Balls of Fate."

"Really?" She snorted at the name.

"Each either has a symbol drawn inside or nothing. If

you draw a blank one, you win. If it has a dragon, I win," Katsuo explained the rules.

"So what do you want if you win?"

"You, for one month, pretending to be my bride."

"Didn't you say 'wife', earlier?"

"It's the same."

No, it's not, she thought.

"Okay… and what do I get if I win?"

"Anything you want," he spread his arms.

Ciara dropped the ball into the basket.

"I want you to help me get back home. Tomorrow."

"We have a deal."

"Aren't we going to shake on it?" Ciara asked.

"What does that mean? Shake on it?"

"You shake hands when you come to an agreement between gentlemen and ladies," Ciara explained and extended her right hand. "It's a tradition in my country."

"All right," Katsuo nodded and put his hand in hers. Ciara noticed how small her own hand seemed in his. His touch was gentle but firm as he shook her hand. When she drew back, she immediately missed his warmth and touch. Her hand tingled, but she decided to ignore it.

"Now, choose," he said, gesturing to the basket between them.

Ciara took a deep breath to center herself then dug into the basket. She rummaged around for a while.

"Have you decided yet?" Katsuo sounded bored, but his eyes were twinkling in amusement.

"Don't rush me," Ciara admonished him. Two more times circling around the basket and she finally drew a ball. She looked at it curiously then up at Katsuo. "How do we find out what's inside?"

"Just twist it sideways, it'll come loose," he said, putting the basket next to him on the floor and leaning on the table. He was so near that his fresh forest scent had reached Ciara's nose. She didn't know what was greater torture: his scent or the scent of food.

She cleared her throat and carefully twisted the ball in her hand. Just as he said, it opened relatively easily.

"What is it? Show me."

Ciara sighed at the image of the dragon in her hand. She showed it to him with a frown.

"You win."

He cracked a smile, and Ciara's heart skipped a beat. He'd never looked so handsome before.

"Wipe that smirk off your face, I'm still not sleeping you."

"Didn't think you would."

Did he actually roll his eyes at her? She shook her head, amused. She reached for the platter, grabbing another rice ball.

"So what's your plan?" she asked after gnawing on a partial rice ball. She was going slow with this one.

"What plan?"

Ciara almost choked on the bite again.

"The plan! You want us to pretend to be married."

"Yes. That's the plan."

"That's the—I can't believe this." She muttered and poured some sake. She sipped it, pondering. "We need to come up with a plan on how to pretend."

"What do you mean?"

"Like... activities for dates? I don't know. Or announcing it? You haven't gone around my back and announced it, have you?" she asked, irritated. She bit into the rice ball as if she was ready to take down a monster.

"I might've let it slip to Orihime, which is what put me —us in this situation," he replied with honesty. Ciara felt a headache forming.

"Who's this Orihime again? Have I met her?"

"She was there when we arrived."

Ciara wracked her brain, then her face brightened as she recalled the beauty.

"Ah, the one in the orange kimono!"

Katsuo nodded after a moment.

"But she's beautiful! Why don't you marry her?" she asked before she could stop herself. *Why would you want to pretend to be with me when you can have a woman like her?*

He looked at her, annoyed.

"I don't. And that's final."

"Okay, I see, it's none of my business," Ciara backpedaled. She gulped down the last bite of the rice ball.

Silence descended on them as they both quietly sipped their sake. It was Ciara who broke the silence.

"It's late, I should go," she said as she tried to stand up again. She made it halfway to the downward dog pose but got stuck. She collapsed back onto the pillows, quietly cursing her clothes. Next, she tried to roll onto her feet and straighten up. She almost made it but lost her balance mid-move.

Shrieking, she fell toward the table, but strong arms embraced her before she could hit the surface. It took a moment for Ciara to realize Katsuo had caught her. She raised her head from his chest and looked up into his eyes.

"Thanks," Ciara said, pushing herself back to her feet. Finally, she found her balance. "I'll get going now."

"See you in the morning," Katsuo said, pouring another drink for himself.

Ciara turned back from the door.

"Good night," she said, before exiting.

He listened to her retreating steps, and they faded quickly. Katsuo sighed and stood up to prepare for bed. He was just pulling off his undershirt when a tentative knock sounded on the doorframe.

"Who is it?"

"Me."

He recognized Ciara's voice easily. He hurried over and slid the door open.

"What is it?"

Ciara's gaze was fixed on his chest, her breath caught in her throat. She blinked rapidly and shook her head. With tremendous effort, she dragged her gaze up to his eyes.

"I'm lost. Can you show me to my room?"

Katsuo was a bit skeptical.

"Please?" she sighed, tired. "Takeru led me here, and I forgot to pay attention. Every corridor here looks the same!"

"Fine, let's go," he said, strolling out of his room half-naked.

Ciara rolled her eyes heavenward as she followed, trying not to burn a hole into his back as he led the way. She quickly caught up to him, but as she got closer, she noticed a long scar on his back. Her hands itched to touch it, but she made a fist and kept her arm at her side. She fell in pace beside him.

12

*K*atsuo led Ciara to her assigned room in silence then bid her goodnight. Before they parted, however, she asked a shocking question. In hindsight, it was to be expected in the situation he found himself in.

"What happened to your wife? Are you divorced?"

His shock must have shown on his face because Ciara gasped. Or maybe *she* was shocked she had asked such a question.

"I'm a widower."

"Oh. I'm sorry."

He nodded. He was sorry, too. He turned to walk away.

"Good night, Katsuo."

He felt a cool breeze sweep along the corridor as he slightly shivered.

"Sleep well," he said and headed for the storerooms.

He needed more alcohol after this and didn't want to bother the servants this late at night. He went to fetch a bottle of sake himself.

He moved from shadow to shadow under the cover of

the night. Katsuo wanted to be alone, and he most certainly wanted to avoid a certain woman or two. He exited the main castle building and crept along the huts scattered along the courtyard. Soon, he had reached the storeroom and grabbed a bottle of alcohol. Just as he was about to leave, a blade blocked his way. Its edge almost touched his neck.

Katsuo growled at the attacker. To be assaulted in his own home! What was Taiki doing? Eyes flashing with anger, he looked at the offender.

"You're coming with me, sake thief," a muffled voice said.

"Taiki. Explain yourself."

The ninja stepped into the light. Surprise reflected in his grey eyes as he drew back his dagger. He pulled down his mask and bowed to Katsuo.

"My lord, may I inquire as to what you're doing here?"

"Helping myself to some sake, as you can see. Now what about the sake thief you mentioned?"

Taiki straightened and explained the situation to him.

"The head maid from the kitchens reported that every now and then, sake goes missing. It's been more frequent lately. That's what I was investigating."

"Very commendable," Katsuo replied, drinking from the bottle. "And what did you discover?"

"You."

"Ah, this is awkward. You found me drinking my sake."

"My lord—"

"You can tell Miyako a certain amount of sake is being transported unfrequently to the pagoda to appease Benten. And we're using more at the moment to pray for her blessings in the upcoming battles."

"As you wish, my lord," Taiki bowed. If he thought his

employer was speaking nonsense, it didn't show on his face.

Katsuo took another sip and pondered over his strange night, from Takeru's crazy idea to keep Orihime at bay to Ciara's reluctance to be part of it. His gaze found the silver sliver of the moon hanging low in the sky.

"Have you found out anything about our new guest?" Katsuo asked Taiki as he handed him the bottle. The ninja accepted the sake but didn't drink.

"You'll be happy to hear I've investigated her."

"Already?" Katsuo nodded approvingly. "I expected nothing less from my head of security. So? What have you found?"

"Nothing."

Katsuo tore his gaze away from the moon and looked at his ninja sharply. A cool breeze swept through the court-yard, reminding him he was half-naked. He crossed his arms to retain what little warmth he had.

"What do you mean? That's so unlike like you."

"I mean there is absolutely no information of her prior to her appearing at Kawayuki's castle."

"Hn. Interesting. And how did she arrive there?"

"I meant *appearing*, as if out of thin air."

Katsuo eyed the sake bottle.

"Have you been drinking?"

"Of course not, my lord! I'm on duty!"

Katsuo looked skeptical but shrugged.

"Well then, find out what happened, if you can."

That was a challenge Taiki couldn't refuse. He bowed deeply.

"As you wish, my lord."

"And please stop with the bowing and the 'my lord' thing. You're my friend. No, you're my family. Stop it."

"Right... sir."

"Eh, better. Good night." Katsuo said as he stood up abruptly and headed back to his room. The night was cold.

"Good night... my lord."

The next morning found Ciara asleep in her futon. It wasn't as comfortable as her bed back home, but once she put half a dozen blankets underneath the sheets, it was almost as good as a mattress.

A knock startled her awake. Ciara stretched and opened her eyes to an unfamiliar ceiling. She shot into a sitting position and looked around wildly.

"Damnit."

Will this nightmare never end? she silently asked, sighing heavily. She closed her eyes, willing reality away. Another knock sounded on her doorframe.

"Milady? I'm here to help you prepare."

That didn't sound good.

"Prepare for what?"

"You are to spend breakfast with Milord and his vassals in the conference room."

Great, an audience to her empty stomach, just what she needed. At least she slept well.

"Come on in." She waved as she stumbled out of her bedding. A servant girl slid the door open and let herself in. She shut the door securely before walking to Ciara and bowing deep.

"My name is Yura, I am here to assist you."

"I'm Ciara."

"Yes, Milady."

Ciara balanced her weight from one foot to another. It was fancy to be called 'Milady', but it made her feel awkward. The pain in her feet reminded her she was still injured.

"Feel free to call me by my name." She saw the girl opening her mouth, probably to protest, but Ciara cut her off before she could begin, "Please."

"As you wish... Ciara-sama."

That was better. Whatever "sama" meant, at least Yura was calling her by name. Ciara smiled at her.

"So what shall we do?"

Yura perked up. She straightened, and that's when Ciara could take a better look at her. She had black hair and brown eyes, a kind face, and seemed to be the same age as Karen. Ciara felt a pang in her heart reminding her how she missed her little cousin.

"I've brought some water to wash your face, then we can do your hair and makeup, and I can help you into a kimono. I've picked a purple one. It'll bring out your eyes, Ciara-sama."

"Wait, wait, too much info, I haven't had my coffee yet," Ciara massaged the bridge of her nose. She held up her other hand and pointed each of her fingers at the ceiling as she counted. "One, thank you, and please show me where the bathroom is. Two, I do my own makeup. Three, how do you know I have purple eyes? Four, I'm sorry if I'm grumpy, but I need my coffee. Please tell me you have coffee here."

"Ko-hi?" Yura asked, hesitant. Ciara sneaked a glance at her.

"You've never heard of coffee."

It wasn't a question, but the girl nodded anyway. Ciara let out a heavy sigh and rolled her eyes heavenward.

"I've never believed in hell, but if there is one, this must be it."

Yura paled at that. Flustered, she bowed repeatedly.

"I'm sorry if I somehow offended Milady. Please forgive me!"

"Oh, no, no, no! Please don't do that!" Ciara immediately bent down to grab the girl's shoulders and help her stand up. "It's not your fault. Don't worry. I'll get by... somehow. What do you use to wake up in the morning?"

"Tea, Milady."

"Ciara."

Yura blinked at her, not understanding.

"I've told you to please call me by my name."

"Ciara-sama. Tea is the best in the morning."

"I see. Is there any chance you can get me some tea before breakfast?"

A bright smile appeared on Yura's face as she nodded, enthusiastic.

"Sure, mil—Ciara-sama!"

"All right, let's do this!"

Tea was better than nothing. She might need a very strong tea to make it through the day, however. She knew cola wouldn't be available, but then, what else had caffeine? How did people get their energy this day and age?

Ciara was helpless on the matter but decided to find it out. After all, she had an entire month to survive here. Without caffeine, it was bound to be hard. She already felt light-headed, just thinking about it.

Yura had someone else prepare the tea while she worked on Ciara's hair and clothes. By the time the tea had arrived, they were almost done. Yura let Ciara sip her tea quietly but couldn't help fidgeting.

"How much time do we have?" Ciara asked, noticing Yura's nervousness.

"Breakfast should start any minute now."

"What? Why didn't you say so?" Ciara jumped up, put the tea back on the tray, and marched to the sliding doors.

"Mi—Ciara-sama!" Yura stumbled after her. "We still need to do your makeup!"

"Oh. What do you use?"

"I have the coal and the fire ready for you," Yura gestured to another tray where something resembling a pencil made of coal and a strange device sat. Ciara paled.

"You're not serious."

Yura cocked her head to the side.

"I don't understand, Ciara-sama."

"I will be fine like this. Thank you for your help," Ciara slid the doors open and stepped out. She turned to the left then the right, not sure which way to go.

"Let me show you the way," Yura offered as she hurried to get in front of Ciara.

"Thanks."

It only took a couple of minutes, but it involved several turns and twists in the corridors to get to the huge meeting room where breakfast was served. Ciara was lost in her thoughts, trying to remember the way, so it came as a sudden surprise when they arrived at the open doors of the meeting room. Yura stepped to the side, and Ciara looked up to see a crowd.

here were two rows of people on both sides of the room, sitting on their knees. She quickly found Katsuo, who sat at the dais at the other end of the room. When he noticed her, he gestured for her to… go away?

Confused, Ciara looked at Yura for confirmation, but she was looking at her toes.

"Do I go in?" Ciara whispered.

"Yes, Milady."

Ciara took a sharp breath. Now was not the time to correct her.

"But he just waved me away!"

Yura looked up, surprised, then glanced at the lord of the castle. Katsuo waved again.

"Milady, he wants you to go to him."

Ciara looked at Yura, but she looked sincere.

"If you say so. I trust you," she said and straightened up before marching across the room.

All eyes turned to her as she arrived in her deep purple kimono. She loved the white streaks across the silk, which turned out to be a pattern for white, Eastern dragons. Nervous, she stumbled, almost unnoticeable, but it was enough to warn her to slow down.

Finally, she made her way to her 'husband', who stood up when she arrived at the dais. All the men followed his example. Suddenly, the huge room felt very small.

"My loyal vassals, it pleases me to introduce you to my beloved." Katsuo reached out and took Ciara's hand to lead her next to him. She smiled at him, covering her nervousness which overtook her as soon as everyone's attention was on her. "This is Ciara. We are to wed in a month."

It took all effort for her not to hiss or yell at him. She couldn't help a sharp glare as she squeezed his hand in warning. Ciara felt her smile turn into a much too sweet and fake one as her thoughts turned to the different ways she could make him pay for that comment. That was most definitely *not* what they'd agreed to.

Katsuo's face was unreadable, making Ciara think he didn't even notice her harsh grip on his hand. She squeezed a little tighter, and he suddenly yanked her close to him. Ciara lost her grip at his unexpected move, making it easy for him to easily retrieve his hand, which he immediately rested on her hip. She was squished to his side.

How lovely. Ciara put a hand to Katsuo's side, trying to push him back, but the man was like solid rock. He didn't even budge. From an outsider's point of view, it looked as if two lovers were smitten with each other. Only Ciara and Katsuo knew what battle they fought behind the scenes.

Not only does he force me to play the role of his fiancée, he changes the terms at the first chance he gets! Ciara used her free hand to pinch Katsuo's back.

He covered his surprised yelp with a cough and immediately let go of her. Ciara smiled at him sweetly as he gestured for everyone to sit down. He didn't look at her until after meal was served.

Half a dozen servants rushed with small tables around the room so everyone would have a tray of freshly cooked food in front of them. Katsuo and Ciara were the first ones to be served.

Katsuo waited until everybody had their own tray in front of them, before shouting, "Itadakimasu!"

Ciara jerked in her seat at the loud voice, but it was lost in the sea of 'itadakimasu' echoing around them and with the movement of grabbing the chopsticks.

She looked at her own tray. A bowl of rice, a cup of pickled vegetables, and a few small grilled fish waited for her on a square plate. Next to them, she found a fork and a knife. She looked around and her suspicion was proved correct when she saw that everybody else had chopsticks. She furrowed her eyebrows and looked around, hoping to catch the eye of a servant, but she didn't have to wait, because at that precise moment, tea was served.

"Excuse me—"

"Yes, Milady?"

"Could you please get me chopsticks?"

The servant girl looked confused. She looked at her lord for confirmation, who looked at Ciara with an expression that said he had found something intriguing.

"Chopsticks, Milady?"

"Yes, chopsticks."

It looked as if the girl wanted to say something, but thought better of it. She bowed and quickly hurried away.

"I thought you would be more comfortable using European cutlery," Katsuo said as he sipped his tea. He was slurping. Everyone was slurping and it was slowly grating on her nerves.

Ciara forced a smile on her face. He couldn't have

known she loved Asian cuisine and frequently used chop-sticks. She had to remind herself that he must be comparing her to European people a few centuries earlier than her time. Still, she was a bit annoyed with him from earlier.

"Thank you for your concern, dear *husband*, but I'm fine with using chopsticks," she replied.

He grinned at her comment.

Maybe it was a bad idea to put sharp objects within her reach because all she could think of at that moment was to grab the knife and—

"Here you go, Milady." The servant kneeled next to her as she handed over the cutlery wrapped in a thin cloth. She reached out with both hands as she gave the bundle to Ciara.

"Arigatō," she said as she accepted the chopsticks with one hand and unwrapped the cutlery. The servant girl bowed and scurried back to her place near the wall.

───

When Katsuo noticed her as she appeared at the entrance, he was caught off guard. She looked completely different from before when she wore servant clothes. The lavish kimono suited her, and he didn't expect her not to wear any makeup. Even with the small, yellowish hues on her face, which had been caused by Kawayuki's rough hands, she looked stunning.

He forgot for a moment that she only agreed to be his bride for a month, nothing more, and did so under pres-sure. He suddenly wanted her all for himself. Later, he realized she had a strong hand. Her grip was crushing, quite unexpected from a woman.

Katsuo's instincts took over as he slipped his wrist out

of her grip and held her against his side. The pinch in his back was the third thing that caught him off guard. One thing was for certain. He never had to guess where he stood with this one. If she was upset, she wouldn't leave him in the dark.

He glanced to the side as Ciara carefully unwrapped her newly delivered porcelain chopsticks. With the movements of an expert, she quickly gripped them and started eating. Katsuo was impressed. He could count on one hand how many Europeans he had come across who could use chopsticks.

For some odd reason, it made him feel proud. He turned back to his own tray of food and continued eating. Breakfast was a peaceful matter as his vassals chatted among themselves. Katsuo took extreme care to finish after everyone else. When he was done, all the dishes were taken away.

"Gochisōsama deshita," everybody murmured at that.

"Hey, I'm still—" Ciara started, but cut herself off when all voices suddenly ceased to murmur. Hesitating, she looked around at the cause of the sudden silence. Katsuo realized he forgot to check her plate. It was rare someone was seated next to him. Ciara still had half a fish on her plate, as she was the last one to start eating.

Silently, he berated himself, but there was nothing to be done. Ciara cleared her throat and put her chopsticks down, quietly enduring the awkward atmosphere that enveloped the room. Katsuo made a note to keep it in mind he had one more person to take into account now.

He sipped his tea, and everyone's cup was refilled after his, but no small talk ensued in the following minutes. Everyone was slurping peacefully, but it was awfully quiet next to him. He risked a glance at the strange woman to see she was drinking the tea in silence. No slurps, no spills.

Was it not to her taste? He raised his eyebrows in question. Maybe it was a Westerner thing.

"My lord, may I?"

One of his generals raised his cup, and Katsuo nodded. The man walked over to them and introduced himself to Ciara. One by one, all his vassals did the same, except one. Katsuo's eyes sought his ninja.

"There's one more person I need to introduce you to," he murmured as the last samurai had left the dais.

"Where is he?" Ciara asked, playing with her teacup. She didn't drink during the introductions. In fact, she was all smiles and pleasant, even to his most grumpy vassals.

"Probably on duty. He's my chief of security and never rests," Katsuo replied, silently wondering the same. Where was Taiki?

"Anyway, thank you for breakfast," Ciara said as she moved to go.

———

"Milord!" A shrill voice cut through the room. Ciara looked up, half-standing in an awkward position because her legs felt like jelly. She had never in her life before sat on her knees for so long. This was going to kill her knees. She needed to find a chair or something, otherwise she would be a cripple in no time.

Ciara straightened up just as Katsuo stood up. She smoothed imaginary wrinkles on her silk kimono.

"Orihime-dono," Katsuo said in greeting. Ciara looked more closely at the woman standing in the doorway. It was indeed the person who greeted them at the gate. Orihime hurried up to them with small steps. Ciara had to bite back a laugh as she saw the other woman wobble. She reminded her of a penguin.

Ciara quickly sobered as she realized she must've been more clumsy than this woman in a dress she wasn't used to.

"To what do I owe the... pleasure of your visit this fine morning?" Katsuo asked politely. There was only a small pause mid-sentence, a most impressive act, considering the circumstances.

"What is the meaning of this?"

"Whatever do you mean, Orihime-dono?" Katsuo asked. He stood next to Ciara at the dais, looking down on Orihime. On one hand, Ciara felt awkward. On the other hand, she agreed to play the part. So, she did.

"Oh my, have you come to congratulate us? How sweet of you!" Ciara widened her eyes innocently and even managed a sincere-looking smile.

"What?" Orihime barked, clearly not expecting this reaction.

"We're honored you're one of the first ones to congratulate us on our upcoming wedding! Aside from these fine gentlemen present in the room." Ciara smiled at Katsuo and grabbed his hand. She jokingly added, "Although I've yet to receive an engagement ring, the matter is as formal as it can be."

"Engagement ring? What is that?" Orihime asked, distracted by the strange words.

Ciara noticed Katsuo looking at her with a puzzled expression.

"Oh! In my home country, when a man asks a woman to be his wife, he gives her a ring. That's called an engagement ring," Ciara explained then shrugged, still holding hands with Katsuo. "Of course, at the wedding, both man and wife give each other rings, but until then... there's the engagement ring! Exciting, isn't it?" She smiled, looking between Orihime and Katsuo.

"Yes, of course," Katsuo replied after a small pause. "I will arrange for a ring for you, I mean, *us*."

"Brilliant, thank you, darling!" Ciara hugged him quickly, then stepped back. "I'm sorry, but we have some matters to attend to. It was lovely to meet you, Orihime."

"Wha—" The woman couldn't get one word in and she looked clearly upset. Ciara grabbed Katsuo's hand again and dragged him through the side door that the servants had used during breakfast to make a quick escape.

She led him through several corridors until finally, he stopped her.

"What was that?"

Ciara felt her hand shaking and quickly let go, but Katsuo grabbed both her hands. He turned her to him and looked into her eyes.

"Answer me."

Ciara glanced to the side, not meeting his eyes.

"I just did what you asked me to, acted as your bride. Hopefully, she'll get out of your hair soon."

"Was it only that?" His tone was sharp, making her look at him. She was momentarily distracted by his penetrating gaze.

"Yes. What else would it have been?" Ciara huffed and tried to retrieve her hands in vain. "Let go of me!"

"Not until you stop trembling."

"I don't have all day to wait here. Let go. Now."

"No."

Ciara breathed out through her nose and closed her eyes. She forced herself to calmly say, "Please. Let go of me."

She waited a heartbeat with her eyes closed, and Katsuo finally let go of her. Ciara sighed and sent him an annoyed look before twirling around and marching off.

*K*atsuo looked after her in stunned silence. He was used to two kinds of women: meek and submissive or loud and demanding. Essentially, all of them wanted to get in his good graces and be lady of Shirotatsu castle.

But this one, Ciara, made him crazy! She did completely unexpected things. She wasn't meek, even when she was unsure of local traditions. She figured out things on the go. And she voiced her opinion confidently but didn't raise her voice unnecessarily, unlike Orihime.

Katsuo suppressed a sigh as he massaged his temples. He couldn't figure out what Ciara wanted. She didn't want to play the part of his fake betrothed. Every woman he'd come across would've jumped at the opportunity, but not her! Maybe it was for the best.

He felt a pang in his chest at the thought and frowned. She made it clear it was all an act whenever she wore that fake smile. Afterward, she either attacked him or retreated but never stayed by his side longer than absolutely necessary.

Breakfast was a small reprieve even though she looked uncomfortable. Was it because of so many new people at one place? Or was it something else? Katsuo looked at his hand, remembering the feeling of hers shaking in his. Was she *scared* of him?

No.

Ciara didn't look scared. On the contrary, she looked annoyed. Katsuo knew from experience from many years spent on the battlefield that people often used anger to cover up their fears. Maybe—

"Lost in your thoughts again, brother?" Takeru appeared out of nowhere and slapped him on the shoulder.

Katsuo blinked at him, surprised. He didn't hear his brother coming up behind. It had been years since he'd been so distracted someone managed to sneak up on him.

"Actually, yes. Did you want something?"

"I haven't had a chance to talk to you this morning because of the training," Takeru explained, "and I'm curious how it went yesterday."

"How what went?"

"You know? Shiara and you?"

"Oh," Katsuo looked around. "Let's go talk in my office."

"Sure."

They arrived soon enough, but they weren't even through the door when Takeru spoke up.

"So what happened? From the whispers of the wind, she agreed, yes?"

"Close the door."

Takeru slid the door closed and sat opposite his brother.

"Tell me what happened!" he repeated for the hundredth time.

Katsuo's fingers drummed on the low table between them. "She agreed."

"Good!"

"Not on her own volition."

"Oh. How that happened?"

"I had to convince her," Katsuo replied, his gaze landing on the basket of balls next to him he still hadn't put away. Takeru followed his line of sight.

"You used *those*?"

"I had no other choice."

"That's so unlike you. Usually, the ladies are all over you, clinging on every word you say," Takeru said, shaking his head in disapproval.

"Not this one. This one drives me crazy." Katsuo said this all matter-of-factly. It was hard to think he had any business with the whole thing.

An excited gleam appeared in Takeru's eyes. "Is she different?"

Katsuo's fingers stopped the drumming, and he looked his baby brother square in the eyes.

"On the surface? Yes. However, all women are the same in the end."

Takeru crossed his arms and leaned back.

"Maybe you've met all the wrong women up till now."

Katsuo snorted.

"You'd better not be so naive on the battlefield, Takeru. Women all want the same, and when I'm gone—"

"Which won't happen for another two hundred years, so no need to—"

"I'm *serious*."

"Me too."

"Takeru"—he immediately shut up, allowing Katsuo to finish his thought—"when I'm gone and you'll be the lord of Shirotatsu, you'll see what I see."

"And what do you see, brother?"

Sadness flashed through Katsuo's eyes, but it was gone in a second.

"Women only want to use your power and influence."

"I respectfully disagree."

"You still have so much to learn, baby brother!"

Ciara wanted to go home. She hated sitting on her knees, she hated the bitter tea, that there was no coffee, she hated she had to play lovebirds with a man so arrogant!

And most of all, she hated the feeling that her hands still tingled where he had touched her. Fuming, she didn't pay attention to where she was going. Even if she did, every corridor looked the same. All she knew was that she was on the ground floor but had no idea how to get back to her room.

She didn't want to ask the servants rushing through the corridors. Already in a bad mood because of the lack of coffee and the fact she didn't have time before breakfast to do her daily yoga exercises, Ciara had a dark expression on her face as she marched through the castle.

Somehow, she found her way outside. She ended up in an unfamiliar spot. On this side of the castle there were no buildings but a sudden drop. This was the part she could see from her window. At the foot of the steep hill, an orchard stretched, split in two by a brook. A bright red bridge connected the two sides.

Ciara found several boots and getas in a neat row near the back door. Her eyes widened, looking at the wooden sandals. How could anyone walk in those, much less conquer this hillside in them? She picked a pair of boots that looked the closest to her size. They ended up being a bit too large for her, though. She waddled along the narrow path leading down to the orchard, winding through the steep hillside. One hand gripped the railing tight, and the other picked up the hem of her kimono.

She wondered if there was a way to obtain some clothes which let her move more freely. The kimonos were wonderful, but they constricted her movements way too much, and she feared getting them dirty or accidentally ruining them. Slowly and carefully, she made her way to the bottom of the castle hill.

Shielding her eyes, she looked up. She had to crane her neck back to see the top of the highest tower from this vantage point. Ciara breathed in deeply, enjoying the scents of fallen leaves and some wildflowers which bloomed in fall. The air was so pure here. She turned to the orchard and walked across the field.

The colored leaves crunched under her feet, but otherwise, silence surrounded her. She breathed in the fresh air, free of pollution, and stopped among the trees, closing her eyes for a moment.

Such silence.

Ciara took another deep breath and felt a smile forming on her face as she turned toward the sun with closed eyes. Suddenly, in her mind, she was transported back to her childhood, to her grandmother's countryside house where she spent entire summers. Mother joined her occasionally on these holidays, when work permitted. It was such a joyous time. Ciara could almost smell Grandmother's chocolate rolls baking in the oven. Her little cousin, Karen used to help her out while Ciara spent time with Grandfather out in the field, gathering wildflowers.

Mother usually appeared on Friday evenings to spend the weekend with them. Karen only spent two weeks of summer vacation there, but Ciara was there the entire time. Later, her grandparents even invested in a synthesizer, which sufficed while she was away from home, from her piano. She missed those days.

Smelling rain in the air, she opened her eyes and realized grey clouds were gathering in the sky, and she was standing in the middle of an abandoned orchard. Shaking her head, she cleared her thoughts, willing the memories away. She sighed and continued her way to the red bridge that caught her attention from above.

It was just as one would imagine, an arched bridge, made of wood and painted red with black color added at the base. Ciara walked to the center and looked down at the babbling brook, leaning her elbows on the railing. Rust-colored leaves scattered the water's surface and floated downstream. She could spend hours watching it.

It was easy to lose track of time.

"Identify yourself!" someone yelled, and she jumped in surprise. A man in black uniform was fast approaching from the side of the castle. Ciara looked around, but there was no one else in the vicinity.

"Are you talking to me?" Ciara knew it was a question with an obvious answer, but she couldn't get over the fact she was accosted in this island of serenity.

"Who else would I talk to? You're the only one here. Identify yourself," the man said. He reached the bridge and stepped onto the red wooden planks. Ciara would say he was handsome if he didn't have a sullen expression on his face. He had a hood on, but she could see his piercing gaze from beneath. His hand was on the hilt of a sword resting at his hip.

"I'm Ciara Coleman. You are…?"

The man narrowed his grey eyes as he looked at her from head to toe then settled his gaze on her face.

"What are you doing here?"

Ciara felt her irritation rise. She crossed her arms. Just

who was he to interrogate her? She shared her thoughts with him.

"I'm the head of security here."

"Are you Taiki?" Ciara asked, her posture relaxing a tiny bit. A sliver of surprise flashed through the man's face, but it was gone before Ciara could be sure she had seen it.

"I am."

"I see... Katsuo was looking for you during breakfast," Ciara said, letting her arms drop down to her sides, and she leaned against the railing.

Taiki tilted his head to the side.

"He was?"

His voice was skeptical.

"I said so, didn't I?" Two could play this game.

"Then maybe we should see him," he said, briskly walking up to her and grabbing her arm firmly.

"Hey! What are you doing?"

"You shouldn't be here."

---

aiki set a quick pace back to the top of the hill. He only stopped for a moment until they got their footwear off then marched on, Ciara jogging behind.

"Hey! Slow down! It isn't easy moving around in this kimono!" she told him, irritated. Taiki slowed his pace a notch. Ciara huffed, but stopped protesting. Her arm hurt a little as he dragged her behind him.

Finally, they reached Katsuo's office. Ciara recognized the door from the day before. Taiki knocked on the doorframe.

"Milord."

There was no reply even though they could hear someone shuffling paper inside. Ciara listened curiously. What was happening?

"My lord?"

Still, no answer. Ciara could hear someone move around.

"Katsuo-sama!" the man said loudly.

"Oh, is that you, Taiki?"

Ciara heard Katsuo's voice through the thin rice paper that made up the door.

"Yes, my lord. I heard you were looking for me. And I caught a trespasser."

"Interesting. Come on in."

Taiki slid the doors open and hauled Ciara in front of him as they both entered the room. Ciara caught Katsuo's eye. He looked at her, then back at Taiki.

"What is the meaning of this?"

"I found her in the orchard."

"*And?*"

That was the end of Taiki's patience, it seemed.

"What do you mean, my lord? She was caught sniffing around the—"

"I wasn't sniffing around!" Ciara cut him off, surprising him into silence. Katsuo was just starting to get used to her unexpected behavior and got over it sooner than his ninja. "I was just taking a walk. Is that a crime?"

Katsuo massaged the bridge of his nose as he let out a sigh. Both Ciara and Taiki looked at him.

"This is why I wanted to formally introduce you to each other." Katsuo looked up at them. "Taiki, meet Ciara, my betrothed. Ciara, meet my head of security, Taiki."

"Your *what*, Milord? Isn't she the one you found in a battlefield close to Kawayuki's place?"

"That is a very accurate observation, Taiki," Katsuo replied. "And you heard that right. She is my bride."

Taiki gaped, which was a rare sigh. Amusement glinted in Katsuo's eyes. The ninja was almost impossible to catch off guard.

"I'm going back to my room," Ciara said abruptly and marched out of the room. Taiki reached out for her arm, but she moved away, and the ninja froze mid-movement.

They heard her angry steps retreating. Taiki turned to his lord.

"Katsuo-sama?"

"Do your thing, I have work to do," he waved the ninja away.

"Yes, Milord."

Katsuo gave a growl at that, and Taiki hastily exited the room, almost bumping into the returning Ciara.

She sidestepped him and poked her head through Katsuo's ajar door.

"I'm sorry to disturb you, but could you please tell me how to get to my room?" Ciara wore a sheepish smile. "It's very confusing here."

"Taiki!" Katsuo said, shuffling the paperwork on his desk.

"Let me show you the way, Milady."

Ciara glared at him.

"Milady now, am I?" she huffed, but followed him.

The rest of the day went relatively normal. Ciara found some baggy pants and a coat inside the small closet in her room and quickly changed. It was amazing to be able to move freely again! She practiced yoga until lunch, which was served in her room.

She ate alone, entertaining herself by gazing out of the window. In the distance, she could see snow-peaked mountains. It was an amazing sight, but eating alone reminded her of her life before Karen had moved in with her. Sadness lingered around her for the afternoon even though Yura happily chatted away while she showed her around the castle courtyard.

There were plenty of huts for storing food and

weapons, another for making pickles, a different one for sake, and so on. The barracks surrounded them, and small gardens could be found between the buildings. There was a huge guest house in the back where Orihime stayed. Finally, Yura pointed out the pagoda.

"How many stories does it have?" Ciara asked, curiously. "Can we go closer?"

"Well, it has only three stories, and it's been here since before my grandmother's time," Yura explained. "We can go closer, but the immediate area is off-limits."

"Really? Why?"

"It's a sacred place for my lord's family."

"I see…" Ciara pondered over what that meant. "Do you live in the castle, Yura?"

"Only for five days. Then I go home, I live in the castle town."

"Oh, when are your days off?"

"The day after tomorrow."

"One day?" Ciara asked, concerned. "You get only one day off after working five days?"

"That is plenty, my lady."

"Ciara."

"Ciara-sama. I'm lucky my lord is so generous with his servants," Yura elaborated. "I have a friend from another village. She used to come here with her family to the market every moon, but I haven't seen her in three seasons because the lord she serves now gives her one day off every moon."

"Really?" Ciara was taken aback. That was inhumane!

Yura nodded. "It can't be helped. I'm honored to serve Kitayama-sama's family."

They arrived at the pagoda, and Ciara looked up at the graceful building. The arched rooftops gave it an airy feel. Small bells hung from the corners, and the building itself was made of stone and wood. At the top of the pagoda rested a finial. It looked like a lightning rod to Ciara's eyes.

"This is the closest we can get. There are guards on the path to the pagoda," Yura explained, motioning to a soldier walking up and down nearby.

"But there is a path. So some people do use it," Ciara said, turning to her with a puzzled expression.

"Only with permission from Milord."

"Is it a shrine?"

"It's a buddhist building, my la—Ciara-sama," Yura quickly corrected herself. "But I heard it was built to pay respect for Benten."

"Benten? Who is that?"

"She's a goddess, the guardian of Milord's family line."

He even has a goddess looking out of him, Ciara snorted. Unbelievable. His family had their own goddess, and he still had women-problems. It seemed even divine protection couldn't save you from everything.

Yura and Ciara spent the rest of the afternoon talking and discovering the castle area. By the time dinner came, Ciara was able to make her way back to her room from the main entrance without getting lost. She counted it as an accomplishment. She wasn't completely hopeless when it came to directions.

Ciara was invited to spend dinner with Katsuo. Yura insisted she wear another nice kimono, but Ciara had had enough of the lavish clothes for the day. She preferred the comfortable outfit she'd found for dinner. It was her understanding it would be just the two of them, so it took her by surprise when she slid the door open and Ayaka barreled toward her.

"Whoa, careful!" Ciara gently admonished as the little girl bumped into her and hugged her middle.

"Are you eating with us?" she asked, smiling up at her.

"Yes," Ciara replied. "But you know, I can't get inside if you hug my legs."

"Oh, sorry." Ayaka let go of her and stepped back. Her grin didn't fade, however. "How is your foot?"

"Better, thanks for asking," Ciara replied as she entered the room. She noticed Katsuo sitting at the low table. "Hello."

"Good evening," he replied.

Ayaka grabbed Ciara's hand and led her to the table, next to Katsuo.

"Is this my seat?" she asked.

"Yes, you sit next to Daddy. Takeru will sit next to me."

"I see," Ciara sat down, cross-legged. When she looked up, she noticed both Ayaka and Katsuo looking at her with a funny expression.

"What is it?"

"Can I sit like that, Daddy?" Ayaka turned to Katsuo.

"No."

Ciara immediately realized her error. She rearranged her legs so she was sitting mermaid-style. She wouldn't bare sitting another minute on her knees like at breakfast. It was cruel!

"What did you do today, Ayaka?" Ciara asked the little girl about her day, trying to ignore Katsuo's presence next to her. She felt awkward after her earlier mistake. She stole a glance in his direction and caught him looking at her. Ciara quickly turned back to Ayaka, listening to her recall the study hours then what she played.

In the middle of it, Takeru appeared.

"Sorry for being late," he said as he stepped in.

"It's all right," Katsuo said calmly. He was silent during the entire time Ayaka was talking. "Let's eat."

he meal was still warm when they lifted the lids from the plates. Unlike at breakfast, where everyone had their own little table, this time they shared one large, low table. The lids hid several plates filled with different kinds of fishes, meats, and there were bowls filled with rice or pickles. One of them had some kind of dumplings.

Ciara felt like an intruder. It was clear for her that Katsuo, Takeru, and Ayaka were a team as the little girl chatted away and the adults moved in sync to put appropriate portions of food on Ayaka's plate. But they looked happy, and Ciara leant back, just looking at them. A small smile grew on her lips at the sight, remembering the times when she and her mother had dinner together.

Katsuo surprised her when he turned to her. "May I?" He gestured to Ciara's plate. She swore her heart skipped a beat.

"Yes, thank you."

Ciara watched as Katsuo selected food for her. It felt odd to be taken care of by a man. For so long, it was only her and her mother. Then her and her little cousin, Karen. Naturally, she had had her share of boyfriends, even some polite ones, but she never truly felt looked after.

Get a grip, it's just food, she silently admonished herself as Katsuo placed the plate in front of her.

"Thanks."

"You're welcome." And he meant it.

She waited with Ayaka until Katsuo and Takeru had picked their meals and then, with a loud 'itadakimasu' from the little girl, they all began eating.

"What's this?" Ayaka asked, looking at a deep-fried shrimp. Its tail was sticking out from the end of the crust.

Ciara was happy to recognize the dish.

"That's tempura. Try it, it's very tasty!"

Katsuo and Takeru looked at her oddly. She noticed their stares, meanwhile Ayaka summoned her courage to try the food.

"What is it?" Ciara asked, blinking at the men.

"How did you know what it was?" Takeru asked.

"I've... tried it before?" Ciara wasn't sure what was the reason for their strange behavior. "Why?"

"It's a new dish from Nagasaki," Takeru explained, glancing at his brother for a moment. "It's the first time it's served here."

"I see."

"Where are you from?" Katsuo asked. "Did you come here through Nagasaki?"

Should I lie and tell them yes? Then at least they wouldn't suspect me why I know new goods in this area. Or shall I tell them the truth? At least part of it? Ciara mulled it over as she chewed on some sticky rice.

"I'm from the US."

"US?" Takeru asked.

"United States of America," she replied.

"Where is it?"

Shoot, has America been discovered yet? I don't even know the century we're in!

"East."

"There's nothing East," Katsuo finally spoke up. "We're the most Eastern country."

"It's so East it's West," she replied and stuffed some meat in her mouth. Her concentration on the conversation stopped as she realized she'd just tried the infamous sashimi. Raw meat. Granted, she'd eaten sushi with raw meat, but this was only meat. Nothing else. As she silently wondered if she'd survive dinner, the men cast her confused glances.

"I don't understand," Takeru finally said. "What do you mean?"

Somehow, Ciara forced the raw fish down her throat. It wasn't half bad.

"If you go to the East far enough, you'll end up in the West," she explained. Ayaka was starting to chew on the tail of the shrimp and Ciara reached out to her. "No, don't eat that part."

The little girl obediently put the tail down and went for another tempura. This time, she picked a vegetable one.

"Do you like it?" Ciara asked.

"Yes, very tasty, like you said!" Ayaka smiled at her.

"Try this," Katsuo put a bowl full of green pods in front of her. Ciara was surprised at his sudden gesture.

"What's this? Beans?" She asked as she picked up one with her chopsticks. Takeru chuckled, which made Ciara look around, puzzled.

"Here," Katsuo picked up a pod with his hands and opened it. "It's steamed soybeans. Edamame."

Ciara reached for the pod between her chopsticks and followed Katsuo's lead, opening it. Tentatively, she put a bean in her mouth, not sure what to expect. There wasn't a rich flavor but a faint salty one. It was quite refreshing after all the meat and rice. Suddenly, she wanted fruit. She idly wondered if it was possible to get some after dinner. Ciara skimmed the table, but unfortunately, no fruits were to be found. She quickly finished off her first edamame pod then reached for the second one.

"Good, isn't it?"

"It's refreshing," Ciara replied as she sent Katsuo a small smile. "Thanks for the recommendation."

The rest of the dinner was spent in a similar fashion, with good-natured conversations. Ciara forgot her earlier worries about not fitting in with the small family and truly enjoyed dinner. It was a more informal event than breakfast had been.

After they'd finished, Ayaka insisted on some reading. Basically, this meant someone had to read a bedtime story for her. She thrust a book into Ciara's hand and pleaded with her eyes.

"I want you to read me a story!"

"Oh, well…" Ciara opened the book. Her brow furrowed as the writing there didn't make any sense for her. It was foreign and reminded her of her peculiar situation. How was it she could understand spoken language but was totally lost when it came to the writing?

"I'm sorry. I can't read this."

"Do you not like it?" Ayaka's lips trembled.

"It's not that. I literally *can't*. I don't understand any of these letters," Ciara brought the book closer to her eyes and squinted. "Are these even letters?"

"You can't read?" Ayaka's eyes were big.

"I can, just not this," Ciara insisted. "I don't know this writing."

"Then you should come to the reading lessons with me!"

"Ayaka," Katsuo cut in. "That is quite enough. I'll read it to you."

"I want Takeru to read."

Ciara swore she heard Katsuo sigh. Ayaka crawled into Takeru's lap with the book, and he started reading out loud. Ciara moved around a little bit to find a more comfortable position sitting on the floor. She fidgeted so much, she lost her balance and bumped into Katsuo who was sitting next to her.

"Sorry," Ciara apologized with a red face. She crawled back to her seat and arranged her legs around until she was settled.

"It's all right," Katsuo replied with a little delay. He didn't seem bothered by Ciara's clumsiness.

Takeru stopped reading the story soon because Ayaka's head was bobbing as she tried really hard not to fall asleep. There was a small protest from her when he declared she was going to sleep, but she let him gather her in his arms and take her to her room. She was too exhausted to protest.

"She's such a sweet child," Ciara mentioned once Takeru had left with Ayaka.

Katsuo nodded in agreement. They looked at each other, and the moment stretched out. Ciara started fidgeting and cleared her throat as she looked sideways. Her gaze caught the door.

"Well, I better go, too. Thanks for dinner," she said as she stood.

"You're welcome," Katsuo replied, also rising. "Do you need help getting back to your room?"

Ciara sighed and hung her head, embarrassed.

"Most probably."

Katsuo escorted her back to her room. They stopped in front of her door, and she turned to him.

"Thank you."

"No problem," he replied. "Sleep well."

"You too."

Ciara stepped into her room, and Katsuo went back the way he came. Their rooms weren't far away, just on the other end of the corridor, but there were two intersections to similar looking corridors, which confused Ciara. She gathered her bathing essentials and ventured out again. She hoped to catch Yura and ask her directions for the bath.

17

*F*inally back to some semblance of order, Katsuo woke up at dawn, went to the pagoda to exercise, then finished the kata just as the sun rose over the Eastern horizon. The soldiers were just warming up in the courtyard by the time he had finished. Takeru bowed when he saw him, and Katsuo nodded in return, not stopping this time.

He was looking forward to some breakfast. Alone. As usual.

But the Universe would not have it. Soon, he noticed pounding footsteps coming for him. He slightly turned to see a random soldier out of the corner of his eye. He was young, and Katsuo didn't recognize him by name but knew he was one of the new recruits. Panic reflected in his eyes as he approached his lord.

"What is it?" Katsuo growled. He might've woken up early each day, but that didn't mean he wanted human interaction before breakfast.

"Th-there's someone at the gates, my lord!"

"And?"

"She insisted on being admitted and wants to meet with you immediately!"

"Did she say why?"

"No, Milord."

"Did she say who she was?"

"Actually, no. But she had *this*." The young soldier lifted a small, wooden square in his hand. A crimson tuft dangled from it. Katsuo grabbed the item with such speed that the soldier couldn't catch his movements. "If I'm not mistaken, this means—"

"Where is she?"

"Still standing at the gates. She said she won't move until you come get her... Milord."

Katsuo nodded and started toward the gates immediately. The soldier had to jog to keep up with him. He couldn't read his lord's expression. They arrived at the gates soon, where the aforementioned woman was taking her time looking around. Katsuo's soldiers eyed her suspiciously.

"You really should find another hobby instead of scaring them."

The woman twirled around, and her silver hair seemed to float with the movement. Her eyes were golden, and she had a brilliant smile on her young face as soon as she saw Katsuo. She held a naginata that was at least two heads taller than her.

"My, you've become"—she paused for a second, searching for the appropriate word—"grumpier."

"Meanwhile, you did not change a bit, Gr—"

"Yuki. You call me Yuki, and thank you. I'll take that as a compliment." Her brilliant smile never faded. She walked up to Katsuo and hooked her arm in his as she started walking to the castle.

The soldiers looked at them incredulously.

"I see you have some new recruits."

"It's wartime. I need the manpower."

"Right, you have that." She nodded, her thoughts seemingly far away.

"I know you usually don't pay attention to these matters, but this has been going on for a few decades now." Katsuo sighed, steering them toward the main entrance. As they went further in, they had come across older recruits who had bowed to them.

"Lady Yuki!" one greeted her with enthusiasm. She just smiled back at him and waved. Katsuo suppressed a smile, watching her interact with the soldiers.

"I suspect he still has a crush over you."

"Bah, don't be silly!" Yuki swatted his arm in annoyance. "It's been two decades. He has most certainly gotten over it."

Katsuo shook his head but didn't comment further on the matter. Fortunately, no one heard their exchange.

"How long are you planning on staying?"

Yuki looked at him sharply.

"I've only just arrived to see my cute grandsons, and you already want me gone?"

"It's not that. It's just… there's a lot that's happened these past few days and—"

A scream tore through the early morning calmness. Katsuo sighed.

"Where did it come from? What happened?" Yuki tensed, hefting her weapon in one hand, ready for combat.

"It came from somewhere inside."

"Maybe the inner courtyard?" Yuki suggested.

They hurried to the castle and through the corridors to arrive at the inner courtyard. A few guards loitered then dispersed as they saw no threat and had seen their lord had arrived at the scene.

Orihime was screaming at one of his servants, Yura. There was a huge upturned basket near them, its contents spilled. Katsuo narrowed his eyes as he realized it was the laundry, including some of Ciara's clothes.

He moved to step in, but before he could say anything, Ciara appeared from a random direction. Next to him, Yuki was watching the scene unfold with mild amusement. They could hear every word.

"What happened?" Ciara asked as she stood between the two women.

"She bumped into me!" Orihime pointed her finger at the cowering Yura. The servant girl was hunched in a exceedingly low bow.

"I'm very sorry, Milady. I didn't mean to—"

"I don't tolerate such clumsiness in my household!"

"How fortunate this is *not* your household," Ciara quipped. Orihime was stunned into silence, her face reddening. Katsuo heard a snort coming from next to him. Glancing at Yuki, he saw she was trying hard not to laugh.

"Get up. Let's gather the clothes." Ciara bent down to help Yura, who immediately jumped up. She knocked her head into Ciara's.

"Ow, ow, *ow*! Careful, Yura!" Ciara admonished the servant girl.

"I'm so sorry, Milady!" Yura went back into a dogeza.

"Serves you right!" Orihime huffed and turned her nose up at the prostrating servant. "But be careful, you might catch her clumsiness!" With that, she twirled around and stalked off.

Katsuo swore he could see Ciara roll her eyes before she turned to Yura. He took a step, but Yuki's arm shot out, creating a barrier before his chest.

"Wait," she whispered.

"Yura, what did I tell you?" Ciara put her hands on her hips.

Yura startled and hunched her shoulders. She mumbled something. Ciara squatted down as much as her kimono let her. She touched Yura's arm, and this time, she was prepared when the girl quickly straightened and avoided being hit by her.

Yura looked as if she was ready to cry.

"I told you to call me Ciara, not 'Milady' or any other variants," Ciara reminded her. She looked around at the scattered clothes. "Now, let's clean this up."

"Oh, no, no, I can't possibly let Milady do this!" Yura protested, but Ciara was already gathering up the items.

"It's no problem. Also, I'd be more willing to listen if you used my name," Ciara reminded her as she bent down to retrieve an obi.

"Let me get those!" Yura quickly grabbed the basket and held it out to Ciara.

"Thanks." She smiled as she dumped the clothing from her arms. She quickly collected the remaining items. "Do you need help?"

"I cannot possibly ask you to—"

"You're not asking me. I'm offering. There's a difference," Ciara said and grabbed one end of the basket amidst Yura's protests. "It's quicker this way. Maybe we can mow down someone else on the way. Though I doubt there's anyone that deserves it more than that—" Ciara coughed "—person."

"B-but—"

"Where are we bringing this?"

Yura gave in and gave her the directions. Together, they walked off with their heavy load. Yuki let her arm drop and turned to Katsuo. Her eyes had a playful glint.

"Who is she? I like her."

Katsuo felt a little mischievous. "That's good, because she's my betrothed."

"Your *what?*" Yuki shrieked. Yura and Ciara were still nearby, and they heard it. They stopped, looking at them. Ciara waved at them while Yura paled. The servant girl started talking very quickly, and, grabbing the entire basket from Ciara, she ran off.

"Yura!" Ciara lost her balance but managed to catch herself last minute. She grumbled at the kimono and pulled up the hem, running after Yura. "Stop!" she cried out, and Yura immediately obeyed.

A strange tingle ran down Katsuo's spine at that moment. From the corner of his eye, he saw Yuki shiver.

"Are you cold?"

"No, it was nothing." She shook her head. Her gaze followed the pair of Ciara and Yura who started walking again.

"Have you had breakfast yet?" Katsuo asked as he steered Yuki in the direction of her rooms.

"I was hoping to spend it with you."

Katsuo nodded. "I'll get Takeru to join us."

"What a lovely idea!" Yuki beamed. "I'd love to catch up with you boys!"

18

"*W*hat got into you, Yura?" Ciara hissed as they hauled their heavy load to a seemingly random empty room. She caught up with Yura in the kitchen, which was on the ground floor, after she had run off again. The room was a flurry of activity, everyone going their own way, but no one collided. It was as if it was a choreographed dance.

"Lady Yuki is here!" Yura shouted as she slid the door open.

Immediately, everything went silent, and everyone froze.

"Lady Yuki? Are you sure, girl?" A middle-aged woman asked from the center of the room.

"I saw her with my own eyes! She's with Katsuo-sama!"

"Already? Why didn't the guards tell us sooner? Everyone, three meals to Katsuo-sama's room. *Now*," she instructed, and the room came into life again.

If Ciara previously thought it was a flurry of activity, that was nothing compared to what ensued after the head chef made her orders known.

"Who is Lady Yuki?" Ciara asked.

"The woman we saw with Katsuo-sama," Yura replied as she turned to her.

"Yes, but that doesn't explain—"

"Hurry up, girl. Either help us or get out of the way, but don't hold us up!" The woman in charge said as she reached them. Then she took another look at Ciara and her brows furrowed. "Who are you?"

Yura paled even more if that was possible.

"This is Ciara-sama, betrothed to Katsuo-sama."

The head chef paled, too, and bowed deeply.

"I'm very sorry, my lady!"

"No worries," Ciara said. "Don't waste your time apologizing. Aren't you in a hurry?"

"R-right." She looked around for a moment, trying to gather her thoughts, then ran off toward the stove, shouting, "Get that off the fire, now! No, don't put it there!"

Ciara saw it better to silently withdraw and be on her way. She would be underfoot if she stayed there. Her new mission was to discover who this Lady Yuki was. She seemed close to Katsuo, as she was hugging his arm and smiling at him. They seemed to be close in age, too, although her silver her tricked her for a moment, but once she got a clearer look at her face...

Ciara shook her head. What ridiculous thoughts! She'd be better off doing her own things rather than worrying about some random woman. It's not like she was truly engaged to Katsuo or had feelings for him. Who would have feelings for such a dangerous and arrogant person? She still hadn't gotten over how easily his sword cut people down on the battlefield. She shivered just remembering it.

Ciara wanted to talk to Yura a bit more, but now that she was preoccupied with the sudden guest, she wasn't sure what to do. Eventually, she decided she'd like to go see the town. She wandered around the castle courtyard until she made it to the gates. But when she reached them, guards had stepped in front of her.

She took a step back, confused.

"Are you saying I'm not allowed outside? Why?" she asked in vain. The soldiers didn't reply. She tried to side-step them, but the one closest to her positioned the spear in his hand so it would act as a barrier. Ciara crossed her arms.

"I'm not a prisoner. Why can't I go outside?" Her anger stirred as they refused to answer. "Are you deaf?"

For a moment, no one moved. Then Ciara huffed and turned around to stalk back to the other end of the court-yard. She was still fuming when she noticed the roof of the pagoda nestled among the nearby buildings. Her curiosity piqued again, she headed towards it. In a few minutes, she finally stood at the beginning of a path paved with big, flat stones leading to the pagoda. There was a guard patrolling nearby, just as Yura said there would be, but Ciara walked on with determined steps.

Her confidence lasted only a moment.

"Halt!" the guard shouted, and she stopped. She could hear his quick footsteps. Ciara looked down at her kimono. If only she wore the pants she had on the day before, then she could have had a chance at outrunning him. No way this attire would get her far.

"The pagoda is off-limits," the guard told her as soon as he arrived.

"Great." Sarcasm was dripping from Ciara's voice. "I can't get to town; I can't even get to a goddamn pagoda! I'd hate to hear how your prisoners feel if this is how you treat guests. Or the lord's bride."

She was either getting to see the pagoda or town, or she was going crazy.

"I'm sorry, Milady, but rules are rules," he said. He actually did sound sorry.

"Whose rules are they?"

"Milord Kitayama-sama's."

"And do you happen to know why it is I can't visit town?"

"You need an escort, Milady."

"I'm a grown woman, I don't need one," she protested.

"That is not for me to decide," the guard said. Seeing her eyes glinting in a dangerous light, he quickly took a step back.

Ciara turned her back to him and strode away with heavy steps. Hopefully, she could make it to the orchard today. That is, if she was allowed to go there. Staying here felt suffocating. Sure, she agreed to be Katsuo's fake bride for a month, but she did not agree to be his prisoner!

A frustrated cry escaped her lips, and someone chuckled nearby. Ciara froze. *Shit. I know that voice.* She turned to the source of the chuckle. It was Orihime. *She's the last person I want to see me like this,* Ciara thought. She didn't know when she started thinking of the other woman as the enemy, but her instincts screamed in warning whenever she was in the vicinity.

"It is a relief to see you, too, get ruffled sometimes, *my lady*," Orihime said with a fake smile. Ciara returned the gesture and felt a grimace forming on her face.

"You're still here? What a surprise. I thought you'd gone back to your household where everything goes according to your wishes," Ciara couldn't help making that comment.

Orihime's smile was like poison. She reminded Ciara of a snake as she sashayed closer. For some reason, she didn't have an entourage shadowing her every move this day.

"Don't be so confident in your ability to keep Katsuodono," she said icily as she leaned closer to Ciara. She grabbed Ciara's arm in a tight grip.

"Hey!"

"Sooner than you think"—Orihime shook Ciara's arm to silence her protests—"you will be begging me to let you serve me as lady of this castle. You won't last a week, you outsider."

"Excuse you!" Ciara yanked her arm out of Orihime's vice-like grip. It tingled where she had held it, but Ciara refused to show more weakness before her. "*Outsider?* Out of the two of us, you're the one who's less welcome here." Even though she said it, Ciara herself wasn't sure what to think. But she'd die sooner than let Orihime see her insecurities.

"Hmph, you Westerners are so barbaric. You wouldn't comprehend the fine nuances of Japanese lifestyle," Orihime mocked in a shrill voice. She opened her fan in one smooth movement and hid the lower half of her face. She glared at Ciara over the rim. "Shoo, shoo! Go back to your country!"

"You have no idea—" Ciara stopped herself before she said too much. Her voice quivered with rage as she made a fist with her hands.

"No idea about what? Finish what you started," Orihime prodded as she cocked her head to the side curiously. "I'm listening."

"You have no idea where you stand with Katsuo, isn't that right? At least I'm aware of my own situation," Ciara shot back. She nodded at Orihime before storming off. When she rounded a corner and was sure the woman could no longer see her, she massaged her abused arm and muttered a curse.

Orihime might have seemed like a fragile flower, but she had poisonous thorns. And for some reason, she somehow always managed to get under Ciara's skin with her arrogance and remarks. They had only met a handful of times and Ciara was already fed up with her behavior.

"Ugh!"

Ciara decided she had had enough for today. She made her way back to her room and collapsed in a heap on the floor pillows. She didn't want to fume more on Orihime or about the feeling she was trapped here, not free to come and go as she pleased. She quickly changed and then settled down on the pillow. Focusing on her breathing, she shoved away her thoughts. It was harder than usual, but eventually, she managed to meditate without interruptions.

19

"*Y*uki!" Takeru's face brightened as soon as he saw the unexpected guest. He hugged her tightly. "It's been so long!"

"And you've grown into a fine young man."

"Are you staying for long?"

"You know me," Yuki smiled. "I can't stay in one place for long."

"Let's discuss this over breakfast," Katsuo said from the background. He was already sitting at the spread table. "I'm hungry."

"Oh, I'd better not make you wait!" Yuki said as she sat down at the narrow end of the low table. Takeru occupied his usual seat opposite his brother.

Finally, they began eating.

"Tell me about her," Yuki suddenly said. Katsuo coughed as a bite went down the wrong way. Takeru looked back and forth between them.

"Who? Orihime? Ayaka? Or Ciara?"

"I see you've been busy, young man."

"It's not like that," Katsuo sighed. He loved Yuki, but her teasing always got the better of him.

"Well then, clear it up for me!" Yuki asked.

"First of all, Ayaka is my daughter."

"Not from *that* person, I presume?" Yuki asked, tense.

"Of course not! I adopted her a few years ago. She's ten."

"She's adorable!" Takeru added with a grin. Yuki's eyes glinted with excitement.

"I'd like to meet her."

"You will," Katsuo reassured her.

"Good. And tell me how you found her. But first, I want to know about your bride."

"You told her?" Takeru asked.

"She knows Ciara is my betrothed, yes," Katsuo said, sending a meaningful look to Takeru.

"What was that?" There was hardly anything that escaped Yuki's sharp eyes. "I know that look meant something. Tell me!"

Katsuo glared at Takeru who narrowed his eyes, not backing down.

"Boys!" Both men gave a start at the admonishing voice of Yuki. "What is going on? We have enough secrets as it is."

Finally, Katsuo gave in. He sighed.

"You sigh an awful lot since I've arrived."

"So you noticed. It's not you, it's this entire situation here."

Katsuo told Yuki about Orihime's sudden appearance and demands and then how they found Ciara on a battlefield and how she helped finding the kidnapped Ayaka. Then Takeru's masterplan to fool Orihime and everyone else along with her, which led to Ciara being fake-engaged to Katsuo.

"But you do like her, don't you?"

Katsuo opened his mouth to protest. Yuki held up a finger to stop him.

"I've seen the way you look at her. Don't try to deny it."

"How do I look at her?" Katsuo seemed taken aback at the discovery.

"You look at her fondly. I've only seen this expression once in your face, before your wedding," Yuki replied. Katsuo tensed at the reminder of his ex-wife. "That is to say, this Ciara is different. I don't have bad feelings about her. On second thought…"

Yuki fell silent, trying to work out what her instincts were telling her. She shook her head.

"Nevermind."

"What is it?" Katsuo asked. "I need to know how much she can be trusted."

"I'm not your hound, boy," Yuki replied. "Danger encompasses her, but not the kind that did that other woman. It's hard to explain."

"Yuki, where have you been travelling?" Takeru asked with sparkly eyes. He had forced himself to be calm so far but couldn't contain his excitement any longer.

"Oh, here and there. I've been back and forth on the Silk Road!"

"The Silk Road?" Takeru's eyes widened. "But no one uses the Silk Road nowadays!"

"Oh, is that so?" Yuki feigned surprise. "I must be a nobody, then."

"Th-that's not what I meant, Granny!"

"I've told you not to call me that!"

"Yuki"—Katsuo put a hand on the woman's arm—"you must be tired from your journey. Would you like to have a nap?"

"Not you, too, Katsuo," Yuki sighed. "Stop treating me like an old lady!"

"We didn't mean to—" Takeru and Katsuo both started at the same time, but Yuki held up her hands.

"Indeed, I must be old if I get offended over such small matters," she said. "Let's forget it. I have some presents for you!"

"Oh?" Takeru's eyes shined with excitement. "From the Silk Road?"

"Yes, from that road nobody uses nowadays," Yuki grumbled as she rummaged in her furoshiki bag. She brought out a bundle and gave it to Takeru. He accepted with both hands. "This is for you."

"It's so light," he said, surprised as he unrolled it. It was an overcoat made of a strange material. "What's this made of? Look, brother, what an odd fabric!"

Katsuo touched the corner of the cloth presented to him. He looked surprised, too.

"It's soft and light but feels thick."

"It's called wool. Brilliant in winter weather!" Yuki said. "I have acquired one for myself as well."

"Thank you!" Takeru said, immediately putting it around his shoulders. Yuki smiled at him before turning to Katsuo.

"As for you…" She brought out another item. Recognition flared in Katsuo's eyes.

"A pistol."

"Exactly. Have you seen one before?"

Katsuo shook his head.

"I've heard about them and seen the drawings," he admitted. "But how did you manage to sneak it here?"

Yuki winked.

"Take it. I heard it's useful for winning battles."

Katsuo took the pistol with both hands as he admired the craftsmanship.

"There are plenty of these in Europe. Here, it comes with a cleaning kit. I'll show you later how to load it," Yuki explained.

"Thank you!" Katsuo said.

"Have you used one of these, Yuki?" Takeru asked, eyeing the strange weapon.

"I have, once or twice."

"Do you have one, too?"

"I don't need one, boy," Yuki laughed. Her fangs became prominent at that moment. She flexed her claws for good measure. "But I wanted to see what it can do. It causes more damage than an arrow in the hand of an expert."

"No wonder Nobunaga makes use of them." Katsuo mumbled.

"Now when can I see my great-granddaughter?" Yuki asked, changing the subject.

"She has classes in the morning, but..." Takeru looked at his brother for confirmation. "We can have lunch together, if you aren't too busy, Katsuo?"

"I have tons of paperwork, but you three go ahead," Katsuo sighed and got up. "Which reminds me, I need to get back to work. See you all at dinner."

He squeezed Yuki's shoulder fondly and exited the room.

They both looked after him.

"When do you think he realizes this is his office?" Yuki asked in the following silence.

Takeru had the nerve to laugh at that.

Katsuo made his way to his personal armory. It was

located inside the castle, unlike the one for his troops. Only he, Takeru, and Taiki had a key to it. Carefully, he placed Yuki's gift on a small table inside the room. He stroked the weapon, marveling at the detailed carvings that broke the smooth surface of the pistol. He wondered if he'd ever use it.

Using a sword was in his veins. Using an arrow came just as naturally to him. But a *gun*? It was such a foreign idea! Nonetheless, he cherished it because it came from Yuki.

After he made sure it was secure, he strolled out of the armory. He locked up the door and headed back to his study. As he crossed the inner courtyard, he remembered the scene from earlier when Ciara rushed to the aid of his servant. He noted he'd never seen Orihime look so angry and nasty. His gut feeling was right when he decided not to trust her. Or women in general.

For a second, he entertained the idea what if the betrothal were *real*? Would Ciara do everything in her power to stay in his good graces and seize power through him? Would she use him? Try to manipulate him? He shook his head. It was futile to think of it since this arrangement was only for a month, no longer. And it was only a fake engagement, nothing more, nothing less.

A knock sounded at the door, making Ciara stir. She opened her eyes and blinked the sleep away. She was lying on the tatami floor, with her lower body on the floor pillow. Ciara moaned as she sat up.

Damn, I fell asleep. She rubbed her eyes.

"Yes?" she asked when there was another knock.

"Ciara-sama, dinner will be served in an hour," Yura said from the other side of the door. "Do you need help getting prepared?"

Ciara stretched, but lying down in an awkward position put a strain on her back muscles. Oh, what she'd do for a hot bath right about now! She sighed, longing for modern conveniences. Then she froze as she remembered Japan had plenty of hot springs and bath houses built in her time. Maybe... just maybe...

"Yura, is there a hot spring nearby?"

She waited with belated breath.

"An onsen? We have one at the bathhouse."

"Yes!" Ciara jumped up, excited, and pulled a muscle in her leg, making her curse.

"Is everything all right, Ciara-sama?" Yura sounded worried. She had a surprised expression on her face when Ciara swung open the door with a grin on her face.

"Let me get my stuff and then you can show me the way to the bathhouse!"

"As you wish, Ciara-sama."

They walked back to the closet in her room, and Yura helped her pick out a yukata and some other essentials before they made their way to the bathhouse. Ciara concentrated hard on mapping out their route from her room. She wanted to be able to visit the bath whenever she wished. She couldn't drag Yura here to show her the way every time she wanted to use the bathhouse.

It was on a lower floor, in the back of the castle. Ciara realized it was on the same side as her room and over-looked the orchard below.

"You will find the towels over there. Please undress here, then you can clean yourself in the next room," Yura explained the rules for her. "After that, you can proceed to the pool. It is very important you enter the pool only after you have cleaned yourself."

Ciara looked at her with a puzzled expression on her face. Why was she stressing this point so much?

"You will find soap and a bucket for water in the next room. Would you like me to assist you?"

"Oh, no, thanks. I can manage it myself!" Ciara even took a step back to make her point. "Thanks for showing me the way.

"You are most welcome," she replied. "And please, don't bring the towels into the pool."

"Of course." Ciara looked after Yura as she exited. What was that strange behavior? She shrugged, placing her clean yukata on a nearby shelf. She grabbed a towel then went behind a folding screen to undress. Wrapping the towel

around herself, she realized it only covered the most inti-
mate parts of her and she had to hold it together at all
times. It was much smaller than what she was used to at
home.

Home.

Ciara sighed and fought the sudden tears. Would
anyone search for her? Maybe Karen. Gods, she hoped
Karen was all right. Would her students miss her? Would
they be angry with her when she'd get back a month later?
If she got back. She sniffled and wiped her eyes. No use in
pondering over things she couldn't change. She took a
deep breath and stepped out from behind the folding
screen.

Putting her used clothes on another shelf, she made
her way to the next room, hugging the towel tightly
around herself. She was in the same room as the pool, but
small stools lined one wall, buckets of water next to
them. She made her way over to the closest of them. A
bar of soap caught her gaze in a container attached to the
wall.

She looked around but couldn't see anyone. Steam
arose from the pool, making it hard to see, but she didn't
hear any movements, either, so she quickly folded the
towel and put it on a free stool. She hastily cleaned her
body as best she could with her limited options. When she
felt clean enough, she grabbed the towel and made her way
to the pool.

She dipped a toe in it. It was extremely hot, and Ciara
debated for a second if she'd be all right entering it. A cool
breeze swept through the room and she shivered. Was she
outside? She quickly made her way inside the pool, leaving
her towel on a stone near the edge of water.

The pool was shallow, so she had to squat to immerse
herself in the water. She waddled her way around, circling

the edge. Halfway through, she happened upon another person. She shrieked at the unexpected meeting.

"Good gods, girl, my ears!"

"Sorry," Ciara apologized quietly. "You surprised me."

"I can hear that."

The steam slowly dispersed, and a familiar face emerged.

"Lady Yuki!" Ciara said, immediately recognizing the woman from the morning. Her silver hair gave her away, and only now did Ciara realize the woman had gold eyes. She looked to be in her early thirties, only a few years older than Ciara.

"Oh, you've heard about me?"

"Not really, only your name," she admitted. "My name is Ciara. Nice to meet you."

Lady Yuki surprised her by offering a hand. Ciara readily shook her hand and smiled at her.

"Call me Yuki."

"I hope you don't mind me asking, but what brings you here, Yuki?"

"I'm visiting family."

In truth, she wanted to know her relation to Katsuo. She remembered how Yuki had hooked her arm into his.

"In this castle?"

"Why all the questions?" Yuki asked. Her voice cut through the thick steam surrounding them.

Ciara shrugged and turned to the side. "Just curious. I didn't mean to pry."

"No need to fret, darling," Yuki said, fixing her bun on top of her head. "I'm just teasing you."

Ciara didn't know whether to be amused or annoyed.

"So?" she pressed.

"Katsuo is a busy man, isn't he?"

"I suppose so?" Ciara had completely lost the thread of

the conversation. She had no idea what this woman was thinking and where was she going with the discussion.

"Do you think you can—" Unexpectedly, she fell quiet, and Ciara felt the water move as Yuki suddenly appeared right in front of her. Ciara jumped back, splashing water around.

"Don't move. Let me see your eyes."

"My eyes?"

"I've never seen such eyes for a mortal," Yuki mumbled as she came closer. Ciara raised an eyebrow in slight offence. What was next? Was she going to insult her, too?

"Don't take this the wrong way, darling," Yuki said, smiling at her. She drew back, finally giving Ciara some much needed breathing room. "I like your eyes. They remind me of the sky at sunrise."

"Thank you. I guess," Ciara said, still uncomfortable with the situation. "You have an unusual eye color, too."

A mysterious smile played on Yuki's lips as she hummed but didn't offer an explanation other than, "It's in my blood."

"So it's the same as me," Ciara replied, settling down on the seat at the edge of the pool. It was carved out from the stone wall of the pool.

She could feel her muscles relax, and she sighed in contentment. This was an excellent idea. She'd definitely have to come every night. Now if only she could remember the way back to her room, that'd be fantastic. She let out a sigh of frustration.

"Why are young people sighing so much?" Yuki grumbled from next to her. Ciara blinked at her. "What's troubling you, darling?"

"Well, I was thinking how relaxing this is and I could come every day, but then I remembered I constantly get lost in this castle! It's like a maze!" Ciara cried dramatically.

Yuki's tinkling laughter made her face redden.

"Sorry," Yuki apologized, wiping a lone tear from her left eye. "I was the same when I first came here. My advice for you is to look up."

"Look up?" Ciara echoed, tilting her head to the side. "What do you mean?"

"Look up when you walk the corridors. You'll see what I mean." She didn't elaborate more.

They spent some time chatting before Ciara felt the hot water was too much for her. She was beginning to feel light-headed and decided to head back to her room. She was extra careful not to slip on the floor with her wet feet. She made her way to the changing room to dress herself. Then she gathered up her dirty clothes to bring them back to her room.

On her way back, she looked up at the ceiling as Yuki suggested.

"That's smart!" she exclaimed, surprised to see markings in different colors. Now she only needed to decode what they meant. Maybe next time, she could ask Yuki.

"Ciara-sama!" Until they met again, she could always count on Yura to rescue her from wandering the corridors aimlessly.

*C*iara was surprised to see another low table set for dinner as she arrived in Katsuo's room. The decor was also different from before, and she soon realized that this was a different room. She wondered if this was Katsuo's own room.

"Come, sit." Katsuo stood up and gestured to the seat next to him. He looked relaxed, wearing a simple black yukata. His light sharp, light brown eyes followed Ciara's movements as she walked over.

"Thanks," she said. "Am I the first one to arrive?"

"It seems so," he replied, just when they heard voices coming from the corridor. "Ah, that must be Takeru and Ayaka."

"How come we're not in the usual room?" Ciara asked as she arranged the pillows around.

"We wouldn't fit there."

Ciara cocked her head to the side in question. She clearly remembered that the day before, they had indeed fit in there. A squeal brought her attention to the door just in time to see Ayaka get tossed into the air.

"Please don't do that," Katsuo asked as Yuki caught the little girl.

"But she likes it!"

Katsuo used his strict stare on her, but naturally, it had no effect. Yuki turned to the little girl.

"Your dad is as grumpy as ever."

Ayaka chuckled and hugged Yuki's neck. Katsuo mumbled something unintelligible as they all sat down around the table. There was a blanket hanging from the bottom of the table and Katsuo tucked his feet beneath it. He noticed Ciara looking at him and lifted the edge of the blanket for her.

"The weather's getting chilly. This kotatsu will keep you warm," he explained. Ciara was happy to sit cross-legged and hide her feet under the table. It was much more comfortable. She sent a small smile as thanks his way before turning back to the others.

They were staring at them, except for Ayaka who was peeking under the lids of the bowls.

"What?"

"Nothing," Takeru coughed and looked away. Yuki had a half-smile on her face as she glanced at Katsuo.

"Let me introduce you two," Katsuo said. "Yuki, this is Ciara, my betrothed. Ciara, this is Lady Yuki, a relative."

Ciara smiled and bowed a little to Yuki, who chuckled.

"What is it?" Takeru looked back and forth between the two. "Have you two already met?"

"Indeed," Yuki said. "Let's eat."

Dinner went by in a good mood, with Ayaka, Takeru, and Yuki chatting. Katsuo was content to just listen to them, and Ciara didn't have anything to add, so she stayed silent. At the end of the meal, Ayaka proposed singing.

"We haven't done that for days!" she added when Katsuo opened his mouth to possibly protest.

"You are right." He gave in. "Let me get the biwa."

"Daddy plays the biwa beautifully!" Ayaka told Ciara proudly.

"Do you play any instruments, Ciara?" Yuki asked.

"I used to, yes."

"Not anymore?"

"I…" Ciara was looking for words. She didn't want to go into details about the accident. It was still hard to talk about it, plus, they had no idea she was from another time. She suppressed a heavy sigh. "I had a hand injury. It's near impossible for me to play again."

"Oh, I'm sorry to hear that," Yuki said with concern in her voice. "May I ask what instrument you've played?"

"A piano," a small smile lingered on Ciara's face as she replied.

"What kind of instrument it is?" Ayaka asked. "It has a foreign name. Is it from the West?"

"That's right. It has a keyboard, which makes small hammers strike wire strings. You can play lots of sounds, with a lot of varieties," Ciara explained. Her right hand rested on the table surface, and it automatically started playing a simple tune when she spoke about her love for the piano. "I have played for many years and had concerts."

"Oh, I want to hear!" Ayaka said.

A bitter smile appeared on Ciara's face.

"Perhaps one day you'll have someone play the piano for you."

"Is it a new instrument?" Yuki asked. "I've never heard of it."

"As I said, it's from the West."

"Yuki's just got back from there," Takeru added and Ciara tensed. "She's just been back from the other end of the Silk Road."

"Oh. Well, yes, it's relatively new."

Ciara racked her brain to remember when the first piano was constructed. It was around the... eighteenth century. Not for the first time, Ciara wondered about the time period. She didn't know much about Japanese history and had no idea where to place herself.

"Interesting," Yuki said. "Next time I go, I must see it myself."

"Do you play any instruments?" Ciara quickly changed the topic.

"I do, although I'm better at singing."

"Shiara said she teaches singing," Ayaka supplied helpfully.

"Really?"

"Yes, I'm a voice trainer and singing teacher."

"Can you teach me? Daddy says I need training."

"Katsuo!" Yuki gasped.

"She needs guidance," Katsuo said, sitting down with the biwa in his hand. "Ayaka, you have a beautiful voice, but you need to learn how to use it."

"See?" the little girl turned to Yuki in all seriousness. Ciara chuckled, good-natured.

"Sure, I can help you if you'd like," she told Ayaka. Out of the corner of her eye, she saw Katsuo looking at her with an expression on his face she'd never seen before.

"What is it?"

He shook his head and strummed the chords on the biwa. Ayaka clapped her hands, excited. He played a bittersweet melody. Soon, Takeru and Yuki joined in, singing the lyrics. It was so beautiful and sorrowful, Ciara felt as if Katsuo was playing on her heartstrings instead of the biwa.

It took a moment for everyone to collect themselves after the last sound died in the room.

"Now a happy one!" Ayaka requested.

Katsuo sent her a smile and started a fast-paced song,

which Ayaka knew and started singing almost immediately. The others joined in, and even Ciara accompanied them with clapping her hands to the rhythm.

A few more songs were played before Ayaka's yawns became so big that she couldn't sing anymore. Her eyes were drooping, and Takeru, as the ever dutiful uncle, gathered her up in his arms and left to put her to bed.

"This was fun! Oh, how I missed these nights!" Yuki said with a bright smile. "When the whole family just sings after dinner. We should do this at the pagoda."

"We're nearing winter, I don't want Ayaka to fall ill," Katsuo said.

"Oh, she won't!" Yuki insisted. "I'm sure the nights still carry warmth. Or maybe we can gather there in the afternoon?"

"Takeru and I have work, Yuki."

"Surely you have some spare time for family?" she asked, her eyebrows arched.

Katsuo groaned.

Ciara suddenly felt as if she witnessed something she wasn't supposed to. She faked a yawn and politely said her goodbyes. On her way back to her room, she pondered over what she'd learned.

So Yuki *was* a relative to Katsuo, but she couldn't exactly put her finger on their relationship. Were they cousins? Aunt and nephew? Although her silver hair at first confused Ciara, she'd gotten used to it. Sometimes Yuki did or said something only old people did, but the next moment, she was like a woman in her thirties.

Ciara shook her head and looked up to the top of the wall where she saw the small green flower painted. Her room was on a corridor with red flowers. How would she find that? She vaguely remembered she was on the same floor, but with all those turns... Ciara picked a random direction and searched for the corridor with the red flowers. She figured that sooner or later, she had to come across them.

"What are you doing?"

Ciara startled as she heard a somewhat familiar voice. She twirled around and saw the man who had dragged her out of the orchard. Taiki, chief of security. She narrowed her eyes and tensed at the sight of him.

"Nothing."

"I highly doubt that."

Ciara didn't reply to that statement. The man sighed and pulled down the mask covering half his face. He took a step toward her.

"Look, I know we didn't get off on the right foot, but it's my job to ensure the security of the Kitayama family," he said.

"Was that an apology?" Ciara asked, confused.

"Not at all."

"Not at all..." she mumbled, repeating him. "Taiki, right?"

"Yes, Milady."

"Maybe you can answer me this. Am I a prisoner here?"

"Of course not, Milady." He looked taken aback. "Why would you think so?"

"Because everything is off-limits!" Ciara blurted out. "I want to see the town! I want to walk around, looking at stuff, and I just can't get outside! Why is that, if I'm not a prisoner?"

"A lady of your station would need an escort."

"So would it be all right if I took someone with me?" she asked, desperate to understand.

"I believe so."

"Anyone?"

"Yes?"

Ciara thought for a moment. Maybe she could get Yura to come with her to town tomorrow. That is, if she didn't have much work to do.

"Is there anything else I could do for you?"

"Now that you mention…" Ciara cleared her throat and hoped the darkness hid her flaming face. "Can you show me the way back to my room?"

"As you wish." He bowed and led the way.

22

*T*he next morning found Ciara doing yoga stretches before the sun rose. She was excited to start the day and determined to finally visit the castle town. By the time Yura had knocked on her door, she was ready to leave.

"Come on in," Ciara said, tying her overcoat. She wore pants today.

"Good morning, Ciara-sama."

"Good morning, Yura. What are your plans today?"

She seemed surprised at the question.

"What do you mean, Milady?"

"I mean, do you need to do some chores, or are you free?"

"Do you need my help with something, Ciara-sama?" Yura asked, curious.

"Would you mind accompanying me? I would like to visit the castle town and was hoping you would come along."

Yura's eyes widened.

"Wearing *this*?"

Ciara looked down at her attire.

"What is the problem?"

"That is not proper."

"I don't really care."

"Milady, you can't go see the townspeople like that!" Yura protested. "Let's change you into a nice kimono and then we can go."

"So you *will* accompany me? I'm so happy!" Ciara quickly hugged the young woman who looked startled with all the attention. She put some distance between them as soon as Ciara let go of her.

"I think the purple-orange kimono would suit you this day."

"But it's difficult to move around with the kimono on!" Ciara said, while Yura rummaged through her closet.

"Here!" The servant girl pulled out a deep purple kimono with orange hues. It looked like the sky at dusk. Ciara's breath hitched.

"This is beautiful!" As if in a trance, she walked closer and tentatively touched the material of the kimono. It was made of silk. "And so soft!"

Yura grinned proudly.

"They made this in the castle town."

"Really?"

"We can visit the shop. But you need to change, Milady. You are, after all, Milord's bride."

I am, after all, his bride, Ciara silently repeated in her mind, as she subjected herself to Yura's assistance.

They were done relatively quickly, and Yura promised to meet her at the gates before she ran off gods-know-where. Ciara made her way to the courtyard and put on a pair of sandals, which reminded her of flip-flops, but more elegant, when she reached the edge of the veranda that ran along the perimeter of the main castle building.

Ciara was used to moving with speed, thus she was frustrated at the slow pace the traditional Japanese clothing allowed her to walk at. Nonetheless, she endured. If that was what she had to do in order to get to town, then she'd have patience.

Just when she reached the gates, Yura appeared. She wore a straw hat and held another one in her hand. Its shape reminded Ciara of a wok pan. She accepted the hat.

"Is this for me?"

"Yes, Milady."

"Ciara, please."

"I'm sorry, Ciara-sama," Yura quickly corrected. "A dark cloud is headed for this area, so it might rain. This will come in handy."

"I see. Thanks."

"You are most welcome," Yura smiled at her. She turned toward the gates. "Shall we?"

"Show me the way," Ciara was way past ready to get out of the castle walls. She and Yura walked toward the guards stationed there, and Ciara half-expected them to cross their spears or block her way like they did the day before, but neither of them moved. The women effortlessly walked through the gates. Ciara let out a sigh she didn't realize she was holding.

"What would you wish to see, Ciara-sama?"

"I trust your expertise, Yura. Show me the must-sees."

"Must-sees?"

"The places one needs to visit when they come to town. Surely, there're some shops or shrines everybody visits when they come here!"

Yura's face brightened.

"Of course! I know where to start!" Yura's walk adopted

a skip as she made her way down the hill to the castle town. Ciara followed her, curious.

Unfortunately, by the time they had reached the edge of town, rain had started to fall. Ciara put her hat on and caught up to Yura.

"You were right about the weather. I don't know what I'd do without you, Yura!"

The girl smiled, looking ahead.

"There is a teahouse nearby. We can stop there and wait until the rain lets up," she suggested. "What do you say, Ciara-sama?"

"I think it's a great idea. Let's go!"

It took a few minutes until they reached the teahouse. The inside was full, but they had a terrace in the back with a roof covering half of it. They picked a table there. Just as they sat down, the rain started to pour even heavier than before.

"Phew, we've just missed the worse of it!" Ciara's eyes widened as she listened to the harsh pitter-patter of the raindrops on the roof. A cool breeze swept through the terrace.

"Welcome to the Golden Dragon teahouse. What can I get for you?" A small waitress appeared next to Ciara.

"What do you recommend on such a rainy day?" Ciara asked the woman. The waitress had bland features, was small in stature, her clothes and hands were impeccably clean, and she had a smile for everyone.

"Some oolong tea to warm up and soothe your spirit."

"Oh, you have oolong?" Yura asked in surprise.

"Yes, we've just received shipment the other day," the

waitress explained. "Thanks to the Lord's hard work, the shipments have come regularly for the last few weeks."

"That's great news!" Yura smiled. "Ciara-sama, what do you think? Oolong is good for health."

"Okay, let's try it! I've heard of it, but never tasted it," Ciara agreed.

The waitress nodded and turned to Yura.

"Would you like the oolong, too, or your usual?"

"I'd like oolong."

The waitress bowed to them.

"I'll be back with your orders soon. Meanwhile, please enjoy this." She put a bowl of biscuits on the table for them.

"Thank you," Ciara said, reaching for the bites.

They sat in silence for a few moments, just enjoying listening to the rain drumming on the roof above their heads. Ciara breathed in deeply, the smell of rain making her smile. She felt at peace.

"Here are your teas. The waitress appeared soon, with a platter in her hand. She placed a cup and a tea kettle in front of each of them.

"May I have some honey, please?" Ciara asked.

Yura and the waitress looked at her funnily.

"I'm sorry, Milady, we don't have honey here."

Now it was Ciara's turn to look surprised.

"How come?"

"Production is low here, Milady. I am sorry!" The waitress bowed low to apologize, making Ciara uncomfortable.

"Please don't do that! It's all right!"

"Thank you, Milady!" The waitress bowed again and walked off. Ciara sat back with a puzzled expression on her face.

"Do you have much honey from where you come from, Ciara-sama?" Yura tentatively asked as she poured some tea for the two of them.

"I've never thought about it this way, but I guess we do."

"Please take these as my apology!" The waitress had returned and put a big bowl of sweet rice cakes in front of Ciara.

"Oh, that's unnecessary!"

"You try these. Eat one before drinking the tea," suggested the waitress. "Sorry for the inconvenience!" She bowed again and scurried off to attend to other customers.

She was like a hurricane, leaving Ciara blinking blindly after her. *What just happened?*

"Mhmmm, these are really good!" Yura picked a small mochi then slurped her tea. Ciara felt a headache coming on. Everyone slurped around her, and it was rubbing off on her. She took a sip from the tea and immediately felt better.

Ah, how she missed this feeling! It was like drinking the first sip of coffee in the morning! Suddenly, all was well in the world! The rain didn't bother her. The loud slurping didn't bother her. The forming headache was of the past. Ciara sighed, content.

I wonder if it has caffeine, she silently mused as she reached for a biscuit before her next sip of tea.

They chatted until the rain let up and the oolong tea had been finished. All the sweets had disappeared as well. It was time to go. Ciara turned to her side where she usually had her purse then froze when she realized she didn't have it with her. Even worse, she remembered she'd never even had a purse ever since she'd arrived here. Which meant she had no credit cards. No debit cards. No money. Although it was highly doubtful she would be able to use any of them here.

She swallowed a cry of frustration and fought the rising panic. She turned to Yura with wide eyes, sure that she was as pale as snow at that moment.

"What's the matter, Ciara-sama?"

She leant closer to the servant girl.

"I forgot to bring money," Ciara whispered.

"Oh, don't worry about it!" Yura said, reaching inside the folds of her clothes. "Milord gave us some coins to spend while in town."

"What?" Ciara furrowed her eyebrows. "When did that happen?"

"I saw Katsuo-sama just before we left. He said to take this," Yura withdrew her hand and a small pouch rested in her palm. "Here."

"Oh, I don't know your currency. It's better to leave it to you," Ciara said, feeling uncomfortable with the whole situation.

"Sure! I'll be back in a moment, Ciara-sama," Yura said with a smile and went to pay for their beverages.

Ciara sat back, looking up at the grey sky. The clouds still lingered, but at least the rain had stopped. Her emotions, however, were in a turmoil. She'd been on a few dates where she was treated to a meal, but she'd never been in such a situation where she got some spending money from someone. Not since high school.

As an adult, she'd never had to ask someone else to pay for something she wanted. She prided herself as an independent person and that she'd never had to rely on a man to buy something for herself. She felt... indebted to Katsuo, and she didn't like the feeling. What if he had ulterior motives?

Ciara frowned as she realized she didn't have a choice. She was stranded in a foreign land, in a time period she was unfamiliar with. She had to rely on Katsuo's goodwill to survive. But how would she repay him? Would he expect her to?

"All done, Ciara-sama!" Yura appeared just when

Ciara's thoughts turned darker. She glanced up at the girl, pushing the bad feeling away.

"Let's go then. I'm sure you have some other things to show me!"

"For sure! There's a market today. You'll love it!" Yura said, leading Ciara out to the main street.

23

"*W*here is Katsuo?"

The young guard was unprepared for the bluntness his lord was referred to, but he immediately recognized the person asking the question because of her silver hair and amber eyes. He didn't know who Lady Yuki was, but even the oldest retainers of his lord spoke of her with reverence.

He understood she was someone he'd better not question. There were rumors. The guard pointed to the pagoda in his daze.

"He's over there, Milady," he added, gulping.

"Good boy." Lady Yuki nodded at him and headed toward the pagoda.

He looked after her, stunned. Even though they'd only exchanged a few words, there was a sense of dread clawing its way along his spine while in her presence. As soon as she was out of sight, his body relaxed involuntarily. He couldn't put his finger on why he felt threatened in her presence. It was basic instinct.

Yuki took her time walking through the courtyard. Not

much had changed since she'd last visited. A few, smaller buildings were erected, others had been renovated, and a new, bigger kitchen was built. She took a mental note to check it out later.

She reached the path leading to the pagoda the same time a woman with her entourage arrived there. Yuki stopped, waiting for them to greet her and step aside so she could continue on her way.

No such thing happened. The woman was vaguely familiar, but Yuki didn't remember when she'd seen her.

"Out of the way," the stranger said.

Yuki lifted an elegant eyebrow at her rudeness.

The woman looked to the side and opened her golden fan to speak to the maid slightly behind her. She didn't bother to keep her voice low.

"It is unbelievable how rude the servants are! One bumps into you, the other refuses to make way for their superiors."

Suddenly, Yuki realized where she had seen the woman. It was immediately after arriving at Shirotatsu castle. She was scolding a servant in the inner court.

"Once I'm lady of this household, these will be the first ones to go! Hmph!"

"I do believe you are mistaken, on many accounts," Yuki replied calmly.

The woman glared at her. She snapped her fan closed and took a step toward Yuki. They were almost toe-to-toe. The pagoda's guard headed toward them.

"About?"

"Your role in this household and mine," Yuki replied without batting an eye.

"Just who do you think you are, daring to talk to me like that!" The woman lifted her fan in a threatening manner.

Yuki narrowed her eyes, which flashed in anger.

"You aim to be Katsuo's bride, or so I've heard. Is that correct?"

"Don't meddle in others' business! And how dare you use his name without an honorific? The punishment I'll give you—"

Yuki couldn't help it. A roar of laughter left her lips.

"Oh, dear." She wiped a tear from the corner of her eye. "You're a thousand years too early for that, brat. And you're dismissed."

With that, Yuki turned away and started down on the path to the pagoda. The guard passed her in a hurry.

"You—!" She heard a shout from behind then a clank. Yuki glanced back for a moment to see the guard holding the scabbard of his katana up, stopping the woman's fan. Her gaze locked with the other woman's, and she sent her a smirk before turning back toward the pagoda.

She immediately frowned. Why in hell was Katsuo letting this person reside in his family's home?

"You! Let me go!" the woman shrieked in the background. Yuki's ears twitched at the shrill sound.

"I'm sorry, Milady. The area is off-limits."

"But she's going there!"

"Naturally. It's Lady Yuki's prerogative."

"What—?"

Katsuo was jarred out of his meditation by sharp voices seeping in through the ajar door. He bowed as he finished his prayers and poured sake into the cup in front of him.

He soon felt the presence of his grandmother.

"What brings you here?" he asked, not turning around.

"Praying to Benten?" she asked instead and settled down next to him.

She clapped once and bowed. Yuki was never one to follow tradition. Katsuo watched her in silence. She was like a statue, hardly moving.

"Don't stare. It's rude."

"Sorry, Grandmother," Katsuo said, looking away. This was the only place where Yuki let him call her by that title.

Soon, she was finished and turned to him.

"Do you come here often?"

"Often enough."

"It's peaceful, isn't it?" Yuki looked back at the altar. A scroll hung behind it, depicting a gorgeous woman with long, flowing black hair. Her eyes were black like the abyss. She wore a simple white kimono with a red sash keeping it in place. She was playing on the biwa, sitting on top of a majestic, snow-white dragon. Yuki sighed. "I've missed this place."

"You are welcome anytime."

"I know."

Comfortable silence descended on them, and they stayed this way for a little while until Katsuo spoke up.

"Why are you here? Not that I don't like it when you visit, but... usually it has to do with something else happening."

Yuki was silent for a heartbeat. She fully turned to him and looked him in the eyes.

"You are right. I really should come without bearing ill news."

Katsuo waited patiently, letting her gather her thoughts.

"There's been some disturbance in the community."

She didn't have to specify which community she was talking about. His eyebrows furrowed.

"How so?"

"You know how they normally don't interfere in matters regarding humans and how they view us of mixed blood."

Katsuo bit back a snarl.

"Easy," Yuki said. "That's the truth of our inheritance. It's foolish not to acknowledge it." She waited until Katsuo settled down before continuing. "This time, it's complicated. Someone from the community is on the move, manipulating humans and instigating this war."

"It's been going on for decades—nay, a century!

"You see what I mean? Who else would have the resources to do something like that?"

"And why are *they* suddenly interested in this human war? They were ignoring it for a hundred years?" Katsuo asked, genuinely curious.

"They think after he or she has conquered the human realm, the next step will be the community. A human is a speck of dust to them. However, if they were to band together, they could do some serious damage," Yuki explained. "You know we keep our origins a secret for exactly the same reason."

"Hard to imagine the all-powerful youkai fearing humans." Katsuo snorted at the idea. "So what can we do?"

"You?" Yuki asked. "Do what you've been doing. Be more vigilant, because another front might be opened in this war. I came to warn you about that."

She stood up, and Katsuo immediately followed. He grabbed her hand.

"You're not leaving already, are you?" he asked. "You've only just got here."

"I have to investigate this matter further. Something just doesn't add up."

Katsuo's pleading eyes made her reconsider.

"There might be some leads here. I can stay a few more days, I guess."

Katsuo wondered, not for the first time, what would happen if his grandmother for once, would be honest with her feelings.

"Thank you, Granny." He hugged her.

"Oh, boy, you embarrass me."

"Shush, I missed you."

Yuki smiled as she patted his back.

24

A few days later, Katsuo was going through the movements for his training. Today, he felt like exercising with a katana. Even though the air was chilly, he warmed up quickly and had to lose his shirt. He was just behind the pagoda, out of sight of everyone.

The quick pace of the kata made his heart race. He felt he had to break the usual routine, otherwise he'd go crazy. All he'd been doing the last couple of days was paperwork, which was broken by the instances he was eating with his family. He hadn't had a chance to spend much quality time with them, and he hadn't had an opportunity to let off some steam. Even though there were a few border skirmishes, they were insignificant enough that his officers stationed there could handle it.

But if nothing happened, he might just get on a horse and ride to the closest enemy border. He concentrated on the way of the sword, expanding his senses, calming his emotions, silencing his mind. After a while, he felt as if he was becoming one with the wind. Bending left and right, cutting through the currents with a sharp blade.

His concentration was broken as he felt eyes on him. Katsuo continued his practice as if nothing was amiss but carefully surveyed his surroundings. Nothing was out of place. He pricked his ears and sharpened his senses as he let his power seep out. He was in the middle of a particularly difficult choreography, twisting himself and twirling the blade so fast it was hard to follow with non-trained eyes.

He heard a gasp, and he unexpectedly let go of the blade, hurling it toward the voice he'd heard. Another gasp and a clatter followed as the sword lodged into a tree behind some huge jars, which mostly contained sake. One of those jars dangerously tipped to the side, and Katsuo hurried to get there in time to catch it.

He saved it the last moment. He let out a breath in relief and returned the jar back to its place. Strange, it was heavier than he would expect. He furrowed his eyebrows and drew the wakizashi from his waistband. Pointing the blade at the top of the jar, he quickly removed the lid.

For a moment, he didn't know whether to laugh or be furious. His *betrothed* was hiding inside one of the jars, peering up at him with a red face. Her eyes were looking up at him innocently even though she was caught in an area off-limits to her.

"Get up," he said, fighting a laugh. His voice sounded raw even to his own ears.

"I can't," she whispered.

"What was that?" Maybe he heard wrong.

"I can't," Ciara repeated, louder this time. "I'm stuck."

Oh, for heavens' sake! He couldn't stop the laughter bubbling up from the deepest part of his soul. *Who hides in a jar and then can't get out of it?*

"Sure, laugh at me all you want. I'll just wait until the

rest of eternity," Ciara grumbled, "or until a gentleman decides to rescue me, while you laugh."

Katsuo wiped a tear from the corner of his eye.

"Come on, I'll help you."

"How?" she asked, eyeing him. She tensed up as he walked closer and bent over her head. He gripped both sides of the jar and it moved to the side. Ciara grabbed the edges and panicked. "No! Wait!"

"Trust me."

"It's hard when I'm stuck here!"

"I'll get you out," Katsuo insisted and the jar fell sideways.

"Waaaaaait!" Ciara screamed and braced for impact. It never came. Carefully, she opened her eyes and realized she was laying on her side, inside the jar, which was quite intact.

"Now what?" she asked, blinking up at Katsuo. He grabbed a small container hanging from his waistband and opened it. It looked like something Ciara would put cosmetics in. Katsuo dipped a finger in it and Ciara realized there was some kind of cream inside the container. "What are you going to do with it?"

Instead of replying with words, he started to rub the cream on the edge of the jar. It smelled awful. Ciara made a face, which Katsuo caught from the corner of his eye. He chuckled.

"Now, give me your hands."

"Both of them?" Ciara asked.

Katsuo nodded and put the container away. He reached out his hands, and Ciara struggled to have both of her arms come free from the jar. One was easy, but two at the same time?

By some miracle, she did it. He tightened his hold on her wrists, and before she could do anything, he pulled on her arms. She shrieked, but by the time the sound left her mouth, she was already free.

Ciara sighed in relief and hung her head.

"That was so embarrassing!" she said, burying her face in… something warm? Her breath hitched and she looked up, fearing the worst. Yep, she had just managed to embarrass herself even further, if that was possible.

She was laying on top of a topless Katsuo who had just saved her from a very troublesome situation. She straightened her arms, putting her palms on his muscled torso.

"I'm so sorry!" Ciara scrambled back, falling on her bottom. She stared at Katsuo with wide eyes. "I'm sorry! I didn't mean to do that!"

"What were you doing there, anyway?" he asked as he sat up without any help from his hands. Damn, the man had abs. Ciara looked away, her face reddening. She realized he was waiting for her reply. Thankfully, he didn't have any sharp objects near him, not that she could see.

She cleared her throat and looked back at him.

"I was just taking a stroll and wanted to see the pagoda. And then you came, and I panicked, and I just… hid."

"Are you aware this place is off-limits? There's a guard on the path here," Katsuo asked. He was still amused at her feeble attempt to hide and how she got stuck in the jar. But she needed to know the boundaries. He reached for the fallen wakizashi and Ciara's eyes widened.

"Yes!" she hurried with her answer. "I did know. I'm really sorry, I just wanted to see this building from up close. It looks so unique! Please don't kill me!"

Katsuo was taken aback.

"*Kill* you? Why would I…?" He realized he was twirling the blade in one hand. Ah, that's why. He put it away in its scabbard then stood to retrieve his katana. He walked back to Ciara who was cowering on the ground. Her hands were shaking badly. He put the katana away, too, and squatted down. Their eyes were at the same level.

"You'd have to do a lot more for me to even consider hurting you," he said. He was surprised to realize he meant it.

"B-but I wasn't supposed to be here."

"Well, as long as you're not a spy... Are you?"

Ciara fervently shook her head.

"Then we're good. Just promise me you won't break any more house rules," he smiled, but it didn't reach his eyes. Even though he put the weapons away, Ciara felt the danger had still not completely passed.

"I'm sorry. It won't happen again," she said, determination lacing her voice.

"Good. Come." He stood up and offered his hand for her. After a moment of hesitation, Ciara took it, and he helped her up. "Let's go back."

He went to get his shirt, put it on, and walked back to Ciara, who was waiting for him patiently. He steered them toward the path leading from the pagoda to the castle courtyard.

"Are you mad at me?" she asked. Her voice was small.

"I'm not happy with you, but no, I'm not mad at you, either."

Ciara let out a sigh of relief and straightened from her hunched posture. For the first time, he looked at her attire. She was dressed like a man.

"Why aren't you wearing a kimono?"

She puckered her lips.

"It's easier to move around wearing these clothes," she admitted. She glanced at him, nervously. "Katsuo, can I ask you something?"

"Sure."

"How do you do it?"

"Do what?"

"You use the sword so easily," Ciara said.

"Years of practice."

"No, I mean…" She sighed in frustration, trying to find the words. "On the battlefield. You fight people, you *kill people*. How do you deal with that?"

Katsuo looked at her, puzzled.

"There is war. If I stopped to mourn every time I cut someone down, I'd be dead in a heartbeat."

"So you just… not think about it?" Ciara asked for clarification.

"That's not quite right, either. How shall I put it?" Katsuo placed a hand to his chin as he thought. "You do what you must in order to protect something important to you. If it's killing someone, then that's it. You know you have to do it. And you put it away to a corner of your mind. Something like that."

"I see…"

"Have I satisfied your curiosity?" he asked, concerned what brought upon this line of questioning. Did she think he was threatening her? She did beg him not to kill her, not that that had been the case.

"Thank you for your honesty," Ciara said, giving him a sad smile. "You gave me plenty to think about."

hey had just passed the guard on duty on the path to the pagoda. He didn't react to Ciara's appearance but bowed to them dutifully. Katsuo made sure to remember his face, however, and tell Taiki to train his guards better.

Ciara seemed harmless enough, but if a dangerous person were to make their way there… Katsuo made a fist with his hands as he remembered that night when Ayaka was kidnapped. It was pure luck and Ciara's determination that his daughter got back safely. The woman was still guilty of trespassing, though, and he didn't intend to let the whole incident slide.

"Well, I'll be going back to my room—" Ciara started to say, but Katsuo shook his head. "What is it?" She asked.

"You didn't think I'd let you off the hook so easily, did you?" Katsuo quirked an eyebrow, and Ciara looked away. The tips of her ears grew red. So she did think he was going to forget what she did. "You knew well that it was forbidden to enter the pagoda area unless you had my prior permission."

Ciara looked down as she nodded.

"I cannot let this go unpunished."

At his words, Ciara froze, and her eyes widened. Katsuo swore he saw her pale.

"W-what do you mean?" Her question came out as a breath. Her big, purple eyes looked up at him, wide in fright.

"Every action has its consequences."

"I know that," she replied, looking away again. She cleared her throat after a moment of silence. "What do you have in mind?" Her voice sounded different from before. Detached.

"I'll think on it. I'll let you know by the end of the day," he replied. A little time for her to think on her actions might do good. "You may go now."

"Yes. Bye."

She hurried off so fast that Katsuo didn't even have the chance to ask if she would need help finding her way back to her room.

Ciara didn't even go to town with Yura that day. She just wandered around the orchard or circled the corridors, careful to avoid people. She had steered clear of Katsuo's office. Finally, when she could take it no more, she visited the bathhouse and relaxed for a long time. Thankfully, her bath was uninterrupted and she was alone and could meditate. By the time she exited the pool, her fingers had wrinkled from the water. She felt warm and happy until the moment she stepped out of the bathhouse and came face to face with a servant she didn't know.

"Milady, please come with me. Milord wishes to speak to you."

"Okay, lead the way," Ciara said, following the man. He bowed when they reached the door to Katsuo's study.

"Milord, Ciara-sama is here," he said, tapping the door.

"Let her in."

Ciara took a breath as the doors slid open for her. Katsuo's voice was just as emotionless as his face was at the moment she looked at him. He did the gesture she had learned meant 'come in' in this country, and the doors quietly slid closed behind her. For a terrible moment she felt like a mouse trapped with a cat. A big cat. Like a lion.

"You called me?" Ciara asked, trying to keep her voice neutral.

Katsuo finally looked up at her and put his paperwork away. He looked taken aback as he gazed at her. Ciara's eyes furrowed.

"What is it?"

"I thought... I didn't..."

It was amusing to see him bewildered for a change, and Ciara had to swallow a smile.

"Were you taking a bath?"

"Yes. It *was* very lovely," she emphasized the past tense.

Katsuo cleared his throat and looked away for a moment before gesturing for her to sit in front of him. Ciara sat on her knees, waiting for him to start talking.

"I've decided what you need to do to make amends for your trespassing this morning-"

"I'm still not sleeping with you," Ciara said firmly.

Katsuo's eyes flashed golden for a moment, but it disappeared before Ciara could confirm what she saw.

"Why do you always jump to that conclusion?" he asked, puzzled. "Do you actually want to sleep with me but are playing hard to get?"

Ciara gaped.

"I'm not!" she immediately protested.

Katsuo mumbled something unintelligible under his breath.

"What was that?" Ciara narrowed her eyes.

"You make me dinner."

"Ummm... what?"

"You make me dinner today, for just the two of us," Katsuo clarified. "You can use whatever ingredients you want from the kitchens. There's just one condition."

"And what is that?" Ciara asked. "I'm not cooking for you naked!"

"Will you stop that for just one second?" Katsuo hit his fist on the table, making Ciara jump. His ears were red.

"It was just a joke," she mumbled.

"A *joke*? So there's a version where you'd actually cook naked then sleep with me?"

Ciara's hid her face behind her hands, but whatever remained exposed, Katsuo could see it turn crimson red.

"Can we just move on and never mention it again?" she asked.

"I'm just continuing what you've started," Katsuo simply said and stood up. He rounded the desk, completely silent, so when he reached for Ciara's hand, she jerked in surprise. She looked at him with huge eyes the color of twilight. As their gazes locked, Katsuo felt some kind of tense energy whirling between them.

"Be careful what you say. The joke might be on you," he said as he held her hands. Ciara's breath hitched, and she didn't move. She felt as if she was trapped by the gaze of a predator.

"You make me dinner tonight. The only condition is that it'll be Western cuisine."

"Oh."

"The head cook can show you where we store the ingredients," he said and stood up, still not letting go of her. He lifted her hand a little, and Ciara rose from her seated position with his help.

"I'm looking forward to dinner," he said with a small smile.

"R-right." Ciara retracted her hand and turned to the door. "See you later, then."

"See you at dinner," Katsuo told her as she exited the room.

26

*C*iara left in a daze, and by the time she realized she wasn't paying attention to where she headed, she had already been lost in the maze that was the castle. Confused, she stopped at an intersection and looked up to find red lines painted on the beam of one corridor and yellow puffs on the other. She had never seen these symbols before. The corridors were empty, not even a guard stood around. This meant she was in the inner parts of the castle, but other than that, she was completely lost.

Sighing, Ciara picked the corridor with the red lines and took a left turn. She had crossed a few intersections but stuck to the red-lined corridor. Just when she was about to think she'd never see another human being in her lifetime and she'd die wandering the hallways of an abandoned castle and archeologists would find her mummified corpse centuries later, she finally heard some voices. She picked up her pace, nearing yet another intersection, but just before she rounded the corner, she stopped as soon as she heard her name being mentioned.

"I want that foreigner, Shiara, out of here!" a hushed voice said. It was probably a woman's voice.

"I can't help you with that," replied a muffled voice. It was hard to discern if it was another woman or a man.

"Don't jest," she said. "Someone with your skills could easily make her disappear."

Ciara put a hand over her mouth to stifle her gasp. Silently, she took a step back, but she was too curious to know more to leave.

"That is true."

Ciara froze on the spot behind the corner. Were they planning on *killing* her?

The person whose voice was muffled sighed before continuing.

"She is under close watch, but I'll see what I can do."

"You better," she hissed in response. "I won't forget your assistance when I'm the lady of this household. I expect you to do your best."

"I'm not your servant," the other person grunted.

"Who do you work for?"

Silence was her answer.

"You better decide where your loyalties lie," she said. "That foreigner and the entire Kitayama family will be out of the picture soon. It'll be too late by then to decide which side you serve. Choose carefully."

Ciara heard footsteps retreating and glanced around in a panic. There was a door ajar, and she silently stepped in. She crouched down behind a furniture. A moment later, a shadow passed the spot where she had been standing. Her heart hammered loudly in her chest as if she'd run a marathon.

She waited until she could hear nothing, then a little more just to be sure, before she carefully crawled to the opening and peeked out. Ciara let out a silent sigh in relief when she realized she was alone. She stepped out from her hiding place and picked another random direction, hoping neither person from the conversation had headed the same way.

Her mind was reeling with what she had heard. People were plotting about killing her! She was in a daze and felt as if she was walking in a nightmare.

"Oof," she grunted as she bumped into someone. She rubbed her nose, which felt most of the impact, and glanced up.

"I'm sorry, are you all right?"

"Yes. I'm sorry, too," Ciara said as she finished rubbing her nose. It still tingled a little. Taiki nodded then side-stepped her to go on his way. "Be careful."

"Wait!" Ciara called after him, and he stopped, turning back to her. "Can you please point me in the direction of the kitchens? I'm afraid I got lost… again."

"It's that way."

"Straight?" Ciara asked, looking in the direction he indicated.

"Yes. Just follow this corridor until you see a purple dot," Taiki pointed upward, referring to the symbols Ciara tried to decipher ever since Yuki had mentioned them. "From then on, it should be easy enough to find the kitchen."

"Thanks," Ciara said, gazing in that direction. "Say—" She turned back to ask something else, but he was already gone. She hadn't even heard his footsteps. Ciara shrugged before turning to the direction of the kitchen.

This time, she didn't get lost.

Katsuo let his family know that he wouldn't be eating

dinner with them today. Takeru had a secretive smile on his face, as if he knew something his brother didn't, and it quickly got on Katsuo's nerves.

Telling Yuki was a more difficult situation. She listened to him then started asking questions after questions.

"Why?"

"I've just told you, because I will eat with someone else."

"Would this someone else happen to be the lovely foreigner staying at your castle?" Yuki asked. She had the same irritating smile playing on her lips as Takeru. Katsuo crossed his arms and stared at her, wiping his features of any emotion.

This only made Yuki smile. Her twinkling laugh enveloped them.

"What is so amusing?"

"Still, I'm just curious why you'd like to spend dinner with only the two of you there?"

"We have some business with each other."

"I see..." Yuki was eyeing him with suspicion in her gaze. Eventually, she looked away. "Well, I hope you'll enjoy dinner. Actually, I won't be attending either."

"Why not? Takeru and Ayaka would love to spend more time with you," Katsuo asked, puzzled.

"I have some business to attend to, too. I'll be nearby, don't worry."

"Are you leaving?"

Yuki turned to her grandson and put her hand on his shoulder.

"Soon, possibly, but not tonight. There are a few inquiries I need to make."

"Regarding... *them*?"

Yuki nodded and let go of him. She looked at Katsuo with a serious expression on her face.

"I see." His voice was sad, and she immediately understood his mood.

"Katsuo, you know I look out for my family," Yuki said.
"And I wanted to visit you. It's just coincidence that this
happened while I was here."

"You told me once there are no coincidences," Katsuo
said.

Yuki sent him a sad smile.

27

*K*atsuo waited in his study, hoping to finish up some tasks before dinner was ready. But the paperwork was completed, and he was hungry. Still, there was no sign of dinner. He picked himself up and went in search for Ciara, heading in the direction of the kitchen. He let his nose lead him the rest of the way.

He smelled cooked meat and something else. It reminded him of noodles, but it had an unusual scent. Intrigued, he quickened his pace and reached the kitchen soon. Katsuo could hear humming over the sound of the bubbling water. As he peeked through the open doorway, he saw Ciara leaning against the counter, watching the pot over the fire like a hawk watches its prey.

She quietly hummed and tapped a rhythm with the long wooden chopsticks in her hand. A few white streaks ran along her face, and she nodded her head to the rhythm. Katsuo was bewildered when she suddenly erupted in singing and dancing. She used the chopsticks to drum on the nearest tabletop whenever the choreography allowed her to do so.

It took all his willpower to remain a silent statue standing in the doorway. He was bewildered, and Ciara was enchanting and beautiful as she danced. Her singing voice sounded heavenly. Katsuo observed her for a few more moments then stepped in just as she made a twirl. He caught her mid-motion, making her lose her balance. As he held her close, Ciara gripped his arms, still holding the wooden chopsticks in her hand.

"Oh. Hi," she said, and he could see red creeping up her neck. She cleared her throat. "How... how long have you been here?"

He started humming the song right from the beginning.

"Oh no!" Ciara buried her face in his chest in embarrassment.

"Your dance was..." Katsuo started, and Ciara hunched. "...very unique."

"Shut up," she mumbled, playfully slapping his shoulder with her free hand. They heard a hiss from somewhere behind Katsuo.

"Oh no! The ravioli!" Ciara jumped out of his arms and ran to the pot over the stove. "Oh no, oh no, oh no! It'll be overcooked!" She looked around frantically.

"What are you looking for?"

"Where I can pour the hot water out?" She asked, eyes wide. Katsuo hurried over to her and grabbed the pot.

"Let me."

In the end, he poured the hot water into an empty basin. By some miracle, he had managed to keep the pasta in the pot without the use of a sieve.

"Thanks, I think you've just saved our dinner," Ciara said, taking the pot from him.

"You're welcome."

Katsuo looked around. The room was a mess; flour covered the entire tabletop, sometimes small bundles of goo smeared it, and a few cracked eggshells were neatly piled in a corner. He looked at Ciara. It was a wonder her hands were clean. She turned around. Even her white apron was clean.

"What is it?"

"Do you need some help?"

"Oh, I'm good," she replied. "Are you hungry? I'm just doing the finishing touches. It'll be done in a few."

"Good to hear."

"So you *were* hungry," she chuckled.

"It's been a long day," he replied.

"I imagine. You sound tired."

"Do I?"

"No worries. You can drink some oolong tea for that."

"Oh, you'll make me some?"

"I didn't say that," she laughed, working on the pasta in the pot. "I'm not sure how to prepare that properly."

"You don't know how to make tea?"

"Of course I do!" she said, indignant. She glanced over her shoulder at him. "It's just... different from home."

Ciara turned back to stir the pot one more time. Katsuo was content to just watch her work. For the first time since before Ayaka had been kidnapped, he felt at peace. He pondered how nice would it be to spend days like this.

"Done!" Ciara stepped back with a huge smile on her face, drawing Katsuo out of his thoughts. "I did what I could, considering the circumstances!"

She stood there, admiring her work for a heartbeat.

"Now, how do I turn the fire off?"

Ciara wanted to tidy up the kitchen before they left, but Katsuo insisted they eat.

"And I pay people to do that for me," was his final argument. Ciara caved in, but not after a small fight ensued, which ended up with Katsuo confiscating the kitchen rag she had found. He used this chance to wipe the streak of flour off her face.

He grabbed the pot while Ciara gathered the plates and Westerner utensils, and they set off for his room. After the tenth servant wanted to wrestle him for a chance to bring the pot full of pasta instead of him, Katsuo picked a less frequented route and they had no interruptions.

"You're just doing this to confuse me, right?" Ciara sighed as they rounded yet another corner, ending up in a seemingly random corridor. Katsuo smiled, glancing at her out of the corner of his eyes.

"And you're enjoying it! Please tell me we aren't going in circles!"

"We aren't," he replied, "but this is the longer route."

"I thought you were hungry."

"Are you getting hungry?"

"Very much so," Ciara replied, hoping to control the rumbling of her stomach. She didn't succeed.

"I can hear that."

"Look who's talking," she mumbled, glancing down.

They took a left turn, and Katsuo suddenly stopped. Ciara didn't notice and bumped into him, losing her balance.

"Oh no!" She tried to keep her balance while still keeping hold of the plates, but her feet felt wobbly. She grabbed the cutlery and lifted her hands high in the air as she felt herself start to fall. She closed her eyes, thinking she might acquire a few bruises at most, but she couldn't repair the plates if they broke. They were decorated with gold stripes, for gods' sake! How much would it cost to replace them?

Ciara felt an arm around her waist as her fall was broken. She opened her eyes and saw Katsuo's face from up close. She was captivated by his amber gaze, and the world seemed to pause completely. Katsuo held the pot in one hand and Ciara with the other. She could feel his muscles through her kimono. He had a strong but gentle grip on her.

"Are you all right?" he asked her quietly. Ciara was distracted for a second. Was it just her, or did his voice truly sound deeper than usual?

Eventually, she nodded and willed her legs to work. She managed to get her balance back, but Katsuo still held her in his arm, and she was mesmerized by his intense gaze. He seemed to be closer than ever. Only an inch more and they could—

The plates rattled, and Ciara quickly glanced to her hands. Why, oh why were they acting up at this time? Such precise timing to ruin the moment!

"I'm sorry, can you—?" Ciara held out the plates between them as much as she could. Her hands trembled uncontrollably.

Katsuo looked at her with a question in his eyes but nodded.

"Sure, can you stand on your own?"

"Yes, thank you."

He let go of her waist and grabbed the plates.

"Sorry," she mumbled.

"Don't worry about it," he said. "But in turn, you will be the one to open the doors for me."

"Sure," Ciara chuckled as she made a fist with her hands, willing the trembles to pass quickly. "I can do that at least."

They arrived at Katsuo's room a few minutes later, and Ciara slid the door open. Her hands still trembled a little, and she wouldn't dare carry any fragile items, but otherwise, the tremors had subsided to a manageable discomfort.

Katsuo put the pot on the table then set the plates next to each other. Ciara was a bit surprised at the arrangement, but it would've been rude to reorganize the sitting chart. Plus, she found she didn't mind the close proximity to Katsuo.

Chill, you're just pretending to be engaged, Ciara told herself, trying in vain to calm her fast heartrate. She kneeled down next to Katsuo and distributed the forks. Meanwhile, Katsuo took off the lid and smelled the steam coming out of the pot. Ciara finished her musing, *But then why does it feel like we're a real couple? Especially with that scene in the kitchen.*

"So what is it called?" Katsuo asked, breaking her train of thought.

"Ravioli. Basically, it's pasta pockets with fillings," she explained. "I filled it with meat."

"Oh, we have something similar here, although the shape is quite different," he observed.

Ciara lifted the wooden chopsticks to get some ravioli out, but her hand wasn't steady, and the pasta dropped back into the pot at every turn. Katsuo put a hand on hers.

"Let me," he said, looking into her eyes, determined. She let go of the chopsticks.

Katsuo carefully fished out the raviolis.

"Thank you," Ciara said and sent him a small smile.

"You're very welcome," he replied, getting some pasta for himself as well. Ciara leaned back and sighed a little. "What is it?"

"I was just thinking how fortunate the trembles came *after* I was finished preparing dinner."

A short silence followed her words as Katsuo finished his task.

"Does this happen often?"

Ciara shrugged helplessly.

"It happens every now and then. Sometimes there's nothing for days then suddenly... *this*," she held out her hand. The trembles had subsided but were still detectable. "Not sure if they'll ever fully go away."

"What happened?" Katsuo asked, genuinely concerned. Ciara looked at him for a long moment, debating how much should she tell him. How much could she trust him? Maybe if she took away anything related to the future...

"I was in an accident. Our car-rriage was hit by another and we..."

For a terrible moment, her ears were filled with screams and her vision with crimson. She squeezed her eyes shut and felt her breath hitch. The sight of the glass shard sticking out of—

"It's all right, you're all right."

Katsuo's hand on her shoulder startled her out of the flashback. She felt her tense muscles gradually relax. As she blinked, a single tear escaped her left eye. Disturbed, she quickly wiped it away but didn't expect to be covered in a big hug the next moment.

Ciara froze on contact, but soon hugged Katsuo back, gradually calming down in his embrace. He stroked her back in silence. She realized all she needed was a hug. When was the last time she was embraced like this? A couple more tears escaped her eyes, but she willed them to be the last ones. She felt completely safe and at ease in Katsuo's arms. It was a foreign feeling.

Finally, she withdrew and wiped at her face.

"Sorry, and thanks." She sent him a smile.

"There's nothing to be sorry about."

"Except maybe the pasta getting cold."

Katsuo chuckled.

"Well then, let's eat! Itadakimasu!"

"Itadakimasu!" Ciara echoed. They both started eating.

After a moment of silently chewing the first ravioli, Ciara couldn't wait any longer and asked Katsuo's opinion.

"It's... *different*," he said, pondering on his reply. "I like it! The flavor is stronger than what I'm used to. Very good!"

"I wish we had cheese, though."

"What for?"

"Back at home, we put grated cheese on it. I think that makes it more delicious," Ciara explained, picking up a ravioli with her fork. "I looked around but couldn't find any kind of cheese in your pantry."

"Judging by your tone, I think I must remedy this."

"You're ought to!" Ciara chuckled. "But I'm glad you like it even without the cheese."

Ciara only ate a small portion, as she wasn't very hungry, but was pleased to see Katsuo finish off the pot completely. They chatted light-heartedly during the meal, and her hand injury wasn't mentioned again.

*A*fter the meal, Katsuo kept Ciara talking, hoping to find out more about where she came from, but the more he heard, the more he became enamored with her. He was so caught up in the topic, he almost missed the signs of Ciara getting exhausted, the drawn-out blinking and her answers getting slower and shorter. When he noticed her stifle a yawn, he realized it must've been quite late.

He enjoyed her company, and despite the hour, Ciara's attention had never waned. As much as he wanted to continue having her in his presence, he had to steer her toward the door. She was having a hard time keeping her head up and rested it in her palms, elbows on the table. Ciara was facing him, and a slight smile played on her lips. Katsuo averted his eyes.

"It's getting late. You should go."

Ciara blinked slowly, as if she was surprised. She straightened and turned around, looking for something, but eventually faced him.

"How do you know?"

"You're sleepy."

"Am not!" she said indignantly then tried to cover her yawn.

"You are. I'll not have my guest exhaust herself."

"Ah, am I your guest? Am I not your fiancée?"

Katsuo stopped for a moment at that unfamiliar word. He repeated after her, prompting her to explain.

"Yes, you are." Katsuo agreed when hearing her words and helped her up. He led her to the door and slid it open for her.

Ciara stood outside, slightly puzzled.

"Your door is over there, just turn to the left" Katsuo pointed to the intersection three doors down. "Would you like me to escort you?"

"I think I can manage," she said, rolling her eyes. Katsuo raised his eyebrows. He was a mere child the last time someone dared to roll their eyes at him. Ciara padded toward her door, and Katsuo turned back to gather the pots and plates. He put them all just outside his door, thinking how great it would be to spend most nights like this one.

A scream tore through the night, immediately alerting him. It came from Ciara's room. Katsuo ignored the ringing in his ears and hurried over to her. She was retreating to the corridor, her face paler than usual.

"What happened?" Katsuo asked and quickly ran his gaze over her form, looking for any sign of injury. Ciara looked at him and pointed inside her room.

"Th-there's…"

He heard a small noise from inside, and Ciara did, too, because she snapped her gaze toward it. She stood at the doorway like a statue, pointing a trembling finger at something in the room.

Katsuo arrived behind her and peeked over her shoulder. He sighed in relief when he saw what caused the fright.

"I really do hope that wasn't a sigh of relief, because—"

"Relax, it's just a snake."

Ciara came out of her shocked stance and turned a sharp gaze on him.

"Did you just hear what came out of your mouth?"

"It won't hurt you. Trust me," Katsuo said and entered the room. Ciara moved away but made sure to have the snake in her sight.

"I trust you, but I don't trust the snake."

Katsuo squatted down to swoop the white snake around his shoulders. He had a firm grip on its neck, keeping its head away. Then he started walking toward the door, and Ciara quickly cleared the way for him. She looked at him with wide eyes.

"How can you be sure it won't hurt you?"

Katsuo stroked the head of the animal.

"It's a symbol of my clan. It won't hurt me."

"Does the snake know that, too? Because to me, it doesn't look like—"

The animal hissed at her, and Ciara shut up. She even jumped a little at the strange sound.

"Nope, most definitely not," she shook her head, retreating.

"That was not very nice." Katsuo looked at the white snake. Ciara suddenly had the feeling he might not be talking to the snake, but her. Or maybe he admonished both of them, as absurd as it sounded. "I'll take care of it. Rest well."

"As if I can after this," Ciara muttered to herself and headed toward her room. She noticed Katsuo going back to his room. "What are you doing?" She hurried after him.

"I'm letting it go."

"In your room?" Her voice sounded near hysterical.

"Not the worst idea, but no," he replied as he reached the window and leaned out, putting his arms outside. The snake didn't move. "Go on. You're free," he urged it, and Ciara was surprised to feel a smile creep up her lips. He was talking to the reptilian like Karen talked to her black cat.

Finally, the snake slithered down his arm and out the window.

"Aren't you going to—" Ciara finished abruptly as she realized there was no glass on the window. It was basically a hole in the wall.

Katsuo turned to her.

"Aren't you afraid it'll climb back in?" As soon as she said it, she realized how foolish it sounded. A grown man, a warrior—no, a *warlord* who was cuddling the snake just moments before, why would he be afraid of it? A shadow of a smile passed his lips.

"Are you laughing at me?" Ciara gasped.

"Of course not."

Katsuo walked over to her and looked at her straight in the eyes.

"I'm not afraid of the snakes. As I've told you, we have family history with them."

"You gotta tell me one day," Ciara said, her interest piqued.

"But not today. It really is getting late," he reminded her.

"Right…" Ciara turned away slowly. She didn't feel safe going back to her room and spending the night there alone. She wasn't sure she'd get any sleep. If a snake could get in, what other dangers would await her?

Suddenly, she recalled Katsuo's arms around her and how safe it felt, being embraced by him. If only—

She shook her head. She had a goal and must not get distracted. She had to get home. The hug was only an illusion. It'd last a couple more weeks, but after that, it'd be gone. She couldn't stay in Katsuo's room.

"Could you…" Ciara glanced over her shoulder at him.

"Yes?"

She gulped down her pride.

"Could you please check my room? If it's not a problem."

"Sure. Stay here," he said then changed his mind. "Or come with me, whichever suits you."

"Thanks," Ciara trudged after him and stood in the doorway as he inspected her room. It only took a couple of minutes for him to check the place.

"No snakes or other unwanted guests in here," he reported when he was done. He walked over to her and leaned closer to her. "You can rest safely."

"Thank you," Ciara said, breathless. He was doing it again. He was too close. She glanced away and cleared her throat as she took a step back and to the side to let him pass. There was a moment of silence, and she got the feeling Katsuo wanted to say something, but in the end, he silently walked away.

"Katsuo," she said just when he was about to turn at the intersection. He stopped on the corner and looked back at her. "Thank you. And good night."

"Thank you for the meal," he nodded with a smile. "Sleep well, darling."

With that, he was gone.

Ciara stood there a moment longer with a hammering heart in her chest. The way he said "darling" to her…

"Stupid," she admonished herself as she forcefully pushed the dangerous feelings away. She slid the door closed behind after she entered her room. "Forget it. Forget him."

29

*I*t seemed whenever Katsuo and Ciara planned on doing something together for the rest of the week, for some incomprehensible reason, Lady Orihime showed up to join them. Ciara was sure she was doing it on purpose.

Whether it be a picnic at lunchtime on the veranda, in a secluded part of the castle, or a stroll in the garden, as soon as Ciara thought they were alone, Orihime soon showed up and spoiled the mood.

Katsuo closed off and ignored her as much as politeness would allow—after all, he was still the host and she was the daughter of an ally, from what information Ciara could pick up on—but Orihime was all over him, which in turn made Ciara cranky and had her making barbs at Orihime. It was ugly, but she didn't have the patience to deal with her day after day.

She hadn't seen Orihime for the last few days, however. As for Katsuo, she only saw him at dinner because he was so busy during the day. She wondered what happened. Did he perhaps put off work to meet her then it piled up? Or was it just busy season for warlords? He wasn't going to go to war soon, was he?

"What a lovely day, Ciara-sama!" Yura's voice startled her out of her thoughts. The servant girl came to Ciara's room that morning as usual. She immediately went to the cupboard to look for a kimono for Ciara. "Shall we go to the market?"

"Oh, is it market day already?" Ciara asked, getting up. She was losing track of time, which was not good. She needed a calendar of some sort. She could've sworn market day was two days later. "Wasn't that supposed to be later? Or did I get my days mixed up?"

"This is not the usual market," Yura chirped as she turned around, with a neatly folded heap of clothes in her arms. Her expression fell as she looked at Ciara. "Are you feeling all right?"

"Yes, as okay as I can be," Ciara replied, yawning. "Sorry. It's just... I've been having these nightmares."

"Multiple?"

"Yes, for a few nights now."

"May I ask what about?"

Ciara picked at her bedding.

"Going home but not reaching it. Stuff like that," she shrugged it off as if it was something insignificant. She didn't want to dwell on it. Her gaze ventured to the window. "But enough about that! It's a sunny day, I see."

"Indeed! Perfect for a walk."

"I think I'll take you up on your offer and go to the market with you. What's so special about it?"

"You'll see." Yura winked at her.

Ciara was mildly amused. Usually, Yura was a wealth of information, so something must be really special about this market for her to be so secretive. She quickly washed up and put the kimono on with Yura's help. She even let the girl apply some light makeup for her.

"Hey, where are we going?"

"To the market, of course!"

"B-but… breakfast?" Ciara asked, her voice tiny. She needed the oolong tea to stay awake. It was the next best thing after coffee.

Yura paled and squirmed.

"If Milady—"

"Ciara."

"If Ciara-sama would like, I was thinking… maybe we could get breakfast at the market?"

"Oh. Good idea. Let's go."

Katsuo felt he was going to go mad if he spent one more minute on paperwork. The last few days had been pretty much the same ever since he had to send Takeru to handle a border skirmish: training in the morning, breakfast with Yuki since she insisted on it, then training the soldiers, paperwork, then a quick lunch, then more paperwork, listening to messengers from the castle town, coming up with strategies to strengthen the borders, listening to reports from Taiki, waiting for news from the battlefield, then finally, dinner where he could spend the time with his family. That was basically the only time he'd seen Ciara for the last few days. He didn't have energy or time to take part in the music after dinner, though. Ayaka's sleepiness gave him an opportunity to use that as an excuse.

He mildly wondered what his grandmother was doing during the day, but he was sure if she got bored or something was not up to her satisfaction, she'd be badgering him. Except he was slowly going crazy. He was used to fast-paced battlefields, and this idleness didn't suit him.

Katsuo took a walk in the orchard, hoping to clear his thoughts and calm his restless soul. He bet he inherited his bustling nature from his grandmother. In his musings, he didn't realize he wasn't alone. It was too late to avoid a certain someone when he noticed Orihime.

"Oh, how nice to bump into you here, Milord." Orihime bowed, and her entourage copied her.

"Orihime-dono. Are you enjoying my garden?"

"Very much so, Milord." She smiled sweetly at him and stepped in his path. "How about you?"

"I was," he replied curtly. Too bad he couldn't have a peaceful walk in his own orchard without someone finding him. "Doesn't your honorable father miss you?"

"He does, but that is the cruel fate of a man who has a beautiful daughter," Orihime said without a hint of modesty. She pretended, though, as she shyly glanced down at her feet. There was a time when he would've played along, maybe even believed her, but he wasn't going to make the same mistake twice. On the other hand, he pondered, he didn't see such manipulation from Ciara. There was a big contrast between the two women's behavior.

"I guess that'll be my fate, too," he replied as he turned to face the castle. "If you'll excuse me—"

"May I ask, what are you wearing, Milord?" Orihime asked she noticed the strange footwear he wore.

"These are boots."

"Are they from the West?" Orihime couldn't hide her grimace.

"They are imported from Joseon[1]."

"Oh!" Orihime's expression transformed into one of interest. "Do you frequently do dealings with them?"

"Do not let it concern you, Milady," Katsuo deflected the question. "However, I have work I need to do, if you'll excuse me." *Finally.*

"Have a good afternoon, Milord." Orihime bowed, entourage in tow. Katsuo hurried back up the muddy hillside. The wooden planks placed there functioned as steps, which made it easier. They'd been having heavy rains for the last few days. Today was the first one where they'd seen the sun.

Katsuo didn't want to return to his study. He wanted to spend some time outside. On a whim, he decided to visit town. It had been a while since he'd observed business there. It would do good and would count as work.

Happy with his decision, he grabbed his weapons and a pouch full of coins before making his way out of the castle gates and down to the town at the bottom of the hill.

As soon as he entered, he realized it was open day. Every month, there was one day when he allowed craftsmen and merchants from other provinces to visit. The market was normally for people from his province to do business, but on this day, everyone was welcome. He even started seeing merchants from Joseon and the West recently. In exchange for a fee, anyone could set up a stall for the day.

More guards patrolled the streets than usual, and there were some officials working in the market to check if every vendor had purchased permission to sell. So far this seemed to be a splendid idea. Business flourished, and he used most of the extra money to make better roads and dams for villages in his territories He was thinking of expanding this event to the next biggest town, on the other side of the province.

Katsuo was curious to see the goods from Western merchants. They had always brought something interesting. His people had some reservations when dealing with the foreigners, and he had, too, but he had successfully established good business relations with a bunch of them. It helped they had no idea they were talking to the daimyō. They acted strange when faced with authority.

As soon as he arrived at the market, he immediately spotted some ceramic ware from Lake Biwa. He made a beeline to the stall, and a set of sake cups soon caught his eye. There were light blue flower petals on a white background. It reminded him of the rainy days in summertime. He ordered the set to be brought to the castle and paid the merchant.

He visited all stalls and bought some toys for Ayaka, a dictionary from a Western merchant, medicine from another, then some ointments from a shady-looking herbalist. Just when he thought he was done, he saw something sparkle in the weak sunlight. He walked closer and saw several elegant hairpins laid out on the table.

"Do you see anything you like, Milord?" The merchant asked. He was from another prefecture, completely clueless that he was talking to the daimyō, but Katsuo liked the man's politeness.

"Maybe," he replied, looking at the different items. A comb caught his eye. It had small flowers attached at the top, encircling a large red lily made from textile.

"I must praise you. You have a very good eye for quality products," the merchant said. "That one was commissioned by a noble lady and took days to perfect."

"What happened?"

The merchant shook his head sadly.

"You know how fluttering the ladies' hearts are, Milord! By the time it was finished, she was no longer interested. It's such a pity, because my wife designed this especially for her."

"How fortunate for me, because I'd like to purchase it," Katsuo replied. "Has your wife designed any other items?"

"She occasionally does, Milord. Would you be interested in commissioning something?"

Katsuo pondered for a moment.

"A hairpin. Nothing elaborate, but something elegant. Something that would look good in a brown hair."

"Oh, is it for a foreign lady?" The merchant asked, and Katsuo looked at him sharply. "I didn't mean anything by that, Milord! Just curious."

"Yes," Katsuo replied eventually. "Maybe something purple to decorate it."

"All right, I'll take note, Milord. It'll be done next open day."

"Can you make it sooner?"

The merchant blinked at him slowly.

"Of course! But I can't come here on other days. Only one day a month."

"How soon can it be finished and sent here if it weren't for that rule?" Katsuo asked. Ciara would be gone by the time of the next open day, and he wanted to give her something to remember him by.

"Hmm…" The man stroked his chin, thinking hard. "Well, it can be done in about a fortnight."

"Brilliant. I'll pay you now for the comb, and when you're done with the hairpin, make sure it gets here as soon as possible."

"I'd love to do that, but as I said, I can't do anything until open day. If the daimyō hears of this, my head will be severed! No business is worth that much, I'm sorry, Milord!"

Katsuo smirked at that. It was always nice to hear people obeyed his rules.

"Don't worry about that," he told the merchant as he

paid him. "Just make sure you deliver on time. I'll make sure you'll get permission to do this business."

"Are you an official working for the daimyō here, Milord?" The merchant asked as he accepted the coins.

"Something like that," he said. "Oh, one more thing…" Katsuo added something else to his order before he bid goodbye and walked away. His next stop was at the book shop. He was certain old man Akira would have some extra paper and ink for him to draw up a quick permission document. Thankfully, Katsuo always had his personal seal with him.

---

1. The country on the Korean peninsula during medieval times

30

*A*fter taking care of the permission for the merchant to visit Shirotatsu castle on business for one time outside of open days, he asked a guard to deliver the document to said merchant. Happy with how the afternoon turned out, Katsuo continued his inspection of the marketplace.

After a while, he got tired of the crowd and visited his favorite teahouse, hidden in a quiet street. He was immediately greeted by a smiling waitress. He didn't even have to order because they knew his usual drink. Katsuo settled down on some pillows in the back of the room where he had a view of the garden but was able to keep an eye on the entrance as well. He was quietly enjoying his tea and the scenery. It was a fine afternoon.

A little while later, laughter crept into the teahouse as two ladies turned up. They were a little too loud for him, but thankfully, the waitress guided them away. Katsuo felt something brush against his side. He glanced down to see the cat of the teahouse rubbing against his tight.

"Well, hello there, futoneko[1]. You look bigger than the last time I saw you," he told the cat, who purred. Katsuo stroked its silky black and white fur. He saw the waitress walking across the room and addressed her, "Mio-chan, what have you been feeding him? He is almost as big as a horse!"

"You jest, Milord." The waitress chuckled. "We feed him the same as always, but I suspect he goes around the neighborhood to ask for more. I can't be sure if our customers give him anything extra either. It's hard to keep him on a diet!"

"It must be great to be a cat in your household," Katsuo remarked, making the small waitress laugh and shook her head at him. Just then, a few other customers walked in, and she went to assist them.

"Katsuo?"

He looked up as he heard his name without an honorific and saw Ciara and Yura standing at the door, looking at him.

"Come, join me," he gestured to his table with his free hand. The waitress led the two women there.

"The usual, Milady?"

"Yes, please," Ciara said, glancing at Yura. "For you, Yura?"

"Me too, thank you," the girl replied shyly.

They settled down, Ciara opposite of Katsuo. Yura huddled next to her, her gaze never leaving the table surface. She looked nervous to sit with her lord. She even moved to stand up, but Ciara put a hand on her shoulder and pushed her down with gentle force and a smile.

"Stay, please."

"A-are you sure, Milady? I wouldn't want to intrude."

"On what?" Ciara asked her. "We're only having tea."

"If you say so." Yura looked outside and effectively extracted herself from the conversation even though her body was sitting there. Ciara noticed Katsuo petting the housecat.

"Whose is the cat?" she asked, curious.

"The teahouse owner's," Katsuo replied. He lifted the fat cat with no effort at all.

"Do you want to pet him?"

"I'm fine, thank you. Maybe after I'm done with the tea," Ciara said, and he retracted the cat.

"What kind of animals do you like?" she asked after a heartbeat of silence. "I assume you must like cats and horses."

"Why do you think so?"

Ciara arched her eyebrows.

"Please, I've seen you interact with them. Do you like dogs?"

"They are useful."

"Hmm... I'm more of a dog-person myself. Although I usually get along well with cats, too," Ciara said. "My cousin, however, she loves cats. Sometimes I fear she'll end up a crazy cat-lady."

Ciara found herself babbling, so it was a relief when tea was finally served and she could busy herself with it. However, she was pleasantly surprised when Katsuo poured some tea for her.

"Thank you," she said, giving him a small smile.

"You're welcome," he acknowledged and sat back, sipping his own tea. Meanwhile, his other hand was busy stroking the fur of the cat in his lap.

"I think he likes you," she couldn't help commenting.

Katsuo looked around then leaned closer to her. His whisper in her ear gave her a slight shiver. "It's because I always give him a bite from my biscuits. But don't tell the owners."

Shocked, Ciara snorted, and the tea caught on her throat.

"Please don't make me laugh while I drink," she pleaded, wiping tears from her eyes. Katsuo's gaze was fixed on her face. "What is it?"

"Your bruises have already faded. It's good to see you laugh."

She wasn't sure how to react to that, so she sent him a tiny smile and drank her tea in silence. They made small talk for the rest of the afternoon until they had run out of tea. Katsuo paid for their beverages, then they headed back to the castle.

"This was a great day. We must come tomorrow, too, Yura!" Ciara said as they exited the little establishment.

"Oh, I…" Yura was looking everywhere but at Ciara.

"What is it?"

She mumbled something under her breath.

"What was that?" Ciara leant closer.

"I believe tomorrow is her day off. Isn't that right?" Katsuo asked as he caught up to them.

"That is right, Milord," Yura bowed.

"Oh," Ciara blinked in surprise. Yura did tell her she had a day off every now and then. "Then enjoy your day off tomorrow."

"You don't mind?" Yura peered up at her. Ciara smiled at her.

"Of course not. Everyone needs rest."

"You may go now, if you'd like," Katsuo added. "I'll escort Ciara back to the castle."

"Yes, Milord. Thank you for your generosity, Milord," Yura bowed low, before saying goodbye and running off.

"She has so much energy," Ciara remarked as she looked after the girl fondly. Katsuo was looking at her, a question on his face. "What is it?"

"Would you like to go back straight to the castle, or will you let me show you something?"

"I'm not eager to get back soon," she replied. "What do you have in mind?"

"Tsk, tsk. It's not a surprise if you know what it is."

Katsuo gently took hold of her hand, placed it in the nook of his arm, and led them back to the market. Most of the stalls had already closed, but a few merchants were still selling their items. One of the Europeans was still there, and he headed for him.

"Do you see anything that catches your eye?" he asked as they stopped. Katsuo thought that Ciara seemed happy to be able to look over goods from her home. She spent a while investigating each item.

"We have some incense from Arabia, small carpets from Persia," Ciara shook her head at each item the merchant listed, "Maybe a jewelry for the lady?"

"Is this—?" Ciara stopped at a jar. "Can I open it?"

"Let me, dear," the merchant said, taking the jar from her hands and opening it in one swift motion. Ciara leant closer to sniff it. Yep, it was honey.

"How much is it?" she asked. The man said an amount and Ciara looked at Katsuo. She still had no idea how the monetary system here worked. He had a frown on his face and Ciara turned back to the merchant.

"Thank you, but that's a bit too much."

"It is very rare."

"Not where it came from," she replied, eyebrows raising. Two can play that game.

"Look, lady, I can give you a discount because you're so lovely. Ten percent."

Ciara crossed her arms. So he was open to bargaining.

"You offend me," she turned her face away. "Maybe for thirty percent—"

"Do you have any idea how much danger I needed to face in order for it to arrive here safely?" His reasoning didn't seem to have an effect on Ciara. "Fifteen percent. And that's final," the merchant said.

"Twenty, and you give me the jar for free," Ciara was not giving him any chance.

"Fine," he spit into his palm and stretched it out for her. Ciara's eyes widened at the gesture. "Come on, do we have a deal?"

"We do."

"Shake on it!"

Ciara gaped. They both turned their head at the tinkling sound of coins. Katsuo was counting the money out on the table.

"Oh, thank you, Milord!" He went to grab his hand, but Katsuo avoided him at the last second. It seemed he didn't want to come into contact with the merchant's spit any more than Ciara did.

"The jar," he reminded the merchant.

"Sure, Milord," the man bowed a few times while giving him the jar of honey.

"Let's go," Katsuo nodded to Ciara who seemed to come out of shock. She hurried over to him and they said goodbye to the merchant who was still bowing to them.

When they were out of earshot, Katsuo commented on the deal. "That was quite impressive. I didn't know you could bargain so well."

"Thanks," Ciara said, eyeing the jar of honey in his hand. "I guess when I really want something, I do everything in my power to achieve that."

"But not shaking hands?"

"He spit into his palm!" Ciara protested loudly.

"I'm beginning to think I was lucky you didn't do the same when we sealed our deal."

Ciara laughed when she imagined the scene. To her surprise, Katsuo allowed a small smile. Her breath caught.

"You smiled!"

"Did not." He immediately wiped it off his face.

"You *did* smile!" She insisted. "Now that's something I've never thought I'd see."

"Why's that?"

"Yuki is right, you can be a bit grumpy. And you take yourself way too seriously," she explained. "And I don't mean any offense. That's just how you are, and that's fine."

"You and I have very different ideas on what is offensive."

"Do tell."

"Maybe another time," he said, putting a hand on the small of her back. "It's getting dark. We should get back to the castle."

"S-sure."

Ciara shivered. Was it because of the chilly air or his light touch? Her heart hammered as she felt tingles from where he touched her. On their way back, however, she got distracted by another merchant. He was from Joseon, wherever it was, and had gorgeous fabrics. Ciara couldn't help caressing the silks and marveling at their intricate pattern.

"Which has caught your eye, Milady?" The merchant asked. "Mayhap the azure one with the cranes? It is indeed beautiful."

Ciara, who was just admiring said material, walked on to check the other silks.

"I think the purple one would suit you," Katsuo said, and Ciara glanced up at him. He had that intense look in his eyes, which made her want to blush. Ciara inspected the material he referred to. It had purple embroidery. It was gorgeous.

"Do you think so?"

"It would go well with your eyes," he replied. She looked up at him, surprised. Katsuo turned to the merchant. "How much is it?"

"You really don't have to..." Ciara trailed off as she realized Katsuo ignored her protest. She sighed, willing away the feeling of warmth in her chest. The indigo silk he'd pointed out would make a gorgeous kimono or dress. But she was not going to be here long enough to wear it. She had to go home, because...

While the men were busy with bargaining, Ciara got lost in her thoughts of conflicting feelings. She paid little attention to her environment and to the silks spread out before her. She certainly felt... *something* when it came to Katsuo, but did he feel it, too? She had to constantly remind herself it was a fake engagement but couldn't help being awed by the person he turned out to be.

But her fate lay in another time and place. She was born hundreds of years in the future and thousands of miles away. She had to get back. Her whole life was—

"Back there... what was it?" Ciara mumbled to herself as she felt a shiver run through her. What would she leave behind if she—

A hand closed over her mouth and nose, and she struggled to breathe. Someone held her from behind with a strong grip and was dragging her away. She couldn't make any noise and flailed toward Katsuo, but his back was turned to her. She locked gazes with the merchant for a moment, but he looked away immediately. Or was that just her imagination?

The world turned black as she ran out of air.

---

1. lit. 'fat cat'; it's not the cat's proper name

*K*atsuo was satisfied when he made the deal. He got a good price for the material. Now he only had to persuade Ciara to go with him to the tailor the next day since it was probably closed already. He turned to tell her his wish and was surprised to see that she wasn't there. He looked around, hoping to see her, but she was nowhere to be found.

"Deliver this at the castle. Today," he told the merchant, distracted.

"That'll be another silver—"

"Forget it," he bit out, grabbed the material, and strolled up to the nearest pair of guards. His afternoon went so well after he had escaped the castle. Why was it turning out this way? His instincts screamed in alarm.

"Have you seen a foreigner woman in a kimono?" he asked the guards as soon as they were within ear-shot. One of them, a man in his late twenties straightened as he noticed him and bowed. The other, who was a teenager, looked between them in confusion but followed his partner's lead.

"A foreigner in a kimono?" The older one echoed. "Yes, I have seen her standing with you, sir."

"I mean, after that! She disappeared. Have you seen anything?"

The man scratched his chin, thinking.

"No, I can't say I have seen what happened." He looked at the teenager next to him. "What about you?"

"I haven't seen a foreigner in kimono."

Katsuo suppressed a growl. His thoughts raced one after another. What had happened to Ciara and how come no one had seen anything? Her scent lingered in his nose and he looked to the side.

"Milord?"

"Boy, take this to the castle," he shoved the bundle of cloth and the jar of honey at the teenager who stumbled to gather the items. Then he addressed the other guard. "You stay in this area in case she comes back. If you see something, report it back to me."

"How will I get in touch with you, sir?"

Katsuo's eyes twitched. They were wasting time. Ciara's scent was fading.

"Just tell Taiki," he said and ran off after the scent.

"That was weird," the teenager said afterward. He received a smack to the back of the head.

"Idiot, that was Lord Kitayama! You better deliver that stuff right away then come back!"

"Eeek!"

She regained consciousness for a moment then lost it. This happened several times during the trip which felt like days had gone by. Finally, Ciara was put down on a flat surface. Her fingers touched wood. She smelled dirt and urine.

Ciara crunched up her nose and pushed herself off the floor despite the sudden vertigo. She put a hand on her forehead, hoping to stop the spinning.

"What did you do to me?" she croaked. Her voice was not unlike her own grandmother with a throat infection.

"Oh, you're already awake? I'm impressed," said a man's smooth voice. Ciara peeked out from between her fingers which were spread over her face. The spinning worsened, so she closed her eyes. She felt sick and couldn't care less if her kidnapper was impressed or not.

I wonder how impressed he'll be when I throw up on him, she idly wondered, finding humor in the situation.

"Do you want me to make it better?"

Ciara squinted, trying to make out his face. He sounded familiar, and she had the feeling she had seen him somewhere before but couldn't recall when exactly. It didn't help that his face was blurred together with the environment. Everything was fuzzy, no matter how many times she blinked. She couldn't even figure out how the room looked or if it was even a room.

"Do you want me to make it go away?" he repeated. She focused on him.

"For free?"

He chuckled.

"Of course not."

Ciara felt like throwing up. She put a hand in front of her mouth and leaned forward.

"Oh dear, I didn't know you'd react so strongly to that smell. If I didn't know better, I'd think you're not human," he mused. His voice moved closer. He squatted down near her, but kept enough distance so that he wouldn't be in the danger zone. Ciara breathed in deeply. The smell in the air made her want to gag.

"Or are you? Are witches humans?"

She jerked at that and turned to fully face him. Still, she couldn't make out his exact features. He had dark hair and a round face, but everything was blurry. Was this how Karen felt when she couldn't find her glasses? This was torture!

"Not in the mood to talk?" He reached a hand out to stroke her hair, and Ciara jerked her head away and scowled at nothing in particular. The man let his hand linger for a moment, before forcefully grabbing her hair and pulling it back. A shriek escaped Ciara's throat before she felt the bile rise in her throat. Throwing up would be a very bad idea, considering her position, so she fought with every ounce of her being to calm her stomach. Something wet rolled along her cheek and she realized she was crying. She didn't want to! Not in front of her torturer!

She could actually hear him smirk when he spoke again: "I can help you. You just need to say the word, and I'll make it all go away."

Like hell.

She managed to spit in his face in her anger, and he angrily dropped her to the floor. More disastrous smells and a worsening headache awaited her.

"I see you want to get right to business."

He dug his elbow into her back, and a sob tore from her at the helplessness she felt. After a moment of silence, he continued his monologue in a calm, chatty manner.

"See, when I brought you through, I thought you could make something useful. You know, magical objects or something, but then I realized I got the wrong witch."

Ciara had a hard time concentrating on his words. She tried to make sense what was happening around her.

"Who are you?" she croaked. "Why are you doing this?"

"Silence! I didn't say you can speak!" He put more weight on his elbow. Now the tears streamed down freely on Ciara's cheek as she cried out. She felt as if her lungs were being crushed. Surprisingly, the man eased up on her back. "As I was saying before I was so rudely interrupted, I got the wrong person. *But* you may be even more useful than her. I can adjust my plans, no worries. So, my question to you. What would you do for the chance to go back home?"

Ciara froze.

"I see I have your attention. *Now*, you may speak."

After a heartbeat of silence, Ciara spoke up. Her voice was but a whisper. "What do you want?"

"Nothing difficult, really. *Sing for me.*"

"What the—?" Ciara turned her head to try and look up at him. She was flabbergasted.

"Don't look at me like that. If you sing me a certain piece at the time and place of my choosing, I will make sure you get home safely."

"Are you serious?!" Ciara asked in disbelief. She couldn't hope—she wouldn't—but all this suffering for just one song?

"I am."

"What song are we talking about?" Her curiosity got the better of her. Going home was within reach, and all she had to do was to sing a song? It was unbelievably lucky!

A dark chuckle left his lips, which made her shiver with a bad feeling. There was a catch, she just felt it in her bones. However, silly as human nature was, she still held onto hope, on the slim chance that it could be that easy to solve all her problems.

"An aria."

"Which one?" Ciara closed her eyes. She suspected the worst.

"Queen of the Night."

32

"*N*o way in hell!" she cried.

"You don't want to go home?"

"I do, but not like that! I must never, ever—"

"And why is that, hm? A fable from childhood, perhaps?" The man leaned down and ran his fingers along her cheeks. His nails were long and sharp, like claws, but he was careful not to break skin. Not this time. "Just a little song, and you can fly home, my bird. Isn't that what you want?"

"I can't. Only very few people can sing the highest note in that aria."

"I know you're able to."

"No, I'm not," Ciara insisted. "And how the hell do you know about this piece when it hasn't even been written?"

"Ah, that hurt! I thought you'd remember me," he replied with a sad sigh. "I guess not. Anyway, do we have a deal?"

"Are you deaf?"

"I'm at the end of my patience, little witch." He raised his voice and dug his fingers into her back. "If you do not want to sing for me, then I have no use for you! Last chance!"

Ciara cried out in pain.

"Stop!" Her voice was stronger than she felt at that moment. She could feel the magic stirring her blood. But her captor held her firmly. "Let me go!"

"That won't work on me," he said, emitting a dark chuckle.

"What?" Ciara stopped struggling for a second. She rarely used her magic, but it had always worked before.

"Oh, you should see the look on your face!" the man said, mirth lacing his voice. He leaned so close Ciara could feel his breath on her face. He whispered into her ear as if he was sharing a grand secret with her. "The blood in my veins is much more powerful than your magic, little witch."

Ciara didn't understand the meaning of his words. What she did understand was that the Voice didn't work on him and she had to think of another way to get out of the sticky situation. She continued to struggle.

Her captor scoffed and gathered Ciara's hands at her back. He gripped her wrists in one hand.

"I'm getting tired of this," he sighed dramatically. "Maybe I should just kill you and kidnap that little blondie. What was her name? Kitty? Carol? Karen?"

Ciara tensed at the mention of her cousin.

"How do you—?" She struggled to get free, but his grip only tightened. She bit her lip to keep from crying out and tasted blood. "How would you know her?"

"How did you think you ended up in war-torn Japan? I thought you were smarter."

He started another monologue, but the pain in her shoulders wouldn't let Ciara concentrate on anything else other than how to get out of this position. She started chanting. It was nonsense, because she hardly remembered anything from her childhood studies, but he didn't have to know that. What mattered was that she had his attention. He leaned down to hear better. She murmured quietly and waited for him to get close enough.

She was momentarily taken aback as her sight cleared a little bit and she saw a slightly pointed ear in front of her. But she didn't let it distract her. Ciara took a deep breath and screamed in that ear with all her might, hitting all the high, painful notes.

Her captor fell back, gripping his ears, and cried out in pain. Ciara immediately used the opportunity to get to her feet and ran away from him. She took a few wobbly steps and looked around. She was in a big room where even the walls were made of wood. She wiped at her eyes, trying to get rid of the fuzziness, but she could only clear her vision for a couple of seconds before it blurred together again. However, it was enough for her to spot a staircase leading up to a door.

She stumbled over to the steps and gripped the railing. She could feel a gust of wind push against her back right before she was hauled to the other end of the room. She landed in a heap, with excruciating pain in her back. For a moment, she didn't even dare breathe, in fear she had broken something and would make the pain worse. But her instincts prevailed, and she sighed. Her breathing was harsh, and she heard loud footsteps before she was kicked in the side.

"Don't. Ever." He emphasized each word with a kick. "Do. That. Again."

Even coughing was painful when he was finished. She heard the metal hiss of a blade being unsheathed. Ciara closed her eyes and prayed for whatever gods listened to rescue her somehow. Her fingers twitched as she gathered her remaining energy and pushed off from the floor to roll away. The blade embedded into the wooden planks just where her head had been. She felt as if the entire universe was spinning, and she couldn't get her bearings.

Ciara kicked out blindly as she heard the man approach, and her feet connected with something. She used this moment to get on her knees. It was hard to manage with her balance off.

Another kick landed on her stomach, and this time, she couldn't fight the urge to throw up. It all happened too fast. She faintly heard the voice of disgust from her captor and shuffling as he moved away. She, too, wanted to get away. The smell was making her nauseous. Again. At least her head had stopped spinning and she could scramble away from that spot.

She grimaced as she looked down on her once nice kimono. Now torn and bloodied, it had spots of vomit over it. She dry-heaved at the sight, desperately trying to fight her instincts.

"Humans are disgusting," she heard the man say. She glanced up to see a somewhat familiar face framed by loosened black hair. But the eyes… these eyes were ruby red, as if a demon had risen from the depths of hell.

She didn't believe in hell or heaven, but the sight before her caused her to tremble. Tremors ran through her body and settled in her hands.

"Why are you doing this?" Ciara asked in a hoarse voice. She wiped the edge of her mouth with the back of her shaking hand. Why did he look so familiar? Where did she see him before?

"I'm just a man making a place for myself in this crazy world," he said.

"Have you ever thought of doing that in a less messed-up manner?" Ciara couldn't help but ask.

"Hn." He smirked at her. The red had seeped back to the

edge of his eyes before it disappeared. Now that he looked more *human*, Ciara noticed his clothing was worn, but he exuded the presence of a powerful person.

She blinked, and by the time she opened her eyes, he was only an inch away from her face. Ciara yelped, and he moved away with a grimace. She could've sworn she heard him muttering 'stinky human'.

"Then what are you?" she asked him instinctively. He was holding his nose as he glanced at her. Ciara was very aware of the blade in his other hand. "You speak as if you aren't human."

"I am not!" he roared as he once again moved close. This time, he put his free hand next to her head, effectively trapping her against the wall behind her. His eyes were once again red as he glared at her. Ciara held his gaze, more afraid of letting him out of her sight than because of having the courage.

"You tremble," he said and leaned closer. He buried his nose in the crook of her neck and took a deep breath. "You smell like fear. I like it." He made a curious sound. *Was he purring?*

It made Ciara want to run, but there was no escape. He leaned back, his irises still red. He brought the katana up to Ciara's neck.

"So you won't help me. You don't want to go home. You don't want to save the other witch," he summarized and, to emphasize his point, pushed the blade deeper into the tender flesh. Ciara felt a slight prickle in her neck. "Because you know, after I kill you here, I will go get her."

"You son of a—"

"Choose your next words very carefully, woman," he said.

Ciara opted for a knee-jerk, but he avoided her meager attempt to attack. As soon as she thought she had some leeway, he leaned his whole body on her. She couldn't move a muscle, and it was starting to get difficult to breathe. Ciara noticed blackness creeping in from the edge of her vision.

"Is your answer still no?"

Ciara couldn't believe him. Was he so dense? Or was it that he wanted something so desperately that, even in this situation, he'd rather use her, no matter how small a chance for her cooperation. At that moment, the sounds of a fight came from above. They both looked toward the door at the top of the stairs.

Ciara felt her heart hammer in her chest. Whoever that was, they could probably help her. She gathered all her remaining energy and screamed for help at the top of her lungs.

Her captor stumbled away, gripping his ears. He even dropped his katana. Ciara's legs gave way, and she slid down on the wall. She put a hand on her throat. It came away with blood on her fingertips.

"Shit."

33

*C*iara's scent gradually became stronger as Katsuo set off after her. He let go of the restriction he usually put on his senses, not caring if someone saw his true nature. Ciara was in danger, and he had to protect her. That was all he knew.

He made his way to the darker side of town, mildly surprised as he hurried through narrow alleys and dodged bumping into suspicious people. He took care to pursue criminals and not to let his castle town be a meeting point for them, but it seemed darkness had a way of creeping into the happiest of places. Katsuo made a mental note to come back to this part of town and remedy the situation as soon as possible.

But first he had to find Ciara. Her spicy vanilla scent got stronger and stronger and led him into a brothel. Another thing he had to evaluate later. He barged in without knocking, and the woman in the foyer shrieked at his entrance.

"What happened, girls?" A middle-aged woman walked in through a side-door to investigate the situation. She was graceful and looked beautiful with all that makeup. Katsuo glared at her and she looked taken aback at the sight of him. She nervously whipped her fan open. "What brings you here, Milord? Would you like some of the girls to accompany you for tea?"

"I'm looking for someone, Madame."

"We've plenty of girls, take your pick."

"A particular someone. She was kidnapped," he clarified.

"Oh, we don't do that here! Everyone is here on their own terms, right, girls?" She looked around, wetting her lips nervously.

"Have you seen a foreigner around here?"

"A foreigner?" The Madame's eyes bugged out of her head. "What a particular taste in women, if I may say so!"

Katsuo closed his eyes for a moment and focused on the sounds. Ciara's scent was all over the place, mingled with incense and smoke twirling about the place. It was difficult to pinpoint the direction of the source.

He heard a scuffle upstairs and almost headed there when he realized it wasn't the sounds of struggle. He felt a headache coming. He hated brothels; all the scents and sounds made him feel sick.

"Are you all right, Milord?" A brave girl, no older than sixteen, had moved close and put a gentle hand on his arm. He grabbed her and twirled her in front of him. She looked frightened by the sudden action.

"Have you seen something suspicious before I arrived here?"

She shook her head violently.

"Anyone?" He turned around, looking at the girls one by one. They couldn't stand his gaze.

"Actually…" someone spoke up and he looked toward the girl. She was a little older than the others and even though she looked intimidated by his presence, she squared her shoulders and held his gaze when he looked at her.

"What did you see?" Katsuo let go of the other girl and approached this one. She looked to be around the same age as Yura.

"I was out back on my break," she started. "And I saw a couple of men dragging an unconscious woman toward the cellars."

"Where?"

"The backyard," she pointed to the end of the corridor. "They were armed, and they had a leader. He was strange."

Katsuo was just about to start heading down on the corridor, but he glanced back at her at this.

"Strange how?" he asked, puzzled.

"He had a weird aura around him."

"Hush, stupid girl!" the Madame chided her. "I warned you not to talk nonsense here!"

"I'm sorry, but it's true," she looked down, her cheeks red. She risked a glance at Katsuo. "Milord, he was the most dangerous out of all of them. He had a certain darkness surrounding him. You must believe me!"

"Enough of this! I'm sorry, Milord, she doesn't know what she's talking about." The Madame nudged the girl. "Stop this nonsense now and apologize!"

"Thank you," Katsuo told the girl, ignoring the other woman and hurried down the corridor.

"Wait, Milord!" The Madame tried to stop him in vain. The girl was right. As soon as he opened the door to the backyard, Ciara's scent grew stronger.

There was a makeshift shed in the courtyard. It was the only thing that looked to be leading somewhere. As he walked closer, Katsuo unsheathed his katana, stopped right outside the wooden door, and pricked his ears. He could hear men inside laughing and telling dirty jokes.

Not wasting more time, he kicked the door in. All three shot up from their seats on the barrels and drew their swords.

"You must be insane to try to take on the three of us!" One of them taunted, making the others laugh.

Katsuo smirked.

"Try me."

A few minutes later, all three were sprawled on the floor, moaning in pain.

"My daughter can fight better than you lot," he said, not impressed with them. He didn't even break a sweat.

"Oh, can she do this, too?"

Katsuo turned just in time to block the attack coming from behind. Clearly, these people had no idea who they were dealing with. Unfortunately, his attacker managed to make him drop his weapon and didn't leave him a chance to recover it.

He had to continue the fight barehanded. His new opponent was a better warrior and had probably had formal training as a soldier. He didn't prove to be much of a challenge to Katsuo, however. Suddenly, he heard a scream from beneath and was reminded of the danger Ciara was in.

This split moment was enough for his opponent to injure him. Katsuo jumped back and held up his right arm. The sleeve of his kimono was torn and a deep gash marred his forearm. Blood dripped steadily from the wound.

He saw red.

Instinctively, he grabbed his injured arm. His opponent charged, blade drawn, and Katsuo swiped at him with a blood-coated left hand. He felt a strange wind, then his opponent screamed as he was thrown back against the wall. He had claw marks over his face and body.

Katsuo looked down at his hand. His fingernails had lengthened into claws, and he flexed them. He knew they could do damage, but this was new, even to him. Was it a technique inherent in his family? He had to use the rare chance that Yuki was here and ask her—

Another scream tore through his musings, reminding him of his mission. He picked up his sword and turned around, facing the door leading downstairs, then kicked it in without hesitation.

*C*iara's scent filled the empty cellar below. It mingled with something nauseating, and it took only a fraction of a moment for Katsuo's heightened senses to understand the situation. Ciara was huddled at the bottom of a wall, and the scent of her blood was lingering in the air, quickly overpowering his senses.

The person who stood a few feet away from her turned around at the sound of the door breaking down. Katsuo froze in shock for a moment as recognition flickered in his eyes.

"Juro?" he asked, barely audible. "Is that really you, Juro?"

The man sent him a smirk.

"You always knew how to make an entrance," he said and hurled a small pouch at his feet. Smoke rose quickly in the closed space, covering the floor within seconds. Even though Katsuo was standing halfway down the stairs, above the cloud of smoke, he couldn't see a thing. However, he could hear Ciara coughing violently on the other side of the room.

He quickly dove into the gray cloud in search of Ciara, relying on his ears to find her. Meanwhile, he kept in mind that Juro was still around, hiding somewhere behind the smokescreen.

Katsuo heard a swish and instinctively ducked. The blade had just narrowly missed his head. It had managed to cut his manbun in half, making his hair cascade around his face. Ciara coughed somewhere in front of him, urging him to reach her. A growl escaped him.

Frustrated, he blindly swung his katana in the direction the attack had come from. His blade connected with another, and a metallic clang echoed, dispersing the smoky cloud a little bit. Katsuo twisted his sword to disarm his opponent; however, he didn't succeed.

"Are you sure you want to risk impaling your lovely bride?" a mocking, bodiless voice asked him. Katsuo threw the katana at his enemy, surprising him.

An angry hiss answered his attempt at slaying him, but it bought him enough time to put some distance between them and reach Ciara. Her coughing had weakened considerably, which did not bode well for her condition.

Katsuo heard a squelching sound under his boots but ignored it. He could hear hurrying footsteps going upstairs, but it was more important to save Ciara than to chase after that traitor. She was more important.

He stumbled, but thankfully, the wall stopped him. A painful moan sounded from near his feet.

"Ciara!" He squatted down immediately, feeling around blindly. The smoke had barely cleared. He could just about make out the silhouette of her form.

She coughed. "Katsuo?" Her voice was hoarse and weak.

"I'm here." He reached out to hold her up. Her arms immediately went around his shoulders, and she buried her face in the nook of his neck. She coughed a little bit. "Come on," he said and gathered her in his arms, ignoring his injury.

He barely registered her weight as he carried her toward the stairs with confident steps. The enemy had already fled, and he was able to see a bit more with every passing second. He could make out the shape of the stairs and quickly climbed them, taking three steps at a time.

As soon as they made it outside, they both sighed in relief. Ciara leaned back and looked at him.

"Thank you."

"You're not out of danger yet," Katsuo said, concern lacing his voice.

Ciara focused on his face. Was it a trick of the setting sunlight or were his eyes of the same gold color as Lady Yuki's?

"Have your eyes always been this color?" she asked, mesmerized. She closed her eyes.

"Ciara, stay with me!" Katsuo shouted as she went limp in his arms.

He spied a gate at the back of the courtyard and hurried over, firmly holding onto Ciara's unconscious form. A restless energy bubbled within him as he navigated through the darkened streets. Night had just fallen, and he was grateful for the darkness. Gathering all his strength, he jumped high in the air. He landed on top of a hut. Momentum made him skip over to another rooftop, then another, until he had reached the last building in town. He climbed the way up to the castle hill in the same manner.

Time was of essence if he were to save Ciara. He was acutely aware of her fading pulse and the despair spreading in his stomach. He reached the castle in record time.

"Halt! Who goes there?!" his soldiers at the gates asked.

"Get a healer!" he yelled, and they recognized his voice right away.

"Aye, sir!" One of them turned to go but was interrupted by a new voice.

"No need. He is already here," Taiki said as he stepped out of the shadows. "He is waiting for you in the conference room."

Without saying another word, Katsuo headed in that direction.

"Would you like me assist you, my lord?"

"No need."

Katsuo didn't even chide him for using his title instead of his name. He couldn't care for anything else at that moment but Ciara's safety.

Ciara struggled to open her heavy eyelids. When she managed to do it, all she saw was a ceiling. She blinked a couple of times, and it got easier to keep her eyes open. It was difficult to breathe, though. Every breath she took required effort. Her limbs ached, but at least her hands didn't tremble. She sighed, and a coughing fit racked her body.

"Careful. Drink this," a woman's soothing voice said as someone held her head up. Suddenly, there was a cup at her mouth, and she sipped at the liquid. Ciara grimaced at the bitter taste.

"Yuck."

The woman chuckled, and Ciara glanced up to see Yuki.

"The healer said you needed to drink it when you woke up."

"All of it?" Ciara could hear the disgust in her quiet

voice. All she could manage was a hoarse whisper, and even that took all her energy.

"Yes, to the last drop!"

Ciara forced herself to gulp down the bitter potion, hoping it would make her better. Yuki carefully put Ciara's head down back on the pillow.

"How long was I out?" Ciara asked.

"A few hours. You'll be fine."

"I don't feel fine," she whispered, putting a hand to her throat. She could feel it was wrapped in a smooth piece of cloth. "Will my voice come back?"

There was a heartbeat of silence before Yuki responded:

"It'll take some time, but it'll heal. Don't worry, it's just a scratch."

Ciara breathed in deeply. A single tear ran down her cheek. She already had to give up on her wishes to play the piano. All she had left was her voice. The Voice.

The fact that she'd recover it eventually was great relief. She closed her eyes, relaxing her body.

"How is he?"

"Katsuo? He'll be fine too. Nothing a good rest can't heal."

Ciara opened one eye to peek at Yuki. She seemed sincere.

"Good," Ciara said curtly and closed her eyes before adding: "Thank you for taking care of me. I appreciate it."

"You have nothing to worry about," Yuki replied. "Now sleep. You need to build up your energy."

35

*T*he next time Ciara opened her eyes, Yuki was nowhere to be found. She stood up, stumbled a bit, but caught herself on a column. She eyed it suspiciously. She didn't remember her room having one. But the need to go relieve herself was too great to be taken aback by such miniscule details.

She padded to the door and slid it open, looking both ways of the corridor, then up to see the symbols. She was on the corridor with small green flowers. At least it was close to her room, allowing her to find her destination easily. After taking care of her business, Ciara padded back to the room. Her back ached, and she felt exhausted from the short trip. Slowly and surely, she made her way back.

After she slid the door closed, she waddled into the room, straight to her bedding, and settled down. She pulled on the cover and cocooned herself in. A moment later, it was ripped from her, leaving her exposed to the cool, early morning air.

"Hey!" she wanted to yell, but her voice croaked. She turned around, confused and hurt, and saw Katsuo, but her mind couldn't fully process the situation. She poked him. "That's my cover."

"No, it's not. Yours is over there." He was half-asleep but pointed a finger to the side. Ciara followed his lead and realized there was another bedding a few feet away from the one she was lying in.

"Oh."

A moment of silence passed.

"Aren't you going to get in?"

She quickly measured it would take way too much effort in her state to crawl to her own bedding.

"Too far."

"What?"

"It's too far. I'm tired." She knew she was whining, but she really was exhausted, and everything hurt. She sniffled.

Katsuo shuffled behind her. "Are you crying?"

"No."

"You are."

"No!"

She certainly felt like crying. Ciara just wanted to lie down, cocoon up, and sleep away all her worries. But her goal seemed to be at an unreachable distance. She picked at the bedding, frustrated.

"Or you can sleep here."

She froze. "And where will you sleep?"

"Here."

"No."

"I'm too tired to move."

"You took my cover."

"Excuse you. Firstly, it was mine," Katsuo said. "Secondly, that was the last of my energy."

"So there would be nothing stopping me from taking your cover now?"

"If my lady wishes to leave me to the harsh cold, then no."

To her surprise, a chuckle escaped her lips. It sounded like a crackle, so she quickly stopped, but her smile lingered. Her head felt heavy. It would be much easier to just stay where she was.

"Okay," Ciara said and pulled up the edge of the cover.

"Ooooh, so cold," Katsuo mumbled, but true to his words, he didn't struggle for the authority over the cover. To his surprise, Ciara lay down next to him and snuggled to his side.

Katsuo opened his eyes.

"Am I still sleeping?" he asked.

Ciara chuckled, peeking at him.

"No, but the other bedding is way too far. I'm afraid you'll have to share."

"I don't mind, but don't you?"

"You can barely open your eyes. Sleep."

"Yes, my lady."

He carefully arranged the blanket so they'd be fully covered. Soon, they drifted off.

Ciara woke up to her own scream. She sat up, panting heavily. Her throat hurt, and she was shaking like a leaf in the harsh wind. She put her head in her hands.

"What happened?" Katsuo asked from next to her. He sat up, too. She looked at him to answer, but her gaze was caught by the item in his hand.

"Is that a *dagger*? Where the hell did it come from?" Ciara was flabbergasted. She acknowledged in the back of her mind that at least her normal speaking voice was back.

"I have my reasons," Katsuo avoided the question.

Ciara quirked an eyebrow.

"Did you have a nightmare?" he asked, changing the subject.

"Yes. Am I still dreaming?"

"No," he put a hand on her shoulder, but as much as she longed for reassurance, she shrugged it off and leaned away.

"Put that thing away!"

Katsuo promptly put the dagger back under the pillow. Ciara shook her head in disbelief then pulled up the cover. Adrenaline was still coursing through her veins, giving her a boost of energy.

"Where are you going?"

"Away from pointy items," she replied without missing a beat.

"Come back," Katsuo said. He managed to get hold of the hem of Ciara's yukata. She was sitting just on the edge of the bedding. She glanced back at him.

"I'm not going back there. I can't sleep with a dagger near me."

"Why?"

"Why? He asks me why… Unbelievable." Ciara muttered, shaking her head. She hid her face behind her hands for a moment before taking a deep breath and steeling herself.

She let her hands down and looked Katsuo straight in the eye.

"Because I can't, that's why!" She tried to move away, but her yukata was caught in Katsuo's firm grip. "Let go of my clothes!"

"Come back." His voice was soft, catching her off guard. Ciara looked into Katsuo's eyes, not understanding the emotion she saw in them. Eventually, she crossed her arms.

"It's the dagger or me."

Katsuo gaped, and Ciara tapped her fingers in the nook of her arm impatiently. He let go of the hem of her yukata. Hurt glinted in Ciara's eyes for a moment before she turned away.

She was half-standing when she heard a thud. Ciara twirled around to see Katsuo looking in the far corner. She followed his gaze to see the dagger embedded in the floor. Now it was her turn to gape.

"I'm not letting you out of my sight again," he said, leaning over and tugging her closer.

"Was that the only one?" Ciara squatted down, not even waiting for a reply.

"Yes."

She looked underneath the pillow then the sheets but couldn't find another weapon.

"Are you satisfied, my lady?"

Ciara huffed and sat down on the edge of the bedding. The adrenaline rush was beginning to wear off. Her limbs became heavy.

"Has anyone ever told you you're a bit possessive? Maybe a little too much?"

"One of my many virtues." He smirked.

"I wouldn't categorize it as such."

Interested, Katsuo moved closer and touched Ciara's face. He looked her in the eye.

"Does it bother you?" His voice was neutral, and Ciara couldn't read his expression.

She shrugged. "As long as you don't want to put me in a tower room for the rest of my life and throw away the keys, I guess it's fine."

"Good idea. Why didn't I think of it?" he mumbled to himself as he rubbed his jaw.

Ciara swatted his shoulder, and he fell back on the bedding. He opened his arms.

"Come here."

"Do you swear you don't have more weapons in the bed?"

"Where would I put them?"

Ciara lifted an eyebrow.

"I swear there's no pointy items here."

She waited a heartbeat before nodding and moving closer to him. "Good."

With that, she crawled back underneath the covers and into his arms.

36

*A*s sunlight filtered through the shutters, the room became gradually brighter. Katsuo usually rose before the sun to do his morning exercises, but today was different. Maybe because he was recovering. Maybe because of the beautiful woman sleeping in his arms.

He took a deep breath, smelling the spicy vanilla scent enveloping Ciara. She fit in his arms perfectly, and he sighed in content. He could hardly remember the last time he felt so at peace.

Regardless, duties awaited him, and he had to get up. Katsuo carefully moved away, but Ciara stirred. She opened her eyes, and time seemed to stop for a long moment as he stared into her purple gaze. As soon as she recognized him, she smiled.

"Good morning."

"Good morning to you, too," he replied in a trance. "Have you slept well?"

"Very well, thanks. You?"

"Yes."

She looked at him for a moment longer before she

glanced away. Her gaze landed on his arm as he leant above her. Ciara narrowed her eyes and gently stroked his forearm. Angry red lines lingered where he was cut. Her light touch sent a spark through Katsuo's nerves.

"You got injured protecting me," Ciara observed, her expression sad.

"It's not your fault. I'd happily do that again. If only I had arrived there earlier…"

She chuckled, looking up at him with a grin.

"What is it?" Katsuo asked, curious at her reaction.

"You know what they say about heroes?"

He shook his head.

"They always arrive at the right time. Not a minute earlier than necessary," Ciara finished.

"What does this mean?" Katsuo leant closer.

"You're officially my hero."

"Hmm…" He mulled it over. "It does have a nice ring to it."

"I'm sorry you were injured. Even your hair is shorter," she frowned, playing with a lock of his dark hair between her fingers. She sounded sad. "Your manbun is gone."

"I told you not to worry," Katsuo repeated and leant down for a brief kiss. They both froze as he drew back. Ciara blinked at him in surprise, and even he seemed shocked at his own reaction.

He cleared his throat and got up. "I'll see you at breakfast?"

"Yes," Ciara replied curtly and sat up. She looked around, unsure for a moment, before she got up.

"See you in a bit," she told him as she exited the room.

Katsuo nodded and went to the corner to wash his face in the basin. The cold water did nothing to clear his thoughts. He mechanically went through his morning routine while his mind raced. Something had changed between them, but what did it mean?

Ciara tiptoed back to her room in a hurry. Fortunately, it was only a short trip from Katsuo's room and she had walked this route many times.

As soon as she slid her door open, she was greeted by Yura.

"Milady!"

"Ciara," she corrected on instinct, shut the door, and walked in confidently as if nothing happened. Nothing happened, anyway, not *really*.

The knowing smile on Yura's face did nothing to calm her nerves. Ciara went to wash her face in the basin.

"Did you rest well, Ciara-sama?"

Yura's question reminded her of how safe she'd felt lying in Katsuo's arms. Then the kiss—

She quickly splashed another handful of cold water over her face before replying, "Yes, thank you. You?"

"Did you…" Yura stood up and hurried over to her. She handed a towel to Ciara, and as she dried off her face, Yura whispered, "Did you spent the night with Milord?"

"Yura!" Ciara gasped. She didn't expect that question from the servant girl. Yura paled at the reaction and immediately bowed.

"I'm sorry, I didn't mean to—"

"It's… fine," Ciara replied and tossed the towel away. "I was just surprised. Yes, I was there."

Yura looked up with a smile.

"I'm so happy for you, Ciara-sama!"

"Really? Why is that?"

"You and Milord Katsuo make such a nice couple, if I may say so."

"Erm…"

Ciara was torn. Yura misread the situation, but she couldn't really tell her the truth since the girl was under the impression the engagement was real. She opted for keeping silent and went over to the closet.

"Let me help you with choosing today's kimono, Milady. I think the midnight blue would fit you well."

Ciara let Yura help her prepare for the day. As she looked into the small handheld mirror, she discovered bruises covered her face. The wrapping around her throat was ragged and soiled with spots of blood.

Yura cleaned the wound, and while she was retrieving new strips of cloths to cover it, Ciara looked at the mirror with judging eyes. The injury on her neck was still visible, but it had already closed. Fortunately, that man didn't manage to make a deep wound. She shuddered inside as flames of rage engulfed her for a moment. Her passion had been playing the piano and that ability was taken away. Was that not enough? Now her Voice was put in jeopardy.

"Are you feeling all right, Ciara-sama?" Yura tentatively asked, coming closer. She set the clean strip of cloths down on a pillow.

Ciara looked at her, pondering.

"I'll be fine, Yura. Everything will be fine."

Katsuo knocked on Ciara's doorframe.

"Enter!"

He slid the shoji open and found Ciara sitting at a low table, looking at herself in the mirror. Yura was behind her, doing the finishing touches on Ciara's hair. For a terrible moment, Katsuo felt as if he was sent back in time, as if he was looking at his late wife just before they wed. Kikyō had often spent time on her appearance. It took up way too much of her time.

"Thanks, Yura."

Ciara's voice drew him back from his memories. He blinked to take in the scene before him. Ciara smiled up at the servant girl.

"You've done a wonderful job. I don't think the bruises are visible. What do you think, Katsuo?" She turned to him.

Katsuo's gaze landed on the silk scarf covering Ciara's throat, and he looked at her face. He could see some bruises forming, but his eyes were better than most men's. Ciara's face fell, and she looked into the mirror with a frown. He was immediately reminded it was not Kikyō sitting before him but a different person.

"You look beautiful," he said, and Ciara's breath caught. She looked at him, surprised to hear those words. Yura quietly withdrew to the background and left the room.

"Thank you," Ciara said, breathless. Her gaze traveled down to his feet and back up, finally settling on his face. "You clean up well, too."

Katsuo chuckled. Yes, Ciara was definitely a different woman.

"Shall we?" He held out his hand to help her stand. Ciara took it but winced as she stood. Katsuo was immediately concerned. "Are you feeling all right?"

Ciara let a small, bitter smile slip.

"It'll be fine. Just a little sore from all those kicks to my stomach."

"Do you want to—"

She cut him off before he could suggest she stayed in her room.

"I'm fine. As a woman, I'm used to dealing with the occasional pain."

Ciara squeezed his hand to let him know it was all right. She smiled up at him and opened her mouth to say something, but her stomach chose that moment to make her hunger obvious. Instantly, her face flamed.

"Let's go." Katsuo suppressed a chuckle and led Ciara to the conference room.

37

This time, Ciara entered through the door at the back of the room, at Katsuo's side. Yuki was on his other arm, and he led both women to the aisle. All three of them were seated there. The layout of the rest of the room was basically the same as how it was on the day Ciara arrived. Except Takeru's place, which was occupied by Orihime.

Katsuo's gaze found the woman, too. He frowned but otherwise didn't comment on it. However, this didn't escape Yuki's attention.

"I invited her," she whispered, hardly audible. Katsuo looked at her in disbelief. "You need to keep up appearances, my boy. Her father is a powerful ally."

"Please don't encourage her," Katsuo asked before he turned to address his vassals.

"Itadakimasu!"

His men echoed his words, and everyone started eating. Ciara reached for her chopsticks with a smile.

"Itadakimasu," she said, amused.

"What is it?" Katsuo glanced at her, curious.

"It was a bit abrupt."

"Abrupt?"

"Yes! I thought you'd say a short speech or something."

"About what?" Katsuo asked.

"I don't know," Ciara replied. "It's nothing. I was just surprised, I guess."

"You guess…"

"Katsu… eat," Yuki murmured from his other side.

Katsuo looked up to see people were yet to touch their food, and everybody looked at him. He started to eat, and the whole room became animated as everybody followed his lead.

"This is definitely not my favorite part of being a daimyō."

"What is?" Ciara asked between two bites.

Katsuo opened his mouth to reply then closed it. For a moment, he looked as if he was caught off guard.

"You don't know?" Ciara blinked at him in surprise.

"I know I don't like paperwork. But what my favorite part is about being a daimyō has never crossed my mind."

"Well, do let me know when you've found your answer."

"You ask the most curious questions, Ciara," Yuki said, overhearing the conversation. "But I'm interested, myself. You'll tell me next time I visit, yes?"

"Are you leaving already?" Katsuo blurted out.

Yuki looked at him calmly. "Why are you so surprised? You know I never linger in one place for long. I'm just waiting for Takeru to get back."

"I see. It was good to see you."

"I'm still here."

"I know, Gra-Yuki."

Katsuo had to catch up on the dreaded paperwork for the rest of the day while Ciara recovered. She managed to have an unpleasant run-in with Orihime after lunch. The woman was gloating over the fact that she had been invited to breakfast by Lady Yuki that morning.

"At first glance, she seems strict, but she's actually very kind once she gets to know you and takes a liking to you," she was explaining excitedly. Ciara wasn't sure if the monologue was directed at her or Orihime's own entourage. She continued, sending a condescending look at Ciara. "Of course, you wouldn't know."

"That's true. I've never noticed she was strict," Ciara replied.

"Hmph!" Orihime snapped her fan shut with a clang. The sound was eerily loud. "At least I know who she is! Come on, let's get out of here. I need some fresh air, free of annoying insects."

She marched away, her entourage in tow. Ciara looked after her, shocked at the elementary-school level insult. She snorted in amusement and shook her head, pushing away the unpleasant memory. In spite of this, a tiny voice piped up, demanding to know what Orihime knew about Yuki. Why was she better informed than Ciara?

Funnily enough, she saw Yuki not long after the strange exchange with Orihime. Ciara was taking a stroll in the courtyard after lunch, and Yuki was heading down the path leading to the pagoda.

"Yuki!" Ciara shouted. Her voice sounded loud in her ears, and both the guard and Yuki turned toward her. Oops.

She hurried over to Yuki.

"Sorry, I didn't mean to be so loud."

Yuki had a kind smile on her face, but it didn't reach her eyes. It was off-putting for Ciara.

"Did you need something from me?" she asked.

"No, I was just happy to see you," Ciara replied. "I wanted to thank you for taking care of me when we got back from…" She drifted off, looking to the side.

"You already did," Yuki said and put a hand on Ciara's shoulder. "Come, let's talk." With that, she steered her toward the pagoda.

"B-but—"

"You look like you have plenty on your mind."

"But the pagoda. We can't—I mean, I can't go there."

"It's all right," Yuki chuckled. "You're with me."

"Are you sure it's okay?" Ciara asked, suspicious.

Yuki nodded. "Don't worry about it."

They walked down the path, passing the guard who offered a bow but didn't question them. Ciara let out a small sigh of relief and followed Yuki happily. She liked the pagoda and didn't have the chance to have a proper look the last time she had been there. Sneaking around didn't make for a great sightseeing program.

Yuki caught her staring at the building.

"This pagoda had been here for generations. It was built before the castle."

"Really?" Ciara gasped. "That's awesome!"

Yuki smiled, ignoring the strange word, and continued. "It is dedicated to Benten, also known as Benzaiten. Have you heard of her?"

"I heard she is a guardian of some sort?" Ciara sounded uncertain.

"She is a goddess, associated with many things, including the arts, music, water, beauty, and so on," Yuki explained. "And she is the guardian of my family. She rides a great white dragon."

Ciara mildly wondered if it was a Western or Eastern dragon then realized she was in Japan, so Yuki was probably talking about the slender Easter dragon with a long body.

"Ever seen a white snake?"

"Oh, yes, more than I ever wanted to! Ever since I've arrived here, they pop up left and right!" Ciara knew she was exaggerating. But only a little bit.

"Interesting," Yuki's eyebrows rose before she continued. "White snakes are often associated with her. You see, under special circumstances, a snake can evolve and transform into a dragon."

Yep, she was definitely talking about an Eastern dragon.

"So what does this all mean?"

"Oh," Yuki blinked, as if waking up. "Sorry, I got a little carried away! My family history is intertwined with Benten's presence, you see. Anyway, what did you want to talk about?"

Yuki picked a spot under a tree and sat down, patting the grass next to her. With a bit of difficulty, Ciara followed her lead. She sighed as she sat down.

"Are you in pain?"

"My muscles are a bit tender, but they're getting better," Ciara confessed then turned to face Yuki. "What do you mean what I wanted to talk about? You said to come talk."

"Well, you looked like you want to talk. Sometimes a listening ear is all we need." Yuki said, before gently prodding: "What's on your mind?"

"Hmm… well…" Ciara tapped a finger to her chin. Should she tell Yuki? She was a cousin of Katsuo, possibly older by the way she talked and behaved. Maybe someone with her insight could help her.

Yuki was waiting patiently for Ciara to gather her thoughts and talk.

"I keep having these nightmares," she blurted out in the

end. She felt silly. After all, she was an adult. She could handle a nightmare or two. She took a deep breath before continuing. "They are getting worse. And they feel so... *real.*"

"Do you want to tell me what they are about?" Yuki asked gently. All her attention was on Ciara. She didn't laugh or mock her, instead, she was understanding.

"I only remember flashes. I keep trying to get home. At first, it is just me, and a shadow chases me. It keeps getting closer, and I *know* that something terrible will happen if it catches me. And recently, Karen appears, too."

"Who is Karen?"

"My cousin. She is a few years younger than me," Ciara explained. "She lived with me while she attended... school. Anyway, I finally reach her, then the shadow splits and chases us both. We keep getting separated and trapped in a dark place, looking for each other and for a way home."

"Do you ever find the way home?"

Ciara shook her head.

"Lately, I end up at a cliff, alone. Then the shadow monster appears. It takes on the shape of a person, but I can't see their features. It keeps getting closer, until—" Ciara voice hitched.

"You fall off the cliff," Yuki finished for her. Ciara nodded and shivered at the memory.

"It all feels too real not to be true. Like a bad omen."

Yuki hugged her.

"I know it seems scary, but... don't forget you have Katsuo."

Ciara glanced up at her, question in her eyes.

"Really?"

"Of course. You're his bride. He'll protect you. Whatever may come, you can count on him," Yuki promised.

"And if it turns out it's nothing more than just a nightmare, all the better."

"Thanks, Yuki."

"You are welcome," she replied, squeezing Ciara.

Ciara closed her eyes and sighed. She felt as if she was brought back in time when she was a child; feeling safe and protected in her mother's embrace. She let the illusion wash over her as she hugged Yuki back.

The other woman didn't know that the engagement was fake. Even though, Ciara desperately wanted to believe Yuki's words about Katsuo.

ocus, Katsuo, focus! he silently reprimanded himself when he read the same paragraph for the fifth time and still couldn't comprehend it. His thoughts weren't there. His kokoro[1] was in a turmoil.

He was reading the reports on his fiefdom's income, listed by products, when suddenly, he remembered Ciara's limp body in his arms as life faded from her. Her face pale, her neck bleeding as he sprinted through town to reach the castle.

Katsuo cried out in frustration and threw the paper down. He picked up another. This time, he reached the koku[2] taxes when his mind showed him the image of Ciara lying in his arms. She was alive and healing, sleeping peacefully next to him. Then they kissed.

"Damnit!" He threw the papers at the door just as a knock sounded.

"Who is it?"

"It's me, brother." There was a moment of silence as Takeru thought through his options. "Is this a bad time?"

"Come on in," Katsuo said. He had a feeling that there wouldn't be a better time that day anyway.

Takeru slid the door open and stared at the stack of papers scattered at his feet.

"What's this? Are you all right, brother?" He squatted down to gather the documents and closed the door behind him. "Katsuo?"

"What is it?"

"I've asked if you're feeling all right," Takeru repeated as he sat down in front of him.

"I just can't concentrate today," he admitted. "Tell me you have news."

"Actually—"

"Oh, you've just got back from the border! How is everything? Are you unharmed?"

Amusement danced in Takeru's eyes.

"Nice of you to notice. I'm back, yes," he chuckled. "You really are distracted. May I ask what happened while I was away?"

"Well... Ciara got kidnapped, and she was almost killed."

Takeru's eyes got as big as lanterns at the unexpected news.

"Is she all right?"

"Yes, she is, considering. She's healing fast."

Takeru sighed in relief. "Thank Benten! I was worried. Did you save her?"

Katsuo nodded.

"So what's the matter?" Takeru focused on his brother's face. He frowned. "What happened to your hair?"

"That was the price I paid for saving her."

Takeru couldn't help a smile.

"There's not a lot of someones I'd cut my hair for. I'm proud of you, brother."

A growl of frustration escaped Katsuo's lips.

"What got you so riled up? You killed the bastards and saved her, right? That's what matters."

"You have the uncanny ability to find the sore spots, do you know that?" Katsuo asked, narrowing his eyes at his little brother.

"What?" Takeru was lost. "Please elaborate, because I don't understand."

"The culprit got away."

"What? How?"

"I got his underlings. I think Taiki collected them afterward. We'll see if we'll get anything useful out of them. But I let their leader escape."

"Why?"

"Ciara was on the brink of death," he replied. "She was more important at that moment."

A small smile appeared in the corner of Takeru's mouth. He looked as if he knew something his brother didn't, and this bothered Katsuo to no end.

"Say what you want, little brother."

"Let me see if I understand correctly. You let a dangerous criminal escape to save Ciara's life?"

Katsuo nodded.

"Then let me ask you this. Why did you decide to do so? Why is Ciara's life more important to you?"

"I—" Katsuo fell silent as he thought about it. He remembered the gripping fear when it seemed Ciara might not make it and would possibly die in his arms. He recalled the tension when the healer patched her up and said she'd live *if* she woke in the next few hours.

He remembered the relief when Yuki told her Ciara had indeed woken up during the night and seemed better. He fell asleep looking at her resting in the bedding across from his. Then he recalled when he heard her sweet voice when she accidentally mixed up the futons and wrestled for his cover. His heart squeezed when she woke up screaming in the early morning hours. He was prepared to slay anything, anyone that was hurting her. He even got rid of the dagger underneath his pillow for the first time in a decade.

And the peaceful feeling in the morning when he woke up with her resting in his arms, that was something he would cherish forever.

"So?" Takeru prodded, shaking him out of his reverie. Katsuo looked at his brother, baffled.

"I think I like her."

Takeru laughed out loud at that.

"You *think* you *like* her?" he echoed. "This is more than that and you know it, brother. Go for it."

"What?"

"I haven't seen you like this since… ever. Not even when you were last engaged," Takeru said carefully.

"This is only a fake betrothal," Katsuo reminded him.

"But do you want it to be?"

———

Ciara was used to breakfasts with Katsuo's most important vassals in the conference room, and she expected the dinner that night would be similar. But this was different. A feast had been prepared for Takeru's safe return from the borders, and Ciara suspected everybody from the castle had showed up. It was messy and loud, and plenty of sake was spilled as the night went on and more people got drunk.

She sat at the dais, in her usual spot on Katsuo's right. Takeru was on his other side, followed by Yuki who was content to let the spotlight shine on Takeru tonight. There was plenty of food, and Katsuo even urged the servants to join them in the celebrations, which they did but dutifully made sure everyone had what they wanted, whether it be food or sake.

The later the night, the louder the bunch of samurai. Some walked up to the dais and chatted with their lord, while others tried to sweet-talk Lady Yuki, who was amused at the situation but wouldn't give her attention to anyone for long.

After their bellies were full, some samurai drew Takeru away from the dais and insisted he drank with them. Poor boy had been lost in the sea of people, and Ciara looked after him with worry.

"Shouldn't you stop them?" she whispered to Katsuo when there was a brief break between his vassals coming up to him. He leaned to the side, closer to Ciara.

"It's all right."

"But he's just a boy. How old is he? Eighteen? I'm not sure he should be drinking this much alcohol…"

"He's already over twenty and has seen many battles. He can hold his sake," Katsuo said proudly.

"Hmm…" Ciara quietly sipped her own drink. It tasted sweet, and she was sure it was made from a fruit. She quickly got distracted trying to figure out the ingredients. She sniffed at the golden liquid.

"What are you trying to do?" Katsuo's amused voice reached her ears. She looked at him with a most serious expression on her face.

"I'm trying to determine what drink this is."

"Let me…" Katsuo leaned toward her to take a closer look. Ciara froze for a moment as she was suddenly reminded of this morning when he unexpectedly kissed her. Her cheeks colored at the memory, but she was sure it was partly because of the alcohol.

"It's called umeshu."

"U-me-shu," she repeated, slowly. Then she downed the contents of the small cup in one go. Katsuo's eyes widened at that.

"It's really nice! What's it made of? Rice, like sake?"

"Plums," he replied, still shocked at how she drank it in one go.

"It's good. Yura—" Ciara turned around to look for the girl.

"My lord—" At that moment, one of Katsuo's vassals appeared at the dais, wanting to exchange some words with him. By the time they had finished, Ciara had disappeared from his side.

---

1. heart, spirit, mind
2. 1 koku is considered 1 person's sufficient rice supply for a year (about 180 liters); a daimyō's wealth is determined by how many koku his territory can produce

39

*M*ost of his guests were passed out in the conference room, as was usual after a celebration. His family had probably headed back to their own quarters, but there was a nagging thought that he should check on Ciara. Katsuo went to her room but found it empty. Her futon was prepared and creasy.

Katsuo was distracted when he realized he was thirsty and headed for the stores for more sake. As he was walking across the inner courtyard, he realized there was a feminine figure sitting on the edge of the veranda. Moonlight shone down on her, bathing her in a silver light. Katsuo thought for a moment he was seeing the patron goddess of his family.

He rubbed his eyes, thinking he might've drunk a bit too much. He held his liquor better than most men, so sometimes it was hard to draw the line. When he looked up next time, the moonlight was half-blocked by a dark cloud, and he realized he wasn't looking at an apparition but Ciara sitting there.

After the initial surprise wore off, he immediately walked over to her. She looked up at his quiet footsteps and offered him a smile.

Goddess, she was beautiful!

"What brings you here?" she asked.

"I'm thirsty."

"I think I can help you with that." She winked and conjured a bottle from somewhere behind her. "Here."

"Thanks," Katsuo sat down next to her, keeping some distance between them. He sampled the drink and a smile appeared on his face as he looked at Ciara. "I see, so that's why you escaped. You've run out of umeshu!"

"Maybe," she replied. At that moment, the clouds had moved, and the moon became visible again. Ciara gazed up as she was once again enveloped by silver light. "It's gorgeous."

"Yes, it is," Katsuo said, looking at her, before glancing up at the silver orb in the sky.

They sat in comfortable silence, moongazing, until he felt Ciara's head land on his shoulder. He glanced at her, trying to figure out if she was asleep, and she wrapped her arms around his.

"Umeshu?" he offered.

She shook her head and inched closer. "Nah, I'm good."

"Are you—?"

"What? Sober?" She chuckled. "I am."

She squeezed his arm before letting go, and he immediately missed her warmth at his side. Ciara looked at him, sheepish.

"Maybe a bit tipsy, not knowing personal boundaries." She looked away, feeling awkward.

Katsuo placed the umeshu bottle on the floor and leaned toward her. He put his hand on her cheek and gently turned her to face him. Darkness surrounded them as clouds blocked the moonlight again. There was just enough light for them to see each other's eyes.

Purple and golden gazes locked, and he heard Ciara's breath hitch.

"You, of all people, don't need to worry about that."

He leaned in but stopped a hair's breadth from Ciara's lips. He was going to do it properly this time.

She glanced down at his lips then back to his mesmerizing eyes. She swore her heart skipped a beat as she moved in for the kiss. Katsuo's hand slid to the back of Ciara's neck as he drew her closer, and her arms wound around his shoulders. For the first time in years, she let go of her worries and let herself get lost in the sensation.

The kiss only lasted a moment, but she felt safe and cherished in Katsuo's embrace and stayed there even after their lips had separated. He rested his forehead against hers, his eyes closed. Ciara's heart swelled with joy.

She felt as if she could take on the whole world, no matter what may come, if Katsuo was by her side. It was a foreign feeling for her, and just as she was about to draw back, Katsuo opened his eyes, his golden gaze capturing her.

Moonlight shone on them, and a cool breeze swept through the courtyard, but they sat there, unmoving. Ciara felt as if she could admire his eyes for eternity and still not have her fill of them. The wind picked up, and this time, it carried the chill of late autumn with it. She shivered.

"Come," Katsuo picked her up, eliciting a squeal from Ciara.

"Wh-what?"

"I don't want you to catch a cold," he said, "and you're still healing."

"I'm fine," she insisted but wrapped her arms around his shoulders. "The alcohol dulled the ache. It wasn't that painful anyway."

Katsuo raised an eyebrow in question.

"It doesn't hurt when—" Ciara cut herself short, embarrassed as she realized where her thoughts had wandered.

"Finish what you've started. I'm eager to hear," Katsuo replied, leaning in and planting a kiss on her forehead.

Ciara stayed silent as he carried her through the winding corridors. Finally, she admitted in a whisper, "It doesn't hurt when I'm in your arms."

She sighed and covered her face behind her hand. "Wait. That came out wrong."

She felt him chuckle at that.

"You worry about the most peculiar things," he said. She peeked at him from between her fingers as Katsuo glanced down at her and his gaze softened. "That's another thing I like about you."

"You like me," Ciara said, as if forgetting they were kissing just minutes ago.

"I thought that was obvious by now," he said, making her blush. She swatted at his shoulder, and he adjusted his hold on her, making her grip his shoulders stronger.

"Relax, I'm not going to drop you."

"Are you sure? I'm not that light."

"You are as light as a feather to me," he replied.

"Are you saying you're strong or that I'm light?"

"As I said, you worry about the most peculiar things," Katsuo repeated as he slid the door open with his foot. "Why can't it be both?"

"Both, huh?" Ciara murmured, lost in thought for a moment. Katsuo gently put her down on her feet. She looked around, disoriented, before she realized they were in Katsuo's room. He touched her arms and looked her in the eye.

"What—?"

"Spend the night with me."

Ciara's breath hitched. She knew very well what he was referring to. He waited patiently while she decided on her answer. She adored him, and the attraction was undeniable between them. They both wanted this. But would she dare make the jump to trust him? To place her heart in his hands and trust him not to crush it?

She hardly felt his hands on her arms, and she was reminded of how safe she had felt when he embraced her. How confident he was holding her. The thought that she might not get another chance to be with him squeezed her chest. Ciara's heart skipped a beat as she realized her soul had already made the choice. She smiled up at Katsuo and kissed his cheek before circling him and heading toward the door to shut it.

Katsuo froze on the spot and hung his head as soon as he heard the door slide shut. So that was it. He was so enamored by her he forgot his role in their arrangement. What was he thinking, desiring her when she so clearly stated, repeatedly that she wasn't going to—

Unexpectedly, graceful arms embraced him from behind, and he glanced back, surprised. Ciara smiled at him, a rosy blush spreading on her cheeks.

"It was drafty," she said, squeezing him for a moment. Katsuo turned around and stroked her face. His hand lingered on her cheek, and she leaned into the touch, closing her eyes for a moment.

"Is that a yes?"

"It seems I must elaborate," Ciara replied with a cheeky smile. She rose on her tiptoes and kissed him with all the passion she dared.

With Katsuo as a partner, it didn't take long for Ciara to let go of insecurities and show him how much she loved him. *I love him,* she realized just when Katsuo planted small kisses on her neck. Joy bloomed in her soul as she embraced him with all her heart.

40

*C*iara woke up fully rested. For the first time in more than a week, the nightmares avoided her, and she curled into the warmth beside her. She sighed, content to just be where she was.

She wanted to stay in bed for a little longer, but her brain kicked in, and she quickly realized something was different from usual. She cracked one eye open. It was still dark, but she could make out Katsuo's silhouette. Her hand rested on his chest, which rose with every breath he took. Carefully, she retreated her hand and looked at his face.

His features were relaxed as he slept peacefully. She admired him and suddenly wished his proposal was real. Even if she had to stay in this foreign land and time, if she was with Katsuo, it wouldn't be so bad. In the end, the fake engagement only depended on whether they made it real. She was afraid to bring it up to him and decided to enjoy for the time being what she could. *It's pointless to worry about tomorrow.*

Katsuo sighed and turned in his sleep, momentarily showing her his back. Ciara's gaze was drawn to the long scar on his back. She had noticed it right away the first time she had seen him shirtless. This time, she let her fingers trace the scar. It had healed as much as it could considering how deep it must have been when he received it. She wondered if he collected it in a battle and what happened.

He shivered at her slight touch, and she stopped for a moment. But the mystery of it held her interest, and she ran her hand along the entire length of the scar. Her hand was at Katsuo's shoulder blade when he suddenly moved and captured her wrist.

Ciara found herself laying on her back, Katsuo hovering over her. His golden eyes flashed in the darkness, and he looked at her with an angry expression. She made herself smaller but stood his gaze.

"Sorry," she said. "I didn't want to wake you up… or upset you."

It looked as if he was battling with something before he let himself relax and rolled back to his side of the futon. He was breathing hard as he stared up at the ceiling. Ciara wasn't sure what made him react this way. Had her actions brought up bad memories?

"I'm sorry," she repeated, curling into his side. She gently laid her head on his chest, waiting for him to calm down.

"Did I hurt you?" he asked after a while.

"What?"

Ciara hardly registered his light touch on her wrist.

"Oh, it's fine. You didn't hurt me," she reassured him. "Did I?"

"Did you what?" He looked at her, puzzled.

"Did I hurt you?" she asked, cocking her head to the side. At least they were talking, that was a good sign.

He quickly shook his head.

"No. It's just, I was… unprepared." He grimaced as he said that.

"Sorry."

"Please stop. You didn't do anything wrong."

She didn't look convinced, and he sat up, cradling her in his arms and giving her a sweet kiss.

"Okay, that was convincing," She chuckled and moved around a little to get into a more comfortable position. "Can I—" Ciara stopped before she could finish the question.

"Go on. Ask me anything."

"I'm just curious what happened," she admitted then quickly reassured him, "You don't have to tell me if you don't want to!"

Katsuo let out a heavy sigh.

"It's okay. Don't force yourself," she said, backpedaling. What was she thinking, ruining a perfect moment like that?

"No, I'll tell you," he decided. "You have a right to know."

Ciara looked at him, interested why he thought so but too curious about the story of the scar to interrupt him now that he was talking. Katsuo gathered his thoughts as he held her in his arms.

"I was married once. For not even a day." He paused.

"What happened?" Ciara asked in a whisper.

"On our wedding night, I was attacked," Katsuo confessed, and Ciara gasped. He continued, "Kikyō attacked me and gave me this scar."

Ciara immediately hugged him.

"I had no idea!" she said, clinging to him. His arms closed around her. "I'm sorry, Katsuo!"

"It happened a long time ago. Still, the scar reminded me ever since then. For some reason, it refuses to heal."

Ciara thought this wouldn't be the best time to comment on how deep it must have been back then. She squeezed him tighter, and Katsuo adjusted his position awkwardly.

"Ah, careful."

"Does it still hurt?" Ciara drew back quickly.

"That's not what I meant," he said with tenseness in his voice. "Stop moving around."

It took a few seconds for Ciara's brain to process what he was referring to.

"Oh. *Oh*." Her eyebrows rose, and she couldn't help the smug smile. She leaned closer to him. "I don't think you mean it."

"I do."

"No, you don't," Ciara confidently stated and met his lips with her own, making Katsuo growl.

"You have no idea what you're doing to me, woman," he said before he kissed her back.

Ciara awoke to the sound of someone quietly moving around and carefully rummaging in the room. Katsuo's heat from beside her was gone, and she reluctantly opened her eyes. She saw him pulling on his shirt.

"Where are you going so early?" Ciara asked, stealing a glance through the window. The sun had just probably risen over the Eastern horizon.

"Ohayō," he greeted her with a small smile.

"Good morning to you, too," Ciara said as she sat up and gathered the sheets around her shoulders. It was getting chilly in the morning. "So?"

"To answer your question, I'm going to train."

"At the pagoda?"

"Yes."

Ciara contemplated for a moment.

"Do you mind if I join you?"

Katsuo looked at her surprised.

"I'll keep out of your way, I promise," she said, standing up. "I've been neglecting my yoga exercises, and it would be nice to do them at the pagoda. That's all."

Or just do something together before the illusion of last night dissipates, she added mentally.

"Sure, come," Katsuo replied. Ciara smiled at him then turned around to look for her yukata. "Give me a sec, I'll be right back!" she said, dressing and running out the door.

41

*K*atsuo looked at Ciara amusement as she ran around the room, gathering pieces of clothing, quickly putting on her yukata *the wrong way,* then rushing out the door. She was like a windstorm.

He chuckled as he retrieved his sword. His gaze landed on the dagger on the table. He still hadn't figured out where to put it now that it was banned from under his pillow. Katsuo held it up, contemplating. It was strange how he felt the need to have it nearby for a decade, and now, it didn't even occur to him to put it back after Ciara demanded he got rid of it.

That seemed like a lifetime ago.

He placed the dagger on the top of the cupboard, next to the basket filled with the balls, and headed over to Ciara's room to fetch her. They didn't speak much on their way to the pagoda, but Katsuo didn't mind. Soon, they came across a group of training soldiers. Takeru was up and about, energetic as always, as if last night's drinking had never happened.

"Good morning, brother, Ciara!" He bowed a little

when he saw them. The soldiers greeted them with a loud shout and a deep bow. Ciara fidgeted next to Katsuo. He noticed that she rarely liked the attention.

"Morning," Katsuo returned. "I see you're already refreshed and have started the day."

"You know me," Takeru beamed at him.

Ciara mumbled something under her breath and both brothers turned to her.

"What was that?" Katsuo asked, leaning close.

"I said it's unnatural. How can you be so cheerful this early in the morning?" she asked.

"You're up, too, aren't you?"

"I am on my feet, yes, but that doesn't mean I'm fully awake," she explained. Takeru looked at her puzzled.

"I don't understand. How can you be up but not awake?"

"It's magic!" Ciara stage-whispered, and everybody froze. She looked around, her eyebrows creasing. "It was just a joke."

There was an awkward silence until Takeru laughed.

"Haha, foreigners!" With that, the soldiers' stance relaxed, and they went back to practicing their moves. Takeru sent a look to Katsuo before he started his walk among the rows of soldiers to instruct them.

Katsuo put a hand on the small of Ciara's back and guided her through the courtyard.

"Do you often joke about magic where you come from?" he asked. He sounded curious, but his voice was strained.

"Well, sometimes. Most people think it's not real. They think science explains everything," Ciara replied. "Why? That was a weird reaction back there."

She was reminded that she was in another time period. Just how could she forget? Thank gods it was Japan and not Europe in the Middle Ages. She wouldn't have lasted a minute there.

"Common folk are superstitious," Katsuo explained. "They believe magic exists and give respect to those who have it. But is also comes with fear. Those who wield magic have power over those who don't. So even if they're respected, they can never really become part of a community. That's why you shouldn't joke about it."

"Hmm…" Ciara pondered over his words. "What about you?"

"Excuse me?"

They were just passing the guard standing on the path to the pagoda. After a brief exchange of greetings, Ciara elaborated.

"You said 'common folk' and were talking about them in third person. That makes me think that you might have different views on the matter?"

A small smile appeared in the corner of Katsuo's mouth. She was perceptive, maybe a bit too much for her own good.

"I am a daimyō," he said, thinking it was a sufficient explanation, but seeing Ciara's confused face, he added, "Just as people who wield magic, we, too, have power over people's fate."

"Does that mean you're okay with someone having magic?"

"It means I can understand the burden."

Katsuo debated how much to tell her. He didn't fear magic because most human magic didn't work on him. He had to be careful with the magic youkai wielded, however.

"Okay, whatever," Ciara shook herself. "It's still too early to philosophize about such things. I haven't had my oolong, yet."

"You should've told me sooner."

"Ah, it's okay. I can manage until breakfast," Ciara waved. "If I can't and fall asleep, I trust you to take care of me."

"As you wish, my lady," Katsuo replied with a smile.

"I wanted to let you know that I'm leaving today," Yuki said during breakfast. Katsuo put his chopsticks down and looked at her. She caught his glance. "Don't be so surprised, boy. I told you I'd wait until Takeru gets back."

"But today is Benzaiten's festival!"

It was Yuki's turn to look surprised.

"Oh, right."

"You won't miss the celebrations in Her honor, will you?" Katsuo asked.

Ciara and Takeru was listening to the conversation, curious.

"You are right," Yuki said. "I can't miss it. Of course, I'll attend."

Now that it was settled, Takeru went back to his meal. Katsuo, however, was not finished.

"What are your plans for today?" he asked Yuki.

"Preparing for the journey. Why?"

"Then would you come to my office after breakfast? There's something I need to ask you.

"Sure," Yuki nodded. If she was surprised by his request, she didn't show it.

Not long after breakfast, Katsuo and Yuki sat down at the table in his office. He poured tea for both of them.

"What is it you wanted to talk about?" Yuki admired the black and gold, lacquered cup in her hands.

"I didn't have the opportunity to bring this up before,

but... when Ciara was kidnapped and I fought, I was injured on my arm."

"I remember," Yuki carefully sipped the hot tea.

"My hand was coated with blood, and I threw it at the enemy to distract them, but what happened was..." Katsuo shook his head as he trailed off, not sure how to describe it.

Yuki put the cup down, her eyes wide.

"You injured them."

"Exactly! It's as if—"

"You inherited the Blood Blades," Yuki said, taken aback.

"Blood what now?"

She cleared her throat.

"The Blood Blades. The magic in your blood transforms it into a weapon if you find yourself in a dire situation."

"How does it work? Do you have this ability, too? Did Father—"

Yuki held up a hand and he fell silent.

"One question at a time. Yes, I do have this ability, and no, your father didn't inherit it."

"How is that possible?"

"Maybe it skipped a generation." Yuki shrugged.

"Do you think Takeru has it?"

"No idea. I'm surprised you have it."

"It is very useful. We should find out," Katsuo said, eager to stand up and find his brother.

"Calm down, boy," Yuki said, using her grandmotherly voice. "It might seem useful, but you can't rely on it."

"What do you mean?"

"You can't train. It's not connected to your will or emotions like your other abilities," Yuki explained. "It's connected to instinct. You might be injured, throw your blood, and nothing happens. It's completely random."

"Oh," Katsuo settled in his seat.

"But once it appears, it could be very powerful, maybe your most powerful ability," Yuki smiled at him.

"I just don't have control over it. Great."

"Katsuo, I know you're used to being in control," Yuki told him, "but there are things we cannot. They make life all the more worth it."

"Are talking about the Blood Blades?"

Yuki slurped her tea. "Maybe."

42

*T*he rest of the day went by slowly as Yuki gathered supplies for her journey, collected her newly sharpened naginata from the blacksmith in town, and decided to pay one last visit to Benten's pagoda.

Unfortunately, she had a hard time getting there, as Katsuo gave permission to selected servants to be on the pagoda grounds for the preparation of the festivities.

Katsuo was holding a strategic meeting with his vassals regarding the information Takeru brought from the Northern border. Taiki had found him later, buried under paperwork, reporting the rise of suspicious people appearing in town. Katsuo was reminded of the thugs in dark alleys when he was looking for Ciara.

"Deal with them," he told Taiki.

"You mean—"

"Keep the streets clean and safe. You can use whatever means to drive them out of town," Katsuo confirmed. "Report back to me when you're finished."

"Yessir," Taiki bowed low and disappeared. Katsuo

didn't even have time to protest at his behavior on this occasion.

A knock sounded on his door, and Takeru looked in.

"Perfect! Just who I need!"

Takeru's face brightened. "How can I assist you, brother?"

"Sit down." As he did, Katsuo put a stack of papers on his side of the table. "These are yours."

"What?" The smile fell off Takeru's face.

"The sooner we get it done, the sooner we can go celebrate."

"But there's no end to it."

"You're right. Maybe I should hire an aide to deal with all this paperwork. This is ridiculous!" Katsuo said, contemplating while putting his seal on a document in front of him. If he had someone to take care of these things, he could spend more time with Ciara. He realized he was getting distracted again.

Takeru sighed and picked up a report to read through, resigned to his fate of spending the entire afternoon in this stuffy office.

Ciara spent the afternoon with Yura, discovering the festive events in town. She was a bit worried with just the two of them going around after all that happened last time she visited the castle town.

After she shared her concerns with Yura, she got a soldier, who was off-duty, to volunteer to keep them safe. Ciara was thankful for the company and the added feel of security.

They stopped at the town square, where a stage had been erected and a handful of people acted out a play.

"Oh, I love this part!" Yura gasped. "This is where Benzaiten descends to the human world!"

Ciara could hear a biwa and a few other instruments in the background as the narrator commented on what was happening. Apparently, as the goddess arrived, an island rose up to meet her feet. Her husband, a white dragon, followed her soon, making people panic. Ciara couldn't hear the end of the story because her attention was drawn to elsewhere.

"Say, Yura, what are they doing over there?" She nodded in the direction of a group of adults and children who were sitting in a semi-circle just on the side of the road. The servant girl followed Ciara's gaze.

"Oh, they're making chōchin." At Ciara's puzzled look, she explained. "Paper lanterns for tonight. There's a narrow river at the edge of town. That's where the procession will end tonight."

"Procession?"

"There's always a procession," Yura said, furrowing her brows. She glanced at the guard just behind her. "Right, Riku-san?"

He nodded. "It starts at the pagoda, Milady," he added. "Usually, Katsuo-sama performs a short ceremony to honor the goddess Benten, then a procession will follow through town so everyone can give their respects and receive the goddess' blessing."

"What's in the procession?" Ciara asked, intrigued.

"The goddess!" Yura said, excited.

"The goddess?"

"You will see, Ciara-sama," Yura said. "It all ends at the river where we let the paper lanterns go. Would you like to see how they make them?"

"That's a great idea!"

Eventually, they ended up making a few paper lanterns

themselves. Ciara couldn't help noticing the looks Yura and Riku exchanged when they thought no one was looking. She smiled to herself, thinking they looked cute together. *I wonder if they're a couple?* she mused as her hands created her first lantern. It was a bit sloppy and ugly, compared to the others surrounding them, but she made it and was happy how it turned out.

The hours went by quickly, and the trio decided to get some food from one of the stalls lining the streets. Yura and Ciara settled on dango while Riku opted for a couple of fried fish. It gave them enough energy to make it back to the castle for the opening ceremony.

"Eeh, it's Takeru-dono this year," Riku remarked as they made their way to the small crowd near the pagoda. Katsuo's most important vassals and some high-ranking officials were invited, but no one stopped the trio when they saw Ciara leading them.

"This is so exciting; I've never seen it from this close!" Yura whispered as they stopped among the men. "Usually, if I'm lucky, I can sneak a peek from one of the castle windows from up there!"

The crowd left a half-circle cleared in front of the pagoda's gates.

"Shh, it's starting," Riku warned, and Yura immediately fell silent.

Takeru appeared from one side and was dressed in white except for the red rope which held his robe together. He was holding something, but Ciara couldn't see it clearly because it blended it with his clothes. Takeru was chanting a beautiful song, but for some reason, Ciara couldn't understand the words.

When he got closer, she was able to make out the white snake winding around his hands. He was cradling the serpent in his arms, not the least bit afraid of it. Ciara looked on, mesmerized by the entire scene. The sound of a biwa played in the background, and Ciara's eyes found Katsuo's form under the trees. His music perfectly complemented Takeru's chanting.

Lady Yuki appeared behind Takeru, wearing a long, flowing dress. It wasn't a kimono, which was known to restrict movements, but something lighter. Its long sleeves and skirt fluttered as Yuki danced. The color of the dress was light blue, like the spring sky or the clear water in a pond. The whole performance reminded Ciara of a dancing waterfall.

Yuki's movements were graceful and complemented the sound of the biwa and Takeru's chanting voice. As she watched, Ciara felt something blooming in her heart. It was as if it was being filled up with hope and joy. A warm feeling spread in her chest and just when she thought she could bear it no more, suddenly, everything stopped.

Katsuo held the biwa, not playing it, and Yuki froze mid-movement for a moment before slowly bringing her arms down to clasp them in a prayer. Takeru was silent as he lifted his arms with the white snake striving toward the sunlight.

"Goddess Benten, patron of our family, guardian of our town," Takeru started. His voice rang out strong and not even insects could be heard. It was as if nature itself was anticipating what came next. "We would be honored to receive your blessings for the coming year."

Takeru finished and kept the snake held up. Ciara sensed everyone hold their breath.

"What are we waiting for?" she whispered, almost inaudible, afraid to break the quiet reverence that seemed to envelope everyone.

Riku, on her right, whispered, "Now we wait for the goddess to answer."

"How do we know if she answers?"

"Watch and wait."

Her curiosity was soon satisfied. The white snake unexpectedly lunged at Takeru, biting his arm. Ciara gasped in shock and looked around, but nobody moved. Did they not see what happened? She steeled herself to break through the ranks of samurai, but before she could do anything, Takeru brought the snake down, carefully embracing it.

"May you shine our path in this coming year. May prosperity find us," he said as he headed for the pagoda. Lady Yuki followed, then Katsuo finished the line. Nobody went in after them.

"Is he all right?" Ciara asked, worried.

"It's part of the ceremony," Yura said. "Don't be concerned, I don't know how they do it, but you won't find a bite mark the next day."

"How do you know?"

Uncharacteristically for her, Yura ignored Ciara's question. Soon, Katsuo and Yuki appeared, a beam on each of their shoulders. A tiny palanquin followed, and Ciara could see the white snake relaxing peacefully on a silky pillow inside. Takeru brought up the rear, holding up two beams with his hands.

The samurai made way for them as they proceeded down the path that led to the castle courtyard. When they reached the common areas, soldiers appeared at their side and each took a beam to support the palanquin and free Yuki, Katsuo and Takeru from their burden. They wore white sashes over their crimson uniforms.

Ciara immediately headed for the trio, but it took her a while to get there because everybody who was at the ceremony was going the same way. The samurai quickly reached the palanquin and gave their respects to Benten, symbolized by the white snake, without stopping the process.

Finally, she could check on the injury.

"Takeru, are you all right?" she hurried over to him, still worried despite Yura's earlier words. He grinned at her, hiding his arm behind his back.

"I'm fine."

"Then why aren't you showing me your arm? And why is your face so tense?"

Takeru sighed.

"Here," he lifted his arm for Ciara to inspect. There was no bite mark.

"Are you really okay?"

"Yes. How did you like the ceremony?"

"It was mesmerizing, all of you were," she glanced around at Yuki and Katsuo.

"It was Takeru's first time performing," Katsuo said.

"Really? Nice work," she beamed at Takeru.

"Thank you. Brother, do you mind if I refresh before joining the procession?"

"Go ahead," Katsuo said. With that, Takeru hurried off. Ciara followed him with her gaze and noticed his arm twitching. The one he didn't show her. She tsked.

"I knew it."

"What did you know?" Yuki asked, coming up beside her. Ciara almost forgot she had an audience.

"He showed me the wrong arm. He looked pale,"

"He'll be fine," Yuki reassured him. "Katsuo has done it plenty of times, and he is here, isn't he?"

"I suppose..."

"I want to confirm I am definitely here," Katsuo remarked, putting a hand on Ciara's hip. His comment elicited a chuckle from the others.

43

*T*he procession advanced slowly through town while the four guards who held the palanquin were changed every hour. They reached the edge of town at sunset, and the river looked like a flaming, fluttering ribbon in the orange-hued sky. The palanquin was set on a stage on the riverbank, giving the opportunity for the rest of the public to pay their respects.

A group of people stood near it, giving out chōchin. A huge pile of paper lanterns was stacked beside them. Ciara stood in line with Katsuo to receive one, hoping her ugly lantern wouldn't make it here.

Alas, she was surprised when she saw Katsuo picking up one from the ground. It was hidden underneath the pile of lanterns. And it was the ugliest she'd ever seen. Even so, she immediately recognized it. Her eyes widened.

"Milord, please have this one," the man next to Katsuo said, offering him a perfect one. "This one's better. That one was made by an amateur."

"I like it," Katsuo insisted.

"A-are you sure, Milord?" the man asked, sweating under the piercing gaze of his daimyō.

"It's all right," Ciara spoke up and offered the perfect lantern in her hands. "Let's switch."

"There's no need. This is perfect in its imperfection. Natural."

"You say the sweetest things," Ciara said, snaking her free hand around Katsuo's arm.

"What are you talking about?" he asked, heading for the next group of people, in charge of lighting the lanterns.

"You know, what he said was true. It was made by an amateur."

"I can see the care with which it was created. I like it."

Ciara gently squeezed his arm.

"I'm happy you do."

Her comment left Katsuo puzzled, but she didn't elaborate. Soon, the sun was completely set, and the riverbank was full of blinking little flames. If one saw it from a distance, they might mistake it for a field of fireflies.

"What happens next?" Ciara asked, excited.

"Takeru arrives and lets the serpent back to the river."

"It came from the river?"

"It didn't. It's just a symbol since Benten is primarily a water goddess."

"Ah, I see." Ciara nodded. "Basically, the serpent symbolizes the goddess, and when you let it into the river, the goddess returns to her usual place. Is that how it is?"

Katsuo looked surprised for a moment.

"You've grasped that quite well for a Westerner."

"I'm going to take that as a compliment."

"It was," he replied, turning toward the stage. "Look, there's Takeru."

Just as he said, Takeru carefully retrieved the white snake from the silky pillow in the mini palanquin and slowly walked toward the river. Everybody fell in reverent silence as he walked amongst them with the representative of the deity in his arms. Katsuo was the first to move, and the crowd parted before him. Ciara followed him as they lined up behind Takeru.

One by one, people quietly joined the procession. Katsuo stopped a few feet behind his little brother as Takeru lowered the white serpent to where soil and water met.

"Thank you for your blessings, beloved Benten," he murmured as the snake slithered out of his hands and into the river.

He straightened and faced his brother who nodded in approval, making Takeru beam with pride. Katsuo walked over to the river with Ciara by his side. A couple of people stood to the side and lit the small candles installed in the lanterns. As Katsuo gently put his on the water, Ciara copied him. The chōchins swayed slightly as they journeyed down the river.

Soon, several other lanterns joined in, and the river became an orange ribbon in the dark night, celebrating the goddess Benten.

"How did you like the festivities?" Yuki asked as she suddenly appeared next to them.

"Today was amazing!" Ciara exclaimed happily.

"Well, there's still a dance and feast waiting for everyone. Make sure you enjoy tonight."

"Thank you, Yuki. You too."

Yuki had a sad smile on her lips.

"I'm afraid I need to depart," she said. She looked up at Katsuo apologetically. "But I'll try to make it back to your wedding day. When will it be?"

"In a fortnight."

"Oh, I might be late, then," Yuki's expression fell at the

news.

"We are happy to have you here whenever," Ciara quickly jumped in. "Right, Katsuo?"

"Indeed."

"You take care of each other," Yuki told them. "And Ciara?"

"Yes?"

"Be careful, darling. The sun might darken but only for a moment."

"Okay?" Ciara looked at her, puzzled. Yuki smiled and waved goodbye. "Take care, Yuki!"

She quickly disappeared among the celebrating crowd.

"Well, that was cryptic," Ciara commented on Yuki's last words.

"She does that." Katsuo chuckled. "You'll get used to it."

Will I? Will I stay long enough to get used to it? Ciara silently wondered, not for the first time. She could definitely get used to waking up in Katsuo's arms each day. But what of her family? Her life in the modern days? If she were to stay, both of them would need to agree it was permanent. Right now, this arrangement was only for two more weeks.

"What's weighing on your mind?" Katsuo asked as he moved closer and put his hand on her waist, half-embracing her.

Ciara shook her head. She didn't want to ruin this perfectly nice evening with her worries.

"Let's see what they have for dinner!"

Unfortunately, they couldn't be alone for long. Someone always needed to exchange a few words with Katsuo. Ciara drifted away a few stalls down. She was debating over the fried octopus balls.

Katsuo was just about to catch up with her when Orihime flitted into his path unexpectedly. She was dressed in a plain, pink kimono. Katsuo took a second glance at her attire.

"Good evening, Orihime-dono," he greeted politely.

"Good evening, Katsuo-sama. I see you've taken a liking to my kimono," she twirled around, her hand gracefully resting on her shoulder as she faced him. "I thought to mingle with the common folk."

"And how has your experience been so far?"

"Why, splendid! It's fun here."

"I'm happy you like the festival."

"Is it every year?"

"Indeed. Why?"

"Oh, nothing, I was just thinking how wonderful it would be to attend from now on," she mused out loud, sneaking a glance at Katsuo from the corner of her eye.

Katsuo groaned inwardly. *Anything, but that!* he thought, forcing a neutral expression on his face, lest he offend Orihime. Too bad she was the daughter of a close ally, otherwise she would've already been sent back to her father. As things stood, that version still offered a solution.

"If you'll excuse me—"

"Oh, look! Dango, my favorites!" She hooked her arm into Katsuo's and dragged him with her to the nearest vendor. "What flavors do you have?"

Katsuo tried to retrieve his arm, but Orihime didn't let go.

"Milord, would you like something, too?" The dango man asked. There went his incognito.

"Thank you, I'll take two," he said, thinking of Ciara.

"Why, thank you, Katsuo-sama," Orihime grinned,

taking one of the sticks with three dangos on them. At least she let go of his arm.

Katsuo froze for a moment at the face of such audacity. Orihime used this chance to bite into the dango, leaving Katsuo with no choice but to acquire another portion for Ciara. He had just about enough of Orihime for that night.

"How peculiar…" Orihime murmured. "These foreigners, that is."

"What are you talking about?" Katsuo followed her gaze and saw Ciara talking to a vendor and a couple of other men standing in a semi-circle around her, speaking with her.

"She's engaged and still flirts with men. Tsk, tsk. I wonder if it's normal from whence she came," Orihime said, throwing away her half-eaten dangos. "If I were engaged to a man of your caliber, I'd never do such a thing."

"Enough."

"I'm sorry?" Orihime blinked up at him innocently.

"Have a pleasant night, Orihime-dono," Katsuo said, leaving her promptly.

44

*H*er eyes lit up as she spotted him coming her way.

"Katsuo!" Ciara exclaimed as soon as she saw him. Her shoulders visibly relaxed at the sight of him. The men who had been so eager to get her attention a few minutes before quietly disappeared in the crowd.

"Is that for me?" she asked as she spied the sticks of dangos in his hand.

"Here," he held out one of them and she took it. Her fingers brushed his as she retrieved the sweets. She smiled at him before turning back to the vendor with the octopus balls.

"Have you ever tried takoyaki?" he asked.

"Not yet. Are they good?"

"One of my favorites," Katsuo said. "Unfortunately, I rarely get to eat it since it's from West Japan."

"Oh, I see," Ciara was eyeing the food, contemplating. Meanwhile, she bit into the dango absentmindedly. She chewed on it for a moment. "This is good, thank you."

"You're welcome."

"Would you like to try the takoyaki?" the elderly man behind the stall asked them.

Katsuo looked at Ciara in question.

"Sure, let's try! I'm feeling adventurous tonight!"

"Two portions," Katsuo said, paying for them. The old man quickly put together two plates for them, using big leaves to tie them up.

"Thank you for your patronage," he said, bowing a little as he held out the packages with both hands.

Katsuo nodded as he took the food and decided to find a calm spot with seats so they could eat in peace. They made small talk while they ate. Then the topic turned a bit more serious.

"Do you think Takeru will be all right?" Ciara asked, still concerned for the youth. "He looked really pale."

"He was fine when he let the snake into the river, wasn't he?" Katsuo asked, a bit irritated. He wasn't sure why he was annoyed with his little brother. He knew the bite would've been painful even though they were immune to the venom. The recovery rate was quicker each time, but this was the first time Takeru had performed the opening ceremony and was bound to need at least a day or two to recover.

"It was dark," Ciara replied. "I couldn't determine how well he was, but if you say so, I'll believe you."

"Good."

Ciara crumbled the empty leaves and hurled them away. She looked at him sharply.

"Why are you in a mood?"

"I always have some kind of mood," he replied, puzzled by the peculiar choice of words coming from her.

"You know what I mean," she said, crossing her arms. When Katsuo remained silent, she sighed and elaborated: "You seem... annoyed. Are you annoyed with me?"

"What? No," Katsuo was quick to reassure her.

"Then why?"

It was Katsuo's turn to let out a sigh. How could he explain it to her when he, himself wasn't sure why he was irritated at Ciara and Takeru. They didn't do *anything*.

"I'm sorry," he said instead, reaching for her hands. Ciara let him unravel her arms and take her hands in his.

"You are an enigma, mister," Ciara said, pulling him closer and gazing into his eyes. "I want to get to know you better and find out all your secrets."

"All my secrets?" Katsuo raised his eyebrows, amused at the thought. "That might be more than you can handle, darling."

"Is that a challenge?" Ciara asked with a grin and quickly planted a kiss on his lips.

Katsuo pulled back immediately, and Ciara felt hurt.

"What—?"

"Anyone can see us," he said, looking around nervously.

At that moment, Ciara was sharply reminded that she was probably centuries in the past. And she was in a completely different culture that most certainly had different views on public displays of affection.

"Sorry," she said, drawing back. She made a mental note of this cultural difference. She tried to respect it even though it felt like rejection when he pulled back.

He stood and helped her up, too. Grasping her hand, he gently nudged her in the direction of the castle.

"I know a place," he said, his voice deeper than usual.

Ciara was thankful for the darkness to hide her blush.

They were awoken in the middle of the night. Ciara was

jarred from her sleep because of something loud, but she couldn't recognize the sound. Katsuo sat up next to her.

"What was that?" she asked, also getting up. Katsuo pricked his ears, and the sound came again.

"Ayaka," was all he said, and he was out of bed the next second. He quickly tugged on a hakama and ran out of the room. It took a moment for Ciara to find her yukata and follow him to the little girl's room.

Katsuo was sitting down, Ayaka in his lap, when she arrived. He was stroking her back to calm her down.

"What happened?" Ciara asked as she approached them. "Did you have a nightmare?"

Ayaka sniffled.

"Yes," she whispered and grabbed onto Katsuo's neck.

"It's all right, we're here," he said, reassuring her. Ciara went around to light a candle and brought it close.

"Do you want to talk about it? It might help," she suggested to the little girl.

"A big raven was trying to eat Takeru," she blurted.

Ciara and Katsuo exchanged a puzzled glance.

"You know, ravens can't get that big in real life," Ciara said.

"But it felt so real!"

"Oh, darling," she sighed, contemplating. She patted the little girl's hair. "Takeru is strong. I'm sure he could win."

Ayaka shook her head.

"Do you want to check on him?" Katsuo suggested, and she fervently nodded. "All right. But be very quiet because he is sleeping. Can you do that?"

"Yes, Daddy," she whispered, still clinging to his neck.

"Are you coming?" he asked Ciara, but she shook her head.

"I'll tidy up here."

Katsuo looked at her strangely, as there was not much

to tidy up in the room, but shrugged. Calming Ayaka down was his priority at the moment.

As soon as they left, Ciara rummaged through the bedding of the little girl.

"Huh. Interesting," she murmured, finding a small pouch hidden in Ayaka's covers. Carefully, she opened it and sniffed it. Her face crunched up. "Ugh, this is definitely that awful concoction."

She put it in the pocket in her sleeve and made Ayaka's bed before returning to her room and hiding the packet in the cupboard. *I'll get rid of it tomorrow,* she decided. She had a pouch of dried lavender and brought it back to the little girl's room.

Someone is agonizing Ayaka with nightmares. But what's the point? I have to find out who would do such a thing.

She put the lavender pouch inside the cover of the pillow and fluffed it before returning to Katsuo's room. Ciara made a mental note to check her bedding as well. There must be some explanation for her own nightmares.

45

*T*he next morning, Ciara quietly slipped out of bed and went back to her room. She had a hard time sleeping after she was awakened by Ayaka's scream. She envied Katsuo's ability to easily fall asleep again.

She quickly changed into comfortable clothes to practice yoga, but before exercising, she combed through all her bedding. There was nothing. She paused, pondering. Was it possible she just had random nightmares and that was all they were? Was her mind playing tricks on her?

Ciara folded up her bedding and put it away. The pouch from Ayaka's room fell down and she bent down to retrieve it. At that moment, Yura knocked on her door. Ciara quickly stuffed the pouch in the cupboard and shut it close.

"Good morning," she greeted Yura.

"Good morning, Mil—Ciara-sama," she replied, bowing a little. "Did I interrupt you?"

"Ah, no, I was just about to do some exercise. Care to join?"

"Eeer…"

"It's good for your health."

"Oolong tea as well!" Yura lifted her hands, and Ciara only now noticed that she was holding a tray. She waved to Yura.

"Oh, come, come, let's have tea."

It was becoming a tradition for them to drink tea in the morning before breakfast. At first, Yura felt self-conscious to share a drink with her lady in the morning, but Ciara insisted they already did so in the teahouse, and it helped her start the day. So Yura could do nothing but accept her kindness.

"I was thinking we could go to town today," Ciara said.

"Again? I think Riku-san is on duty today, however…" Yura frowned.

"You like him?"

"What?" The girl blinked. "Who? Riku-san? No way, Milady!"

"Oh, I thought… Nevermind," Ciara shook her head. "Anyway, I think it'd be fine if it's just the two of us."

"No, no, I'll find someone to come along. But who would—"

"Why don't we ask Taiki?"

"Taiki-dono?" Yura's eyes widened, and she visibly shivered.

"What's wrong?" Ciara was alarmed at the girl's reaction.

"He's scary. He has this dangerous aura around him, I can't explain," she whispered.

"Well, he *is* a ninja."

"Is he?"

"Umm…" It was Ciara's turn to be self-conscious. "You didn't know?"

"I thought he was just a soldier."

"If he looks like a ninja and acts like a ninja, he's probably a ninja, Yura."

"Oh."

"I'll ask him. I'm sure he would be happy to help out his lord's betrothed," Ciara mused. Yura was right. She wasn't fond of Taiki, either, but he got the job done, and if Katsuo trusted him, then she was going to do so, too.

After breakfast, Ciara wandered the corridors, wondering how to get a hold of Taiki. She went to a guard walking past and asked for directions.

"I can escort you to his office, Milady, but there is no guarantee he'll be there," he said. "He always appears in the most unexpected places."

"I see. Nonetheless, please lead me there. I'm feeling lucky today!"

"As you wish, Milady."

He led her to an unfamiliar part of the castle. As she walked, Ciara glanced up at the ceiling, seeing red lines for the corridor. Somehow, she had a feeling that she'd already seen this marking somewhere.

"Here, Milady."

"Thank you," she said, and the guard promptly left. Ciara pondered for a moment how she'd get back to familiar territory but decided to take one step at a time. She knocked on the door, but there was no answer.

"Taiki?" she asked, knocking again. She waited a minute before sliding the door open and poking her head through. "Taiki?"

The room was dark and windowless. No wonder the ninja didn't spend too much time in here. Ciara looked around the best she could, but there was no sign anyone had been here recently.

She saw a small shadow creeping around. It looked like an animal, and Ciara stepped into the room, moving closer to it. She squinted to see more clearly. The black shadow froze and turned to her. Two ears twitched on top of its head, and she realized it must be a cat.

"Her, kitty, kitty!" Ciara crouched and waved to the cat. When it didn't move, she tried to wave the Japanese way. "Here, kitty, kitty!" She idly wondered if the cat could understand her, or was there a different calling in Japanese?

The cat took a step toward Ciara. She waited patiently.

"Can I help you with something, Milady?"

Ciara jumped in fright and twirled on her heels. She put a hand on her heart as she stood up.

"Jesus Christ, Taiki, you scared me!"

He inclined his head but didn't comment. Ciara ignored her frantic heartbeats and looked around for the cat, but it had already disappeared. She went back to business and asked Taiki if he could lend someone to come with Yura and her to town.

"In light of recent... events, I'd feel safer if someone who is trained to fight would come with us. That is, if it's not a big imposition on your resources."

"It's not impossible," he replied and sidestepped her to walk over to his desk.

"Oh," Ciara followed him. "That's great, thank you."

"I'll have them meet you at the gates."

"Excellent. Thanks, Taiki," Ciara gave him a smile.

"Is that all?"

"Eeer, yes. I won't keep you from your work any longer," Ciara hurried to the door. Taiki's gaze followed her like a hawk.

"How did you get here?"

"I'm sorry?"

"How did you find my office?" The ninja rephrased.

"A guard pointed it out to me."

"Please don't let yourself in if I'm not here." His voice was polite, but Ciara could feel a threatening aura emanating from him.

She nodded stiffly. "I'm sorry."

Taiki waited for a moment before asking her if she'd be able to find her way back.

"Or course!" Ciara chuckled and quickly exited. "Thanks!" she shouted over her shoulder, already in the corridor.

Taiki sighed. "That's the wrong way."

*C*iara quickly realized she headed in the wrong direction and turned around but only managed to make herself more lost. She had no idea which part of the castle she was wandering around.

The corridors were dark, and the only light source were windows, but even those were scarce in this part. As she looked up at the ceiling, trying to make out the symbol, she froze. It was three red spirals. Damn. She was absolutely sure she hadn't seen that one before.

"Come on!" she begged to the Universe to show her a way.

Chills ran down her spine as she heard a terrifying growl coming from somewhere on the left. She was nearing an intersection of corridors and froze at the sound. She even held her breath, waiting, tense.

I'm one with the wall, I'm one with the wall, Ciara chanted in her head, closing her eyes for a moment. It would be amazing to be able to become invisible at this moment. She wondered if there was someone in her family who would have that ability. Or if it was something she could learn. If she ever made it back to her time, she was going to do some research.

She jumped as she heard a whimper. Opening her eyes, she tiptoed to the intersection and very slowly peeked into the darkness. It was like gazing into the abyss. For a moment, she felt as if even time had stopped, as nothing moved.

Then she heard the growl again. It sounded closer this time.

"Eep!" She retreated behind the corner and clamped a hand on her mouth.

Oh gods, it's too late, isn't it? She prayed to whatever gods were listening to save her. She closed her eyes in terror as she heard a hiss, even closer. *This is it, isn't it? I'm going to be eaten by an ancient Japanese monster!*

She heard hardly audible footsteps and opened her eyes, surprised, then turned to the intersection. She saw someone's arm reaching out from the corridor and screamed.

The other person shrieked as well and quickly backpedaled. They were just as startled to have run into someone as Ciara was.

"He-hello?" Ciara asked the darkness. A person, she could deal with. A monster, not so much. She started to think that these adventures in feudal Japan weren't very good for her heart. "Are you hurt?"

She heard some shuffling, and as she looked into the abyss, she couldn't see anyone. But she heard the retreating footsteps.

"Wait!" she took a step into the darkness.

Gold eyes flashed at her, and she stood there as if lightning had struck her. The person growled, which jarred Ciara out of her frozen state.

"I'm lost! Can you help me?"

"Are you not afraid?" The sound was a mixture of a growl and human voice. It wasn't easy to understand. She couldn't decide whether it belonged to a woman or a man.

"I just want to get back to the part of the castle I know," Ciara insisted. "I'm sorry to have disturbed you."

She heard a strange noise. Were they chuckling?

"I can show you the shortest way," they said, "But…"

"But what?"

"It's this way, into the darkness," they explained. "Are you brave enough for that?"

The person held out their hand, which was just about visible by the faint light coming from the intersection. Ciara looked at it, hesitating. The person had long nails, bordering on claws, and a few strange marks, which looked like scales, dotted their hand.

"No?" The hand retracted.

"Wait!" Ciara held onto the hand and looked into the gold eyes of whoever was there. She only knew two people who had eyes like those. And one of them had already left the castle. "Please help me."

There was a heartbeat of silence before he replied, "All right. Don't let go. Your eyes can't see in this darkness."

"And yours can?" she asked, genuinely curious.

"My eyesight is better, yes."

"And—"

"No more questions," he interrupted her, "or you can find your way out by yourself."

"Sorry," she murmured as she let him lead her through the dark corridors. His hands were as cold as the wind sweeping across the place. It took quite a few minutes for them to reach an intersection with a lit corridor. The light was blinding. He let go of her hand and pointed to the intersection.

"Turn to the right and go straight. You'll end up in the inner courtyard soon."

"Thank you, Katsuo," Ciara replied, taking off.

"You're welcome, but I'm not him," the mysterious person replied.

Ciara twirled around, eyes wide.

"What?" she asked the darkness, but she didn't get a response this time. She felt goosebumps on her arms, staring into the abyss and quickly turned around to follow that person's directions.

If it wasn't Katsuo, then who was it? No one else was supposed to have gold eyes in this place now that Yuki had left.

She heard a shout.

"Ciara-sama?"

"Yura? Is that you, Yura? Where are you?" Ciara picked up her pace.

"Yokatta[1]! I've found you!"

"I got lost," Ciara shouted back. She felt she was getting closer to where Yura was. "Keep talking. I'll follow your voice!"

"I'm here! Did you find someone to come with us?"

"Yes! Taiki said—Oh." Ciara stopped yelling as she almost bumped into Yura who was just rounding a corner. She switched to her normal voice. "He said we'll meet our guard at the gates."

"Brilliant. Let's go and change then we can—"

"Yura, I'm not going to change. Not this time," Ciara insisted. "My clothes will be fine."

"But—"

"Yura. Stop." She'd used her Voice on the girl accidentally a couple of times before, but this was the first time it was intentional. The change was apparent, and Yura immediately fell silent as she froze on the spot. "Let's go. I will not change."

"A-as you wish, Milady."

"Ciara," she corrected.

"Ciara-sama. This way," Yura gestured ahead of them, and in a few steps, they were in the inner courtyard.

"Ah, finally something familiar!"

---

1. usually translated as 'thank goodness'

"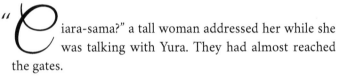iara-sama?" a tall woman addressed her while she was talking with Yura. They had almost reached the gates.

"Yes?"

"I'm Shizuru. I'll be your guard today."

Ciara took another look at the woman, realizing she was wearing the uniform of the soldiers. Her hair was neatly arranged in a bun on top of her head, and her expression was strict.

"Thank you. Were you waiting long?"

Shizuru blinked, surprise crossing over her face.

"Not at all."

Ciara sighed in relief and smiled at her and Yura.

"Let's go then!"

Their guard promptly followed them as they made their way down the castle hill.

"Where do you want to go first, Ciara-sama?" Yura asked.

"It's been a while since we've been to the teahouse. Let's start there!"

They had a lovely time there. During their idle chat, Ciara snuck a few nibbles under the table to the cat.

"So tell me, Shizuru, how long have you worked at the castle?" Ciara asked, curious.

"Ten years."

"Ten?" Ciara looked taken aback. "But you look…"

Shizuru and Yura looked at her, expectant.

"Maybe twenty-ish?"

"I was around Ayaka-dono's age when I arrived at the castle. My family couldn't afford to raise me."

Ciara nibbled on some edamame. She wanted to know what happened but didn't want to bring up painful memories. She sighed. "I'm sorry. It must've been really hard for you."

"It can't be helped," Shizuru shrugged, "I'm probably better off here. I have accommodation and meals twice a day. That's more than what I could've achieved had I remained at home."

"Are there other women working as guards?" Ciara asked. "You're the first one I've met here."

Shizuru frowned but dutifully replied, "At the moment, I'm the only one, yes."

"I see."

"Why do you ask, if I may inquire, Ciara-sama?"

"Oh, no need to be so formal with me," Ciara waved. "I was just curious. It must be a bit tiring, surrounded by testosterone all day."

"Tesutosuteron?" Yura and Shizuru asked, butchering the foreign word.

"Oh, I mean men. They can be a bit tiring."

"Well, I sometimes pop over to the servant quarters to have a chat with the girls," Shizuru explained before turning to Yura with rapt interest. "Which reminds me. Have you already done the deed?"

Yura paled.

"Chicken."

"Hey!"

"What? What happened?" Ciara asked, curious.

"Yura and I had a bet. She lost."

"I did not!" Yura protested. "Well, only a little bit."

"You either lose or don't. There's no 'little bit,'" Shizuru said. "It's like being pregnant. Or dead. You can't be 'just a little bit' of either."

Ciara snorted into her tea at the simile.

"She's got a point, you know."

Yura pouted, crunching her nose.

"I'm going to give you a deadline," Shizuru said.

"Fine," Yura huffed.

"Today."

"What?"

"Why is she panicking?" Ciara asked. "Shizuru, what did you bet on?"

"She has to ask out the guy she likes."

"Stop! It's so embarrassing just thinking about it!" Yura hid her flaming face behind her hands.

"He's on pagoda duty in the evening," Shizuru shared.

"Stop it!"

"All night."

"Shizu!"

Ciara couldn't help but laugh. Yura was so adorable being embarrassed like that. *Oh, youth!* She reminded her of Karen.

She frowned, sipping the last of her tea. All her mirth had suddenly vanished as she remembered her little cousin. She was back home, safe, but for how long? If that sadist's words could be trusted, then Karen would be in danger rather soon. She had to get home. But Katsuo...

Ciara sighed, and the others looked at her, surprised.

"Are you feeling unwell, Ciara-sama?" Yura inquired.

"No, it's just... I want to have a walk. Are you finished, ladies?"

Soon, they left the teahouse. Ciara didn't have a particular destination in mind this time. She just wanted to walk around a little bit and clear her head. Maybe discover the town more.

Unexpectedly, Shizuru came up beside her.

"I'd advise you to choose another direction, Ciara-sama."

"Oh, why is that?"

"This road leads to the most dangerous part of town."

"I somehow doubt Katsuo would let such a place exist here," Ciara insisted but stopped walking.

"Milord is adamant in making this town as safe as possible, but shady people are hard to get rid of. Also, we'll soon reach the entertainment district."

"Entertainment...?" Ciara questioned, her eyebrows furrowing.

"Brothels," Shizuru clarified bluntly.

"What?" Ciara paled a little. That was most definitely not the destination she had in mind. She took another glance at the road stretching before them. On one side, there was a big stone building with red lanterns adorning the entrance. Someone was walking up the steps leading to the door.

Ciara could just make out his profile; to her shock, she recognized Katsuo. *What the hell is he doing in the red-light district?* She saw crimson for a moment as she turned around, her head held high, and marched in the opposite direction. There was no more question in her mind. She chose Karen over Katsuo.

Yura and Shizuru exchanged a glance, not understanding what happened. They failed to notice Katsuo heading into a brothel. The rest of the afternoon was soured, and they quickly made their way back to the castle.

Ciara was fuming inside. She just didn't understand why he would do something like that. Why would he do that to her? Was she not enough for him? Or was it just that she forgot the lessons life had taught her? She could never count on men; they'd always leave. Starting with her father then all the past boyfriends and suitors.

She thought Katsuo was different.

She thought they shared something.

She thought, just maybe, their fake engagement had changed into something... more.

It's just a fake. She sighed, fighting her tears. *You have no standing in being jealous. You knew what you've agreed to when you made the deal,* she reminded herself.

Ciara's fist met the column next to her as she stopped in the middle of the corridor. It hurt, damn it!

If I'd known earlier— She quickly stopped that thought. Would she have done anything differently? It was an undeniable fact that she had fallen for Katsuo. She knew she shouldn't have but couldn't control her feelings, and now she was left to face the consequences.

48

*K*atsuo made his way up to the entrance and stopped for a moment. The last time he had been here, he was running to save Ciara from a gruesome fate. He had almost been too late.

This time, he was going to repay his debts. Collecting his thoughts, he entered the foyer, and immediately, half a dozen girls appeared at his side.

"What can we do for you, Milord?"

"Would you like tea?"

"I can give you a massage." One girl winked at him. "I'll even give you a discount."

"I have business with the Madame. Fetch her."

The girls fell silent.

"*Now.*"

"A-as you wish, Milord!" One of them waved to a child servant. "Go get the Madame. Did you not hear?"

The little girl ran off, leaving a stack of clothes on the floor.

"Useless," the woman mumbled, thinking no one heard her. Her eyes narrowed as her gaze followed the fleeing child. When she turned back to Katsuo, she had a sweet smile plastered on her face. "May I escort you to the meeting room, my lord?"

"You may not."

The woman gasped, shocked. Tears clouded her eyes, and she ran off, sniffling loudly. Katsuo almost rolled his eyes at the obvious pretense.

"Milord! How good to see you again!"

He heard the Madame and turned in her direction. She was gracefully walking toward him, arms open. She had a long kiseru in one hand. It was an elaborately carved bamboo pipe. "What can I do for you?"

"I prefer to speak somewhere private."

She took one long look at him before taking a drag from her kiseru.

"Of course. This way."

She led the way to a nearby meeting room.

"Would you fancy a drink, Milord?"

"No, thank you."

The Madame nodded at someone behind him, and the door closed quietly. They sat down at the table.

"I'm listening," she said, puffing out a small smoke ring.

"You remember a few days ago when I came here looking for someone."

"Yes."

"One of your girls told me where to find the culprits."

The Madame tapped her chin with the end of the pipe. Her face brightened after a moment.

"Right! I remember! What about her?"

"I'd like to buy her debt."

The Madame's eyes widened so much she looked as if she was a bug.

"Excuse me?"

"You heard me. I do not like to repeat myself."

"So you… you mean to buy her debt? What will you do with that girl?"

Katsuo smirked and crossed his arms.

"That is none of your concern, is it?"

They stared at each other.

"All right." The Madame blinked and told him the amount.

"Here." Katsuo pulled out a pouch full of coins from the sleeve of his kimono. "This should cover it and some more. Now, bring her here."

The Madame put the kiseru in her mouth and took a drag. She reached for the pouch and opened it. Her jaw slacked, the pipe hitting the table, forgotten.

"Do we have a deal?"

"Very much so, Milord. It was a pleasure doing business with you."

"The girl. Now."

"Of course!"

The Madame quickly got up and hurried to the door. She shouted for a servant to fetch the girl.

"But she is with a client—"

"I don't care! Get her *now* if you want to eat dinner."

"Y-yes, Madame!"

"Finally."

Katsuo didn't have to wait for long. A slightly disheveled girl showed up soon. The Madame, who had gone back to sitting behind the table, straightened, and a disapproving look was written over her face.

"What do you think you're doing, presenting yourself like that?!" she shrieked.

Katsuo put up a hand, and she fell silent. His ears were hurting. He looked at the girl, who hastily bowed to him. It was indeed the same girl who had helped him find Ciara.

"Gather your belongings. You're coming with me."

"Erm… what?"

"Don't bring shame on me now," the Madame grumbled. "You heard what he said. Get your stuff."

"R-right." She walked off in a daze.

"Hurry up!" The Madame shouted after her. Katsuo heard the girl's footsteps pick up.

"Are you sure you want that on your hand? That girl is trouble, I tell you," the Madame said, tossing the pouch from one hand to another.

"I won't back out from our deal."

"Suit yourself, Milord," she said, standing up. "Well, I have work to do. Have a pleasant day."

Katsuo inclined his head as she exited the room. He only had to wait a few minutes before the girl appeared. She only had a small bundle wrapped in furoshiki[1].

"I'm finished."

"Good."

Katsuo stood and strolled outside. The girl hesitated a moment before following him. They didn't talk until after they stepped outside the building. She stopped at the threshold, shading her eyes with her hand from the sun's glaring. It wasn't even a very bright day.

"What is it?"

"It's strange to be able to walk out of here," she admitted before looking at him. "I don't understand what's happening."

———————————————

1. wrapping cloth

49

"*C*ome."

She started off slowly but quickly increased her walking speed and caught up to Katsuo. She followed a step behind him. Katsuo led her to the main street and stopped at an intersection.

"You are free."

"What?"

"I thank you for helping me the other day," he said. "I have bought your debt from the Madame. You're free to do as you please."

She couldn't seem to comprehend.

"Are you saying I don't have to work there?"

"Yes."

"And you don't want to… use my services?"

"No."

She shook her head and leaned against a wall.

"Is it that hard to believe?"

"Yes. I mean, it's been something I've dreamt of. I've worked hard to get rid of my family's debt, but… wow… what do I do now? It was the only way to live up till now."

"Here," Katsuo held out his hand. A small pouch rested there, full of coins. "This will be enough to get you started. I'm sure there's something you want to do."

The girl stared at his open hand but didn't take the pouch. Katsuo waved it in front of her.

"Take it."

She shook her head.

"You don't want to?" Katsuo's eyebrows furrowed. "Why?"

"If I may be so bold... I'd like to ask for something else," she said, her voice barely above whisper.

"What is it?"

"Let me work for you."

Katsuo didn't leave much time for her to convince him. He had no doubt he wouldn't have anything to gain by employing a former prostitute. He offered the pouch of coins again.

"I can cook," she said.

"I have cooks."

"I can sew clothes."

"Not interested," he replied and turned away.

"Wait, Milord! I can dance and sing, entertain you and your soldiers."

"No need."

"I know some herbs to treat wounds."

"I already have a healer. Look"—Katsuo was at the end of his patience—"just accept these coins and start a business or whatever. I can't help you with employment."

The girl bit her lips.

"What if I told you I'd spy for you?"

Katsu raised an eyebrow.

"And how would you do that?" His voice was amused. How would she gather information or infiltrate enemy strongholds? Would she be able to assassinate a warrior?

He had to snort at the idea of the frail woman succeeding in any of these tasks.

"I've learnt a thing or two while working at the house," she replied. "I can gather information like no one."

Katsuo crossed his arms. He doubted she could add anything to Taiki's information network, but more spies always came in handy. However, he doubted her abilities, and he had no idea if she could be trusted.

"Like what?"

"I could tell you about those men who kidnapped that person you were looking for."

He moved too fast for the human eye. One moment, they were standing a few feet apart, and the next, the girl was slammed into the supporting pillar of a hut with Katsuo's fingers around her neck. She blinked in surprise.

"Choose your next words *very* carefully."

The girl gulped, but she seemed perfectly calm otherwise. She didn't struggle, nor did she cower in fear. It was all or nothing, and she had nothing to lose at this point.

"They were under the impression that they were following Kawayuki's orders," she said, "when in truth, the person behind it all is someone different."

"Who?"

"I don't know their name, but it's someone with incredible power."

"And how would you know this?"

A wry smile appeared on her full lips.

"Many travelers stop at our house, especially on open days. Men are so easy to manipulate after a few cups of sake."

Katsuo held her gaze for a moment longer, seeking deception. She seemed to be telling him the truth. He surprised her with his sudden laugh, as he retreated a couple of steps. She put a delicate hand to her neck.

"Does this mean you don't believe me?"

"Quite the contrary," Katsuo replied when his laugh subsided. "You may come. But first, let's get you something more… appropriate to wear. Follow me."

Katsuo walked her to the tailor who made the castle uniforms. He always had a few in stock, just in case. Katsuo wasn't disappointed this time, either. He took one look at the girl once she was changed, nodded, then paid for three sets of uniforms for her, before they continued their way to the castle.

"You are to tell no one of your origins, is that clear? I don't want my soldiers and servants getting distracted."

"Yes, Milord."

"Take the rest of the day to familiarize yourself with the accommodations and your peers. Your training will begin tomorrow. You are to report to Taiki, my Chief of Security, first. He will tell you the rest. What is your name?" He had just realized he'd never even asked.

"Rui."

"I'm counting on you, Rui."

"I won't disappoint you, my lord."

50

*H*e came back with a woman, after visiting a brothel. Unbelievable! It didn't take a genius to draw the obvious conclusion. Ciara had just managed to catch a glimpse of them before she turned back to examining Takeru's arm. She had a dark expression on her face as she ran a finger where Takeru's injury was supposed to be. His skin was smooth, as if the snakebite had never happened.

"Amazing."

"Do you believe me now when I say I'm fine?" Takeru asked with a half-smile, withdrawing his arm.

"Maybe. It's hard to believe," she replied, honest. "But it must've hurt."

"Nothing I couldn't handle." He puffed out his chest, proud.

"But you're not keen on doing this next year, too, are you?"

"If brother allows me, I'd be happy to do it again." He nodded at Katsuo who had just arrived.

"Good afternoon," he greeted.

"Good afternoon, brother."

"Oh, hi," was Ciara's curt reply. For some reason, Takeru could feel tension in the air between the two, but his brother seemed ignorant.

"Right, I was just about to head to the… eerr… training ground. See you later!" Takeru said and quickly disappeared down a random corridor.

"How has your day been?"

"Quite well," Ciara said. "I went into town with Yura and Shizuru."

"Ah, you got Shizuru. She is a fierce one."

"They showed me around," Ciara continued, but Katsuo didn't seem to catch on.

"It's nice, isn't it?"

"Some parts, yes. If you'll excuse me." Ciara quickly finished the conversation and walked back to her room. Standing in front of her door, she realized she didn't want to go in and instead headed for the orchard. She was sure the crisp air would calm her down.

She was just so angry with Katsuo. Why did she have to suffer so? Ciara sighed, turning her face to the sky and closing her eyes.

It's because I killed Mother. I do not deserve happiness. I'm still not forgiven.

She felt tears gathering in the corner of her eyes, but hastily wiped them away before they could fall. She walked deeper into the orchard, concentrating on the sights. Most of the leaves had already fallen, and those that remained were the color of rust. Everything reminded her of evanescence. Nature, her mother, even her relationship with Katsuo.

All gone in a moment.

The rain pelted down as it grew late. Katsuo couldn't get the image of Ciara examining Takeru's hand out of his mind. He tried to recall all the times he had seen Ciara with another man. She was always polite, smiling kindly. Just how many men held her attention? He was a fool.

Frustrated by his thoughts, he went to meet Taiki. Usually, the ninja visited him, but today, he felt like venturing to the dark side of the castle. The heavy rain and the gloomy atmosphere complemented his dark mood beautifully.

He had just entered the corridor where Taiki's office was when the ninja suddenly appeared beside him. He always knew when Katsuo was seeking him out.

"Milord."

Katsuo growled at him. "We've been through this."

"My apologies, Katsuo-sama," Taiki amended. He inclined his head.

"Let's talk in your office."

The ninja had a few tricks, making sure it was impossible to spy on their conversations.

"As you wish."

They quickly reached his office, and he opened the door for Katsuo to enter. He slid it closed securely once they entered. They settled around his low desk.

"What can I do for you, Katsuo-sama?"

"I brought a new person to the castle."

Taiki nodded. "Rui from the town brothel."

Katsuo wasn't surprised his chief of security already had intel on the woman.

"She will be under your guidance."

Taiki's eyebrows rose in surprise. "May I ask why?"

"I want you to evaluate her potential."

"As?"

"As someone who could be useful. Whether it's gathering intelligence or fighting, whatever you see fit for her."

"Understood," Taiki replied. From his tone, Katsuo knew he had questions but wouldn't want to outright challenge his lord's decision. Under normal circumstances, Katsuo would ask his opinion, but not now.

"Do you have anything to report?" *Might as well get some work done while I'm here,* Katsuo thought.

"Nothing of importance. Just some stupid rumors going around town and among the servants."

"About?"

"It's nothing you need to worry about, Katsuo-sama. Some foolish talk about time-travelling witches."

"That does sound far-fetched. Well"—Katsuo stood —"I'll let you get back to your work. I'm counting on you."

"Mochiron[1], Katsuo-sama."

Two sets of eyes followed Katsuo out of the office. Taiki's cat watched from the shadows between cupboards, its green eyes glinting momentarily in the darkness of the room. It growled softly.

"Patience," Taiki admonished. "You'll soon be free to wander around as you please."

The cat shot out from between the furniture and landed in Taiki's lap. He stroked its black fur and was rewarded with the sound of purrs resonating in the room.

"You won't have to hide for long."

---

1. of course

51

*C*iara didn't mind the rain. It was like having a cold shower but with a chilly wind. She sneezed as she made her way back to the castle. She had waited too long, until her toes felt like icicles, before heading back. Her hands trembled and she slowly climbed the hill.

It felt as if all energy was drained from her. A hot soak in the bathhouse sounded heavenly at the moment, but she wasn't sure if she deserved it.

A huge sneeze left her. She sniffled. Deserving or not, she had to get into hot water if she didn't want to fall ill in medieval times. Who knew if she'd die here from catching a cold? She didn't want to risk it, no matter how depressed she felt.

Ciara hurried to her room to grab a change of clothes before going to the bathhouse. Steam swirled around in the changing room when she entered. She quickly changed out of her soaked clothes and wrapped a towel around herself. She was cold and sneezed as she entered the shower area.

"Oh."

Ciara looked up at the surprised voice of Katsuo. He was just drying his hair with a towel but covered himself up when he noticed Ciara entering the room.

"Ciara, darling—"

She cut him off swiftly. "Are you finished, or have you just arrived?"

"I've just finished," he replied.

Ciara nodded then walked over to a stool the farthest away from him, but didn't sit down. She glanced back over her shoulder at him.

"Well?"

"Well what?"

"Aren't you going to go?"

Katsuo's eyebrows furrowed. "Are you mad?"

"I'm not!" As if to emphasize her point, she sneezed.

Katsuo had just noticed her hair dripping wet.

"Have you been out in the rain?" He took a step toward her, but she held up a hand, stopping him.

"Yes. Now, if you'd just leave me alone, I could warm up."

"I could help—"

"No thanks. You've done enough." The words had just slipped past Ciara's lips before she realized it. She froze. There goes pretending everything was all right.

"What do you mean?" Katsuo walked closer, and Ciara backed away. He stopped a few feet away from her. "Why are you mad at me?"

"I told you—"

"I don't believe that."

Ciara's eyes flashed in warning, but he continued, "What is it? Why are you putting distance between us?"

"*I'm* putting distance between us?" Ciara's voice was sharp like a dagger. With every word, it twisted Katsuo's heart. "You go pick up a prostitute, have the audacity to bring her home, *and* to top it off, you pretend *I'm* the problem here?"

"What—" Katsuo took a step back at the impact of Ciara's words. "You misunderstand."

"There's nothing to misunderstand here."

"Let me explain."

"I know our engagement is only a fake one, but you could've waited at least until the month was up. No one, *no one* has ever humiliated me so much!" Ciara rambled, pinching the corner of her towel together. She was getting cold.

"Ciara—"

"No, I'm done!" she said and sneezed. Katsuo used this opportunity to talk.

"When you were kidnapped, you were held in that brothel."

"What?" Ciara's face was full of disbelief.

"There's a shed in the backyard. It had a hidden stairway to the room you were held in," Katsuo quickly explained. "I'd never lie to you, believe me."

"That still doesn't explain what you were doing at the brothel today. I *saw* you. Then you turn up with some random woman. What's your explanation for *that*?"

She sniffled, feeling another sneeze coming soon. She crunched up her nose.

"That woman saw you being carried off. If she hasn't told me where to go, I may not have arrived in time."

"That's it?" Ciara asked.

"Yes."

"So what is she doing here?" Her eyes narrowed.

"I bought her."

"You did *what*?"

"I paid off her debt because she helped us. I never intended to bring her here."

"Yet you did."

"I wanted to give her some money to start a new life, but she insisted on being employed by me," Katsuo replied. "She might be an asset."

"An asset." Ciara inclined her head. "I see."

"So? Do you understand?"

"What I do understand, Katsuo"—Ciara's eyes smothered him—"is that you are a warlord, yet you cannot seem to stand by your original decision when it comes to this woman."

"Ciara—"

"Don't!" She raised her hand, backing away. "Please don't. Leave me alone, I don't want to catch a cold."

Katsuo waited for a heartbeat before nodding.

"I don't want you to fall ill, either. We'll talk later."

With that, he turned and walked to the changing room, his steps confident. Ciara snarled at his back. *We'll see about that.*

She quickly started scrubbing herself. She couldn't wait to get into the hot water.

52

*K*atsuo was determined to clear things up after the usual family dinner. Ciara completely misunderstood his intentions, and he admitted to himself that maybe his choice of words was not the most fortunate under the circumstances. Ciara was in a bad mood, cold, and agitated. Of course she wouldn't see reason that easily.

A full meal and the company of Ayaka would surely put Ciara in a better mood. That was when he was going to talk to her. She would see sense in his words.

He had a meeting with one of his vassals just before dinner, but it was a boring matter. Katsuo cut the meeting short and walked back to the main building for dinner. However, he ran into Orihime in the courtyard.

"Good evening, Katsuo-sama! How lovely to meet you here!"

"Good evening, Orihime-dono," he replied. "How come you are taking a stroll alone?"

"Believe me or not, my lord, I tire of constant company.

I let my maids take the evening off," she replied, fanning herself.

"How generous of you. If you'll excuse me—"

"How is Ciara-dono?"

"Pardon?" Katsuo thought he misheard her.

"How is Ciara-dono? She looked down when she got back from town earlier," Orihime hid her face behind her fan. "Does Milord know what happened?"

"Nothing in particular." Katsuo chose his words carefully. "I've just met her not long ago. She seemed fine."

Lies, lies, lies. But he would take care of it.

"Oh, I'm happy to hear," Orihime said, snapping her fan closed. She mustered a smile. "Maybe she was just lonely, being so far away from her home."

Katsuo tried to figure out what she was not saying. He didn't have much luck.

"Are you homesick, Orihime-dono?"

"Oh, Milord, I miss home, yes, but such is the fate of a woman who is of age!" She dramatically put a hand on her forehead. "I'm sure Ciara-sama misses her family very much so."

"No need to worry. Have a nice evening," Katsuo said, finally excusing himself.

"You, too, Milord," Orihime bowed and went on her way. Katsuo heard a chuckle coming from her but was too eager to get back to the main building and get dinner over with to pay attention to the strangeness of it.

He quickly arrived at his room, and to his surprise, he was the last one to get there.

"Daddy, where have you been?" Ayaka immediately ran to him. He lifted her up and walked in. "I had a meeting. Have you been waiting for me?"

"Yes. I'm so hungry!" the little girl told him. He let her down.

"Then go, eat!"

She hurried over to the table and sat down next to
Ciara. The only available seating was next to Takeru, and
Katsuo walked over there. Clearly, Ciara was still angry at
him. He would make amends.

Dinner itself was an awkward matter, and even Ayaka's
adorableness couldn't alleviate the tension between Ciara
and Katsuo. The little girl noticed something was amiss
and tried to make everyone join in on her conversation
about the most random things only a child could come up
with, and even though all adults had participated, Ciara
refused to talk to Katsuo for longer than a few short
sentences.

At the end, even the family singing had been postponed
to another time. Takeru picked Ayaka up to tuck her to
bed, and Ciara stood up to leave.

"Well—"

"Stay." Katsuo was on his feet in a second.

"What?" Ciara's voice was full of incomprehension.
"You're not serious, are you?"

"I don't joke about these things. I want to have a proper
conversation with you," Katsuo said, but Ciara still didn't
budge. "This afternoon was a disaster. You refused to
listen, and I fumbled my words. Allow me to make
amends."

Ciara's jaw went slack. She didn't expect Katsuo to say
this, and she could see the reason behind his words. His
words were almost as good as an apology. Plus, she misunderstood his intentions a moment ago. It was only fair she
heard him out.

"Okay," she said, looking him in the eyes. "Talk to me."

"Let's sit down, shall we?" Katsuo asked, gesturing
toward the pillows.

"I'm fine."

"Fine." Katsuo let out a small sigh and stayed on his feet. Gathering his thoughts, he continued. "As I was saying, that woman had helped me find you when you were kidnapped. I went back to pay my dues."

"And she had a debt and you paid it off," Ciara supplemented. "See? I listened."

"Indeed. Then I intended to send her on her way with some allowance, but she refused to do that. Instead, she insisted on being employed by me."

"Why?"

Katsuo blinked.

"I'm a daimyō."

"And?"

"It's an honor to be employed by me," Katsuo said, puzzled at her reaction. There was no arrogance in his voice, he just stated a matter of fact.

"Oh," Ciara nodded, understanding dawning on her. "So? You have plenty of servants and soldiers here."

"She insisted."

"And you felt like you had to comply, because…?"

"At first, I didn't want to, but she was very persistent."

Ciara waited for the rest; however, Katsuo seemed to have said what he wanted.

"That's it?" she asked in disbelief.

"Yes. Nothing more, nothing less."

"I still don't agree."

"I didn't seek your permission."

Ciara tensed for a moment. Of course he wouldn't. What was she to him? Just a convenient excuse for unwanted marriage proposals. She wasn't his partner, not really.

"I see," she said with some difficulty. "Well, if that was all—"

"Ciara." Katsuo grabbed her hand as she turned to leave.

She glanced back at him over her shoulder. "Are we on good terms now?"

She felt blood rush to her head at the question. Her eyes narrowed. "Far from it."

"Why?"

"I still don't understand. I feel like there's something you're still not telling me," she replied.

Katsuo looked into her eyes with a serious expression.

"I'm not the only one with secrets."

"What?" Ciara swayed a little. "What do you mean?"

Katsuo could feel her heartbeat pick up under his fingers on her wrist. Ah, so he was right.

"You refuse to talk about your past. Every time I ask about what happened to you or about your homeland, you shut the conversation down. Why can't you talk to me?"

"That... you wouldn't understand," she replied, looking away. She tried to retrieve her hand, but Katsuo refused to let go. His grip was gentle but firm.

"Try me, or are you a spy?" he said as his eyes flashed gold for a moment.

"There!" Ciara pointed at him. "What was that?"

"What was what?" Katsuo asked, letting go of her suddenly. He even took a step back.

"Your eyes. Sometimes they're brown, and sometimes they're gold like Yuki's. Why do they do that?"

He immediately clammed up.

"See? And you ask me why I don't tell you everything. Trust goes both ways, Katsuo," Ciara said, twirling around and ramming straight into the cupboard.

"Ow," she massaged her painful nose and glared at the furniture, but at that moment, the basket on top, which had been balancing on the edge, had toppled over and spilled its contents on her.

"Are you all right?" Katsuo asked, immediately moving closer.

"I'm fine," Ciara held out her free hand. The other was still nursing her nose. "What was in there, anyway?"

She looked down to see white balls rolling around the floor. Plenty were still intact, but there were some which had opened during the fall.

Ciara was just about to dismiss them, when she realized she was seeing dragons. All the opened balls had a dragon symbol inside them. Slowly, she squatted down and picked up a closed ball.

"Ciara—" Katsuo tried to get the ball from her, but she turned away, quickly opening it. It had a dragon inside, too. Her eyes flashed with rage. She held up the ball for Katsuo to see it.

"I bet you have an explanation for this, too?"

Katsuo opened his mouth then closed it. He tried again, but no sound came out.

"Have a nice life with Orihime," she said as she threw the ball at him and marched out of the room.

Katsuo stood there frozen, looking after her.

"Hells!"

That was *not* how he imagined the evening would go.

53

*C*iara ran to her room, but when she got there, she had no idea what to do. She wanted to scream, to break something, to cry, to do *something* and get revenge on Katsuo for tricking her into an unfair agreement.

How dare he? *How dare he?* He never intended to play by the rules. The game was rigged before it started. It was all a game to him, while for her... she truly believed their feelings were mutual. That she had finally found someone who would be a partner. Someone she could trust.

She screamed in frustration.

"Screw it!" She picked up a vase and hurled it at the wall.

The clatter echoed in the room, and when it died down, the silence hurt. She walked over to the low table in the corner of the room and rummaged around to find some paper and a writing utensil. She found a brush and a block of solid ink.

"How do I even—?" Ciara tried to figure out how to use it, and her gaze landed on the broken vase. Water seeped to the tatami mat beneath it. She stood up and went to the water basin on the other side of the room. She carried the jug back to the desk.

She found a small dish and put the block of ink in it before pouring some water over it. The ink slowly colored the water. Too slow for her taste, but there was nothing she could do.

Ciara grabbed the brush and made her best effort to write down a note with the items available to her. When she was done, she quickly read through it once more. Uncertainty filled her chest. What if no one could understand? She didn't know Japanese and still wasn't completely sure how it was possible that she could speak it. It probably had something to do with that Kawa-something person with the black teeth.

"Bleh," she grimaced as she remembered. Damnit, but it was the only chance she had. She had to go back there and find the mirror if she wanted to get back home. She wasn't even sure how long it would take or which direction to go.

She couldn't even remember that guy's full name!

Ciara folded the note and left it on the desk. She turned around the room that had been hers for weeks. It was nice while it lasted. Too bad her experience ended like this.

She realized there was nothing she could bring with herself. She was already wearing comfortable clothes. The only thing she might need on her journey was money. She went back to her desk where she knew Yura had hidden the pouch full of money they had been using when visiting town.

She shook it and could hear the coins jingle inside. Nodding, she hid it in the folds of her clothes and headed out. She did not spare another glance to her room. Her confident steps led her to the courtyard and toward the gate. It was already dark, and a chilly wind swept through the castle grounds.

"Halt! Who goes there?"

"Ciara."

"My lady! Forgive me, I did not recognize you," the soldier bowed. "How can I be of service to you?"

"I want to go to town."

The guard exchanged a glance with his partner.

"At this hour?"

"Yes."

"I'm sorry, but no one leaves the castle grounds after sundown unless they have special permission from Milord," he replied.

"I have."

"May we see it?" The other soldier asked.

"Oh. You didn't say *written* permission."

"That's what he meant."

"I see. Well, then, I'll be back soon with his special written permission," Ciara said, turning around.

"Milady," the guards bowed as she walked away from them.

Damn. How do I get out of here? It really is like a fortress. Can I climb the walls, I wonder? Ciara took a right turn and investigated her chances. Unfortunately, guards patrolled the walls every few minutes, and it had been a long while since she had climbed a tree, which was way easier than scaling a wall.

She was just weighing her chances when someone unexpectedly spoke to her.

"How unusual to see you outside the main castle after dark."

"Oh, Orihime," Ciara acknowledged her. Great, just what she needed.

"Why the sour face?"

Ciara didn't reply. Her attention was on the walls,

contemplating. Orihime followed her gaze, and it took her only a moment to figure out Ciara's intentions.

"Do you want to leave the castle grounds? I might know a way."

"What?" Ciara snapped her head to the side to look at Orihime. Her need to get out overwhelmed the suspicion she felt toward the woman. "What did you just say?"

Orihime smiled sweetly. "As you may be aware, my accommodations are at the guest house, tucked in the other corner of the courtyard. However, that means less patrolling guards. I can show you the part of the wall they ignore."

"Really?"

"There's even a tree reaching outside."

Ciara narrowed her eyes.

"Where's the catch?"

"Catch? I'm afraid I don't understand," Orihime inclined her head. Her eyes were wide, innocent.

"Why would you help me, when we both know you don't like me?"

"Well… you escaping means one thing. You want to be as far away from Katsuo-sama as possible, which coincides with my will. So why wouldn't I help you?"

Ciara though for a moment then nodded.

"You have a point. Okay, show me the way."

"Follow me," Orihime said, taking the lead.

54

"*Y*ou can do this. You can do this," Yura told herself as she walked along the abandoned corridors. She held a flask in her hand, filled with the freshly brewed oolong tea. "Just ask him if he'd like some tea. If he says no, you can just give him the flask and go away."

She stopped mid-stride.

"Wait, no, that isn't quite right!" She shook her head. "I'm so confused!"

Yura hid her face behind her free hand. She was nervous, but a deal was a deal, and she wasn't going to bring shame to her name by not holding up her end of the bet. She took a deep breath, straightened, and opened her eyes.

"I can do this," she whispered as she marched on toward the pagoda, where fate awaited her.

"We'll have a celebratory drink together later, and you can tell me about it," Shizuru told her at dinner.

"But we don't know if he'd agree."

"Why wouldn't he?" another servant piped up. She was a few years older than Yura. *"He's crazy if he doesn't go out with you."*

"Either way, we'll be having a drink," Shizuru ended the argument. *"Whether it be in celebration or to drown our sadness, it depends on you."*

"What? Our sadness? It's my *heart on the line!"* Yura protested.

Shizuru smirked at her. *"Go make him yours."*

"Shizu!"

Yura shook her head as she remembered. Shizuru sometimes came off as demanding, maybe even aggressive, but her heart was in the right place. Soon, Yura saw the pagoda and could make out the figure standing guard near the path leading to it.

Damnit, her nerves were acting up again.

"Keep calm, deep breaths," Yura told herself. "You can do this. I can do this. Here I go!"

She stepped toward the path confidently. She made it to a few paces before she was distracted by nearby voices.

Is that Ciara-sama? What is she doing here? Yura stopped and altered her course, following Ciara's voice. Soon, she heard someone else. *Orihime-dono?* Yura's eyes got big. She had to do something to help her lady!

She hurried over to the scene, catching up to the women quickly.

"Ciara-sama!"

Ciara startled as she heard Yura's voice. She looked over her shoulder.

"Yura? What are you doing here?"

"I… I heard you and wondered…"

"Wondered what, servant?" Orihime bit out.

"Hey, don't talk to her like that!" Ciara admonished.

"Psssh," Orihime turned her face away.

"What is it, Yura?"

"I thought… maybe Milady—I mean, Ciara-sama would need some assistance."

"That's sweet of you, but I'm fine, thank you."

"Oh. But…" Yura's gaze found Orihime who had turned her back on them.

"Are you coming or not? I don't have all night."

"Sure, your majesty," Ciara said, sarcasm dripping from her voice. "Yura, you don't need to—"

"I'll help!" she quickly jumped in.

"She doesn't need your help," Orihime said, disdain coloring her voice.

Yura frowned, but her expectant gaze was on Ciara, who was reminded of a puppy. She couldn't just leave Yura behind, not like this. Ciara sighed.

"Please don't tell anyone until morning, but I'm leaving."

"L-leaving?"

"I'm going back home."

"Why?"

"None of your concern, girl," Orihime replied.

"I can speak for myself, no need to butt in," Ciara told her, irritated.

"I'm helping you. You either come now or you'll lose your advantage," Orihime explained. She nodded toward Yura. "That is, if that servant girl can keep her mouth shut."

"Yura, please go back to your room, and don't tell anyone—"

"May I come?"

"I'm sorry?" Ciara blinked in confusion.

"May I come with you?"

"Why would you do that? You have a life here."

"I can't let Milady go alone. You're not familiar in these lands. Anything could happen to you!"

Ciara smiled and walked over to Yura. She put a hand

on the top of the girl's head. "You're very kind, but I'm an adult. I can deal with it."

"I remember when you arrived with Katsuo-sama," Yura whispered. "You were pale as a ghost. And I can see it in your eyes—"

"See what?"

"Pardon me for saying this, Milady, but you don't know war. You don't know how to survive here."

Ciara gasped in surprise. Yura was far more perceptive than she gave her credit for.

"Yura—"

"Oh, gods, I can't take this anymore," Orihime groaned. "Take care of them."

"What—?" Both Ciara and Yura snapped their head in her direction, but the only thing they could see was a shadow descending on them. It was already too late for them to react.

Their world turned to black as they lost consciousness.

Orihime sighed in relief.

"Finally! That chatter was starting to give me a headache!" She massaged her temples with delicate fingers. She looked at the figure dressed in black who had knocked out Ciara and Yura. His face was obscured by a mask.

"I see you've come to a decision. Good choice, coming to our side."

The person inclined their head.

"Now, we have to get her to Juro."

"Consider it done. What about the servant?"

"Do as you wish. I don't want to manage such miniscule tasks."

"I see," he said, bending down to pick up Ciara's limp body. Orihime was already walking away, not sparing another glance at her victims.

55

"*W*here is she?" Katsuo asked a servant he had waved over. They were in the conference room with everyone present – except his dear betrothed. "Get her, now!"

"Yes, Milord," the servant bowed low and scurried off in search of Yura, who was responsible for Lady Ciara.

Katsuo frowned and crossed his arms, waiting. Takeru, who sat in the first row, nearest to the dais, looked up at him with question in his eyes. Katsuo glanced away. His vassals seemed to be patiently waiting, but he knew better. It was such an insult, not respecting their precious time and making them wait! If Ciara's goal was to humiliate him in front of his servants, then she was doing well. His eye twitched as he remembered last night.

Okay, so maybe it was partly his fault. Still, that didn't give her permission to make fifty or so hungry men wait. He was just about to stand up and go hunt her down himself when the servant from before hurried to his side.

"You are alone," he observed, not pleased.

"Milord, I can't find Ciara-sama! What's stranger, I

can't find Yura, either! She was supposed to assist Ciara-sama."

"You checked the room, the bathhouse, the courtyard, everything?"

"Yes, Milord, forgive me, Milord, I couldn't find them!" Poor servant went into a dogeza, so helpless that she couldn't find Ciara.

Katsuo stood, and the murmur in the room died down. Rage radiated off him in waves.

"I will not be able to join you this morning," he said, tenseness in his voice. "Enjoy breakfast."

With that, he quickly made an exit through a side door. Takeru was behind him a moment later. Thanks to his sharp ears, he overheard the servant's quiet words.

He followed Katsuo out into the courtyard.

"Brother, what happened?"

"How would I know?"

"Did you have a fight yesterday?" Takeru asked, stopping Katsuo in his tracks.

"How—?"

"I have eyes," Takeru sighed. "There was tension between you two last night, but I had hoped you'd clear it up. Apparently, I thought wrong."

Katsuo turned around and kept walking.

"Hey, where are you going?"

"To the pagoda."

"Why?" Takeru quickly caught up to him.

"That's the only place she couldn't check. And I've caught Ciara there once already."

"Oh."

They reached the pagoda soon. Both Katsuo and Takeru let go of the restraints on their powers to check with their senses if there was anyone else nearby.

"Correct me if I'm wrong, but I can only sense the guard over there."

"Same here," Katsuo said, heading for the guard. He yelled to him as soon as he was within hearing distance. "Have you seen anyone here?"

"Aside from you, Milord, and Takeru-sama? No. But I've just arrived not too long ago."

"Who was posted here last night?" Takeru asked.

"Riku, sir."

"I'll go check with him," Takeru offered. "Then I meet you in your office?"

"Meet me at Taiki's."

"Sure."

By the time they had arrived at Taiki's, the ninja already had some news.

"As usual, I'm amazed at the speed you work," Katsuo said, sitting down.

"Hey, what did I miss?" Takeru asked, out of breath as he arrived.

"Nothing, we were just starting. What did you discover?"

"Riku saw no one last night."

"Taiki?" Katsuo turned to his chief of security.

"She seems to have avoided most patrols. But the guards at the gate did say she tried to get outside after dark."

Katsuo furrowed his eyebrows.

"Did she say where she wanted to go?"

"To town," he said. "But the few guards patrolling town, as per your earlier request, didn't see anyone like her."

"So where did she go?" Takeru asked. "Or was she kidnapped? Like Ayaka?"

Katsuo and Taiki tensed.

"We need to investigate that possibility," Katsuo nodded. "I hope not, but…"

"It is highly unlikely," Taiki said. "It is known that she is to be wed to you. No one in their right mind would attempt to kidnap her. Again."

"Taiki's right," Takeru agreed with the ninja. "It was a silly idea."

"So no one has seen or heard anything, and she is not on castle ground?" Katsuo asked for clarification.

"That is correct, Milord."

"If she fled, where would she go?" Takeru asked, contemplating.

Katsuo mumbled something.

"What?"

"Home. She wanted to go home," Katsuo replied.

Taiki and Takeru exchanged a glance.

"Back to that strange country in the East that is West?" His brother asked. "Then let's go to Nagasaki and—"

"No."

"What do you mean, Katsuo?"

"I said no. She's made her decision."

"What if she's in danger?" Taiki asked.

"I don't care," he said, standing up and leaving swiftly. Silence descended on the room for a moment.

"Hey, Taiki, do something for me, will you?"

"Anything you wish, Takeru-sama."

"Find out where she headed."

"Are you worried?" Taiki furrowed his eyebrows.

"Who wouldn't be?" Takeru asked, standing up. "I'm sure brother feels the same way, but he's too stubborn to admit it."

The ninja inclined his head. "I'll report to you as soon as I find something."

"Good. See you later."

*C*iara awoke to a massive headache. She was lying on a rough and cold surface. She opened her eyes but could hardly see anything. She wondered for a moment if she had lost her sight until she saw a faint light trembling in the corridor before her.

Metal bars obscured her view, and she stood up too quickly.

"Ow," she winced, putting a hand to her forehead. She could feel a bump that hurt when she touched it.

Closing her eyes for a moment, she tried to remember what happened. After dinner and the fight with Katsuo, she fled. She couldn't get out of the castle grounds, and Orihime had so kindly offered to help her.

She should've known better than to trust someone like her.

Her nose crunched up at the foul smells, mold and urine mixed together with the distinctive smell of soil. She could hear water dripping somewhere. It echoed in the empty corridor.

As Ciara's eyes adjusted to the faint light, she looked

around in the room. It was definitely a prison cell, some-where underground. There were no windows, and she had no idea if it was day or night. She wondered how long she'd been out. She was alone in the small cell, and as she looked around, she found a blanket thrown in a heap in one corner and a basin in another.

She looked at it, disgusted.

"I hope that's not the toilet. Ugh."

Well, you got what you wanted. You got away from Katsuo. Now only if I could figure out where I am...

"Is anyone there?" a voice asked from the cell across from Ciara's.

"Yura? Is that you?" she asked.

"Ciara-sama? Thank the Goddess you're all right!"

"Are you hurt?"

"My ankle hurts a little, but it's nothing serious," Yura was quick to reassure her. "Are you?"

"A little bump to the head but otherwise okay. Do you know where we are?"

"In someone's dungeons."

So Yura had no idea, either.

"Do you remember anything? I think we were knocked out mid-sentence," Ciara asked her.

"That's the last thing I recall," Yura replied. She shuffled around, then there was silence, which she couldn't stand. "Don't worry, Ciara-sama, Katsuo-sama will surely come and rescue you."

"That's the thing, Yura. I don't think he's coming."

There was a heartbeat of silent tension.

"What do you mean, Ciara-sama?"

"We had a fight."

Yura seemed to ponder over it.

"Was that the reason you wanted to leave?"

"Yes."

The girl sighed. "I'm sure as soon as Katsuo-sama realizes you've disappeared, he'll come to the rescue. You might have fought, but he still cares for you."

Ciara didn't think so but couldn't crush Yura's hope.

"Maybe you're right."

"I know I am!"

Ciara felt a pang in her heart. She knew Katsuo was not coming, not after what happened between them. Did she make the right decision? Running away seemed like the only option at the time.

But what if Katsuo was telling the truth? She shook her head. No way was he that naive. She made the right decision. Ciara nodded. If only she wasn't kidnapped, or at least if Yura was left alone! Why did they have to drag her here, too?

She was so lost in her thoughts that she hardly noticed the approaching footsteps.

"Ah, you're awake."

It was the voice of the man who had held her captive and wanted her to sing the aria. As a voice coach, Ciara had the uncanny ability to recall voices she'd already heard. He brought a candle with him, and Ciara stumbled as she recognized his face.

"You!"

He grinned, his canine teeth sharper and longer than usual.

"Now you see me. We've never finished our lesson, have we?"

Ciara gulped down a whimper.

"We didn't even get started. You pushed me through a mirror, remember?"

She crossed her arms, her anger growing. She was starting to see a pattern. The new student with a shitload of money, asking her to come to his home. Then he pushed her through the mirror, she was sure of it. He appeared again, just a week or so ago, kidnapping and torturing her.

He chuckled darkly.

"That was quite fun, wouldn't you agree? It set you off on the adventure of a lifetime!"

"Did you get your dramatic flair from watching too much TV?"

He hit the bars of her cell so violently that Ciara involuntarily took a step back. His eyes glowed red in the candlelight.

"Don't mock me, little birdie. I can come in there and make you sing a song of pain."

Yura whimpered in the other cell, making him look over his shoulder.

"Silence, little vermin. You'll get your turn, don't worry."

A sob escaped Yura, and Ciara's stomach clenched.

"What do you want from me? The aria, I'll give you an aria!" She took a step toward him, wanting to protect Yura somehow. The girl was completely defenseless.

"Later, maybe. I just wanted to chat with you."

"How generous of you," Ciara replied. It took great effort not to roll her eyes. "Any topic in particular? Like why you kidnapped us?"

"I'll do you one better." He leaned on the bars, watching Ciara like a hawk. A sadistic glint entered his gaze. His eye color had changed back to black. "Aren't you curious what I am?"

"An asshole?" Ciara blurted out before she could stop herself. She knew it was dangerous to provoke him, but she decided not to make his job easy. His eyes flashed red, and this time, they remained that color.

"Have you ever heard of youkai, little birdie?"

Yura gasped in her cell, but Ciara stayed quiet. She had

no idea what he was talking about, but she didn't like being at a disadvantage. He continued with a smirk twisting his lips.

"Oh, this will be good!" Anticipation shone in his eyes. "Youkai are demons. Monsters that come out at night and eat naughty children!"

Ciara raised her eyebrows.

"At least that's what human mothers tell their children." He shrugged. "But the demon part is true. Youkai are faster, stronger, and better at everything than mortals. To the human eye, they have eternal life and magical powers. But you know about magical powers, don't you, little birdie?"

Ciara crossed her arms and glared at him.

"Is this your idea of torture? To bore me to death with folktales?"

Oh, she was intrigued, but he didn't have to know that. So youkai was a supernatural species which lived for very long and had magic. She wasn't as shocked as she thought she would be. Was it because of her witch heritage? Because she had magic, it wasn't such a huge stretch that there would be others with the same skills.

"You don't seem surprised," he said, observing her and completely ignoring her jab. Ciara shrugged at him. "Here's the fun bit. Most of them look like monsters, but the most powerful youkai can disguise themselves as humans."

There was a brief silence.

"Like me."

"Right." Ciara's voice was flat. She had been feeling something strange surrounding this man, but what he said didn't make any sense. "Prove it."

"Oh, I see you're not satisfied with the diabolical eye color," he said. He tapped his fingernails on the cell bars.

They were long, like claws. "Don't worry, little birdie, you'll see plenty of youkai power."

He reached toward the lock and froze midway as he looked up. "Damn him. It seems I need to cut our rendezvous short, little birdie."

He turned around and withdrew, walking off, taking the light away.

"Just one more thing for you to think about," he shouted from the end of the corridor. "Have you ever wondered how Katsuo saved you?"

"Hey!" Ciara shouted after him, but he had already disappeared. She turned to the other cell. "Yura, are you all right?"

"I'm so scared, Ciara-sama. I want to help, but I'm so scared."

"It's okay," Ciara said, squatting down. "We'll come up with something. We need to escape."

Yura was silent for a moment.

"But we can't. We are powerless before the youkai."

"Yura, don't tell me you believe his words!" Ciara gasped. "He talks nonsense!"

"Youkai… are real, Ciara-sama," Yura said, her voice confident. "They are powerful. They *eat* people like us. We can't escape."

"Yes, we can!" Ciara insisted. "This is his game, don't you see? To make you so scared, you wouldn't even *think* of escaping! Don't make his job any easier, Yura! Get a hold of yourself!"

They were silent for a long while.

"But what if…"

Ciara waited for her to finish.

"What if he was right?"

"About what?"

"About Katsuo-sama. What if he's youkai?"

Ciara sighed. "Even if he was, has he ever mistreated you?"

"No."

"Did he ever wanted to eat people?"

"No, but he is very vicious in battle, or so I've heard," Yura replied.

"Well, he *is* a warlord," Ciara said. "Hey, why I am the one defending him? Weren't you the one who wanted him to come save us?"

Yura didn't reply for a long time.

"I'm scared, Ciara-sama. I'm scared if it's not true because then he'd have no chance to rescue us. And I'm scared if it's true because then that would mean Katsuo-sama is a youkai."

"Katsuo is still Katsuo. That won't change," Ciara said with finality in her voice.

57

*T*aiki found Katsuo in his office after lunch. He was writing a letter.

"What did you find out?"

"All evidence suggests that Ciara-sama and Yura are headed toward Kawayuki's estate."

The brush in Katsuo's hand paused, hovering over the paper. He looked at the ninja.

"Are you sure?"

"Yes, Milord."

A drop of ink fell, ruining the letter. Katsuo put the brush into its holder with measured movements. The next moment, he crumpled the paper with all his repressed emotions.

"What do you want to do about it?"

"Nothing." Katsuo's eyes flashed gold for a second, but it was gone too quickly to be noticeable.

"Nothing? She might be a spy!"

A vein throbbed in Katsuo's forehead. She might betray him, but a small part of him didn't want to believe that. He didn't want to kill her. At least she didn't pull out a dagger on him. If they met again, that'd be a problem for another day, but he wasn't going to pursue her.

"Katsuo-sama!" a new voice joined them. The men turned to the door, and Rui stood there. She bowed to them and greeted Taiki, too.

"While cleaning Ciara-sama's room, I found this." She held up a small pouch.

Katsuo held out his hand, and she put the pouch there. He opened it and saw grass.

"What is this?" It had an awful smell.

"It's a lesser known concoction to induce nightmares and creates fatigue."

"Where did you find this?"

"Among Ciara-sama's bedding. It wasn't hidden inside, so I assume it must've been used on someone else?"

"Maybe when Ayaka had nightmares a few days ago."

"Right, maybe," Katsuo gave the pouch back to Rui. "Did you find anything else?"

Rui blinked, her face passive.

"No, Milord," she said after a brief pause, but her jaw was tense.

"This all points toward Ciara being a spy for Kawayuki," Taiki summarized. "Considering Yura is with her, she might be—"

"No way!" Takeru had just arrived, hearing the last couple of sentences. "Yura has been working here for years, and I can't imagine Ciara doing something like this. It's a set-up!"

Katsuo wanted to believe that, too. But as daimyō, he was responsible not only for himself and his family, but his whole household, inclusive of servants and soldiers alike. Not to mention the townsfolk. If Kawayuki were to get information on his defenses or worse, military strategies, then it would be a disaster.

He decided to check if there were any missing reports or planners after everyone filed out of his office. He needed to know what to expect.

"We need to carefully weigh all the evidence," he told his little brother.

"I say our instincts are just as crucial! Like in battle!" Takeru insisted. Katsuo inclined his head. Their grandmother had used to teach them about that. What would Yuki do in such a situation?

"We know when Ayaka was kidnapped, they had help from the inside," Katsuo said, before turning to the ninja. "Taiki, any developments on that matter?"

His chief of security shook his head.

"Not yet."

"That's unusual for you." Takeru furrowed his eyebrows.

"Milord!" a new voice shouted down the corridor.

"What now?" Katsuo groaned, hurling the crumpled paper away. A moment later, Riku appeared in the doorway. He looked surprised for a second to see such a crowd in Katsuo's office.

"What is it?"

"There is a man at the gates, probably looking for you, Milord."

"Probably?" Taiki echoed. "You're trained better than that."

"Forgive me. They gave us a description of who they were looking for, and it fits you, Milord. He says he has merchandise for you?"

"Ah, I almost forgot!" Katsuo stood up. "I'll go meet him now. Everybody else, out! We'll have a strategic meeting in an hour. Gather everyone."

"Yes, sir!"

"Rui."

"Yes, Milord?"

"Walk with me," Katsuo said as he marched outside.

The woman silently followed him. When Katsuo was sure that no one would overhear them talking, he looked at Rui.

"Here's your opportunity to prove yourself."

"What do you wish of me, Katsuo-sama?"

"Find out who is the mole."

"You want me to assist Taiki to—?"

"No," Katsuo said as he stopped in the middle of the corridor. He fully turned toward the woman. "Rui, I want you to do your own investigation. Leave Taiki out of it. I want to know what *you* can do."

"Understood."

"Good. Now, go."

"Just a moment, Katsuo-sama." Rui pulled out folded up note from the folds of her kimono. "I found this in Ciara-sama's room. I believe it is for your eyes only."

Katsuo looked at the paper as if it was on fire. Eventually, he slowly reached out to take it.

Rui sent him a smile before hurrying off.

Katsuo took a deep breath before opening the note. He squinted. He could read the letters but not the language.

"Damnit!"

He tucked the note inside his pocket for later inspection before heading to the gates. The jewelry-maker merchant waited there patiently, standing underneath a maple tree, admiring its changing colors. A couple of guards stood to the side, eyeing him.

"We meet again," Katsuo said as he arrived.

The merchant's eyes brightened as he saw him.

"Indeed, we do. After all, I promised to make you some unique jewelry," he said, taking off the sack from his back. He quickly found what he was looking for.

"This is the hair ornament for the foreign lady. It is decorated with gems resembling lilac. What do you think, Milord?" The merchant asked as he handed the jewelry to Katsuo.

Katsuo held the precious ornament in his hands, admiring its simplistic beauty. It would've looked stunning in Ciara's hair and would have brought out her eye color.

His heart clenched at the thought. How could he feel so conflicted? Life was easy before her. If someone betrayed him, they died. Now? Even though she ran away, straight into the arms of his enemy, he didn't want harm to come to her. And he still didn't want to believe that she was capable of being a turncoat. What on earth had happened to him?

"It is stunning," he said honestly.

"Thank you, Milord, I'm happy you think so."

"Has your wife designed it?"

"Indeed!" The merchant grinned happily. "She was very eager to come up with ideas!"

"What about the other thing I've asked for?"

"Right here, Milord." The merchant gave him a small box.

Katsuo opened it and peeked inside. There was a simple silver ring with one precious stone in it. A curly design was carved into the band.

"Perfect."

His choked on the word. It would've looked perfect on Ciara's finger.

It was the engagement ring she had asked for. He wanted to surprise her, to ask her to marry him for real.

But that was not meant to be.

"Thank you," he said, giving the merchant the payment.

"How long was your journey?"

"About a week, Milord."

"You must be exhausted. You may spend the night here."

The merchant's eyes bugged out of its sockets.

"*Here*, sir, in the—the Shirotatsu castle?"

"Yes. Do you mind accommodation in the barracks?"

"I would be honored! But would the lord of the castle agree?"

Katsuo smiled, amused. He clapped a hand on the merchant's shoulder before gesturing a soldier over.

"Escort him to the barracks and give him an empty room. He may dine with the others."

"As you wish, my lord. This way," the soldier turned to the shocked merchant.

They were already a few paces away when the man turned back to look at Katsuo.

"Are *you* the lord of the castle, Milord?"

"Have a nice afternoon," was all Katsuo said as he headed off to the conference room. He had a strategic meeting to attend.

58

*K*atsuo swung the sake jug then leaned back to the wall of the hut behind him. It was the storage building for alcohol, standing in the castle courtyard. He looked up at the sky, seeing only a sliver of the moon. A chilly breeze swept across the courtyard, reminding him that winter was just around the corner.

The sake kept him warm, except for his heart. That couldn't be healed so easily. He looked down to his other hand and twirled the ring between his fingers. Was it his destiny to be betrayed by women he loved?

"Milord?" A hesitating female voice interrupted his thoughts. He glanced up to see Rui and quickly hid the ring in his pocket.

"Yes?"

"Oh, nothing, I was just on my way to the barracks when I saw someone sitting here, looking—" she cut herself off.

"Looking what, Rui?"

There was a heartbeat of silence.

"You looked as if you needed some cheering up. I'm

sorry if it's not my place to say. I'm still learning the rules here."

"You will find that I value action over proper etiquette."

"Noted."

She was lingering just out of reach.

"How is your accommodation?"

"Very fine, Milord, thank you," she replied. "I have a lovely roommate."

"Shizuru."

"Yes."

"She's a capable person," Katsuo said, taking a gulp from his sake jug before offering it to Rui. "Care to share a drink with me?"

"Gladly, Milord."

"Katsuo is just fine."

"Thank you, Katsuo-sama," Rui replied, drinking straight out of the jug. She found Katsuo looking at her amused. "What is it?"

"I was just thinking how natural you seemed. You seem to like it here."

"Indeed, I do," she replied, giving back the sake jug. "I've been here only a day and a half, but so much happened!"

"Like what?"

"Eer..." Rui glanced to the side. She wasn't sure if it was wise to bring up Ciara. Clearly, her lord was drinking because of all that concerning the lady. Rui quickly thought up something to say. "The note! Did you read it?"

That was what she wanted to ask as soon as she realized it was Katsuo who sat there then decided she shouldn't touch the subject. Now that was the only topic she could think of. She silently berated herself, but what was done was done.

"Ah, yes, the note. I can't read it."

"What?"

"I can read in four languages, but this one is out of my league."

"May I?" Rui held out a hand.

Katsuo shrugged.

"Why not?" He fished the note out of his pocket and gave it to her. He was watching as she was reading. "It's not Portugal. I don't know other Westerner languages. Even that one is a challenge."

"That's because it's in English."

"English?" Katsuo tapped his chin with his finger. "Now I remember! The two new ships that had arrived in Nagasaki! One of them is from the British Empire."

"Indeed, Milord. And it just so happens that one of my former patrons had done some business with them."

"Which means?"

"I can read this," Rui said.

Katsuo's eyes widened. Maybe it wasn't such a bad decision to take her in.

"Read it to me."

"Dearest Katsuo, our agreement might've started as something fake, but I came to realize that my feelings are— I'm sorry, it's really hard to read it here—*true*. It says true." Rui took a breath. "That my feelings are true, but I see now that I have no future here. I need to get back home. There's someone I need to protect. I'm sorry it turned out this way. Love, Ciara"

Rui gave the note back to Katsuo.

"A few words were smudged," she observed but otherwise didn't comment on the contents. Katsuo stroked the edge of the paper in his hand, contemplating. She loved him.

"Oh, wait, there's something else on the back!" Rui said, and squinted to make out the words. "P. S. Give Yura more days off. She deserves it. I'm going to miss her." Rui leaned back, furrowing her brows. "Didn't you say Yura-san went missing with Ciara-sama?"

Katsuo's breath hitched.

"I think we've just made a great mistake," he said, immediately on his feet. "Thank you for your assistance, Rui. I'm counting on you with the other matter, too."

Rui stood up and bowed.

"I'm on it, Katsuo-sama. By the time you get back, I'll have it all figured out."

Katsuo smirked.

"That's what I expect from you."

He hurried off to Takeru's room with the note and the conviction to go after Ciara. She was in trouble, and he was going to save her.

59

*C*iara was jarred awake by the sounds of metal scraping against metal as someone unlocked her cell. She was sitting at the bottom of a wall, half-awake. Strong hands grabbed her.

"Hey!" She had a hard time getting her bearings. By the time she became aware of her surroundings, two soldiers were already dragging her away.

"Let me go!" She kicked to the side, but her feet met empty air.

"Quiet!" ordered one of the men before Ciara was pinched in the shoulder.

"Ow!" Ciara whimpered as his grip tightened, and she gritted her teeth against the pain. Damnit. Why did she leave Shirotatsu castle? Maybe Katsuo was sincerely explaining what happened with that woman, but he had already lied to her once about an important thing, so she couldn't have been sure.

Ciara unexpectedly stumbled, and vise-like fingers sank into her arms. That was going to bruise. That is, if she managed lived long enough for that to happen.

"Don't struggle. It's useless," one of them told her.

"I'm not! You're just going too fast!"

"Shut it!" The other soldier backhanded her. It reminded her of the time when she had arrived in this area. That Kawa-something dude had a bad habit of backhanding anyone he was annoyed with.

Soon, they arrived in a huge room which was even bigger than Katsuo's conference room. A dais sat at the far end, and the room was richly decorated. Strips of silks hung from the corners of the room, giving it an airy feeling. Ciara's eyes narrowed as they zoomed in on the two figures standing in the middle of the room.

Blackteeth and the man who had lured her to this time. She was yet to figure out the latter's name.

"Welcome, welcome! You were missed," Kawayuki said, opening his arms.

"The feeling isn't mutual," Ciara spat. The grip on her shoulder tightened, and she winced.

"Careful, I need her conscious!"

"Forgive us, Milord," one of the soldiers keeping Ciara in place said.

"Actually, you're dismissed." Kawayuki waved at them. Ciara couldn't see behind her, but she still felt the grip on her arms. "What are you waiting for? Go!"

"Yes, sir!" The two of them let go of Ciara and hurried off.

"Now. Where were we?" Kawayuki mused, tapping a finger to his chin. "Ah, right!"

Ciara didn't even see the slap coming. She fell to the ground from the force of it, and before she could catch her breath, Kawayuki grabbed her hair and forced her to look up. His face was only inches away, and she wanted to gag at the putrid smell of his breath. She couldn't look away from the sight of his black teeth.

"I think this is where we left off. You double-cross me again and won't live to see tomorrow. Are we clear?"

Ciara was silent.

"Are we clear?" he repeated, emphasizing each word.

"Y-yeah," Ciara bit out.

"Good." He let go of her and pushed her head down with the same movement.

Ciara caught herself on her elbows and snuck a glance at the silent person standing to the side. His face was mildly amused. She snarled at him, but Kawayuki didn't catch that.

"Juro here says that you can't enhance objects. Is that true?"

"Yes."

"But I sense magic from you. And you will help me."

"No way in hell."

"What's your magic, huh?" Kawayuki squinted at her, as if that would help him figure it out.

"She has the Voice," Juro helpfully supplied. Ciara glared at him under her messy hair.

"What does that mean? Does she make illusions as she speaks?"

"Worse. She can control minds with her voice."

"Oooh, interesting. Too bad for you, darling. I'm full of protective amulets. You see, I'm a bit of a magician myself," Kawayuki said, full of himself. Ciara's fingers involuntarily twitched, and she looked down to see the start of tremors.

Not now! she pleaded with her body, but soon, even her arms shook.

"It is thanks to my majestic and vast powers that we are able to converse right now."

"You forgot the alphabet." Ciara couldn't help the remark. It felt good to knock his ego down a notch or two.

It felt good for two full seconds before his hand collided with her face yet again.

"Stupid little wench! Show some respect!"

"For whom? You?"

"You'll help me, or you'll die!"

"Never! I'll never help you against Katsuo!"

"Do you think he cares for you? Do you think he'll come for you?" Kawayuki mocked her. "Poor little thing. He thinks you're a spy. *My* spy. If he comes, it'll be to kill you."

Ciara gasped. "Lies!"

"Want to bet your life on it?" Kawayuki cocked his head to the side, scanning her face. "I'll do you one better. Juro, bring her."

The enigmatic person called Juro, who seemed to be the catalyst for everything that had happened to her so far, walked over to a partition screen and dragged someone out from behind.

Ciara's eyes widened as she recognized Yura. She was gagged, and bruises had already started forming on her face. Ciara picked herself up and took a step toward her.

"Halt!" Kawayuki said, grabbing her arm.

She looked at him. "Let her go! She has nothing do to with this!"

"She is your dear servant, isn't she? She has everything to do with this."

He nodded to Juro, who unsheathed his katana and put the blade to Yura's neck. Yura screamed into the gag and struggled to get free. Juro leaned in and whispered something in her ear which made her freeze immediately. With wide eyes, she looked at Ciara, pleading.

"You can help her," Kawayuki said. "All you need to do is help me."

"I—" Ciara chocked on the words. She didn't want to

help Kawayuki, but she couldn't let herself be responsible for ending another life. She closed her eyes and tears slid down her face. "I'll help you."

"What? I couldn't hear you."

"I'll do what you want."

"Excellent. Let her go," Kawayuki told Juro.

Yura was pushed forward, and Ciara met her halfway. She pulled away the gag, and the girl sobbed in relief.

"Ciara-sama! I'm so sorry!"

"No need to be sorry," Ciara said, giving her a sad smile. "I can't let anything happen to you. It was my choice."

"If only—" Yura started, but her breath hitched midsentence. Her eyes widened as she looked down. The end of a sharp blade protruded from her stomach.

Ciara looked on in shock. Yura's face was deathly pale. As the blade was withdrawn, a painful expression flashed across her face and she collapsed.

"Yura!" Ciara grabbed after her. She caught her but couldn't hold her for long, as her own strength quickly seeped away. She sat down hard with Yura's head in her lap. She stroked the girl's hair.

"I'm so sorry, Yura. I'm so sorry." Ciara's own sobs echoed in her ears. Yura coughed, and blood trickled from the corner of her mouth. With palpable effort, she lifted her hand. Ciara held it in her own.

"Don't be... sad," Yura said with a small, bloody smile. "It's my time. Happy... to have known... you."

"Yura!" Ciara shouted, gripping her hand as it went limp. "Yura!"

"The next will be someone closer to you if you don't follow my orders," Kawayuki said, but Ciara didn't react. Her tears continued to flow silently. She had no more words after witnessing such a brutal scene. To give someone hope just to take it away at the last second was such a cruel thing to do. Her mind had a hard time catching up, and she prayed that Yura would blink away the emptiness in her eyes and sit up. And then they could once again have tea in the morning together. But… she stayed immobile, her eyes staring into nothing.

"Take her away. I can't do anything with her in that state." Kawayuki waved, and Juro followed his instructions.

Ciara felt hands snake under her arms and lift her up. She was stood on her feet and didn't protest when she was dragged away, her feet following familiar movements as she stumbled along. Her mind was elsewhere. She couldn't see anything but Yura's pale face, blood trickling from her mouth. It was just as vivid as her mother's bloodied, lifeless body had been next to her in the driver's seat. The two images overlapped in her mind.

60

"*T*akeru, I need you to stay here and strengthen the castle's defenses. That includes showing our unwanted guests the door," Katsuo said as he stepped into his brother's room without so much as a knock.

Takeru was just about to go to bed. He was wearing a simple yukata, and his hair was down. But his eyes were alert as soon as Katsuo started speaking.

"You want to kick Orihime out? Why the sudden change of heart? And with Ciara gone—"

"I'm going to get her."

Takeru grinned.

"Finally, you big idiot."

"I would appreciate it if you'd abstain from name-calling," Katsuo said, his eye twitching.

"Fine," Takeru said, heading for the door.

"What are you doing?"

"I'm kicking Orihime out just as you asked."

"You can't. It's the middle of the night!"

"Oh, you mean I have to wait till morning?" Takeru asked, disappointment lacing his voice.

Katsuo sighed as he massaged his temple.

"I get where you're coming from, but please learn a little diplomacy, brother. You'll need it when you'll run your own castle."

"My own—what are you implying?"

"Takeru, focus, *please*," Katsuo said. "I'll go rescue Ciara and Yura. You send Orihime back to her father and concentrate on the castle's defense. Clear?"

"Yes. Except one thing, brother," Takeru contemplated. "What made you decide to go after Ciara? You were ready to abandon her just hours ago. Moreover, you suspected she and Yura might be spies."

"I found a note she wrote," Katsuo said. "Its contents made me reconsider. If you have questions, I'll leave at sunrise, so you can ask me then."

"Right. See you at dawn."

Katsuo nodded and hurried off to meet with Taiki. As if by magic, the ninja appeared when Katsuo was crossing the inner courtyard in the castle.

"Ah, just who I wanted to see! Walk with me, Taiki."

"My lord."

They were on their way to Katsuo's office when they came across a soldier.

"Excuse me, Milord, Taiki-dono," he said, stopping them. "I was wondering if there's any news of Yura... and Ciara-sama, of course."

"Riku, this is not the time nor the place to ask," Taiki admonished.

The soldier bowed in apology.

"I'm sorry to have bothered you, my lords."

"Do you want to help Yura?" Katsuo unexpectedly asked.

"Pardon?" Riku looked up at him in wonder.

"You want to help?"

"Yes, Milord! If I can be of service to you, I'd do anything to assist you!"

"Good. Come with us," Katsuo decided and continued to his destination. Taiki and Riku followed him closely. The ninja sent an annoyed glance at his subordinate, but he didn't question Katsuo's decision out loud.

The three of them arrived at Katsuo's office in minutes.

"Close the door," he instructed as he took a seat at the low table. He gestured for the others. "Sit."

When they did so, Katsuo shared his thoughts with them:

"We're going to rescue Ciara and Yura."

"Rescue?" Taiki asked, looking at Riku then back at Katsuo. "I'm afraid I don't understand. Just hours ago, you said they were spies and we needed to come up with a defense plan in case she talks to Kawayuki."

"New information has been brought to my attention," Katsuo replied. "I now firmly believe—no, I *know* they weren't spies. If they were heading toward Kawayuki's castle, it's safe to assume it wasn't on their own free will. And he probably already has them. We have to move quickly."

"What do you intend to do, Milord?" Riku asked.

"Half of our forces will depart in the morning. The rest stay here under Takeru's command to defend the castle. Taiki, I'm counting on you to create a distraction when we arrive at Kawayuki's."

"Consider it done, Milord."

"While the main forces fight Kawayuki's, two smaller teams will sneak in and rescue the ladies," Katsuo said. "Riku, you'll be leading one of them."

The soldier bowed low.

"Thank you, Milord. You honor me."

"Be as discreet as possible. Remember, we'll be there to

rescue them, not to kill Kawayuki, though I might as well do if I come across him."

Katsuo's eyes flashed gold, and this time, it didn't escape Taiki's attention. Riku noticed the change, too.

"We leave at dawn. Prepare your men."

"Hai[1]!" Taiki and Riku shouted as they rose and bowed to Katsuo. They hurried off to relay his orders to the troops.

Katsuo got up and exited his office but didn't return to his quarters. He went straight to his personal armory. He unlocked the door, and the faint light from the corridor fell on the gift he had received from his grandmother.

He walked inside and picked the pistol up, looking at it with a critical eye.

"You might just be of use sooner than I'd imagined," he said, once again admiring the handiwork of the craftsman who had made detailed carvings on the weapon's surface.

He needed all the help he could get. But first... Katsuo opened the drawer and took out a small, wooden box. There were bullets inside. First, he needed to familiarize himself with the pistol. Yuki had left him instructions, and this was as good as any time to catch up and deepen his knowledge on Western firearms.

There were still a few hours until dawn, and sleep would probably evade him tonight, no matter what he tried. Might as well use the time for something useful. He gathered all the things he needed and left the armory, locking the door.

Dawn came earlier than expected. Katsuo had yet to fire the pistol even though he had learned everything that was in the papers Yuki had left him. He finished his task just as the Eastern horizon started to lighten.

He cursed, not noticing how quickly time had gone. He hastily freshened up and headed for his office. He grabbed a servant on his way to help put on his armor. With all the straps, it would take too much time without assistance.

Just as dawn broke, he marched to the gates. He weaved his way through his retainers and soldiers. Everyone was alert and ready for a fight. Takeru waited for him with his horse.

"I took the liberty of preparing him. Thought you'd be busy," he greeted him.

"I appreciate it," Katsuo said, patting the horse's side. "Are you ready?"

"Are you asking me or the horse?"

"Both." Amusement danced in Katsuo's eyes at his brother's reaction.

"I don't know about him, but I'm as ready as I'll every be," Takeru replied.

"Any questions?"

"How much longer do I have to wait to kick *her* out?"

"As soon as we're gone." Katsuo lifted himself up on the horse, a smile playing in the corner of his mouth.

"Splendid," Takeru's eyes had a golden hue to it as he reached out to grab his brother's arm. "Have a good hunt, brother."

"This is a rescue mission, Takeru."

"Of course it is."

Katsuo smirked. "But you know me too well."

He turned his horse around, and Takeru retreated to the side, out of the riders' way.

"Men! We will face Kawayuki again. I want it to be the last time. Be as swift as the wind when you fight. Show them no mercy."

"No mercy!" his soldiers yelled after him. The orange color of early sunrise painted their crimson uniforms, making it seem as if a sea of flame had come to life in the castle courtyard.

"Let's go!"

A loud battle cry resounded, waking everyone who had still been sleeping. As they set off, hundreds of hooves beat the dusty road. The city folk thought it was an earthquake. Scared, they fled their homes, but when they saw their lord leading their troops through the main road in the middle of the city, they cheered loudly.

---

1. yes

he sun had just left its zenith in the sky when they arrived at Kawayuki's castle. The forest had grown smaller since the last time they were there. Kawayuki had cut down trees around his castle to see approaching enemies ahead of time.

"We'll need that distraction sooner than I thought," Katsuo told Taiki when they heard the report from their recon team. "In fact, we can start with that."

"I will make the preparations." The ninja inclined his head. "Please wait for my signal, Milord."

"All right. Let's not draw this out more than necessary."

Katsuo and Riku parted from the main group with their small teams and circled around the perimeter of the remaining forest. They tied their horses near the edge.

Riku followed his lord to the border of the forest and plains. From there, they could see the main gate where Taiki would attack with the bulk of Katsuo's forces. However, there was a small side entrance in the wall for servants, which was located right in front of Katsuo and his team.

"What are your orders, Milord?" Riku asked while the others tended to the horses.

"Your team will check the holding cells beneath the castle. If they're not there, search the side buildings for any sign of Ciara and Yura. Remain undetected."

"Understood." Riku nodded. "What if we're detected?"

"Already giving up?"

"No, sir. I like to be prepared for the worse, just in case," Riku replied.

"This is the first time you lead men, is that right?"

"Yes, sir. It is an honor."

"Use your own judgement on what to do. The answer may vary depending on immediate circumstances."

"Right. Thank you, Milord," Riku said, but he looked nervous. Katsuo clasped the young man's shoulder. "You'll do fine. I've seen you fight."

Katsuo turned to the others and waved them over.

"As soon as we receive the sign from Taiki, we will make our move. We reach the castle grounds together, then we'll split up. My team will head to the main castle building while those with Riku will check the holding cellars and outer buildings. Any questions?"

No one spoke up.

Katsuo nodded. "Good."

He turned back to watch the guards strolling on top of the wall. He also noticed a small group of Kawayuki's soldiers patrolling the area near the gates. Soon, they would be distracted by Taiki's attack. Everything depended on the timing.

Very soon, they heard the battle cry and watched as the main force stormed the castle. Looking up at the walls, they could see immediately that most of the guards ran over to the main gates, only a couple of them remaining at their posts, but even their attention was on the plains.

Since the group of Kawayuki's soldiers outside the gate was taken by surprise and the numbers overwhelmed them, they were sent reinforcements. That was when Taiki made the distraction to command the attention of Kawayuki's men.

A big explosion resounded in their ears, and a thick smokescreen enveloped the area. It even reached Katsuo's position, although it had thinned out by that time. Wordlessly, he ordered his men to advance forward. He gestured for the lone archer in their group to keep an eye on the guards on top of the walls.

Unfortunately, the smoke had almost cleared away when they were only halfway through the plains. One of the guards had spotted them, but before he could alert the others, he was shot by Katsuo's archer. And arrow protruded from his neck as he silently fell. The archer neutralized another guard while they continued forward.

Finally, they reached the side door.

"How do we get in? They have it barred from the inside!" one of the soldiers said.

"Patience," Katsuo replied.

They waited for a full minute until they heard a scuffle from the other side of the door. Wood scraped against wood as the bar was lifted, and finally, the door opened.

A young man stood there in servant's clothes, pale and shaking like a leaf as he faced the intruders.

"Good job. Now, scram!" Katsuo threw him a pouch full of coins. The servant bowed low and waited until everyone filed in before running toward the forest.

Katsuo led them to the castle itself, and they used another servants' entry the man from before had left open for them.

"Join us upstairs in you don't find them," Katsuo told Riku before they parted.

The soldier nodded and gestured for his men to follow, heading toward the cellars while Katsuo started to methodically check every room until they reached the conference room on the other side of the floor.

What they found there made the blood boil in Katsuo's veins. The conference room was void of life. No one was there, except the body of young woman.

At first, Katsuo was afraid it was Ciara's, but when he got closer, he was relieved to discover that it wasn't her. His relief didn't last long, though, because he did recognize the young woman who was killed there.

"Yura," he said in disbelief. Despite lying in a pool of her own blood, Yura had a small smile gracing her face as she stared lifelessly at the ceiling. They hadn't even bothered to cover her.

Katsuo kneeled and closed her eyes with measured movements. Rage was building inside him, and it took a tremendous effort to force himself to stay calm. Yura was a capable servant and a nice person. His household would be a sadder place without her.

"Milord?" he heard Riku's voice from behind as he arrived with his team. "We didn't find them in the—*Oh, gods!*"

Riku collapsed on his knees next to the girl.

"Y-Yura…" he breathed, tentatively reaching out to touch her face. He was almost as pale as her. His hands trembled. "No."

Katsuo stood, determined to hunt down Kawayuki. Who knew what he would do to Ciara if he killed a bystander? He didn't deserve forgiveness.

A sob escaped Riku.

"I was going to court her. I was working for a promotion, then I was going to ask her to–" he choked on his words. Only Katsuo heard his whispers. "She had such a beautiful soul."

Katsuo put a hand on Riku's shoulder and squeezed it reassuringly.

"We will give her the proper burial she deserves," Katsuo promised, "but first, let's hunt these monsters down."

Riku nodded and wiped his tears. He stood up and turned to his lord. His eyes were red, but his gaze was sharp and determined. His hands weren't shaking anymore.

"I would be *my pleasure* accompany you, Milord."

62

*Y*ura died, Yura died, Yura died. This one thought repeated itself in a loop in Ciara's head. She thought someone shouted at her but couldn't hear it because of the endless chant inside her mind.

It's my fault. But I don't want to end up like her. I didn't want any of this to happen! A sob escaped Ciara, which she tried to hide as she put a fist to her mouth. Her hand trembled as she realized she may not have much time left in the world of living. She closed her eyes for a moment, centering herself. *Yura died, Yura died—STOP IT!*

Her feet automatically walked on as she was dragged away to an unknown location. She focused on her breathing. It took some effort, but her thoughts gradually cleared up and her mind silenced. Taking a deep breath, she opened her eyes.

She had to concentrate on escaping. Guilt could come later. Otherwise, she knew she wouldn't see another day.

Ciara snuck a glance to the side. Juro was keeping a firm grip on her arm. He was looking ahead, not paying any attention to Ciara, which was excellent for her in the case of a surprise attack.

Precisely at that moment, Juro glanced at her. He smirked at her dumbfounded expression.

There went that chance.

Using all her strength, Ciara retracted her hand, but Juro kept a firm hold on her wrist. As she struggled to break free, they stopped in the middle of the corridor.

"Finally, she wakes up," he mocked, dragging her closer. As he leaned in, their noses almost touched. He flashed a grin, and Ciara was reminded of a vampire for a moment as she noticed his long canine teeth. Looking up, she could see red seeping into his irises.

"Let me go," she said with more confidence than she felt.

"How about no?" Juro pretended to think for a heartbeat. "How about you comply so no one else has to die because of you?"

Ciara was careful to make her expression impassive. She didn't want him to know just how much that statement hurt and how much she agreed with that. Her dark thoughts would only hold her back and give him an opening. In order to survive, she had to ignore those feelings.

"Oh, how very impressive," she said instead, "putting blame on others when it's your fault."

Juro narrowed his eyes, shaking Ciara's hand and lifting it between them. He tightened his grip. Ciara gritted her teeth against the pain.

"You don't want to go down that road, little birdie."

"I know exactly what kind of road I'll take," Ciara shot back as her instinct took over and she bit down on his hand, hard.

The attack took him by surprise and momentarily, his grip lessened. Ciara used it to rotate her arm to the side in his fist, and just when his grip tightened again, she was in a position to twist his arm to the side. As he concentrated on their hands, Ciara quickly kicked out, aiming for his solar plexus with her knee.

It landed a few inches below, which was probably more painful than she had originally aimed for. Good riddance. Juro bent double, but he still didn't release her. Just when Ciara thought all her fighting back was pointless, a tremendous sound shook the castle. At that moment Juro's grip lessened so much that Ciara used that moment of distraction to free herself.

The samurai had no idea what had just happened, but Ciara could recognize a huge explosion. She used this chance to run.

She had only taken a few steps when she reached an intersection and found herself face-to-face with dozen soldiers. They looked ready to attack.

It's now or never! Ciara decided to test her powers. Magic stirred her blood as she yelled out:

"Protect me!"

The soldiers immediately stepped around her and made a protective wall between her and Juro.

"As you wish, my Queen."

*What the f—*Ciara shook her head. *Not the point. Run!* she told herself as she sprinted through the corridors.

She had no idea where she was going, but all the while, she felt a silent threat following her. Ciara wasn't even sure whether she was going in circles. She assumed she was down at the cellars and looked for a staircase.

After several long minutes, she found one and hurried upstairs. More soldiers awaited her. Slightly out of breath, she gestured behind her.

"Protect me!"

"As you wish, my Queen."

Seriously, what's up with that? she silently wondered as she ran on. However, a small smile appeared on her face. At least she could use her ability and for once didn't have to worry about the consequences. She had hoped the soldiers would be an obstacle for Juro, and he probably wouldn't kill them. They were his men, after all.

Ciara circled around but couldn't find the exit. However, she had come upon another staircase, this one leading up. She contemplated, standing in front of it, until she heard the sounds of struggle getting closer behind her.

"Shit." She ran upstairs to evade the battle. She ran for as long as she could, along shortening corridors. As she turned a corner, she saw something big and dark at the end of the passageway. It growled and looked as if an animal had stepped out from a nightmare. It was as big as a person, and it had fangs as long as Ciara's arms. Her eyes widened as she caught a glimpse of the creature. It reminded her of one a prehistorical feline she had learned about in school.

It noticed her.

When it lunged, Ciara backpedaled and ran back the way she came. The Voice only worked on humans. She couldn't use it on that animal or whatever creature it was! Up ahead, the sounds of fighting reached her ears. Too many people were in one place, and if she was truly unlucky, then Juro or Kawayuki was there, too.

Ciara slid open a random door to her left and barreled inside. She shut the door closed and prayed the creature didn't see through the thin paper walls. Her breath hitched as she saw its silhouette slowly move on the other side of the door. It had the gait of a predator.

It took its time walking down the corridor and toward the fight. The minutes crawled slowly as the creature finally disappeared from sight. Ciara pricked her ears. She was expecting screams soon. The creature should arrive at the fight in the next minute or so.

She glanced around the room, looking for something useful. Any weapon would give her reassurance in this situation, even if she had no idea how to use it. Her gaze landed on a familiar mirror.

"No way!" she gasped. Mesmerized, she walked over. As if in a trance, her hand lifted, and she stroked the strange symbols on the frame of the mirror. Her breath made small clouds on the shiny surface. Tentatively, Ciara reached out to touch it. Just before her fingers connected with the silver surface of the mirror, she stopped.

Here was her chance to go home and leave behind this crazy world with its insane samurai residents. She could go back to modern times, continue teaching, and...

Be as miserable as she had been for the last few years.

Her fingers twitched at that thought.

Or she could stay here. In constant danger but, hopefully, by Katsuo's side. Would he even want that? Did *she* want that? Her throat constricted at the thought that he might not care. That he'd choose someone else. Then again, the last few days, before he showed up with a stranger at their home, had been blissful. She didn't remember the last time she was that happy. It was probably before the car accident. She felt empowered. She felt cherished. It was an amazing feeling.

What should I do? she mused, hand hovering over the smooth surface of the mirror. She looked at her reflection. Dark purple irises gazed back at her. Then her reflection rolled her eyes, as if she was annoyed with her. Ciara was so surprised she took a step back. Her reflection's expression darkened as she looked at Ciara, challenging her. Ciara had no idea what her reflection expected of her.

A loud, metallic clang coming from behind her alerted

Ciara that the fight had arrived outside her room. She looked at the door in fear. A blade ripped vertically into the paper covering the door. Ciara gasped and took a step back. She bumped into the mirror.

"No!" she cried, as Katsuo's face flashed through her mind. She expected to be transported back to her own time and country, but nothing had happened.

Ciara inched away from the mirror, and when she judged she was a safe distance away, she let out a sigh of relief. Her reflection stared at her with an irritated expression. Ciara cocked her head to the side, and the reflection followed then pointed behind her.

Ciara ducked at the last second and quickly jumped to the side. She twirled on her feet to see Kawayuki grasping at the air where her torso had been. He snarled as he realized she had escaped his grip. He moved toward her, but Ciara danced away.

"Get back here, little witch!"

"Leave me alone!"

"Don't you want to go back?" he asked. Ciara hesitated for only a second before deciding to ignore him and run away. She heard his steps echoing behind her.

She jumped through the ripped paper door and found herself in the midst of a fierce fight in the corridor. She rolled on the floor, among several pairs of feet, until she hit the wall. The breath rushed out of her, but the skirmish around her didn't stop.

Kawayuki's soldiers fought with Katsuo's. Ciara's heart skipped a beat. Had he come to save her? Hope flared in her chest. Hope for a future together with Katsuo.

She had to find him.

*K*awayuki burst out of the room to chase after her.

"Defend me!" she yelled out. The fighting stopped immediately, and all samurai turned toward Kawayuki, their swords raised high. Even his own soldiers faced him.

Ciara smirked and couldn't help but taunt him. "Next time, make sure you're not the only one wearing an amulet," she said. "Then again, I doubt there'll be a next time."

She rushed off, leaving Kawayuki to deal with more than a dozen soldiers. He cursed after her, but Ciara brushed off his threats easily. She found another staircase leading up. She had no choice in the matter as she ran upstairs, further from Kawayuki.

Eventually, after long, long minutes of escaping and running around randomly, evading soldiers to the best of her abilities, she found herself at the top of a tower. Her face paled as she realized this was exactly what stupid people did in horror flicks. They ran upstairs while Ciara threw popcorn at the TV and shouted at them, 'Idiot, you can't escape that way!' How ironic it was that she ended up in the exact same situation.

She turned back, but it was too late. She could hear the sound of fighting on the floor below. Her only option was to bar the entrance leading to the tower. She struggled to lift the heavy wooden door but eventually managed. She let go of it, and it closed with a loud bang. Ciara looked around and spotted a log standing in the corner. Quickly, she brought it back and slid it in the bracket, effectively locking herself up in the tower.

"Phew!"

Ciara backpedaled as someone lunged at the door from the other side. She had just made it in time. She turned around and bumped into something.

"Ow," she stepped back, massaging her nose. Her eyes widened as she realized she was standing face-to-face with Kawayuki. He grinned his black teeth at her.

"I was beginning to think you were avoiding me."

"I was," Ciara admitted readily and took two steps back. "How did you get up here before me?" She was sure she was running ahead of him.

"It's pointless, my little birdie," she heard from behind and twirled around. She was stuck between Juro and Kawayuki.

"How—?"

"It was a clever trick, using our soldiers against us like that," Kawayuki said. "But it was rather pointless, as you can see. Thank you for demonstrating your power. Now I can use it against Kitayama."

"You wish."

"Oh, I have many wishes," Kawayuki said then nodded to the samurai. "And Juro here, too. Isn't that right?"

"I'm here only to follow your orders, Kawayuki-sama." He bowed.

Ciara backed away, aiming for the door behind her. She couldn't get to the barred door, but maybe she had a chance if she went outside. As soon as she looked through the doorway, she felt her hopes crumbling. A cold gust of wind blew up, making her shiver. She glanced to the side to see there was only a narrow path leading around the tower with a low wall running around the edges. She could see a huge battle unfold below between Kawayuki and Katsuo's men.

"What are you looking at?" she heard Kawayuki ask before she was backhanded.

She was so fed up with him.

Katsuo led Riku and their men through the castle, methodically going from room to room as they broke into small groups on each floor. Whoever stood in their way met their end early. As they got deeper into the compound, however, the strangest thing happened.

They met a group of Kawayuki's soldiers already wounded, some dead, some still alive. Their injuries were bad, but not fatal.

"What happened here?" Riku asked as they made their way upstairs. He was looking around at the enemy soldiers, tumbling left and right, nursing their wounds.

"Must protect…" Katsuo heard one of them mumble. "Must protect… Queen," he said as he lost consciousness.

Katsuo found one who was still conscious and used the tip of his katana to tilt the soldier's head. He was mumbling the same thing over and over.

"What are you talking about?"

"Protect… her," he murmured, half-conscious.

"It's useless, Katsuo-sama." One of his men stepped up

next to him. He was trained in medicines. "It looks as if they are under the influence by something. They aren't aware of what goes on around them."

"Like a spell?"

"Or badly administered medicine," he supplied.

Katsuo withdrew his blade and thought for a moment.

"Stay here with someone and make sure you save as many as you can. I want to know what happened. But be alert. They're to be prisoners."

"As you command, Katsuo-sama!" He bowed and quickly gathered two more men to handle the task at hand.

"Where do we go from here?" Riku asked. "We're almost at the top floor."

"Then we—" Katsuo started but suddenly fell silent. When Riku was about to ask him, he raised his hand to make him quiet.

Katsuo pricked his ears. He heard Ciara's voice. She was singing a strange song, muffled by many layers of doors and furniture. It was coming from directly above him, possibly two or three floors up.

He looked up as if he could see through the wooden planks separating each floor. The voice rose, as if Ciara was screaming. Katsuo cursed and ran off, leaving his men behind.

Riku stood there, frozen for a moment.

"What do we do?" one of the men asked him.

"One with me, the rest of you continue to search of the castle.

"Yes, sir!"

Ciara could smell rain in the air and stepped outside, backing away. Kawayuki was slowly walking toward her with deliberate steps. Juro was nowhere to be seen, and that worried Ciara more. Just what was he planning?

She saw something move out of the corner of her eye. A white crow perched atop the railing, looking down at her as if in disdain. It was a majestic creature. Ciara blinked in surprise, locking eyes with the bird for a moment. Its ebony eyes flashed with green for a split second. Ciara blinked in disbelief, but before she could do anything, the crow jumped into the wind and sailed away. In its place, Ciara could see Juro's face.

Damn. They had cornered her while she was distracted by the rare bird. She felt a gust of wind hit her back as her legs bumped into the low wall running on the edge. There was no escape.

"Stop!" she ordered, using her Voice. The men stopped for a second before they chuckled at her feeble attempt at controlling them.

"I've told you, little birdie. It has no effect on me," Juro said.

"Neither does it affect me," Kawayuki added, fingering the thin chain around his neck. "What will you do? You either comply, or you'll be thrown off from here."

"If you kill me, then you won't get what you want," she said, trying to stall for time and come up with an idea. She could see no way out of this sorry situation. The men stopped a few feet away from her. There was no room for her to back away anymore and they felt they could take their time with her.

"What a cruel woman," Juro said. "After killing Yura and countless soldiers, you're going to kill your own blood, too?" He smirked. "Have you already forgotten my promise to hunt your cousin down? If you don't help us, I'll make sure she will."

Ciara's mind went blank for a moment as guilt washed

over her. And Juro didn't even know the worst of it, that she had already spilled the blood of her mother.

The wind was laughing at her.

You're not going to believe him, are you? It was as if her mother was whispering in her ear. She had often used the wind to deliver short messages to Ciara when she was still alive. Rain started to fall in tiny drops. *Let it go.*

The smiling face of her mother flashed before Ciara's eyes. She looked happy as white light engulfed her. *Show them how wrong they are. I believe in you.*

A big sigh tore from Ciara as if a great weight had been lifted off her, and she felt dizzy for a moment. She caught herself on the low wall at the last minute.

"Haha, look at her. She can't even stand up straight!" Kawayuki mocked, laughing.

"Let's end this," Juro said, lifting his sword. Ciara met his gaze head-on. There was no hesitation in her eyes.

"You wanted a song, didn't you?" The rain pelted down harder, but she ignored it.

Juro paused, curious to see what happened next. In the background, a loud bang resounded, as if something was trying to open the locked door.

"What are you waiting for?" Kawayuki shouted. "Idiot!"

Blackteeth unsheathed his katana and lunged for Ciara. She screamed, and even though both had protection from her Voice, the men froze for a moment at the sudden, high-pitched sound. It wasn't a random scream, but the highest note from the aria Juro so desperately wanted her to sing. The pounding on the door became more violent and desperate.

The men's momentarily distraction gave her enough time to start singing the part of the aria without words and full of high notes. She aimed all her anger and despair at Juro, who looked to be the more dangerous of them.

Kawayuki shortly lost consciousness, falling into a heap next to her, but Juro endured. His katana fell to the floor as he covered his ears, but the clank of the sword was lost in the aria's passionate high notes. He stumbled back as the wind picked up and swirled the small raindrops around Ciara. Everything converged around her as if she was the eye of the storm as she sang, giving it her all.

Juro fell on one knee as Ciara reached the highest note. The swirl of violent wind and sharp raindrops turned against Juro and unleashed their fury on him. It was as if countless tiny blades had cut into his skin. Ciara swung her arms in Juro's direction as she finished. Mini icicles hurled themselves in his direction, injuring him. He fell to the floor, bleeding from countless wounds.

Ciara's legs gave way, and she fell back, ending up on her bottom, her back to the wall. She was panting from exertion, and her throat felt as if it was on fire.

"You never knew that was a powerful spell, did you?" she croaked, smirking at him.

The blood around Juro gathered in one spot and shot out like a spear, cleanly penetrating his left shoulder. It splattered on the wall behind him, and he screamed in pain as he clutched his injury.

At that moment, another loud bang came from the direction of the door. Ciara glanced over, seeing the heavy wooden door break into pieces, and saw Katsuo emerge from the stairway below. His eyes were molten gold as he looked around. Ciara opened her mouth to shout for him, but nothing came out. She struggled to get up, but something grabbed her leg.

Her mouth opened in a silent scream as she turned back and saw that Juro had a firm grip on her ankle. He had a sinister look on his face as he glared at her, momentarily ignoring his wound. Ciara's voice was temporarily gone, which was the price paid for using such a powerful spell combined with her special ability. Juro's grip tightened, making her tear up at the pain. She repeatedly hit his hand but to no avail.

The next moment, a boot came down on Juro's arm, and he screamed, immediately letting go of Ciara's leg. She was hurled around, and by the time Ciara had regained her composure, she was standing behind Katsuo on the other side of the small tower room.

64

"*A*re you all right?" Katsuo asked, keeping Juro in his sight. Ciara touched his shoulder and squeezed it in reassurance.

He glanced back at her. She nodded with a small smile. Up close, she could swear his gold eyes were glowing, but she couldn't decipher the emotion behind his gaze.

"Good. Stay behind me," Katsuo told her, turning back to face Juro. Just in time, too, because Juro had just thrown a shuriken at them. Katsuo quickly parried it with a swift motion of his katana. The throwing star embedded itself into the wall.

"Not today, Juro. You will pay for all your crimes," Katsuo spat, taking a step toward him. Ciara let go of him and looked around to see if there was anything she could use as a weapon. Unfortunately, she didn't find anything useful.

"I should've killed you the first time we met."

"Oh, spare me the dramatic speech, would ya?" Juro cut him off. "It wasn't personal. Unfortunately for you, you just happened to be at the wrong place and time."

"You made it personal as soon as you came into my house *and* turned my betrothed against me," Katsuo replied while casually flicking the blood off his blade in one swift movement. He took up a fighting stance. The weight of the katana in his hand was familiar and reassuring.

"You're just too straightforward." Juro shook his head. "That's going to be the end of you."

Katsuo lunged at him, sword raised, and Juro met him halfway, blocking his attack mid-air. His left arm hung by his side, useless, but he was adept at using single-handed techniques. The blades strained against one another as opposing forces collided. Katsuo's grip tightened on the hilt and felt the pressure in his arms as he pushed back.

"Is this all you got?" Juro grinned at him, showing off his pointed teeth. He put more pressure behind his sword, completely ignoring his bleeding wound. Katsuo sneered as he was forced to take a step back. His fangs were visible, too.

"You're not the only one with surprises," he said, letting go of the constraints on his youki. Juro was taken aback, but he quickly counterattacked with his own demon energy. Two powerful forces collided, sweeping across the tower room and hurling everything away in its path, including some possessions of their owners.

The soldiers who were about to climb up the stairs and come through the door were pushed back by the invisible force and fell downstairs. Ciara was thrown back to the wall by the pressure surrounding the two. Her instincts flared, creating a protective energy enveloping her. Suddenly, she was free and able to breathe again. It was as if she had been in a vacuum when the two youki collided. She could still feel the power swirling around the room, making her skin tingle.

Finally, Juro gave a hard push with his katana, and

Katsuo was thrown back but landed on his feet. Small dirt particles grated under his palm as he skidded to a stop. He was tense as he gripped the hilt of the sword tightly.

"Hah." Juro attempted to wipe away the blood on his face but only managed to smeared it. The cuts from Ciara's aria storm weren't healing as fast as he thought, and the injury on his left shoulder throbbed. The scent of blood in the air was becoming thicker.

He pointed his sword at Katsuo. "Pathetic. You have so little youkai blood in you, yet you act so arrogant. Let me rectify not giving you a proper lesson last time."

Juro lifted his sword, red energy seeping from his hands and running alongside the blade. It only took a moment for the red aura to engulf it. The katana pulsed as he prepared for a powerful attack.

In the background, Ciara's eyes widened, and a shiver ran down her spine. Was there nothing she could do? Oh, how she wished at that precise moment that she had continued to practice the family tradition! She would have been able to use spells and defend against such attacks. She looked at Katsuo in panic.

His eyebrows furrowed as he debated on a counterattack, lifting his sword. At that moment, Juro swung his katana and let the red energy loose. A crescent-shaped light shot forth from the blade, heading straight at Katsuo. He held his katana diagonally before him, gripping the handle with both hands.

The impact forced him back a few steps, and he growled at the painful sensation as it ripped into his skin, but he couldn't have dodged. Ciara stood right behind him, and he couldn't let her get hurt. He gritted his teeth as he gathered all his power and, with great effort, pushed the red energy aside. It collided with the wall to the right and immediately disintegrated it. Dust whirled at the impact.

Katsuo glanced down, seeing the numerous gashes on his arms.

"Aw, how sweet, protecting your little birdie," Juro mocked, lunging at him. Katsuo blocked as he swung his katana and counterattacked the next second. They were quickly engaged in a sword fight. To Ciara's eyes, it resembled an intricate dance. She could recognize a move or two from Katsuo's morning exercises, but it was hard for her to follow their movements.

"Is this your limit?" Juro yelled the next time their blades met. Katsuo didn't grace him with a reply. "How disappointing. Time to finish playing." Juro let go of his katana and a small blade slid out of his sleeve. He flung his hand to stab his opponent. Katsuo noticed it at the last moment and dodged, the dagger grazing his neck. He quickly jumped back and put a hand on his fresh injury. He could feel the blood leaking beneath his palm and its metallic scent tickled his nose.

Juro sneered, throwing the knife at Katsuo, but he easily easily parried it. However, this move gave enough time for Juro to retrieve his sword. He pointed the katana at Katsuo. The blade was starting to be enveloped in the red energy again.

"This is it. If you have any last tricks, I suggest you use them now."

"You talk too much," Katsuo shot back, moving his hand away from the wound on his neck. Ciara looked on worriedly as blood gradually seeped out from the cut, coloring Katsuo's clothes. Juro hadn't reached an artery, but if unattended, the wound could quickly become dangerous. Ciara wordlessly reached out but didn't move from her place next to the wall. The youki pressure was still too much to allow her to walk.

"How sweet, trying to help him when it takes all your

effort just to remain standing." Juro was immensely enjoying the situation. With a surprising move, he threw another dagger using his left hand, aiming for Ciara. *So he can still use his left arm*, Katsuo thought as he caught the dagger mid-air and flung it right back at Juro.

"That's not gonna work on m—" He was cut off as Katsuo followed the dagger with his katana. Juro gritted his teeth as he was forced to defend himself. By this time, the red energy had already completely enveloped his blade.

"You were saying?"

"Still not enough."

Juro kicked Katsuo in the stomach, sending him flying back. He hit the wall next to Ciara, who stood frozen at the rapid movements around her. Her eyes couldn't follow the fight properly.

"Know your place!" Juro yelled, swinging his katana and letting the red energy loose with a shout.

This attack was more powerful than the one before. Ciara could feel it in her bones as the crimson crescent-shaped energy headed for them.

There was nothing she could do.

Katsuo jumped in front of her and stabbed his katana into the floor before him. The wide side of the blade faced Juro's attack. Katsuo wiped the blood from his neck and threw it at the oncoming attack. Small blades formed from his blood, but they did little to slow the energy heading for them.

Damnit, Katsuo cursed as he silently swore to protect Ciara. He gripped the hilt of the sword with his bloody hand. Power pulsed through him and into the katana as his blood dribbled down from the handle to the blade. His instincts flared just as the crimson attack reached him.

White light exploded from Katsuo's sword, clashing with the crimson energy. He could feel it push against him, and he knew if he relented, Ciara would be hit by the attack. He couldn't let that happen, so he endured until the last of the crimson light dissipated.

The clash was way more powerful than the first time Juro and Katsuo's youki clashed. Its intensity pressed against the surroundings and Katsuo could hear Ciara gasp for air in the background. A loud crash deafened them for a moment as the two energies nullified each other.

Katsuo reeled to the side, grabbing his katana to steady himself. He was panting heavily as he stared at Juro. The power from their clashing energies didn't even phase the bastard, and the small injuries Ciara had inflicted on him before were gone. His only visible wound was the hole in his left shoulder, but even that was healing rapidly.

Damn youkai and their self-regenerating abilities.

"Judging from your appearance, you don't have any energy left for, well, anything!" Juro laughed like a maniac. "Die already!"

Ciara was shocked at the display of strange powers, but her instincts urged her to ignore everything and concentrate on surviving. She sent a worried look toward Katsuo, wishing for a miracle. Her Voice was gone, her other magical abilities lay dormant and rusty, and she had no idea how to wield a sword.

She'd never felt so useless in her life.

Juro lunged at Katsuo, sword drawn, and Ciara instinctively jumped at him, trying to protect the man she loved.

"Wait for your turn, birdie," Juro snarled as he kicked Ciara away with a careless move. She landed in a heap, a few feet away. Tears of pain and frustration blurred her vision for a moment before she sat up. Her middle hurt, and it was hard to breathe, but she persisted. She would attack again and again even if she were to die—

Her fumbling hands found something solid on the

floor. She snapped her head to the side to see a pistol there. Ciara's eyes widened, and she could feel excitement rushing through her veins as she realized she had a chance. It had been long since she had last used a gun, but her grandfather had made sure she could use one anytime, anywhere.

A painful groan came from the direction of Katsuo. She looked up, alarmed. He was dodging Juro's attacks as best he could, but he had cuts on his arm and torso more times than Ciara could count. Juro was clearly overpowering him; she had to make her move *now*.

Ciara lifted the pistol and gave it a quick glance as she hastily stood. She had no time to properly check the weapon and prayed that whomever it belonged to had taken care of that. She aimed the pistol at Juro, but he was moving too quickly.

She shouted at him, but no voice left her lips.

Damn it all! She stomped her heel on the wooden floor in anger. Katsuo glanced at her from the corner of his eye and grabbed Juro's haori, throwing him off balance.

"What?" A surprised yell escaped Juro as Katsuo moved him between himself and Ciara.

She smirked.

Perfect.

And fired the pistol.

65

*T*he recoil was bigger than she had anticipated, and she was thrown back toward yet another wall.

I'm starting to think these walls have a secret grudge against me. Ciara sighed, gritting her teeth against the expected pain, but it didn't come. Stunned, she opened her eyes, not understanding why she landed softly.

"Are you all right?" Katsuo asked. Ciara looked up and to the side. He was standing right behind her, half-hugging her. Her eyes widened as she realized he had cushioned her crash.

He was looking ahead but glanced at Ciara when she didn't respond. She quickly nodded and turned back to see what had happened to Juro. Smoke swirled around where he had been standing, and it took a while to clear. When it receded, Ciara's heart skipped a beat. Juro was struggling to get up into a sitting position. He was gripping his side, blood seeping through his fingers.

"Damn. I did not expect that."

"It would be wise to retreat," said someone behind him,

still enveloped in smoke. His voice was eerily familiar. Katsuo's grip on Ciara's shoulder tightened.

"Don't order me around, shinobi," Juro spat as he finally got to his feet. The air completely cleared of smoke, and two figures emerged, standing behind Juro.

"Taiki," Katsuo said emotionlessly. He didn't want to assume anything. He didn't want to ask anything. He just wanted to believe his friend and long-time ally was still trustworthy. A huge, black cat stood next to him. It reached up to his shoulders. Ciara recognized the creature from the hallway.

"Have you finished with the battle below?" Katsuo asked eventually.

"Funny," Juro laughed then winced at the pain in his side. "You see him here and that's the first thing you ask?"

Katsuo ignored him, staring at Taiki, silently begging that his eyes were deceiving him.

"Tell me this isn't true. Tell me you haven't been aiding him all this time."

Taiki was silent as he looked away. Katsuo couldn't see his expression because of the mask covering his face, but he noticed Taiki's eyes had narrowed.

"I'm sorry, Kitayama-sama."

"Don't look so surprised," Juro told Katsuo. "After all, we already knew each other before you met us. Or have you forgotten? Dear me, how deceptive human memory is!"

"You scum!" Katsuo instinctively flung blood blades at Juro, but Taiki was there to parry them with his katana. Juro smirked from behind him.

"I admit you caught me off guard today. Both of you. It's your win this time. However, it shall not happen a second time," Juro swore, turning his back to Katsuo and Ciara before wobbling over to the black cat.

"Let's go," he told Taiki.

The ninja threw something between them, and red smoke filled the tower room. Ciara coughed as it enveloped them. Katsuo couldn't see anything but remembered that the wall next to them had collapsed and brought Ciara to the pathway outside.

"Damn him. What was in that?" Katsuo cursed, coughing.

As the smoke gradually cleared, they caught a glimpse of the black beast flying away on a cloud and carrying two forms on its back. Juro's betrayal hurt a decade ago, but it was nothing compared to the anguish Katsuo felt at Taiki's actions.

He trusted him. He was his closest friend. He was his right hand. He was like family. He grew up as if he was another little brother. Katsuo could feel his heart being squeezed as he looked after Taiki's retreating form. Had all those years meant nothing to him?

A gentle touch on his chest drew his attention away, and he glanced at Ciara. She was looking up at him with a bitter expression, mirroring the pain in his heart. She raised her hand to caress his face. She was saying something, but no sound came out of her mouth, and he couldn't read the words from her lips. It was as if she was speaking a different language.

"What happened to your voice?" Katsuo asked, alarmed.

Ciara gave him a lopsided smile and waved her hand.

"No, it's important!" He grabbed both her shoulders and shook her a little. "What did they do to you?"

She laughed soundlessly and shook her head. She pointed to her chest. Katsuo's eyebrows furrowed, not understanding. Ciara let out a frustrated sigh and looked away for a moment trying to remember if there was another way she could let him know. She recalled Yura's gesture whenever she was talking about herself. Her heart squeezed as the girl's face flashed in her memory. Ciara pointed to her nose.

"*You* did something?"

She nodded.

"Why?"

She looked at him pointedly and gestured around them at the crumbling tower room. Suddenly, she found herself enveloped by Katsuo's arms.

"I'm sorry I was too late," he told her. Ciara shook her head. *It was all right.* She squeezed him in reassurance, and they stayed that way for a few moments.

Too soon, they heard a scrambling sound coming from the exit, and Riku's head popped out of the gap on the floor. He quickly ascended, sword in hand, looking alert.

"They're gone," Katsuo informed him, before his gaze found Kawayuki lying on the other side of the room. "Except that one."

"What would you like me to do, Milord?" Riku asked as he took a stance above the fallen samurai.

"What about the battle down below?"

Riku went to the short wall and looked down. His face was tense.

"Total chaos, sir. It seems our men are being pushed back," Riku observed. He added quietly. "What in the world is Taiki thinking?"

"He's not there."

"Excuse me?" Riku looked up at Katsuo in surprise.

"Don't expect to see him again," the daimyō said and let go of Ciara before walking over to the fallen Kawayuki. He glanced down at the samurai. "And I have no need for prisoners."

He raised his katana. Ciara's eyes widened as she realized what he was about to do. He was too quick for her to protest or stop him. All she could do was look away at the last second. She heard metal meeting the wood floor and something rolling away. She squeezed her eyes shut, but the sounds didn't leave much room for interpretation.

She gripped the low wall next to her to steady herself. Her whole body was trembling as all the adrenaline left her system and shock set in following the horrors of the last couple of hours. She fell to her knees, breathing hard. She survived. Katsuo survived. Yura died. Blackteeth had died. Taiki betrayed them. But they survived.

"Take her to a secure room," Katsuo told Riku as he saw the state Ciara was in. "I'll finish the battle quickly."

"As you wish, Milord," Riku walked over to Ciara and squatted down next to her. He held out his hand.

"Milady?"

Ciara looked up at him, her eyes focusing on his face.

"If you would come with me…"

She glanced at Katsuo.

"He will join you later. Let's get you out of here, shall we?" Riku's smile was tense. A heartbeat later, Ciara put her hands in his and let him help her get to her feet. The trembling had subsided, but she was still wobbly on her legs.

66

They stayed at Kawayuki's castle for a few days. Ciara waited in a room guarded by Riku and a handful of soldiers, until Katsuo's army had won and they had subdued all enemy. She wasn't told of the details how it happened, but servants' whispers confirmed that after she had been escorted from the tower room, Katsuo joined the soldiers outside—accompanied by Kawayuki's head.

After that, the battle quickly came to an end. Kawayuki had maybe a handful of loyal followers who were enraged at his death, but most of his soldiers lost the will to fight. Kawayuki's followers were quickly dealt with, and those who didn't wish to continue the fight were disarmed and locked away in a cell. Too many people were in too few cells.

Ciara knew from Katsuo that he still hadn't decided what to do with the captured soldiers.

"We don't take prisoners," he told her that evening. Ciara's eyes widened, and she grabbed his arm. There was no need for more bloodshed. Katsuo looked at her, contemplating. "For samurai, it is a great shame to lose and survive the fight. Falling in battle is the most honorable death everyone could hope for."

Ciara shook her head, completely pale. She couldn't understand. At least you had hope that things would be better as long as you lived. But if you died... What was the point of fighting?

"I don't expect you to understand how honor works for us," Katsuo said with a sad smile as he gently stroked Ciara's cheek. She leaned into the touch, listening to his voice. "It is also true that the victor decides what to do with the defeated. I have not decided yet."

Ciara put a finger on his lips, immediately silencing him. Katsuo looked at her in surprise. She withdrew her hand and wagged her index finger, tutting. Katsuo looked at her, amused, curious to see what she planned to do. He didn't have to wait for long as Ciara's lips met his in a passionate kiss. She always surprised him when she did that. He wouldn't have expected that from any other woman.

The next day, Ciara was allowed to roam the castle grounds freely, as Katsuo's soldiers guarded everywhere. She looked for the mirror, but it was nowhere to be found in the main building. She even checked the shrine where she had first emerged, but it wasn't there either.

Disappointed, she made her way back to the castle. She wasn't upset because she couldn't go back. She was disappointed because if she had the mirror, she would be reassured no one else could use it. It meant Juro wouldn't try to find Karen and drag her into his deadly schemes.

She shivered as she contemplated the possibility that he would go after her little cousin now that his plans for her had fallen through. Her feet led her in a random direction while she was lost in thought. A painful groan and shuffling sounds had jarred her awake.

Ciara looked up and around. How the hell did she end up in the dungeons? The blood in her veins froze as she suddenly recalled her time spent in this place. She had been here with Yura...

Before sad memories could overtake her, another groan reached her ears. She ventured deeper and realized all the cells were full, more than full, actually. Several of Kawayuki's soldiers sat in each one. They didn't have enough space for all of them.

Ciara gaped at the sight of them. Some of the soldiers simply stared vacantly at the wall. Most of them put their heads in their hands. However, a few of them had caught her gaze and sneered back. There were one or two with a sad expression on their face, as if begging her do to something. To end their suffering.

She quickly escaped the dungeons and hunted down a few guards. A little while later she returned with them, each of them carrying either water or cooked rice. She gestured for the prisoners.

"Do you want to give this to them, Milady?" one of Katsuo's soldiers asked her, furrowing his eyebrows.

She nodded.

"I'm not sure Milord—"

Ciara's eyes flashed in anger as she put a hand on her hip. The soldier stopped talking. Ciara pointed at the bucket of water in his hands and waved her hand impatiently.

"As you wish," he replied and yelled to the others, "Feed and water them."

Ciara rolled her eyes at the phrase but was glad they were complying. She was there the entire time with the soldiers, looking at the prisoners. When they were done with their meager portions, Ciara pointed out a few of them and gestured for Katsuo's soldiers to get them out of the cell.

They were all moderately injured. She led their little procession to the healer. A field medic was assisting him and a few other, less injured soldiers. When Ciara appeared in the doorway with several wounded prisoners and a handful of Katsuo's soldiers behind her, the healer's expression was hilarious.

"What do you want?" he asked in a curt manner. Ciara raised an eyebrow and pointed to the prisoners' injuries.

"You want me to treat their wounds?" he asked, incredulous. "Why? They'll be—"

Ciara held up her hand, stopping him.

"What?" He furrowed his eyebrows.

"Show some respect," the soldier on Ciara's right said. "If Milady wishes you to treat the prisoners' wounds, then you will do so."

Ciara nodded for emphasis.

"I only answer to Katsuo-sama," the healer said, straightening up.

Ciara's fingers twitched in annoyance. She took a deep breath to calm down, but it proved difficult.

"What's with the commotion over here?" a familiar voice asked from behind the small group.

Riku! Ciara's eyes lit up, hoping he would be able to put some sense into the healer. They couldn't just leave them like that.

"Milady wishes for the healer to treat the prisoners, but he refuses to do so."

"Oh, why is that?"

"I only follow Katsuo-sama's orders."

Riku tapped his chin.

"I seem to recall that you serve the Kitayama family. Am I wrong?"

"That is correct. What are you trying to say?" The healer was getting visibly annoyed. "I have patients I need to see, you know!"

"Yes, five of them right here," Riku said, gesturing to the prisoners. "Ciara-sama is practically part of the Kitayama family, which means you answer to her as well. Now do your job."

"When I talk to Katsuo-sama—"

"Argh, this is worse than a Brazilian soap opera!" Ciara cried out. She looked surprised for a moment before a big grin appeared on her face. "Hey, my voice is back!"

"Unfortunately for me," the healer mumbled under his breath. Ciara glared at him.

"I kindly ask you to treat them," she said.

"But they're prisoners!"

"And so what?"

Silence met her words. Even the prisoners looked dumbfounded at her reasoning.

"So what? Can't you see they're in pain? You're a healer, aren't you? It doesn't matter for a true healer whether they're treating friends or enemies. Are you saying you're not a real healer?"

"I refuse your accusations!"

"Then do your job," Ciara said, her eyes flashing dangerously. She let a small amount of power seep into her voice, but it was enough to make the healer do what she wanted. She looked at the soldiers accompanying her. "Please stay here and make sure everything is safe."

"Where are you off to?" Riku asked as she exited the room.

"I have a lot to discuss with Katsuo. Do you happen to know where he is?"

"May I show you the way?"

"That would be great. Thank you, Riku."

"My pleasure, Milady."

They quickly made their way through the corridor, and Riku led her outside to the courtyard.

"Was she…" Riku started, but couldn't finish the sentence.

"Sorry?" Ciara glanced up at him.

Riku gulped as he gathered his wits.

"Was she alone, I wonder?"

"Who?"

"Yura."

Ciara froze at the name, stopping in the middle of the courtyard. She looked at Riku as if seeing his face for the first time.

"I'm so sorry," she said with sadness covering her features. "She… I… I can't believe it happened." Ciara sniffled, quickly wiping away a few stray tears. With great effort, she forced herself to stop the tears. "I was there with her. I wish she didn't follow me that night."

Riku looked at her for a long moment before turning away and starting walking again.

"Don't worry yourself over it, Milady. She simply chose to follow you. It's not on you."

Ciara nodded, but her throat was so constricted she couldn't form any words. She silently followed Riku to the barracks.

*C*iara stood in the doorway for a long moment, not knowing how to announce she was there. Katsuo was moving slowly around the room with paper and brush in hand. There was a soldier by his side, also taking notes. They didn't notice her silent presence.

"Hey," she said in the end, pushing away from the doorframe. Both men turned their heads. "What are you doing?"

Katsuo's eyes brightened. He shoved the paper and brush to the aide's hands and rushed over to Ciara.

"I thought I'd never hear your voice again!"

"No need to be so dramatic." Ciara smiled at him.

"I'm not," he replied, and before she could continue their little argument, he kissed her.

The soldier in the background did a quick turnabout and silently wondered how to disappear into thin air. He cleared his throat, quite embarrassed.

Katsuo withdrew and looked Ciara in the eyes.

"Now that we can have a proper conversation, let me tell you how much of an utter idiot I was."

The soldier slowly inched toward the window after determining that escape through the door was impossible. He dropped the scrolls and the writing brushes at hearing his lord's words.

Ciara and Katsuo looked at him.

"Oh, right, you were here," Katsuo said, as if just remembering his aide's presence. "You may go."

"Thank you, Milord." He bowed and rushed out of the room as if rabid wolves were chasing him.

Ciara chuckled as she looked after the retreating guy.

"Where were we?" Katsuo asked.

"You were just saying how you had been an utter idiot," Ciara helpfully supplied. "Can't wait to hear more."

Katsuo grabbed both her hands in his. His gentle touch had a calming effect on Ciara's soul.

"Even though you've never given me reason to doubt you, I ended up questioning your motives," Katsuo said. "I'm sorry."

"I'm sorry, too." Ciara's voice was sincere. "I let my misgivings get the better of me. I'm ashamed it took so little to arrive at the wrong conclusion. Although, you were acting pretty suspicious."

"I didn't think you'd see it that way," Katsuo replied with a bitter smile. "In hindsight, I can understand now."

There was a heartbeat of silence.

"We're both idiots," Ciara concluded, chuckling. "I think we should stick together." Then she hastily added, "If that's okay with you!"

Katsuo laughed heartily and squeezed her hands before letting go. He fished something out of the pouch hidden in his sash. Ciara watched, curious.

"I know you still have questions—I do, too—but we'll have time to discuss them later." He held out his hand and opened his palm. There was a small, elegant silver ring in it. A precious stone sat in the middle and a pattern curved along the band. "That is, if you decide to stay with me."

Ciara gasped and her hand flew to her heart. She looked at Katsuo with wide eyes.

"What do you say, shall we make it a real engagement?" He smiled at her, hopeful.

She wanted to say yes. Her heart screamed YES. Naturally, she blurted out the first thing that came to mind after arriving at this conclusion. "I'm a witch from the future."

Katsuo blinked, but he didn't seem that surprised. It was more like he finally received the last and most important piece of a puzzle. Understanding dawned on his face.

"So that was it."

"What?" Ciara looked taken aback. She had expected more of a reaction. "Is that it? You're not going to freak out?"

Katsuo chuckled.

"Would you 'freak out', if I said I was part youkai?"

"Was that that strange power?" Ciara asked, her eyebrows furrowing. Katsuo nodded, and she said, "But you're still Katsuo, aren't you?"

His eyes flashed gold, and a small smile played in the corner of his mouth.

"Certainly. And I'm still waiting for your answer."

Ciara collected herself. He seemed to be okay with her and had strange powers himself. They made a peculiar couple. Finally, her brain's excuses were silenced. She grinned at him.

"Yes." Ciara reached for Katsuo's hand. He captured her fingers in his own.

"Yes what?"

"Yes, I want to stay with you. Yes, I want to make it real. And yes, I want to know more about you."

"Glad to hear we're on the same page," Katsuo slipped

the silver ring on Ciara's finger. She was so overwhelmed as joy blossomed in her heart she felt tears well up.

"What's wrong?" Katsuo asked, alarmed at the reaction.

"Nothing! There's nothing wrong!" Ciara replied, flinging her arms around his shoulders and attacking him with a kiss.

After taking inventory, Ciara was sad to realize that there was no trace of the mirror. That evening, she told Katsuo about how she had arrived here. They were sitting in a room near the top floor and had just finished eating dinner.

"I remember the mirror was here when we fought them," she told him. "I don't know where it had disappeared to!"

"Do you want to go back?" Katsuo asked, his voice carefully neutral.

"Of course not!" She waved and leaned close to hug him for emphasis. She had already made her decision to stay in this time period. "I'm content here... with you." She felt a blush creep up her neck but didn't retract her words. She truly was content in Katsuo's arms.

"Then why are you so focused on that mirror?"

"Because it's a gateway to my world, and he... did you say his name was Juro?"

Katsuo nodded.

"Juro threatened my cousin if I didn't help him. I don't know how it works, but he can use the mirror to get to her. What if he kidnaps her like he did with me?"

"I see..." Katsuo seemed to be contemplating something. "Then I'll use my resources to locate the mirror. If we have the mirror, your cousin should be safe, correct?"

"I suppose," Ciara nodded. "But how are you going to get that info? Taiki was the one with the information net."

She winced, because as soon as Taiki's name left her lips, Katsuo's expression darkened.

"I'm sorry," she said, snuggling to him. He hugged her back.

"It's okay. I have to face it." Katsuo planted a kiss on Ciara's head. "He might've been the head of operations, but in the end, all those people work for me. Don't worry about it."

Ciara decided to place her trust in him and let him deal with the logistics of finding the whereabouts of the mirror. It was such a strange and reassuring feeling, not having to solve everything on her own. She had someone on her side, supporting her.

"Why do you still think Juro wants to kidnap your cousin?" Katsuo asked. "It's obvious you're not going to help him, and I can protect you, so that threat doesn't work now."

Ciara let out a deep sigh.

"I've told you I'm a witch, right?" she asked, and Katsuo nodded. Ciara continued. "It runs in the family. We have traditions, but there's something else. Each one of us has inherited a special ability. Mine is the Voice."

Katsuo got goosebumps as he remembered when he first heard her use it. He and Yuki were standing in the courtyard when a strange magic crawled over their skin. It had no effect on them; however, the change in Yura's behavior had been immediate.

"Whenever I use it, I can make people do what I want. I don't like it," she crossed her arms.

"But you had to use it when Kawayuki captured you."

Ciara nodded.

"Do you regret it?"

"No." Ciara's reply was immediate. "I did what I had to do. That was my only chance, and I'd do it again. Preferably before anyone got hurt."

She fell silent as her thoughts turned toward Yura.

"What about your cousin?"

"Karen's ability is to give powers to items. Originally, Kawayuki thought I was the one who had that power."

"What do you mean she can give power?" Katsuo's interest was piqued.

"Special powers. Like, she can bestow healing powers on a soap so every time you use it, it heals your injuries. Or make a stuffed animal speak."

"That sounds awfully disturbing."

Ciara laughed.

"Probably because the stuffed animal I talk about is something different than what you imagine! I'm talking about toys!"

"Less creepy, but still disturbing," Katsuo settled on that. "Does this mean she can use her powers on weapons?"

"Bingo. She can make it so the arrow would never miss its target. Or a sword could be covered in flames to deal more damage."

"That is a very valuable ability in this age of endless wars," Katsuo observed. "I see why Juro wants her power to himself."

Ciara tensed, and Katsuo kissed her forehead.

"Fear not. We'll figure out where the mirror is and get it so Juro won't be able to use its powers, and your cousin will be safe."

"Thank you," Ciara squeezed his arm, trusting his words.

68

*D*uring their ride home, Ciara and Katsuo had plenty of time to talk. She was riding with him at the front of the procession and was suddenly reminded of the time when they met. They had come to rescue Ayaka, and, incidentally, Ciara had joined them in their journey to Shirotatsu castle.

"Don't you want to ask me about stuff?"

"Stuff?" Katsuo echoed the strange word.

Ciara shrugged.

"About the future. Aren't you curious what it's like?"

"We live here and now," Katsuo replied. "Of course, it'd be interesting to know about the future, but I don't want to lose focus of what's important."

"And that is?" Ciara sat up and twisted around to look him in the eye.

"What's important is right in front of me," he said seriously. Ciara looked away, blushing.

"Gods, so cheesy!" She chuckled.

Katsuo cocked his head to the side. "Would you prefer I don't share my thoughts with you?"

"No, no, please continue to do so," she said, settling down in his arms again. "I'm just not used to this side of you. But I like it."

Katsuo smiled as he heard her words.

"And I enjoy your reactions," he admitted. That earned him a pinch in the side. "Ouch!"

"Yep, definitely a reaction to enjoy," Ciara grinned, happy with herself.

"Please don't do that unless you want us to be thrown off," Katsuo said, his voice tense.

"Then don't tease me so!"

"Fair enough. I'll leave the teasing for when we're back on the ground," he promised.

"Hey!"

Katsuo chuckled at her feeble protest. Ciara's thoughts wandered as she calmed down.

"Do you remember the first time we met? We took the same route, but it's so different now."

"Of course, the leaves have fallen off the trees."

Ciara snorted.

"That too. It was only a few weeks ago, but it feels so much longer," she admitted. "Doesn't it?"

Katsuo thought for a moment.

"It does." There was a small pause before he added. "But I like the change."

"The fallen leaves?" It was Ciara's turn to tease him.

"Yes, the fallen leaves." He chuckled. His hand, which rested on Ciara's waist, gently squeezed her side. "You're not so nervous on the horse now."

"Because you're here."

"You were nervous the first time."

"Because you *were* there."

"I think I'll need a dictionary to understand you."

Ciara laughed at that. Something cold hit her nose. She looked up, squinting.

"Is that *snow*?"

Katsuo glanced up for a moment.

"It seems so." He glanced back at his men. "Pick up the pace!"

He turned back and moved his arm to a more secure position around Ciara's middle and leaned forward. Ciara followed his movements.

"Hold on tight."

"Right." She was able to get that one word out before her whole world blurred. Katsuo set a ruthless pace in order to reach Shirotatsu castle as soon as possible. The time for talking had passed, and Ciara missed her opportunity to ask Katsuo regarding the youkai topic.

She didn't mind getting to the castle soon, though. It was very chilly, and she was sure she'd be freezing her butt off if Katsuo wasn't directly behind her, shielding her from the worst of the chilly air. She could only hope he wouldn't end up catching a cold.

Ciara couldn't wait to get home.

By the time they'd arrived at Shirotatsu castle, snow was falling in big flakes, and most of the roads were already covered white. Ciara sneezed as they made their way through the castle gates, but she had no time to deal with the cold because Ayaka ran up to them, worried. She was wearing a warm overcoat, looking like a doll.

"Daddy! Shiara!"

Katsuo was just helping Ciara down from the horse when Ayaka barreled into his legs.

"Ooof, careful, Ayaka," he warned. "I don't want to drop Ciara."

"Sorry," the little girl said, drawing back. Katsuo set Ciara on her feet, and they both turned to the little girl.

"Have you looked after the castle, Ayaka?" Ciara asked, smiling at her. She sniffled.

"Yes! Everything is in order!" she reported before turning to Katsuo with a wide grin on her face. "I've missed you!"

"We missed you, too!" Katsuo bent down to hug his little girl.

Takeru was just arriving, having given Ayaka a head start.

"I've cleaned the guest house," he said. "You might want to consider some allies, too, now that you've doubled your territories, brother. Congratulations on that, by the way."

"Much appreciated," Katsuo replied.

Ciara suppressed a sneeze, which didn't slip his notice. He set Ayaka down and put a hand on Ciara's back.

"Let's go inside before we catch a cold."

She sent him a grateful glance, and Ayaka started to take off her overcoat. "Here, you can have this, Shiara."

"Oh, no, no! Keep it. It's too small for me, but thank you," Ciara said, quickly putting the coat back on the little girl. "I'm fine."

"If you're sure?" Ayaka hesitated for a moment before snuggling in the warmth of her clothes. She turned to Katsuo. "Daddy, will we eat dinner together?"

"Is it that time already?" Katsuo looked up at the sky. The dark clouds made it difficult to gauge the time.

"Well, we still have time before that," Takeru replied. "But it is a fair question from Ayaka."

"Sure. But let us warm up first," Katsuo said.

"I'll make sure the onsen is empty, brother."

"My thanks." Katsuo's last word were drowned out by a huge sneeze.

"Sorry," Ciara sniffled. "I couldn't—" Another sneeze. "Dang it."

"Let's go." Katsuo shepherded his little family into the castle.

69

*A*s Ayaka ran ahead, dragging Ciara along, they chatted between themselves. Takeru used this opportunity to talk to his brother.

"As per your instructions, I've pulled back everyone from the field," he reported. "What happened? I couldn't help but notice someone's missing."

Katsuo narrowed his eyes.

"Taiki deserted us. He had joined forces with Juro. Actually, no, that's not accurate." Katsuo's face darkened as he recalled the conversation in the tower room. "He's been on his side all along."

"Masaka[1]!" Takeru yelled in surprise. Ciara glanced back at them. It only took one glimpse at Katsuo's face for her to guess the topic at hand. She sent them a sad look before turning back to Ayaka, keeping her attention away from the talk.

"There's no way to know for sure how much damage he did," Katsuo continued.

"Surely you didn't gather our spies here in one place to…" Takeru couldn't even finish the thought out loud.

"Of course not. We do need damage control, though. Can you assist me with that?"

"It'd be my pleasure, brother. Thank you for your trust."

"Silly." Katsuo ruffled his little brother's hair.

"Hey!" he protested. His ponytail was all messed up, and he had to unbind his hair before tying it up again. It was still tangled, though.

"Get Rui to help you."

"*That* woman?"

"I've made Taiki look into her, so one of the spies should have info regarding her. Double check. If everything works out fine, bring her in. She might be useful."

"Understood," Takeru replied, already thinking up a solution. He hesitated for a moment, before continuing. "Actually, she came to me the other day, saying she had some information regarding the mole. I might as well ask her about it."

"Aaah, this is heavenly!" Ciara sighed in content as she submerged herself in the warm water.

"I thought you said witches don't believe in heaven," she heard Katsuo's voice from the side.

"Where did you come from?" Ciara shrieked, disappearing up to her chin in the water. She crossed her arms in front of her body. As futile gesture as it was, it seemed to reassure her.

Katsuo was sitting on a flat rock, leaning his head back and just enjoying the hot spring. Snow was falling, but the water was so hot that it melted before it reached the pool. Fog covered the surface, making it hard to see.

"I've been here since before you got here."

"Pervert," Ciara mumbled, looking away. Katsuo chuckled.

"You worry about the most peculiar things. It's not like we haven't seen each other naked before."

Ciara was thankful for the warm water because she could blame her blush on the high temperature. She remained silent.

"Come on, there's nothing to be embarrassed about," Katsuo said, looking straight at her. Ciara gazed back into his golden eyes and was suddenly reminded of the sight in the tower room.

His eyes back then looked like molten gold. He had fangs, claws, and there was a strange energy surrounding him. At the onsen, he looked calm, but she could still feel a curious aura around him. It drew her closer, and she slowly made her way over to him.

"Your eyes are gold."

He looked surprised then blinked. His eyes returned to their normal, dark brown color.

"You don't have to hide it. I like it," Ciara was quick to reassure him. "Is this something to do with what you said? With the youkai stuff?"

Katsuo nodded.

"Will you tell me about it?" Ciara asked tentatively. It seemed like a touchy subject for him. Katsuo seemed to carefully consider his answer, but she was patient. She sat down next to him, bringing her legs to her chest, and looked up at him curiously.

"You told me, because you're a witch, you have special abilities," he started. "It's similar for me. Because I'm part youkai, I have some special powers, too. I've often heard Westerners refer to them as demons or spirits," Katsuo explained. "There are different classes of youkai; however, the most powerful and intelligent lot of them can take on a human form. And they retain their special powers even in that form."

"Does this mean one of your ancestors was a youkai?" Ciara's eyes were big.

"My great-grandfather was a full-blooded youkai, yes. For some incomprehensible reason, he fell in love with a human woman." He thought back to what little information Yuki had told him in the past. "It rarely happens, or so I've heard. Youkai are extremely powerful beings and live for a very long time. And most of them despise mortals. They'd rather not take part in humans' affairs."

Ciara looked at him, contemplating.

"But you want to keep this a secret."

"I have no other choice. I am more human than youkai, and a daimyō at that. I don't want to give my enemies any openings. If word got out, everyone's life in this household would be in danger. Humans fear everything that's different."

"Or stuff they don't understand," Ciara interjected.

"Exactly," Katsuo nodded. "So you know."

Ciara sighed.

"That's why I don't advertise being a witch. It's been hard enough living with this eye color," she confessed as she looked up at him.

"Funnily enough, I've never thought it strange that you had purple eyes," Katsuo admitted. He reached out to stroke Ciara's face.

"You probably thought it was just a normal thing for Westerners, huh?"

"Who knows?" Katsuo said, leaning closer. He touched his forehead against hers. "I'm just happy I've found you."

"Me too," Ciara replied with a smile. "Even though I suspect neither of us was too fond of the idea of living under one roof at the beginning."

"Can you stop speaking, please? I'm trying to enjoy the moment here."

She quickly kissed him on the lips.

"I bet you are."

———————————————

1. No way!

EPILOGUE

*N*ight had fallen, and the head priest was just about to sit down to share his dinner with the two miko who had worked with him at the shrine on the side of a rarely travelled road.

It was a small sanctuary for those who had suffered from the constant war and wanted a place to rest and recuperate before they continued their journey. The shrine was dedicated to a lesser known, local shintō deity who protected travelers.

Their evening respite was interrupted by a loud bang as the door to the shrine was kicked in. Two figures stood in the dark outside, one bending over in pain. The priest immediately stood up and approached the strangers with caution.

"We need your help," was all the man on the left said. He was supporting his companion.

"What happened?"

"He was shot by a Westerner's pistol," he replied. "Can you help?"

"Bring him in," the priest replied as he turned around

and directed the two priestesses to prepare a futon and to bring medicine and equipment. Thankfully, he had had experience treating wounds, even the kinds caused by these new weapons the Westerners had brought with them.

The two strangers were suspicious, but he didn't judge them. After all, it was his mission to help anyone in need, no matter their background. The injured man looked like a samurai while his companion's attire reminded the priest of the rumored shinobi.

By the time he finally got the bullet out of the samurai's wound, a windstorm had arrived, flinging the wooden shutters on the windows. The two miko went around to secure all windows and the door. Soon, the rain's quick pitter-patter could be heard. It was as if they were under rapid gunfire.

Sweat trickled down the priest's forehead as he prepared to use his holy powers to close the wound on the samurai's side. But as soon as his hand hovered over the injury and he let the power flow through his fingertips, electricity burned him. He quickly withdrew his hand, his expression grave.

"What is it?" The samurai's companion asked. A small shadow moved on his shoulder, and the priest only realized just now that they were accompanied by a cat. Not just any cat, but a two-tailed one. He gulped, thinking over his options.

Thunder rumbled in the background as if warning him. The fact that his holy powers didn't work on the samurai meant he had a significant amount of monster blood in his veins. The two-tails was another sign his own life and the lives of his priestesses were in jeopardy. Lightning flashed and illuminated the entire room for a moment. The sharp, grey eyes of the shinobi scrutinized him closely.

"Mayu, bring some bandages," the priest directed the miko, and she hurried off right away. He turned to the shinobi. "We need to stop the bleeding then bandage him. Can you help me with that?"

The stranger nodded, waiting in silence. The priest couldn't help but think that he was being evaluated and his life was hanging on a thin thread. He wouldn't turn someone away who was in need, but he didn't want to risk the lives of everyone here, either.

Soon, they had managed to stop the bleeding and wrap the wound, and the priest and miko had retreated into another room. Their dinner had long gone cold.

Meanwhile, the samurai's eyes flickered open in the other room.

"Taiki?"

"I'm here. How are you feeling, Juro-dono?"

"Been better." He coughed. "Damn. That little bitch did something unexpected."

"The bullet has been extracted. Your wound should heal soon."

"How are the preparations coming along?" he asked, reaching for his haori and pulling it close. His hand disappeared into a pocket.

"I hid the mirror before we left. It's in a safe place," Taiki replied dutifully.

"Bring it here."

"Understood." The ninja didn't comment, but Juro could see the question in his eyes.

"We don't have much time left until the solar eclipse. If we miss this chance, it will set my plans back for years." Finally, his hands found the item he'd been looking for. His fingers closed around the cold, smooth surface of the egg-shaped jewel hidden inside his pocket. A smirk appeared on his face. "And we can't have that."

I hope you enjoyed the journey to a fantastical 16th century Japan in *Sword and Mirror*. If you did, I would appreciate it if you could leave a review.
Book 2, *Smoke and Jewel* will be out on Leap Day! Pre-order here: https://books2read.com/u/m2reOk

Youkai Treasures series:
Sword and Mirror
Katsuo's side story | Ciara's side story
Smoke and Jewel

http://kategrove.net

Katsuo's side story can be found at most online retailers, and you can
sign up for my newsletter to receive **Ciara**'s side story for free:
http://kategrove.net/freebookciara

If you liked Sword and Mirror and would like to support me, here is the link to **advanced chapters of Smoke and Jewel**. Yes, you can read as I write. Yes, this means you can read it *before* *anyone* *else*: https://www.patreon.com/kategrovewriter

---

Find Me On:

a amazon.com/author/kategrove

f facebook.com/kategrovewriter

BB bookbub.com/profile/kate-grove

🐦 twitter.com/kategrovewriter

g goodreads.com/kategrove

AUTHOR'S NOTE

I'm not going to tell you the story of my life but rather, the story of this book. It started in 2017, as I was trying to decide which story to write during National Novel Writing Month and *of course* a new idea popped into my head. There's this advice you've probably heard if you've ever ventured near writers: 'write what you know'. To which my usual reaction was: 'Okay, but hey, I like fantasy. It's not like I can actually travel to another world and experience it, I have to use my imagination'.

Then it clicked. At that time, I was re-watching an old favorite. *Japan.* I love Japan. I've *studied* Japan. Hopefully, that means I know enough of Japan to write about it! And so the avalanche had been, once again, started by that very same anime which had put me on the road to acquire a BA in Japanese language and culture.

There are about 60000-70000 words of Sword and Mirror which will never, ever see the light of day. By November 2018, I had a new outline, and ready to rewrite. Yes, I've started all over from scratch. It seemed easier than to edit what I had.

And I don't regret. It is better, shinier, and more coherent, thanks to all the work, rewrites and test-runs.

I wanted to write a fantasy with romance, an adventure of a lifetime, and a mystery to solve, with a healthy dose of humor. I can only hope you've found it your liking. It gave me a headache just thinking what I should call it, but romantic fantasy is what describes it best.

There will be more books. Not sure how many, but this series is definitely going to be longer than a trilogy. I'm working on Book 2 at the moment, *Smoke and Jewel*, and I've decided to publish it on Leap Day, because I couldn't pass up the opportunity.

(Pre-order here: https://books2read.com/u/m2reOk)

I'm happy with how *Sword and Mirror* turned out and I sincerely hope that you enjoyed reading it, and maybe, just maybe I've managed to take you away to a faraway land, full of fun adventures and a little bit of romance for a few hours.

Thank you.

Printed in Poland
by Amazon Fulfillment
Poland Sp. z o.o., Wrocław

57548253R00249